❧ To Love a Rogue ❧

"How many times has he proposed to you?" Mr. Beaumaris inquired.

"He is the most odious man," Arabella said, unable to resist a laugh, "and seems to think he has only to persevere."

"You must make allowances for him," Mr. Beaumaris said. "If he did not believe you to be a wealthy woman, he would cease to trouble you."

"Had it not been for you, sir, he would never have known it!" Arabella said indignantly.

He was silent.

"Perhaps we should go back into the ballroom," she suggested after a moment.

"Don't be alarmed!" he said with a touch of asperity. "I have not the slightest intention of embarrassing you!"

Her color rushed up; she turned away her head in confusion, her lip trembling.

"I am not, I hope, such a coxcomb as to distress you by repeated solicitations, Miss Tallant," he said. "But if your sentiments should undergo a change, one word, one look would be sufficient to apprise me of it."

These words, delivered, almost made her heart stand still.

GEORGETTE HEYER

ARABELLA

HarperPaperbacks
A Division of HarperCollinsPublishers

HarperPaperbacks   *A Division of* HarperCollins*Publishers*
10 East 53rd Street, New York, N.Y. 10022

Copyright © 1949 by Georgette Heyer
Copyright © renewed 1976 by George Ronald Rougier
All rights reserved. No part of this book may be used or
reproduced in any manner whatsoever without written
permission of the publisher, except in the case of brief
quotations embodied in critical articles and reviews. For
information address HarperCollins*Publishers*,
10 East 53rd Street, New York, N.Y. 10022.

This book is published by arrangement with Heron
Enterprises Ltd.

Cover illustration by Deborah Chabrian

First HarperPaperbacks printing: November 1992

Printed in the United States of America

HarperPaperbacks and colophon are trademarks of
HarperCollins*Publishers*

10 9 8 7 6 5 4 3 2 1

❧ Chapter 1 ❧

THE SCHOOLROOM IN THE PARSONAGE AT
Heythram was not a large apartment, but on a bleak
January day, in a household where the consumption of
coals was a consideration, this was not felt by its occupants to be a disadvantage. Quite a modest fire in the
high, barred grate made it unnecessary for all but one
of the four young ladies present to huddle shawls round
their shoulders. But Elizabeth, the youngest of the Reverend Henry Tallant's handsome daughters, was suffering from the earache, and, besides stuffing a roasted
onion into the afflicted orifice, had swathed her head
and neck in an old Cashmere shawl. She lay curled up
on an aged sofa, with her head on a worn red cushion,
and from time to time uttered a long-suffering sigh, to
which none of her sisters paid any heed. Betsy was
known to be sickly. It was thought that the climate of
Yorkshire did not agree with her constitution, and since
she spent the greater part of the winter suffering from
a variety of minor ills her delicacy was regarded by all
but her Mama as a commonplace.

There were abundant signs, littered over the table in
the center of the room, that the young ladies had retired

to this cosy, shabby apartment to hem shirts, but only one of them, the eldest, was thus engaged. In a chair on one side of the fireplace Miss Margaret Tallant, a buxom fifteen-year-old, was devouring the serial story in a bound volume of the *Ladies' Monthly Museum* with her fingers stuffed in her ears; seated opposite to Miss Arabella, her stitchery lying neglected on the table before her, sat Miss Sophia, reading aloud from another volume of this instructive periodical.

"I must say, Bella," she remarked, momentarily lowering the book, "I find this most perplexing! Only listen to what it says here: 'We have presented our subscribers with fashions of the newest pattern, not such as shall violate the laws of propriety and decorum, but such as shall assist the smile of good humor, and give an additional charm to the carriage of benevolence. Economy ought to be the order of the day'—And then, if you please, there is a picture of the most ravishing evening gown—do but look at it, Bella! And it says that the Russian bodice is of blue satin, fastened in front with diamonds! *Well!*"

Her sister obediently raised her eyes from the wristband she was hemming, and critically scanned the willowy giantess depicted among the fashion notes. Then she sighed, and once more bent her dark head over her work. "Well, if that is their notion of economy, I am sure I couldn't go to London, even if my godmother invited me. And I know she won't," she said fatalistically.

"You must and you shall go!" declared Sophy, in accents of strong resolution. "Only think what it may mean to all of us if you do!"

"Yes, but I won't go looking like a dowd," objected Arabella, "and if I am obliged to have diamond fastenings to my bodices, you know very well—"

"Oh, stuff! I daresay that is the extreme of fashion, or perhaps they are made of paste! And in any event this is one of the older numbers. I know I saw in one of them that jewelry is no longer worn in the mornings, so very likely—Where is that volume? Margaret, you have it! Do, pray, give it to me! You are by far too young to be interested in such things!"

Margaret uncorked her ears to snatch the book out of her sister's reach. "No! I'm reading the serial story, and you shan't have it!"

"Well, you should not. You know Papa does not like us to read romances."

"If it comes to that," retorted Margaret, "he would be excessively grieved to find you reading nothing better than the latest modes!"

They looked at one another; Sophy's lip quivered. "Dear Meg, do pray give it to me only for a *moment!*"

"Well, I will when I have finished the *Narrative of Augustus Waldstein,*" said Margaret. "But only for a moment, mind!"

"Wait, I know there is something here to the purpose!" said Arabella, dropping her work to flick over the pages of the volume abandoned by Sophia. " 'Method of Preserving Milk by Horse-Radish . . . White Wax for the Nails . . . Human Teeth placed to Stumps . . .' Yes, here it is! Now, listen, Meg! 'Where a Female has in early life dedicated her attention to novel reading she is unfit to become the companion of a man of sense, or to conduct a family with propriety and decorum.' There!" She looked up, the prim pursing of her lips enchantingly belied her dancing eyes.

"I am sure Mama is not unfit to be the companion of a man of sense!" cried Margaret indignantly. "And *she* reads novels! And even Papa does not find *The Wanderer* objectionable, or Mrs. Edgeworth's *Tales!*"

"No, but he did not like it when he found Bella reading *The Hungarian Brothers,* or *The Children of the Abbey,*" said Sophia, seizing the opportunity to twitch the *Ladies' Monthly Museum* out of her sister's slackened grasp. "He said there was a great deal of nonsense in such books, and that the moral tone was sadly lacking."

"Moral tone is not lacking in the serial I am reading!" declared Margaret, quite ruffled. "Look what it says there, near the bottom of the page! 'Albert! be purity of character your duty!' I am sure he could not dislike that!"

Arabella rubbed the tip of her nose. "Well, I think he would say it was fustian," she remarked candidly. "But do give the book back to her, Sophy!"

"I will, when I have found what I'm looking for. Besides, it was I who had the happy notion to borrow the volumes from Mrs. Caterham, so—yes, here it is! It says that only jewelry of very plain workmanship is worn in the mornings nowadays." She added, on a note of doubt: "I daresay the fashions don't change so very fast, even in London. This number is only three years old."

The sufferer on the sofa sat up cautiously. "But Bella hasn't got any jewelry, has she?"

The observation, delivered with all the bluntness natural in a damsel of only nine summers, threw a blight over the company.

"I have the gold locket and chain with the locks of Papa's and Mama's hair in it," said Arabella defensively.

"If you had a tiara, and a—a cestus, and an armlet to match it, it might answer," said Sophy. "There is a toilet described here with just those ornaments."

Her three sisters gazed at her in astonishment. "What is a cestus?" they demanded.

Sophy shook her head. "I don't know," she confessed.

"Well, Bella hasn't got one at all events," said the Job's comforter on the sofa.

"If she were so poor spirited as to refuse to go to London for such a trifling reason as that, I would never forgive her!" declared Sophy.

"Of course I would not!" exclaimed Arabella scornfully. "But I have not the least expectation that Lady

Bridlington will invite me, for why should she, only because I am her goddaughter? I never saw her in my life!"

"She sent a very handsome shawl for your christening gift," said Margaret hopefully.

"Besides being Mama's dearest friend," added Sophy.

"But Mama has not seen her either—at least, not for years and years!"

"And she never sent Bella anything else, not even when she was confirmed," pointed out Betsy, gingerly removing the onion from her ear, and throwing it into the fire.

"If your earache is better," said Sophy, eying her with disfavor, "you may hem this seam for me! I want to draw a pattern for a new flounce."

"Mama said I was to sit quietly by the fire," replied the invalid, disposing herself more comfortably. "Are there any ecrostics in those fusty old books?"

"No, and if there were I would not give them to anyone so disobliging as you, Betsy!" said Sophy, roundly.

Betsy began to cry, in an unconvincing way, but as Margaret was once more absorbed in her serial, and Arabella had drawn Sophia's attention to the picture of a velvet pelisse trimmed lavishly with ermine, no one paid any heed to her, and she presently relapsed into silence, merely sniffing from time to time, and staring resentfully at her two eldest sisters.

They presented a charming picture as they sat poring over their book, their dark ringlets intermingled, and their arms round each other's waists. They were very plainly dressed, in gowns of blue kerseymere made high to the throat and with long tight sleeves, and they wore no other ornaments than a knot or two of ribbons at the throat; but the Vicar's numerous offspring were all remarkable for their good looks, and had very little need of embellishment. Although Arabella was unquestionably the beauty of the family, it was pretty generally agreed in the neighborhood that once Sophia had outgrown the overplumpness of her sixteen years she might reasonably hope to rival her senior. Each had large, dark, expressive eyes, little straight noses, and delicately molded lips; each had complexions that were the envy of less fortunate young ladies, and that owed nothing to Denmark Lotion, Olympian Dew, Bloom of Ninon, or any other aid to beauty advertised in the society journals. Sophia was the taller of the two; Arabella had by far the better figure, and the neater ankle. Sophia looked to be the more robust; Arabella enchanted her admirers by a deceptive air of fragility, which inspired one romantically minded young gentleman to liken her to a leaf blown by the wind; and another to address a very bad set of verses to her, apostrophizing her as the New Titania. Unfortunately, Harry had found this effusion, and had shown it to Bertram, and until Papa had said, with his gentle austerity, that he considered the jest to be outworn, they had insisted on hailing their sister by this exquisitely humorous appellation.

Betsy, brooding over her wrongs, found nothing to admire in either sister, and was weighing the advantage of cosseting from old Nurse against the possibility of being called upon to amuse Baby Jack, were she to remove herself to the nursery, when the door burst open and a stout boy of eleven years, in nankeens and a frilled shirt, and with a mop of curly hair, precipitated himself into the room, exclaiming loudly: "Hello! Such a kickup! Mama is with Papa in the study, but *I* know what it's all about!"

"Why, what has happened?" exclaimed Sophia.

"Don't you wish you knew!" said Harry, drawing a piece of twine from his pocket and beginning to tie it into a complicated knot. "Watch me tie this one, Meg! I know six of the chief knots now, and if Uncle James does not get Captain Bolton to take me on his next commission it will be the most infamous, swindling thing I ever heard of!"

"But you didn't come to tell us that!" said Arabella. "What is it?"

"Nothing but one of Harry's hums!" said Margaret.

"No such thing!" retorted her brother. "Joseph Eccles has been down to the White Hart, and brought back the post with him." He perceived that he had succeeded in riveting his sisters' attention on himself, and grinned at them. "Ay, you may stare! There's a letter from London, for Mama. Franked by some lord, too: I saw it."

Margaret's book slipped from her fingers to the floor; Sophia gave a gasp; and Arabella flew up out of her chair. "Harry! Not—oh, not from my godmother?"

"Oh, ain't it?" said Harry.

"If it comes from London, it must be from Lady Bridlington!" declared Sophia. "Arabella, I do believe our fortunes are in a way to being made!"

"I dare not suppose it to be possible!" said Arabella, quite faintly. "Depend upon it, she has written to say she cannot invite me!"

"Nonsense!" replied her practical sister. "If that were all, pray why should Mama take the letter to my father? I regard the matter as settled already. You are going to London for the season."

"Oh, if it could be so indeed!" said Arabella, trembling.

Harry, who had abandoned knotmaking in favor of trying to stand on his head, overbalanced at this moment and fell in a heap on the floor together with a chair, Sophia's workbox, and a handscreen, which Margaret had been painting before succumbing to the superior attraction of the *Ladies' Monthly Museum.* Beyond begging him not to be such an ape, none of his sisters censured his clumsiness. He picked himself up, remarking scornfully that only a girl would make such a fuss about a mere visit to London. "The slowest thing!" he said. "I should like to know what you think you would do there!"

"Oh, Harry, how can you be so stupid? The balls! The theaters! Assemblies!" uttered Arabella, in choked accents.

"*I* thought you were going to form an eligible connection," said Betsy. "That is what Mama said, for I heard her."

"Then you had no business to be listening!" said Sophia tartly.

"What's an eligible connection?" demanded Harry, beginning to juggle with several reels of sewing silk, which had spilled out of the workbox onto the floor.

"I'm sure I don't know!"

"I do," offered the invalid. "It's a splendid marriage, of course. And *then* Bella will invite Sophia and Meg and me to stay with her in London, and we shall *all* find rich husbands!"

"That I shall certainly not do, miss!" declared Arabella. "Let me tell you that no one will invite you anywhere until you have a little more conduct!"

"Well, Mama *did* say it," argued Betsy, in a whining voice. "And you need not think I do not know about such things, because—"

Sophia interrupted her ruthlessly. "If, Betsy, you do not desire me to tell Papa of your shocking lack of delicacy, I advise you to take yourself off to the nursery—where you belong!"

This terrible threat did not fail of its object. Complaining that her sisters were disagreeable cats, Betsy went as slowly from the room as she dared, trailing her shawl behind her.

"She is very sickly," said Arabella, in an excusing tone.

"She is a precocious brat!" retorted Sophia. "One would have thought that she would have had more elegance of mind than to be thinking of such things! Oh, Bella, if only you were to be so fortunate as to make a Splendid Marriage! And if Lady Bridlington is to bring you out, I am sure I do not see how you can fail to! For," she added nobly, "you are by far the prettiest girl *I* have ever seen!"

"Hoo!" interpolated Harry, adding his mite to the conversation.

"Yes," agreed Margaret, "but if she must have diamond buttons, and tiaras, and—and those things you spoke of, I don't see how it can be done!"

A damped silence greeted her words. Sophia was the first to recover herself. "Something," she announced resolutely, "will be contrived!"

No one answered her. Arabella and Margaret appeared to be dubiously weighing her pronouncement; and Harry, having discovered a pair of scissors, was pleasurably engaged in snipping short lengths off a skein of darning wool. Into this pensive silence walked a young gentleman just emerging from adolescence into manhood. He was a handsome youth, fairer than his elder sister, but with something of her cast of countenance; and it was manifest, from the alarming height of his shirt collar, and the disorder of his chestnut locks, that he affected a certain modishness that bordered on dandyism. The Knaresborough tailor who enjoyed his patronage could not aspire to the height of art achieved by Weston or Stultz, but he had done his best, and had indeed been greatly assisted by the admirable proportions of his client. Mr. Bertram Tallant set off a coat to advantage, and was blessed with a most elegant pair of legs. These were at the moment encased in a pair of buckskin breeches, but their owner cherished in one of his chests of drawers a pair of yellow pantaloons which he had not yet dared to display to his Papa, but which, he rather fancied, turned him into a veritable Tulip of Fashion. His top boots, on which he expended much thought and labor, were as refulgent as could be expected of boots belonging to a gentleman whose parents were unhappily unable to supply their second son with the champagne indispensable for a really good blacking; and the points of his shirt collars, thanks to the loving hands of his sisters, were so stiffly starched that it was only with great difficulty that he could turn his head. Like his elder brother James, at present up at Oxford, prior to taking Orders, he had been educated at Harrow, but he was at present domiciled at home, working under his father's guidance with a view to passing smalls during the Easter vacation. This task he had embarked on without enthusiasm, his whole ambition being to obtain a cornetcy in a Hussar regiment. But as this would cost not a penny less than eight hundred pounds, and the termination of the long war with Bonaparte had made promotion unlikely, unless by expensive purchase, Mr. Tallant had decided, not unreasonably, that a civil occupation would prove less ruinous than a military career. He intended that Bertram, once provided with a respectable degree, should adorn the Home Office; and any doubts which the volatile disposition of his offspring might have engendered in his mind of his eligibility for that service, he was nearly able to allay by the reflection that Bertram was, after all, not yet eighteen, and that Oxford University, where he himself had passed three scholarly years, would exert a stabilizing influence on his character.

The future candidate for Parliament heralded his entrance into the schoolroom with a muted hunting cry, followed immediately by the announcement that some people were unfairly favored by fortune.

Arabella clasped both her hands at her breast, and raised a pair of speaking eyes to his face. "Bertram, is it *indeed* true? Now, don't try to roast me—pray don't!"

"Lord, yes! But who told you?"

"Harry, of course," replied Sophia. "The children know everything in this house!"

Mr. Bertram Tallant nodded gloomily, and pulled up

his sleeves a trifle. "You don't want him in here: shall I turn him out?" he inquired.

"Ho!" cried Harry, leaping to his feet and squaring up to his senior in great humor. "A mill!"

"Not in here!" shrieked his sisters, with one accustomed voice.

But as they had no expectation of being attended to, each damsel made a dive to snatch her own particular property out of harm's way. This was just as well, since the room, besides being small, was crowded with knick-knacks. The brothers struggled and swayed together for a brief minute or two; but since Harry, though a lusty lad, was no match for Bertram, he was very soon thrust outside the room and the door slammed against him. After dealing the scarred panels a few kicks and threatening his senior with gruesome reprisals, he took himself off, whistling loudly through the convenient gap occasioned by the loss of one of his front teeth, and Bertram was able to remove his shoulders from the door and to straighten his cravat.

"Well, you are to go," he informed Arabella. "I wish I had a rich godmother, that's all! Much old Mrs. Calne ever did for me, except to give me a devilish book called the *Christian Comforter,* or some such thing, which was enough to send a fellow to the dogs directly!"

"I must say, I think it was excessively shabby of her," agreed Margaret. "Even Papa said that if she had thought you had a taste for such literature, she might have supposed that you would find it upon his shelves."

"Well, my father knows I have no turn in that direction, and this I will say for him, he don't expect it of me!" said Bertram handsomely. "He may be devilish strait-laced and full of old-fashioned notions, but he's a right one at heart and don't plague one with a pack of humbug!"

"Yes, yes!" said Arabella impatiently, "but does he know of this letter? Will he let me go?"

"I fancy he don't like it above half, but he said he could not stand in your way, and must trust to your conducting yourself in society with propriety, and not allowing your head to be turned by frivolity and admiration. And as to that," Bertram added, with brotherly candor, "I don't suppose they will think you anything out of the way among all the nobs, so there's precious little chance of its happening."

"No, I am sure they will not," said Arabella. "But tell me the whole! What did Lady Bridlington say in her letter?"

"Lord, I don't know! I was trying to make sense of a whole rigmarole of Greek when Mama came in, and I wasn't listening with more than half an ear. I daresay she'll tell it all to you. She sent me to say she wants you in her dressing room."

"Good gracious, why could you not have told me that before?" cried Arabella, stuffing the half-finished shirt into a workbag and flitting out of the room.

The Parsonage, although built on two stories only, was a large, old-fashioned house, and to reach Mrs. Tallant's dressing room Arabella was obliged to traverse several corridors, all carpeted with a worn drugget, and all equally drafty.

The living of Heythram was respectable, being worth some three hundred pounds a year, in addition to which the present incumbent was possessed of a small independence; but the claims of a numerous family made the recarpeting of passages more a thing to be dreamed of than an allowable expense. The Vicar, himself the son of a landed gentleman, had married the beautiful Miss Theale, who might have been expected to have done better for herself than to have thrown her cap over the windmill for a mere younger son, however handsome he might be. Indeed, it had been commonly said at the time that she had married to disoblige her family, and might, if she had chosen, have caught a baronet on her hook.

Instead she had fallen in love with Harry Tallant at first sight. Since his birth was genteel and her parents had other daughters to dispose of, she had been permitted to have her way; and apart from wishing sometimes that the living were worth more, or that Henry would not put his hand in his pocket for every beggar who crossed his path, she had never given anyone reason to suppose that she regretted her choice. To be sure, she would have liked to have installed into the Parsonage one of the new water closets, and a Patent Kitchen Range, or, like her brother-in-law up at the Hall, have been able, without feeling the pinch, to have burned wax candles in all the rooms, but she was a sensible woman, and even when the open fire in the kitchen smoked, and the weather made a visit to the existing water closet particularly disagreeable, she realized that she was a great deal happier with her Henry than ever she could have been with that almost forgotten baronet. She naturally concurred in his decision that whatever became of their daughters, their sons at least must receive every advantage of education; but even while employing every shift of economy to ensure the respectable maintenance of James and Bertram at Harrow, she was gradually building her ambitions more and more on the future of her eldest and most beautiful daughter. Without precisely regretting the circumstances which had made it impossible for herself to shine farther afield than York and Scarborough, she was determined that Arabella should not be similarly circumscribed. Perhaps it had been with this hope already at the back of her mind that she had invited her school friend, Arabella Haverhill, who had contracted such a brilliant match, to stand as godmother to her infant daughter. Certainly her resolve to send the younger Arabella to make her début into society under the aegis of Lady Bridlington was of no very recent date. She had maintained throughout the years an infrequent but regular correspondence with her old friend, and was tolerably certain that fashionable life had in no way impaired the easy good nature which had characterized the plump and cheerful Miss Haverhill. Lady Bridlington was not herself blessed with daughters—she was, in fact, the mother of only one child, a son, some seven or eight years older than Mrs. Tallant's daughter—but from her friend's point of view this was a decided advantage. The mother of a family of hopeful girls, however good-natured, would not be in the least likely to take under her wing yet another young female in search of an eligible husband. But a widow in comfortable circumstances, with a strong inclination for all the amusements of fashion, and no daughters to launch upon the world, might reasonably be supposed to welcome the opportunity of chaperoning a young protégée to the balls, routs, and assemblies she herself delighted in. Mrs. Tallant could not conceive it to be otherwise. Nor was she disappointed. Lady Bridlington, crossing several sheets of gilt-edged notepaper with her sprawling pen, could not imagine why she should not have hit upon the notion herself. She was excessively dull, and liked nothing in the world so much as having young persons about her. It had long been a grief to her, she wrote, that she had no daughter of her own; and as she had no doubt that she would love her dearest Sophia's girl on sight, she should await her arrival in the greatest impatience. Mrs. Tallant had had no need to mention her object in sending Arabella to town: Henry Tallant might consider that Lady Bridlington's letters betrayed little but folly and frivolity, but her ladyship, however lacking in mental profundity, had plenty of worldly sense. Sophia might rest assured, she wrote, that she would leave no stone unturned to provide Arabella with a suitable husband. Already, she hinted, she had several eligible bachelors in her eye.

It was small wonder, then, that Arabella, peeping into

her mother's dressing room, should have found that
admirable lady lost in a pleasant daydream.

"Mama?"

"Arabella! Come in, my love, and close the door!
Your godmother has written, and in the kindest way!
Dear, dear creature, I knew I might depend upon her!"

"It's true then? I am to go?" Arabella breathed.

"Yes, and she begs I will send you to her as soon as
may be contrived, for it seems that Bridlington is traveling on the Continent, and she is quite moped to death,
living in that great house all alone. I knew how it must
be! She will treat you as her own daughter. And, oh, my
dearest child, I never asked it of her, but she has offered
to present you at one of the Drawing Rooms!"

This dizzy prospect took from Arabella all power of
speech.

She could only gaze at her mother, while that lady
poured out a list of the delights in store for her.

"Everything I could wish for you! Almack's—I am
sure she will be able to procure for you a voucher, for
she knows all the patronesses! Concerts! The theater!
All the *ton* parties—breakfasts, assemblies, balls—my
love, you will have such opportunities! You can have no
notion! Why, she writes that—But never mind that!"

Arabella found her voice. "But, Mama, how shall we
contrive? The expense! I cannot—I *cannot* go to London
without any clothes to wear!"

"No, indeed!" said Mrs. Tallant, laughing. "That
would present a very odd appearance, my love!"

"Yes, Mama, but you know what I mean! I have only
two ball dresses, and though they do very well for the
Assemblies in Harrowgate, and country parties, I *know*
they are not modish enough for Almack's! And Sophy
has borrowed all Mrs. Caterham's *Monthly Museums,* and
I have been looking at the fashions in them and it is too
lowering, ma'am! Everything must be trimmed with diamonds or ermine, or point lace!"

"My dear Arabella, don't put yourself in a taking! *That* has all been thought of, I assure you! You must know that I have had this scheme in my mind for many a long day." She saw her daughter's face of mystification, and laughed again. "Why, did you think I would send you into society looking like a rustic? I am not quite such a zany, I hope! I have been putting by for this very occasion since I don't know when."

"Mama!"

"I have a little money of my own, you know," explained Mrs. Tallant. "Your dear Papa would never use it, but desired me to spend it only as I liked, because I used to be very fond of pretty things, and he never could bear to think I might not have them when I married him. That was all nonsense, of course, and I'm sure I very soon gave up thinking of such fripperies. But I was very glad to have it to spend on my children. And in spite of Margaret's drawing lessons, and Sophy's music master, and dearest Bertram's new coat, and those yellow pantaloons which he dare not let Papa see—my love, was there ever such a foolish boy? As though Papa did not know all along!—and having to take poor Betsy to the doctor three times this year, I have quite a little nest egg saved for you!"

"Oh, Mama, no, no!" cried Arabella, distressed. "I would rather not go to London at all than that you should be put to such dreadful expense!"

"That is because you are sadly scatterbrained, my dear," replied her mother calmly. "I regard it as an investment, and I shall own myself extremely astonished if a great deal of good does not come of it." She hesitated, looked a little conscious, and said, picking her words: "I am sure I do not have to tell you that Papa is a Saint. Indeed, I don't suppose there is a better husband or father alive! But he is not at all practical, and when one has eight children to provide for, one must have a little worldly sense, or I don't know how one is to go on. One need have no anxiety about dear James, to be sure; and since Harry is set on going to sea, and his uncle is so obliging as to use his influence in his behalf, *his* future is settled. But I own I cannot be happy about poor Bertram; and where I am to find suitable husbands for all you girls in this restricted neighborhood, I have not the least notion! Now, that is speaking more plainly than perhaps Papa would like, but you are a sensible puss, Arabella, and I have no scruple in being open with you. If I can but contrive to establish you respectably, you may bring out your sisters, and perhaps, even, if you should be so fortunate as to marry a gentleman of position, you might be able to help Bertram to buy his commission. I do not mean, of course, that your husband should purchase it precisely, but he might very likely have an interest at the Horse Guards, or—or something of the sort!"

Arabella nodded, for it was no news to her that she, as the eldest of four sisters, was expected to marry advantageously. She knew it to be her duty to do so. "Mama, I will *try* not to disappoint you!" she said earnestly.

❧ *Chapter 2* ❧

IT WAS THE CANDIDLY EXPRESSED OPINION of the Vicar's children that Mama must have had a great work to prevail upon Papa to consent to Arabella's going to London. Few things were more reprehensible in his eyes than vanity and pleasure-seeking; and although he never raised any objection to Mama's chaperoning Arabella and Sophia to the Assemblies at Harrowgate, and had even been known to comment favorably upon their gowns, he always impressed upon them that such diversions, innocent in themselves, would, if indulged in to excess, inevitably ruin the character of the most virtuous female. He had himself no taste for society, and had frequently been heard to animadvert severely on the useless and frivolous lives led by ladies of fashion. Moreover, although he was not in the least above enjoying a good joke, he had the greatest dislike of levity, could never be brought to tolerate idle chatter, and if the conversation turned upon worldly trifles would never fail to give it a more proper direction.

But Lady Bridlington's invitation to Arabella did not take the Vicar by surprise. He knew that Mrs. Tallant had written to her old friend, and however little he ap-

proved of the chief motive behind her resolve to launch
her daughter into society, certain of the arguments she
employed to persuade him could not but carry weight.

"My dear Mr. Tallant," said his lady, "do not let us
dispute about the merits of an advantageous match! But
even you will allow that Arabella is an uncommonly
handsome girl!"

Mr. Tallant allowed it, adding reflectively that Arabella put him forcibly in mind of what her Mama was at
the same age. Mrs. Tallant was not impervious to this
flattery: she blushed, and looked a little roguishly, but
said that he need not try to bamboozle her (an expression she had picked up from her sons).

"All I wish to point out to you, Mr. Tallant, is that
Arabella is fit to move in the first circles!" she announced.

"My love," responded the Vicar, with one of his humorous looks, "if I believed you, I should perhaps consider it my duty to show you that an ambition to move
in the first circles, as you call them, could never be an
ideal I could wish any of my daughters to aspire to. But
as I am persuaded that you have a great many other
arguments to advance, I will hold my peace, and merely
beg you to continue!"

"Well," said Mrs. Tallant seriously, "I fancy—but you
must tell me if I am mistaken!—that you would not regard with any degree of complaisance an alliance with
the Draytons of Knaresborough!"

The Vicar was plainly startled, and directed an inquiring look at his spouse.

"Young Joseph Drayton is growing extremely particular in his attentions," pronounced Mrs. Tallant, in a
voice of doom. She observed the effect of this, and continued in the blandest way: "Of course, I am aware that
he is considered to be a great catch, for he will inherit
all his father's wealth."

The Vicar was betrayed into an unchristian utterance. "I could not consent to it! He smells of the shop!"

"Exactly so!" agreed Mrs. Tallant, well satisfied. "But he has been dangling after Arabella these past six months."

"Do you tell me," demanded the Vicar, "that a daughter of mine encourages his attentions?"

"By no means!" promptly responded the lady. "Any more than she encourages the attentions of the curate, young Dewsbury, Alfred Hitchin, Humphrey Finchley, or a dozen others! Arabella, my dear sir, is by far the most sought-after belle of these parts!"

"Dear me!" said the Vicar, shaking his head in wonderment. "I must confess, my love, that none of these young gentlemen would be welcome to me as a son-in-law."

"Then, perhaps, Mr. Tallant, you cherish hopes of seeing Arabella married to her cousin Tom?"

"Nothing," said the Vicar forcibly, "could be further from my wishes!" He recollected himself, and added in a more moderate tone: "My brother is a very worthy man, according to his lights, and I wish his children nothing but good; but on several counts, which I need not enumerate, I should not desire to see any of my daughters marry their cousins. And, what is more, I am very sure that he has quite other designs for Tom and Algernon!"

"Indeed, he has!" corroborated Mrs. Tallant cordially. "He means them to marry heiresses."

The Vicar bent an incredulous gaze upon her. "Does my daughter affect any of these young men?" he demanded.

"I fancy not," replied Mrs. Tallant. "That is to say, she does not show any marked preference for any one of them. But when a girl sees no other gentlemen than those who have been dangling after her ever since she left the schoolroom, what, my dear Mr. Tallant, must be the end of it? And young Drayton," she added musingly, "is possessed of a considerable fortune. I do not mean that Arabella would consider *that*, but there is no denying that the man who drives a smart curricle, and can afford to be begging a female's acceptance of all the most elegant trifles imaginable, has a decided advantage over his rivals."

There was a pregnant silence, while all the implications of this speech sank into the Vicar's brain. He said at length, rather wistfully: "I had hoped that one day a suitable *parti* would present himself, to whom I might have given Arabella with a thankful heart."

Mrs. Tallant threw him an indulgent glance. "Very likely, my dear, but it would be a great piece of nonsense to pretend that such things happen when one has made not the least push to bring them about! Eligible *partis* do not commonly appear as by magic in country villages: one must go out into the world to find them!" She saw that the Vicar was looking a little pained, and laughed. "Now, do not tell me that it was otherwise with us, Mr. Tallant, for you know very well I met you first at a party in York! I own it was not in the expectation of my falling in love with you that my Mama took me there, but in your turn *you* will own that we should never have met if I had sat at home waiting for you!"

He smiled. "Your arguments are always unanswerable, my love. Yet I cannot entirely like it. I believe Arabella to be a well-behaved girl enough, but she is very young, after all, and I have thought sometimes that her spirits might, lacking wiser guidance, betray her into unbecoming conduct. Under Lady Bridlington's roof, she would, I fear, lead a life gay to dissipation, such as must make her unfit afterwards for rational society."

"Depend upon it," said Mrs. Tallant soothingly, "she is by far too well-behaved a girl to occasion us a moment's anxiety. I am sure, too, that her principles are too sound to allow her to lose her head. To be sure, she can be a sad romp, and *that,* my dear sir, is because she has not yet enjoyed the advantages of town polish. I am hopeful of seeing her much improved by a season spent with Bella Bridlington. And if—mind, I only say if!—she were to contract a suitable alliance, I am sure you would be as thankful as anyone could be!"

"Yes," agreed the Vicar, sighing. "I should certainly be glad to see her comfortably established, the wife of a respectable man."

"And *not* the wife of your Dewsbury!" interpolated Mrs. Tallant.

"Indeed, not! I cannot suppose that any child of mine could attain happiness with a man whom I must—with reluctance—think a very vulgar fellow!"

"In that case, my dear," said Mrs. Tallant, rising briskly to her feet, "I will write to accept Lady Bridlington's most obliging invitation."

"You must do as you think right," he said. "I have never interfered with what you considered proper for your daughters."

Thus it was that, at four o'clock on this momentous day, when the Vicar joined his family at the dinner table, he surprised them by making a humorous reference to Arabella's projected trip. Not even Betsy would have ventured to have mentioned the scheme, for it was generally supposed that he must disapprove of it. But after grace had been said, and the family had disposed themselves about the long table, Arabella began, not very expeditiously, to carve one of the side dishes, and the Vicar, looking up from his own labors in time to see her place a slightly mangled wing of chicken on a plate, remarked, with a twinkle: "I think Arabella must take lessons in carving before she goes into society, or she will disgrace us all by her unhandiness. It will not do, you know, my dear, to precipitate a dish into your neighbor's lap, as you seem to be in danger of doing at this moment!"

Arabella blushed, and protested. Sophia, the first to recover from the shock of hearing Papa speak with such good humor of the London scheme, said: "Oh, but, Papa, I am sure it will not signify, for ten to one all the dishes are served by the footmen in grand houses!"

"I stand corrected, Sophia," said the Vicar, with dry meekness.

"Will Lady Bridlington have many footmen?" asked Betsy, dazzled by this vision of opulence.

"One to stand behind every chair," promptly replied Bertram. "And one to walk behind Arabella everytime she desires to take the air; and two to stand up behind my lady's carriage; and a round dozen, I daresay, to form an avenue in the front hall anytime her ladyship increases her covers for guests. When Arabella returns to us, she will have forgotten how to pick up her own handkerchief, mark my words!"

"Well, I don't know how she will go on in such a house!" said Betsy, half believing him.

"Nor I, indeed!" murmured Arabella.

"I trust she will go on, as you not very elegantly phrase it, my child, exactly as she would in her own home," said the Vicar.

Silence followed this rebuke. Bertram made a grimace at Arabella across the table, and Harry dug her surreptitiously in the ribs with his elbow. Margaret, who had been wrinkling her brow over her father's words, ventured at last to say: "Yes, Papa, but I do not precisely see how she can do so! It must be so very different from what we are accustomed to! I should not be surprised, for instance, if she found herself obliged to wear her party gowns every evening, and I am sure she will not help with the baking, or starch shirts, or feed the chickens, or—or anything of that nature!"

"That was not quite what I meant, my dear," responded the Vicar repressively.

"Will she not be made to do any work at all?" exclaimed Betsy. "Oh, how much I wish *I* had a rich god-mother!"

This ill-timed remark brought an expression of grave displeasure to the Vicar's face: it was evident to his family that the picture, thus conjured up, of a daughter given over wholly to pleasure was not one he could contemplate with anything but misgiving. Several darkling looks were cast at Betsy, which boded ill for one tactless enough to call down upon her sisters a lecture on the evils of idleness; but before the Vicar could speak, Mrs. Tallant had intervened, calling Betsy to order for chattering, and saying cheerfully: "Well, and I think Papa will agree that Arabella is a good girl, and deserves this indulgence more than any of you. I am sure I do not know how I shall manage without her, for whenever I want a task performed, I know I may rely upon her to do it. And—what is a great deal to the point, let me tell you all!—she never shows me a pouting face, or complains that she is bored, or falls into a fit of the sullens because she is obliged to mend her old gown instead of purchasing a new one!"

It could scarcely be expected that this masterly speech would please the three damsels to whom it was pointedly addressed, but it had the happy effect of softening the Vicar's countenance. He glanced at Arabella, who was furiously blushing and holding her head bent over her plate, and said gently: "Indeed, I am disposed to think that her character is well established among us as one who wants neither sense nor feeling." Arabella looked up quickly, her eyes brightened by tears. He smiled at her and said in a teasing voice: "If she will not let her tongue run like a fiddlestick, nor express herself in terms which I might almost suppose she learns from her brothers, nor play pranks like a hoyden, I really believe I may indulge the hope that we shall not hear from Lady Bridlington that she is sunk quite beyond reproach in London!"

Such was the relief of his children at escaping one of Papa's homilies that this mild jest was received with a flattering degree of appreciation. Bertram seized the opportunity afforded by the general outcry of laughing protests to inform Betsy in a savage undervoice that if she opened her lips again he would most faithfully drop her in the middle of the duck pond on the morrow, which promise so terrified her that she sat mumchance throughout the rest of the meal. Sophia, with real nobility of character, then asked Papa to explain something she had read in Sir John Malcolm's *History of Persia*, which the Vicar, whose only personal extravagance was his purchase of books, had lately added to his library. This was a happy inspiration: while her contemporaries gazed at Sophia in stupefaction, the Vicar, becoming quite animated, expounded at length on the subject, quite forgetting the immediate problems of the hour, and reducing his other offsprings to a state of speechless indignation by saying, as he rose from the table, that he was glad to find that he had one daughter at least of a scholarly turn of mind.

"And Sophy never read a word of the book!" Bertram said bitterly, when, after enduring an evening in the parlor under the scourge of having passages from Sir John Malcolm's memorable work read aloud to them, he and his two elder sisters had escaped to the sanctuary of the girls' bedchamber.

"Oh, yes, I had!" retorted Sophia, sitting down on the end of her bed and curling her legs under her in a way that, could her Mama but have seen it, would certainly have called down reproof upon her head.

Margaret, who was always sent up to bed before the appearance of the tea tray and thus had been spared the greater part of the evening's infliction, sat up, hugging her knees, and asked simply: "Why?"

"Well, it was that day that Mama was obliged to go out, and desired me to remain in the parlor in case old

Mrs. Farnham should call," explained Sophia. "I had
nothing else to do!"

After regarding her fixedly for several moments, her
brother and sisters apparently decided that the excuse
was reasonable, for they abandoned the subject.

"I declare I was ready to sink when Papa said *that*
about me!" remarked Arabella.

"Yes, but you know, Bella, he is very absent-minded,"
said Sophia, "and I fancy he had forgotten what you and
Bertram did on Boxing Day, and what he said about your
inclination for finery when you pulled the feathers out
of Uncle's peacocks to furbish up your old bonnet."

"Yes, perhaps he had," agreed Arabella, in a damp-
ened tone. "But all the same," she added, her spirits
reviving, "he never said I had no delicacy of principle,
which he said to you when he discovered it was you,
Sophy, who put one of Harry's trousers buttons into the
bag in church that Sunday!"

This was so unanswerable that Sophia could think of
no retort to make. Bertram said suddenly: "Well, since
it is decided that you are to go to London, Bella, I'll tell
you something!"

Seventeen years' intimate knowledge of her younger
brother was not enough to restrain Arabella from demanding eagerly: "Oh, what, pray?"

"You may get a surprise when you are there!" said
Bertram, in a voice of mystery. "Mind, I don't say you
will, but you *may!*"

"What can you possibly mean? Tell me, Bertram!—
dearest Bertram!"

"I'm not such a saphead! Girls always blab everything!"

"I would not! You know I would not! Oh, Bertram!"

"Don't heed him!" recommended Margaret, sinking
back onto her pillow. "It's all humbug!"

"Well, it's not, miss!" said her brother, nettled. "But
you needn't think I mean to tell you, for I don't! But

don't be surprised, Bella, if you get a surprise before you have been in London very long!"

This ineptitude naturally threw his sisters into whoops. Unfortunately their mirth reached the ears of old Nurse, who promptly sailed into the room and delivered herself of a shrill homily on the general impropriety of young gentlemen who sat on the ends of their sisters' beds. Since she was quite capable of reporting this shocking conduct to Mama, Bertram thought it prudent to remove himself, and the symposium came to an abrupt end. Nurse, blowing out the candles, said that if this came to Mama's ears there would be no London for Miss Arabella; but apparently it did not come to Mama's ears, for on the morrow, and indeed on all the succeeding days, nothing was talked of in the Parsonage (except in Papa's presence) but Arabella's entrance into the Polite World.

The first and most pressing consideration was the getting together of a wardrobe suitable for a young lady hopeful of making a successful début. Earnest perusal of the fashion journals had cast Arabella into a mood of despair, but Mama took a more cheerful view of the matter. She commanded the houseboy to summon the ubiquitous Joseph Eccles up to the Parsonage, and desired the pair of them to fetch down from one of the attics two formidable trunks. Joseph, who had been employed as the farmhand by the Vicar since the first year of his marriage, considered himself the mainstay of the establishment and was only too ready to oblige the ladies; and he lingered in the dressing room, proffering counsel and encouragement in the broadest of Yorkshire dialects until kindly but firmly dismissed.

A pleasing aroma of camphor pervaded the air as soon as the lids were raised from the trunks, and the removal of a covering of silver paper disclosed treasures innumerable. The trunks contained the finery which Mama had worn (she said) when she was just such a giddy puss

as Arabella. When she had married Papa she had had no
occasion for such fripperies, but she had not been able
to bring herself to give them away, and had packed them
up and well-nigh forgotten all about them.

Three ecstatic gasps shuddered on the air as three
rapt young ladies dropped down on their knees beside
the trunks and prepared to rummage to their hearts'
content.

There were unimagined delights in the trunks: curled
ostrich plumes of several colors; branches of artificial
flowers; an ermine tippet (alas, turned sadly yellow with
age, but it would serve to trim Sophy's old pelisse!); a
loo mask; a whole package of finest thread lace; a tiffany
cloak, which set Margaret peacocking round the room;
several ells of ribbon of a shade which Mama called in
her young days *opéra brulé,* and quite the rage; scarves of
gauze, lace, and blonde, spangled and plain; a box containing intriguing knots of ribbon, whose names Mama
could not quite remember, though she rather thought
that that pale blue bunch was A Sign of Hope, and the
pink bow A Sigh of Venus; point-lace tuckers, and lappet
heads; a feather muff; innumerable fans; sashes; a scar-
let-flowered damask mantua petticoat—what a figure
Mama must have looked in it!—and a velvet cloak,
miraculously lined with sable, which had been a wedding
gift to Mama, but which she had scarcely worn, "because, my loves, it was finer than anything your aunt
possessed, and, after all, she was the Squire's wife, and
dreadfully inclined to take a pet, so that I always took
care never to give her the least cause to be offended. But
it is a beautiful fur, and will make a muff for Arabella
besides trimming a pelisse!"

It was fortunate that Mama was an indulgent parent
and so very fond of a joke, for the trunks contained,
besides these treasures, such old-fashioned garments
that the three Misses Tallant were obliged to laugh.
Fashions had changed a great deal since Mama was a

girl, and to a generation accustomed to high-waisted gowns of muslin and crêpe with little puff sleeves and demure flounces round the hems, the stiff, voluminous silks and brocades Mama had worn, with their elaborate undergowns, and their pads, and their wired bodices, seemed not only archaic, but very ugly too. What was this funny jacket, with all the whalebone? A Caraco? Gracious! And this striped thing, for all the world like a dressing gown? A lustering sack—well, it was certainly very like a sack, to be sure! Did Mama wear it in *company*? What was in this elegant box? *Poudre à la Maréchale!* But did Mama then powder her hair, like the picture of Grandmama Tallant, up at the Hall? Oh, not quite like that! A *gray* powder? Oh, Mama, no! And you without a gray hair to your head! How did you dress it? Not cut *at all*? Curls to the waist at the back? And all those rolls and puffs over the ears! How could Mama have had the patience to do it? So odd as it must have looked, too!

But Mama, turning over half-forgotten dresses, grew quite sentimental, remembering that she had been wearing this very gown of green Italian taffeta, over a petticoat of satin, *soupir d'étouffe* (unaccountably missing), when she had first met Papa; remembering the pretty compliment paid to her by that rejected baronet when he had seen her in the white silk waist Sophia was holding up (it had had a book muslin train, and there should be somewhere a pink silk coat, very smart, which she had worn with it); remembering how shocked her Mama had been when she had seen that rose-colored Indian muslin underwear which Eliza—your aunt Eliza, my loves—had brought her from London.

The girls did not know where to look when Mama sighed over a cherry-striped gown and said how pretty it had been, for really it was quite hideous, and it made them feel almost uncomfortable to think of Mama's being seen abroad in such a garment. It was beyond laughter, so they sat respectfully silent, and were pro-

foundly relieved when suddenly she shook off this unaccustomed mood, and smiled, and said in her own brisk
way: "Well, I daresay you think I must have looked like
a dowd, but I assure you I did not! However, none of
these brocades is of any use to Arabella, so we will put
them up again. But that straw-colored satin will do famously for a ball dress, and we may trim it with some of
the point lace."

There was a dressmaker in High Harrowgate, an elderly Frenchwoman, who had originally come to England as an émigée from the Revolution. She had very
often made dresses for Mrs. Tallant and her daughters,
and since she had excellent taste and did not charge
extortionate prices, except during the short season, it
was decided that she should be entrusted with the task
of making all Arabella's gowns. On the first day that the
horses could be spared from the farm, Mrs. Tallant and
her two elder daughters drove to High Harrowgate, taking with them three bandboxes full of the silks, velvets,
and laces which had finally been selected from Mrs. Tallant's hoard.

Harrowgate, which was situated between Heythram
and the large town of Knaresborough, was a watering
place renowed more for the excellent properties of its
medicinal springs than for the modishness of its visitors.
It consisted of two straggling villages, more than a mile
apart, and enjoyed a summer season only. Since up-
wards of a thousand persons, mostly of valetudinarian
habits, visited it then to drink the waters, both villages
and their environs boasted more hotels and boarding-
houses than private residences. From May till Michael-
mas, public balls were held twice a week at the new
Assembly Rooms; there was a Promenade, standing in
the middle of an agreeable garden; a theater; and a
lending library, much patronized by Mrs. Tallant and
her daughters.

Mme. Dupont was delighted to receive a client in the

middle of January, and no sooner learned the reason for
the bespeaking of such an extensive wardrobe than she
entered into the spirit of the adventure with Gallic enthusiasm, fell into raptures over the silks and satins in
the three bandboxes, and spread fashion plates and rolls
of cambric and muslin and crêpe before the ladies' eyes.
It would be a pleasure, she said, to make for a *demoiselle*
with such a *taille* as Mademoiselle Tallant's; already she
perceived how Madame's satin polonaise could be trans-
formed into a ball dress of the most ravishing, while as
for the taffeta overdress—alas that the elegant toilettes
of the last century were no longer in vogue!—she could
assure Madame that nothing could be more *comme il faut*
than an opera cloak fashioned out of its ample widths
and trimmed with ruched velvet ribbon. As for the cost,
that would be a matter for arrangement of the most
amicable.

Arabella, who in general had a decided will of her
own, as well as very definite ideas on the color and style
of her dresses, was so much shocked by the number of
gowns Mama and Mme. Dupont seemed to think indispensable for a sojourn in London that she scarcely
opened her lips, except to agree in a faint voice with
whatever was suggested to her. Even Sophia, who so
often earned reproofs from Papa for chattering like a
magpie, was awed into comparative silence. Not all her
study of the fashion plates in the *Ladies' Monthly Museum*
had prepared her for the dazzling creations sketched in
La Belle Assemblée. But Mama and Mme. Dupont were
agreed that only the simplest of these could be *convenable*
for such a young lady. One or two ball dresses of satin,
or orange-blossom sarsenet, would be needed for grand
occasions, but nothing could be prettier, said Madame,
than crêpe or fine jaconet muslin for the Assemblies at
Almack's. Some silver net drapery, perhaps—she had
the very thing laid by—or a Norwich shawl, carried negligently across the elbows, would lend a *cachet* to the

plainest gown. Then, for a morning half-dress, might she suggest a figured French muslin, with a demitrain? Or perhaps Mademoiselle would prefer a Berlin silk, trimmed with silk floss? For carriage dresses, she would recommend fine cambric, worn with a velvet mantle and a waterloo hat, or even a fur bonnet, ornamented— Mademoiselle's coloring made it permissible, even imperative!—with a bunch of cherries.

Morning dresses, afternoon dresses, carriage dresses, walking dresses, ball dresses—it seemed to Arabella and Sophia that the list would never come to an end. "I cannot imagine how you will find time to wear the half of them!" whispered Sophia.

"Shoes, half-boots, reticules, gloves, stockings," murmured Mrs. Tallant, conning her list. "Those will do for another day. You must take the greatest care of your silk stockings, my love, for I cannot afford to buy you many pairs! Hats—h'm, yes! What a fortunate thing it was that I kept all my old ostrich feathers! We shall see what we can contrive. I think that will do for today."

"Mama, what will Bella wear when she goes to the Drawing Room?" asked Sophia.

"Ah, pour ça, alors, la grande parure!" cried Madame, her eye brightening.

Mrs. Tallant crushed these budding hopes. "Full dress, to be sure, my dear: satin, I daresay. Feathers, of course. I do not know if hoops are still worn at Court. Lady Bridlington is to make your sister a present of the dress, and I know I may depend upon her to choose just what is right. Come, my dears! If we are to call upon your uncle on our way home, it is high time we were off!"

"Call upon my uncle?" repeated Sophia, surprised.

Mrs. Tallant colored slightly, but replied in an airy way: "Certainly, my love: why should we not? Besides, one should never neglect the observances of civility, and I am sure he would think it very odd in me not to apprise him of Arabella's going to London."

Sophia knitted her brows a little over this, for although there had always been a good deal of coming and going between the two boys at the Hall and their young cousins at the Vicarage, visits between their respective parents were rare. The Squire and his brother, while remaining on perfectly amicable terms, scarcely possessed a thought in common, each regarding the other with affectionate contempt; while the late Lady Tallant, besides laboring under all the disadvantages of a jealous temper, had been, even in her charitable brother-in-law's estimation, a very underbred woman. There were two children of the marriage: Thomas, a bucolic young man of twenty-seven; and Algernon, who held a commission in the 9th Regiment, stationed at present in Belgium.

The Hall, which was situated in a pretty little park about a mile from the village of Heythram, was a commodious, unpretentious house built of the prevailing gray stone of the district. Comfort rather than elegance was the predominant note struck by its furniture and decorations, and it bore, in despite of the ministrations of an excellent housekeeper, the indefinable air of a residence that lacked a mistress. The Squire was more interested in his stables than in his house. He was generally thought to be a warm man, but careful; and although he was fond of his nephews and nieces, and always good-naturedly mounted Bertram during the hunting season, it was rarely that his affection led him to do more for them than to give them a guinea apiece every Christmas. But he was a hospitable man, and always seemed pleased to welcome his brother's family to his board.

He came bustling out of the house as soon as the Parsonage carriage drew up at his door, and exclaimed in a loud voice: "Well, well, if it's not Sophia, and the girls! Well, this is a pleasant circumstance! What, only the two of you? Never mind! Come in, and take a glass

of wine! Bitter cold, ain't it? Ground's like iron: don't
know when we shall get out again, damme if I do!"

Talking all the time, he led the ladies into a square
parlor in the front of the house, breaking off his conversation only to shout to someone to bring refreshments
into the parlor and to be quick about it. He then ran his
eye over his nieces and said that they were prettier than
ever, and demanded to be told how many beaux they
could boast between them. They were spared the necessity of answering this jocular question by his instantly
turning to Mrs. Tallant and saying: "Can't hold a candle
to their Mama, though, I swear! I declare, it's an age
since I've clapped eyes on you, Sophia! Can't think why
you and poor Henry don't come up more often to eat
your mutton with me! And how is Henry? Still poring
over his books, I dare swear! I never knew such a fellow!
But you shouldn't let him keep young Bertram's nose
glued to 'em, my dear: that's a good lad—regular devil
to go, nothing bookish about him!"

"Bertram is reading for Oxford, Sir John. You know
he must do so!"

"Mark my words, he'll do no good there!" said the
Squire. "Better make a soldier of him, as I did with my
young rascal. But tell him to come up to the stables here,
if he wants to see a rare piece of horseflesh: great rumps
and hocks, grand shoulders! Don't mind the boy's trying
him, if he likes to, but he's young yet: needs schooling.
Does Bertram mean to come out when this frost breaks?
Tell him the bay has a splint forming or you may call me
a Dutchman; but he may ride Thunderer, if he chooses."

"I think," said Mrs. Tallant, with a faint sigh, "that his
Papa does not wish him to hunt any more this season.
It quite takes his mind off his book, poor boy!"

"Henry's an old woman," replied the Squire. "Ain't it
enough for him to have James as bookish as he is himself? Where is that lad? Up at Oxford, eh? Ah well, each
man to his taste! Now, that other young rascal of yours—

what's his name? Harry! I like the cut of his jib, as he'd say himself. Going to sea, he tells me. How shall you manage it?''

Mrs. Tallant explained that one of her brothers was to use his interest in Harry's favor. The Squire seemed satisfied with this, asked jovially after the health of his godson and namesake, and set about pressing cold meat and wine upon his guests. It was some time before any opportunity offered of breaking to him the reason of the visit, but when the spate of his conversation abated a little, Sophia, who could scarcely contain herself for impatience, said abruptly: "Sir, do you know that Arabella is going to London?''

He stared, first at her, and then at Arabella. "Eh? What's that you say? How comes this about?''

Mrs. Tallant, frowning reprovingly at Sophia, explained the matter. He listened very intently, nodding and pursing up his lips, as his habit was when he was interested; and after turning it over in his mind for several moments, began to perceive what an excellent thing it was, and to congratulate Arabella upon her good fortune. After he had wished her a great many town beaux, envied the lucky one who should win her, and prophesied that she would shine down all the London beauties, Mrs. Tallant brought his gallantry to an end by suggesting that her daughters would like to go to the housekeeper's room to visit good Mrs. Paignton, who was always so kind to them. The style of the Squire's pleasantries was not just to her taste; moreover, she wished to have some private talk with him.

He had a great many questions to ask her and comments to make. The more he thought about the scheme, the better he liked it; for although he was fond of his niece and considered her a remarkably handsome girl, he did not wish her to become his daughter-in-law. His understanding was not quick, nor had he much power of perception but it had lately been borne in upon him that his heir had begun to dangle after his cousin in a marked manner. He did not suppose that Tom's affections were deeply engaged, and he was hopeful that if Arabella were removed from the neighborhood, he would soon recover from his mild infatuation and make some more eligible lady the object of his gallantry. He had a suitable girl in his eye for Tom, but being a fair-minded man he was obliged to own that Miss Maria was cast very much in the shade by Arabella. Nothing, therefore, that Mrs. Tallant could have told him would have met with more approval from him. He gave the scheme his warmest approbation, and told her that she was a sensible woman.

"Ay, you need not tell me! This is your doing, Sophia! Poor Henry never had a particle of sense! A dear, good fellow, of course, but when a man has a quiverful of children he needs to be a little sharper than Henry. But you have all your wits about you, my dear sister! You are doing just as you should: the girl's uncommon handsome and should do well for herself. Ay, ay, you will be setting about the wedding preparations before the cat has time to lick her ear! Lady Bridlington, eh? One of the London nobs, I daresay: couldn't be better! But it will cost a great deal!"

"Indeed, you are right, Sir John," said Mrs. Tallant. "It will cost a very great deal; but when such an opportunity is offered, every effort should be made to take advantage of it, I believe."

"Ay, ay, you will be laying your money out to good purpose!" he nodded. "But can you trust this fine lady of yours to keep half-pay officers and suchlike out of the girl's way? It won't do to have her running off with some penniless fellow, you know, and all your trouble wasted!"

The fact that the same thought had more than once crossed her mind did not make this piece of plain speaking any more agreeable to Mrs. Tallant. She considered it extremely vulgar, and replied in a repressive tone that she believed she might depend on Arabella's good sense.

"You had better drop a word of warning in your friend's ear," said Sir John bluntly. "You know, Sophia, if that girl of yours were to catch a man of property—and damme, I don't see why she shouldn't!—it would be a great thing for her sisters! Ay, the more I think on it the better I like it! It is worth all the expense. When does she go? How do you mean to send her?"

"As to that, it is not yet decided, Sir John; but if Mrs. Caterham holds by her original scheme, and lets Miss Blackburn go next month—you must know that she is the governess, I daresay—she could travel with Arabella. I believe her home is in Surrey, so she must go to London."

"But you won't send little Bella on the stagecoach!"

Mrs. Tallant sighed. "My dear sir, the cost of posting is too great to be even thought of! I own I do not like it, but beggars, you know, cannot be choosers!"

The Squire began to look very thoughtful. "Well, that won't do," he said presently. "No, no, we can't have that! Driving up to your grand friend's house in a hackney! We shall have to contrive a little, Sophia. Now, let me see!"

He sat staring into the fire for some minutes, while his sister-in-law pensively gazed out of the window and tried not to let her mind dwell on what her sensitive husband's feelings must be, could he but have had the least idea of what she was doing.

"I'll tell you what, sister!" said the Squire suddenly. "I'll send Bella to London in my traveling carriage, that's what I'll do! No sense in wasting money on posting: it don't matter to the girl if she spends some time on the road. What's more, those post chaises can't take up all the baggage I'll be bound Bella will have with her.

Ay, and this governess of yours will have a box as well, I daresay."

"Your traveling carriage!" exclaimed Mrs. Tallant, rather startled.

"That's it. Never use it myself: it hasn't been out of the coachhouse since my poor Elizabeth died. I'll set the men on to furbish it up: it ain't one of those smart, newfangled barouches, but it's a handsome carriage—I bought it for Eliza, when we were first married, and it has my crest on the panel. You would not be comfortable, sending the girl off with strange postboys, you know: much better to let my old coachman drive her, and I'll send one of the grooms along to sit up beside him, with a pistol in his pocket in case of highwaymen." He rubbed his hands together, well pleased with the scheme, and began to estimate how many days it would take a strong pair of horses—or, at a pinch, even four—to reach London without getting knocked up. He was inclined to think the plan would answer very well, and that Arabella would not at all object to resting the nags a day here or there upon the road. "Or she might travel by easy stages, you know!" he said.

Upon reflection, Mrs. Tallant perceived that this plan had much to recommend it. Against the evils of lingering in the various posting houses along the route must be set the advantages of being driven by a steady, trustworthy coachman, and of being able, as the Squire had pointed out, to carry all the trunks and bandboxes in the carriage instead of having to send them to town by carrier. She thanked him, therefore, and was still expressing the sense of her obligation to him when the young ladies came back into the room.

The Squire greeted Arabella with great joviality, pinching her cheek, and saying: "Well, puss, this is a new come-out for you, eh? I'll swear you're in high gig! Now, here's your mother and I have been putting our heads together, and the long and the short of it is you are to go to London in prime style, in your poor aunt's carriage, and Timothy coachman to drive you. How will that be, my lass?"

Arabella, who had very pretty manners, thanked him and said everything that was proper. He appeared pleased, told her she might give him a kiss and he would be satisfied, and suddenly walked out of the room, adjuring her to wait, for he had a little something for her. When he came back, he found his visitors ready to take their leave of him. He shook hands warmly with them all, and pressed into Arabella's a folded banknote, saying: "There! that is to buy yourself some fripperies with, puss!"

She was quite overcome, for she had not expected anything of the sort; colored, and stammered that he was by far too kind. He liked to be thanked, and beamed at her and pinched her cheek again, very well satisfied with himself and her.

"But, Mama," said Sophia, when they were driving away from the Hall, "you will never let poor Arabella go to town in that antiquated carriage of my uncle's!"

"Nonsense!" replied her mother. "It is a very respectable carriage, and if it is old-fashioned, I daresay it is none the worse for that. No doubt you would rather see her dash off in a chaise-and-four, but it would cost as much as fifty or sixty pounds, besides what one must give the postilions, and is not to be thought of. Why, even a pair of horses, so far as we are from London, would mean thirty pounds, and all for what? To be sure, it will be a little slow, but Miss Blackburn will be with your sister, and if they are obliged to stay a day in an inn to rest the horses, you know—she will be able to look after her, and I may be comfortable in my mind."

"Mama!" said Arabella faintly. *"Mama!"*

"Good gracious, my love, what is it?"

Arabella dumbly proferred the Squire's banknote. Mrs. Tallant took it from her, saying: "You would like me to take care of it for you, would you? Very well, I will do so, my dear, or you would be squandering it on presents for your brothers and sisters, perhaps!"

"Mama, it is a bill for *fifty pounds!*"

"No!" gasped Sophia.

"Well, that is certainly very generous of your uncle," said Mrs. Tallant. "If I were you, Arabella, I would embroider a pair of slippers for him before you go away, for you will not like to be backward in any little attention."

"Oh, no! But I never dreamed—I am sure I did not thank him half enough! Mama, will you take it for my dresses, please?"

"Certainly not. *That* is all provided for. You will find it very much more comfortable in London to have this money by you—indeed, I had hoped your uncle might give you something to spend! There will be little things you may want to purchase, and vails to the servants, you know, and so on. And although your Papa would not like you to *gamble* precisely, there may be loo parties, and naturally you would wish to play. In fact, it would be awkward if you did not."

Sophia opened her eyes at this. "Papa does not like any of us to play gambling games, ma'am, does he? He says that cards are to blame for many of the evils—"

"Yes, my dear, very likely! But a loo party is quite a different thing!" said Mrs. Tallant, somewhat obscurely. She fidgeted with her reticule for a moment and then added, a little consciously: "I should not tease Papa with telling him the whole history of our doings today, girls. Gentlemen do not take the same interest in such things as we do, and I am sure he has very much more important things to think of."

Her daughters did not pretend to misunderstand her. "Oh, I would not breathe a word to him!" said Sophia.

"No," agreed Arabella. "And *particularly* not about the fifty pounds, for I am sure he would say it was too much and I must give it back to my uncle! And I don't think I *could!*"

❦ *Chapter 3* ❦

IN THE END, IT WAS NOT UNTIL AFTER THE
middle of February that Arabella set out to accomplish
the long journey to London. Not only had Mme. Dupont
taken more time to make the necessary gowns than had
been anticipated, but there had been many details to
arrange besides; and Betsy had not failed to delay preparations by contracting a putrid sore throat and low fever.
It was felt to be typical of her. While Mrs. Tallant still
had her hands full, nursing her, Bertram, succumbing to
temptation, took French leave of his books and his Papa
and enjoyed a splendid day with the hounds, which cul-
minated in his return to the Parsonage on a farm wagon,
with a broken collarbone. A gloom was thrown over the
house for quite a week by this mishap, because the Vicar
was not only vexed but deeply grieved as well. It was not
the accident which upset him, for although he did not
hunt himself now, he had done so regularly in his youth,
but (he said) the want of openness to play truant, and
afterward take the consequences, than to ask his leave to
do something of which one knew well he would not
approve.

"How *can* you explain anything to my father?" Bertram demanded of his sisters in a despairing tone. "He would only be more hurt than ever, and give one a thundering jaw, and make one feel like the greatest beast in nature!"

"I know," said Arabella feelingly. "I think what makes him look so displeased and sad is that he believes you must be afraid of him and so dared not ask his leave to go. And, of course, one *can't* explain that it isn't *that!*"

"He wouldn't understand if you did," remarked Sophia.

"Well, exactly so!" said Bertram. "Besides, you couldn't do it! A pretty botch I should make of telling him that I didn't ask leave because I knew he would look grave and say I must decide for myself, but did I feel it to be right to go pleasuring when I have examinations to pass—oh, you know the way he talks! The end of it would be that I shouldn't have gone at all! I hate moralizing!"

"Yes," agreed Sophia, "but the worst of it is that whenever one of us vexes him, he very likely falls into the most dreadful dejection, and worries himself with thinking that we are all of us heedless and spoilt, and himself much to blame. I wish he may not forbid you to go to London because of Bertram's wretched folly, Bella!"

"What a bag of moonshine!" exclaimed Bertram scornfully. "Why the deuce should he, pray?"

It certainly seemed a trifle unreasonable, but when his children next encountered the Vicar, which was at the dinner table, his countenance wore an expression of settled melancholy, and it was plain that he derived no comfort from the young people's cheerful conversation. A somewhat thoughtless inquiry from Margaret about the exact color of the ribbons chosen for Arabella's second best ball dress provoked him to say that it seemed to him that among all his children only James was not wholly given over to levity and frivolity. Unsteadiness of character was what he perceived about him; when he considered that the mere prospect of a visit to London sent all his daughters fashion-mad, he must ask himself whether he was not doing very wrong to permit Arabella to go.

A moment's reflection would have convinced Arabella that this was the merest irritation of nerves, but her besetting sin, as her Mama had frequently told her, was the impetuosity which led her into so many scrapes. Alarm at the Vicar's words for an instant suspended every faculty; then she exclaimed hotly: "Papa! You are unjust! It is too bad!"

The Vicar had never been a severe parent; indeed, he was thought by some to allow his children a shocking degree of license: but such a speech as this went beyond the bounds of what he would tolerate. His face stiffened to an expression of quelling austerity; he replied in a voice of ice: "The unwarrantable language you have used, Arabella; the uncontrolled violence of your manner; the want of respect you have shown me—all these betray clearly how unfit you are to be sent into the world!"

Under the table, Sophia's foot kicked Arabella's ankle; across it, Mama's eyes met hers in a warning, reproving look. The color surged up into her cheeks; her eyes filled; and she stammered: "I beg your p-pardon, P-papa!"

He returned no answer. Mama broke the uneasy silence by calmly desiring Harry not to eat so fast; and then, just as though nothing untoward had occurred, began to talk to the Vicar about some parish business.

"What a dust you made!" Harry said presently, when the young people had fled to Mama's dressing room, and poured out the whole story to Bertram, who had had his dinner brought to him there, on the sofa.

"I am *sick* with apprehension!" Arabella said tragically. "He means to forbid me!"

"Fudge! It was only one of his thundering scolds! Girls are such fools!"

"Ought I to go down and beg his pardon? Oh, no, I dare not! He has shut himself up in the study! What shall I do?"

"Leave it to Mama!" said Bertram, yawning. "She's as shrewd as she can hold together, and if she means you to go to London, go you will!"

"I would not go to him now, if I were you," said Sophia. "You are in such an agitation of spirits that you would be bound to say something unbecoming, or start to cry. And you know how much he dislikes an excess of sensibility! Speak to him in the morning, after prayers!"

This course was decided on. And then, as Arabella afterward confided to Bertram, it was more dreadful than all the rest! Mama had done her work too well: before the Vicar's erring daughter could utter a word of her carefully rehearsed apology, he had taken her hand and said with his sweet, wistful smile: "My child, you must forgive your father. Indeed, I spoke to you with grave injustice yesterday! Alas that I, who preach moderation to my children, should have so little control over my own temper!"

"Bertram, I had rather by far he had *beaten* me!" said Arabella earnestly.

"Lord, yes!" agreed Bertram, shuddering. "What a shocking thing! I'm glad I wasn't downstairs! It makes me feel like the devil when he gets to blaming himself. What did you say?"

"I could not utter a word! My voice was *wholly* suspended by tears, as you may imagine, and I was so afraid that he would be vexed with me for not being able to contain my feelings better! But he was not. Only fancy— he took me in his arms, and kissed me, and said I was his dear, good daughter, and oh, Bertram, I'm *not!*"

"Well, you need not put yourself in a pucker for that," recommended her matter-of-fact brother. "He won't

think it above a day or two. The thing is that his dejected
fit is at an end."

"Oh, yes! But it was much, much worse at breakfast!
He would keep on talking to me about the London
scheme—teasing me, you know, about the giddy life I
should lead there and saying that I must be sure to write
very long letters home, even if I cannot get a frank for
them, for he would be so much interested to hear of all
my doings!"

Bertram stared at her in undisguised horror. "He did
not!"

"But he did! And in the kindest way, only with that sad
look in his eyes—*you* know! Until I was ready to give up
the whole scheme!"

"My God, I don't wonder at it!"

"No, and to crown all—as though I had not borne
enough!" disclosed Arabella, hunting wildly for her
handkerchief, "he said I should want something pretty
to wear in London, and he would have a pearl pin he
wore when he was a young man made into a ring for
me!"

This staggering intelligence made Bertram's jaw
drop. After a moment's stupefaction, he said resolutely:
"That settles it! I shan't come downstairs today after all.
Ten to one, if he saw me he would start to blame himself
for my frisk, and I should be driven into running away
to enlist, or something, because, you know, a fellow
can't stand that kind of thing!"

"No, indeed! I am sure all *my* pleasure has been quite
cut up!"

Since Papa's tender mood of forbearance showed
every sign of continuance, Arabella fell into such an
abyss of despondency that she was only saved from re-
nouncing the London scheme by the timely intervention
of Mama, who gave her thoughts a more cheerful direction by calling her into her bedroom one morning and

saying with a smile: "I have something to show you, my love, which I think you will like."

There was a box lying open upon Mama's dressing table. Arabella blinked at the flash of diamonds, and uttered a long-drawn: "Oh-h!"

"My father gave them to me," said Mrs. Tallant, sighing faintly. "Of course I have never worn them of late years, for I have no occasion to. Besides, they are scarcely suitable for a clergyman's wife. But I have had them cleaned, and I mean to lend them to you to take with you to London. And I have asked Papa if he thinks I might give you Grandmama Tallant's pearl necklet, and he sees no objection to it. Your Papa has never cared for sparkling stones, you know, but he thinks pearls both modest and becoming to a female. However, if Lady Bridlington takes you to any dress parties, which I am sure she will, the diamond set would be just the thing. You see, there is the crescent to set in your hair, and a brooch, and the bracelet as well. Nothing pretentious or vulgar, such as Papa would dislike, but I know the stones are of the finest water."

It was impossible to be dejected after this, or even to contemplate abandoning the London scheme. What with the trimming of hats, hemming of handkerchiefs, embroidering of slippers for the Squire, the arrival of her gowns from Harrowgate, and the knitting of a new purse for Papa, together with all the ordinary duties which fell to her lot, Arabella had no time to indulge in morbid reflections. Everything went on prosperously: the Caterhams' retiring governess expressed herself all willingness to chaperon Arabella on the journey; the Squire discovered that by driving only a few miles out of the way she could spend a day or two with her aunt Emma, at Arksey, and so rest the horses; Bertram's collarbone knit itself again; and even Betsy recovered from her sore throat. Not until the Squire's carriage actually stood at the Parsonage gate, waiting to take up the trav-

elers, with all the trunks strapped securely behind it, and
Mama's dressing case (also lent for the occasion) placed
tenderly within the vehicle, did the mood of depression
again descend upon Arabella. Whether it was Mama's
embrace, or Papa's blessing, or Baby Jack's fat little
hand waving farewell which overcame her, it would have
been hard to say, but her feelings were quite overset,
and it was a lady dissolved in tears whom Bertram thrust
forcibly into the carriage. It was long before she could
be composed again, nor was her companion of much
support to her, since an excessive sympathy, coupled,
perhaps, with the natural melancholy of a female
obliged by circumstances to seek a new post, caused her
to weep quite as bitterly in her corner of the capacious
carriage.

While familiar landmarks were still to be observed out
of the windows, Arabella's tears continued to flow, but
by the time the carriage had reached an unknown countryside they had ceased, and after sniffing cautiously at
the vinaigrette proffered in a trembling hand by Miss
Blackburn, she was able to dry her wet cheeks, and even
to derive a sensible degree of comfort from the opulence
of the huge sealskin pillow-muff lying on her lap. This,
with the tippet round her throat, had been sent to her
with her aunt Eliza's love—the same who had once given
Mama a set of pink Indian muslin underwear. Even
though one had never left one's home before, one could
not be wholly given over to wretchedness when one's
hands were tucked into a muff as large as any depicted
in *La Belle Assemblée*. So large, indeed, was it, that Papa—
But it would be wiser not to think of Papa, or any of the
dear ones at home, perhaps. Better to fix one's attention
on the countryside, and one's thoughts on the delights
ahead.

To a young lady who had never been farther afield
than to York—and that only when Papa had taken her
and Sophia to be confirmed in the Minster—every new

thing seen on the road was a matter for eager interest
and exclamation. To those accustomed to the rapid
mode of travel achieved by post chaises, a journey in a
somewhat ponderous carriage drawn by two horses,
chosen more for their stamina than their speed, would
have seemed slow beyond all bearing. To Arabella it was
adventure, while to Miss Blackburn, inured by long custom to the horrors of the stage, it was unlooked-for
comfort. Both ladies, therefore, soon settled down to
enjoy themselves, thought the refreshments they were
offered at the various halts excellent, found nothing to
complain of in the beds at the posting houses, and could
not conceive of a more delightful way of undertaking a
long journey. They were made very welcome at Arksey,
where Aunt Emma received them with the greatest kindness, and the exclamation that Arabella was so like her
dear Mama that she had nearly fainted away at the sight
of her.

They spent two days at Arksey before taking the road
again, and Arabella was quite sorry to leave the large,
untidy house, so kind had Aunt Emma been, and so jolly
all her cheerful cousins. But Timothy coachman reported the horses to be quite fresh and ready for the
road again, so there could be no lingering. They set
forth once more, followed by the shouted good wishes
and many handwavings of Aunt Emma's family.

After all the fun and the hospitality at Arksey, it did
seem to be a little tedious to be sitting all day in a
carriage, and once or twice, when a post-chaise-and-four
dashed by, or some sporting curricle with a pair of quick-
goers harnessed to it was encountered, Arabella found
herself wishing that the Squire's carriage were not quite
so large and unwieldy, and his horses less strengthy and
rather more speedy beasts. It would have been pleasant,
too, to have been able to have had a fresh pair poled up
when one of Uncle John's cast a shoe, instead of having
to wait in a stuffy inn parlor while it was reshod; and

Arabella, eating her dinner in the coffee room of some posting house, could not quite forbear a look of envy when some smart chaise drove into the courtyard, with horses sweating and ostlers running out with a fresh team for the impatient traveler. Nor could she help wishing, once she had watched the mail coach sweep through a turnpike, that Uncle John had provided the groom not with a horse pistol, for which there did not seem to be the slightest occasion, but with a yard of tin, that he might have blown up for the pike in that same lordly style.

The weather, which had been cold but bright in Yorkshire, worsened as they drove farther south. It was raining in Lincolnshire, and the landscape looked sodden. Not many people were to be seen on the road, and the prospect was so uninviting that Miss Blackburn said that it was a pity they had not had the forethought to provide themselves with a traveling chessboard, with which, in default of looking out of the windows, they might have whiled away the time. At Tuxford they were unlucky enough to find the New Castle Arms without a bed to spare, and were obliged to put up at smaller and by far less genteel inn, where the sheets had been so ill-aired that Miss Blackburn not only lay and shivered in her bed all night but arose in the morning with a sore throat, and a tickling at the back of her nose which presaged a cold in the head. Arabella, who for all her air of fragility rarely succumbed to minor ailments, was not a penny the worse for the experience, but her north country soul had been offended by the dust she had seen under her bed, and she was beginning to think that it would be a relief to reach her journey's end. It was vexing to discover, just as she had packed Mama's dressing case and was ready to leave the inn, that one of the traces needed repair, for it had been arranged that they should spend the following night at Grantham, which, the guidebook informed her, lay some twenty-nine or thirty miles on from Tuxford. She hoped very much that the coachman would not decide that his horses could go no farther than to Newark; but since he was something of a despot and had no opinion of fast traveling, it seemed more than likely that he would. However, the trace was mended in fairly good time, and they reached Newark in time to eat a late luncheon. Here, while he baited his horses, the coachman fell out with one of the ostlers, who asked him whether it was the King's state coach he had there; and this so much affronted him that he was quite as anxious as Arabella to reach Grantham that evening.

It was raining again when they left Newark, and the atmosphere was dank and chilly. Miss Blackburn wrapped herself up in a large shawl and sniffed unhappily as her cold gained on her. Even Arabella, who was largely impervious to climatic conditions, suffered a little from the many drafts that crept into the carriage, and wriggled numbed toes inside her half-boots of crimson jean.

The carriage bowled along at a sedate pace for several miles, the tedium being enlivened only at the Balderton turnpike, where, recognizing a Johnny Raw in the coachman, the pike-keeper made a spirited attempt to extort a fee from him. But although Timothy coachman might never have set foot beyond the boundaries of Yorkshire before, he was harder-headed than any of these soft southern folk whom he despised so profoundly, and he knew very well that the ticket bought at the last toll-gate opened all the pikes to him until the next, south of Grantham, was reached. After an exchange of personalities which made Miss Blackburn utter little moans of dismay and Arabella—regrettably—giggle, he won a signal victory over the pike-keeper and drove through with a triumphant flourish of his whip.

"Oh, dear, I am becoming so tired of this journey!"

confided Arabella. "I could almost wish to be held up by a highwayman!"

"My dear Miss Tallant, pray do not *think* of such a thing!" shuddered her companion. "I only hope we may be spared any sort of accident!"

Neither lady's wish was destined to be granted her. No such excitement as a holdup awaited them, but a little way short of the Marston turnpike the perch of the carriage broke, and the body fell forward upon the box. The Squire's traveling carriage had stood too long in his coachhouse.

After the coachman had delivered himself of a long, self-exculpatory monologue, the groom was sent off to take counsel of the pike-keeper, half a mile down the road. When he returned, it was with the pleasing intelligence that no adequate assistance was to be hoped for in the next village: it must be sought in Grantham, five or six miles farther on, where a conveyance could no doubt be hired to fetch the ladies in while the perch was mended or replaced. The coachman then suggested that his passengers, both of whom were standing by the roadside, should climb up into the carriage again to await deliverance, while the groom took one of the horses and rode on to Grantham. Miss Blackburn was meekly ready to follow this advice, but her charge thought poorly of it.

"What! Sit in that horrid, drafty carriage all that time? I won't do it!" she declared.

"But we cannot continue to stand in the rain, dear Miss Tallant!" said Miss Blackburn.

"Of course we cannot! Either way, I am persuaded you would catch your death! There must be a house hereabouts which would lend us shelter! What are those lights over there?"

They plainly shone from the windows of a residence set a little back from the road. The groom volunteered the information that he had noticed some lodge gates a few steps back.

"Good!" said Arabella briskly. "We will walk up to it, ma'am, and beg them to give us shelter for a little while."

Miss Blackburn, a timorous soul, protested feebly. "They would think it so strange of us!"

"No, why should they?" returned Arabella. "Why, when a carriage had an accident outside *our* gates last year, Papa sent Harry out at once to offer shelter to the travelers! We cannot shiver for an hour or more in that horrid carriage, ma'am, with nothing to do! Besides, I am shockingly hungry, and I should think they would be bound to offer us refreshment, would not you? I am sure it is dinnertime, and past!"

"Oh, I do not think we should!" was all Miss Blackburn had to say, and it seemed so stupid to Arabella that she paid no heed to it but desired the groom to escort them to the lodge gates before riding off to Grantham. This he did, and the ladies, dismissing him there, trod up the short drive to the house, one of them murmuring disjointed protests, the other perceiving no reason in the world why she should not claim a hospitality anyone in Yorkshire would have been eager to offer.

❧ *Chapter 4* ❧

IT WAS AT ABOUT THIS MOMENT THAT THAT erratic young sprig of fashion, Lord Fleetwood, fixed his friend and host, Mr. Beaumaris, with a laughing eye, and demanded in a rallying tone: "Well! You promise me a rare day with the hounds tomorrow—by the bye, where do we meet?—but what—*what*, Robert, do you offer me for my entertainment this evening?"

"My cook," said Mr. Beaumaris, "is generally thought to be an artist in his own line. A Frenchman: I think you will like his way of dressing a Davenport chicken, while some trick he has of flavoring a Benton sauce—"

"What, did you send Alphonse down, then, from London?" interrupted Lord Fleetwood, momentarily diverted.

"Alphonse?" repeated Mr. Beaumaris, his finely chiseled brows lifting a little. "Oh, no! this is another. I don't think I know his name. But I like his way with fish."

Lord Fleetwood burst out laughing. "I expect if you discovered a cook with a way of serving game which you liked, you would send him off to that shooting box of yours and pay him a king's ransom, only to kick his heels for three parts of the year!"

"I expect I should," agreed Mr. Beaumaris imperturbably.

"*But,*" said his lordship severely, "I am not to be put off with a cook! I came here in the expectation of finding fair Paphians, let me tell you, and all manner of shocking orgies—wine out of skulls, y'know, and—"

"The lamentable influence of Lord Byron upon society!" interpolated Mr. Beaumaris, with a faint, contemptuous smile.

"What? Oh, that poet fellow that has set up such a dust! Myself, I thought him devilish underbred, but of course it don't do to say so. But that's it! Where, Robert, are the fair Paphians?"

"If I had any Paphians in keeping here, you don't imagine, do you, Charles, that I would run the risk of being cut out by a man of *your* address?" retorted Mr. Beaumaris.

Lord Fleetwood grinned at him but replied: "None of your gammon to me! It would take ten times my address to cut out a—a—dash it, a Midas like you!"

"If my memory does not err, all that Midas touched turned to gold," said Mr. Beaumaris. "I think you mean Croesus."

"No, I don't! Never heard of the fellow!"

"Well, most of the things I touch have a disheartening way of turning to dross," said Mr. Beaumaris, lightly, but with a note of bitter self-mockery in his languid voice.

This was going a little too deep for his friend. "Humdudgeon, Robert! You can't bamboozle me! If there are to be no Paphians—"

"I can't conceive why you should have supposed there would be!" interrupted his host.

"Well, I didn't, but I can tell you this, my boy!—that's the latest *on dit!*"

"Good God! Why?"

"Lord, how should I know? Daresay it's because you won't throw your glove at any of the beauties who have been setting their caps at you any time these five years. What's more, your *cheres amies* are always such devilish high flyers, dear boy, it puts notions into the heads of all the old tabbies! Think of the Faraglini!"

"I had rather not. The most rapacious female of my acquaintance."

"But what a face! What a figure!"

"And what a temper!"

"What became of her?" asked his lordship curiously. "I haven't laid eyes on her since she left your protection."

"I think she went to Paris. Why? Had you a fancy to succeed me?"

"No, by Jove, I couldn't have stood the nonsense!" said his lordship frankly. "She'd have had me rolled up within a month! What did you have to give for those match-grays she used to drive all over town?"

"I can't remember."

"To tell you the truth," confided Lord Fleetwood, "I shouldn't have thought it worth it myself—though I'm not denying she was a curst fine woman!"

"It wasn't."

Lord Fleetwood regarded him, half curious, half amused. "Is anything worth while to you, Robert?" he asked quizzically.

"Yes, my horses!" retorted Mr. Beaumaris. "And, talking of horses, Charles, what the devil possessed you to buy one of Lichfield's breakdowns?"

"That bay? Now, there's a horse that fairly took my fancy!" said his lordship, his simple countenance lighting up with enthusiasm. "What a piece of blood and bone! No, really, Robert—!"

"If ever I find myself with a thoroughly unsound animal in my stables," said Mr. Beaumaris ruthlessly, "I shall offer him to you in the happy certainty that he will take your fancy!"

Lord Fleetwood was still protesting with indignation

and vehemence when the butler entered the room to inform his master, rather apologetically, that a carriage had broken down outside his gates and the two ladies it bore were desirous of sheltering for a short time under his roof.

Mr. Beaumaris's cool gray eyes betrayed no emotion, but his mouth seemed for an instant to harden. He said calmly: "Certainly. There should be a fire in the saloon. Tell Mrs. Mersey to wait upon the ladies there."

The butler bowed and would have withdrawn, but Lord Fleetwood checked him, exclaiming: "No, no, too shabby by half, Robert! I won't be fobbed off so! What do they look like, Brough? Old? Young? Pretty?"

The butler, inured to his lordship's free and easy ways, replied with unimpaired solemnity that one of the ladies was both young and—he ventured to think—very pretty.

"I insist on your receiving these females with a proper degree of civility, Robert!" said his lordship firmly. "Saloon, indeed! Show 'em in, Brough!"

The butler glanced for guidance toward his master, as though he doubted whether the command would be endorsed, but Mr. Beaumaris merely said with his usual indifference: "As you please, Charles."

"What an ungrateful dog you are!" said Lord Fleetwood, when Brough had left the room. "You don't deserve your fortune! This is the hand of Providence!"

"I should doubt of their being Paphians," was all Mr. Beaumaris found to say. "I thought that was what you wanted?"

"Any diversion is better than none!" replied Lord Fleetwood.

"What a singularly infelicitous remark! I wonder why I invited you?"

Lord Fleetwood grinned at him. "Now, Robert, did you think—*did* you think—to come Tip Street over me? There may be plenty of toadies ready to jump out of their skins at the very thought of being invited to the Nonpareil's house—and no better entertainment offered than a rubber of piquet, I dare swear—"

"You are forgetting the cook."

"But," continued his lordship inexorably, "I ain't among 'em!"

Mr. Beaumaris's habitual aspect was one of coldness and reserve, but sometimes he could smile in a way that not only softened the austerity of his countenance but lit his eyes with a gleam of the purest amusement. It was not the smile he kept for social occasions—a faintly sardonic curl of the lips, that one—but those who were honored by a glimpse of it generally revised their first impressions of him. Those who had never seen it were inclined to think him a proud, disagreeable sort of man, though only the most daring would ever have uttered aloud such a criticism of one who, besides possessing all the advantages of birth and fortune, was an acknowledged leader of society. Lord Fleetwood, no stranger to that smile, saw it dawn now, and grinned more broadly than ever.

"How can you, Charles? When you must know that almost your only claim to fashion is being noticed by me!"

Arabella entered the room to find both its occupants laughing, and thus had the felicity of seeing Mr. Beaumaris at his best. That she herself was looking remarkably pretty, with her dusky curls and charming complexion admirably set off by a high-crowned bonnet, with curled ostrich feather tips, and crimson ribbons tied into a bow under one ear, never entered her head, since Mr. Tallant's daughters had always been discouraged from thinking much about their appearance. She paused on the threshold while the butler murmured her name and Miss Blackburn's, quite unselfconscious, but looking about her with a kind of wide-eyed, innocent interest. She was very much impressed by what she saw.

The house was not a large one, but she perceived that it was furnished with a good taste which was as quiet as it was expensive. Her quick scrutiny took in Lord Fleetwood, who had put up an instinctive hand to straighten the Belcher necktie he affected, and passed on to Mr. Beaumaris.

Arabella had one brother who aspired to dandyism, and she had thought that she had seen in Harrowgate gentlemen of decided fashion. No one she had ever seen approached the elegance of Mr. Beaumaris.

Lord Fleetwood, or any of his cronies, could have recognized the tailoring of that coat of olive-green superfine at a glance; Arabella, to whom the magic name of Weston was unknown, was merely aware of a garment so exquisitely cut that it presented all the appearance of having been molded to its wearer's form. A very good form, too, she noted, with approval. No need of buckram wadding, such as that Knaresborough tailor had inserted into Bertram's new coat, to fill out those shoulders! And how envious Bertram would have been of Mr. Beaumaris's fine legs, sheathed in tight pantaloons, with gleaming Hessian boots pulled over them! Mr. Beaumaris's shirt points were not as high as Bertram's, but his necktie commanded the respect of one who had more than once watched her brother's struggles with a far less complicated arrangement. Arabella was not perfectly sure that she admired his style of hairdressing—he affected a Stanhope crop—but she did think him a remarkably handsome man, as he stood there, laughter dying on his lips and out of his gray eyes.

It was only a moment that he stood thus. She had the impression that he was scanning her critically; then he moved forward and bowed slightly, and begged, in a rather colorless tone, to know in what way he could be of service to her.

"How do you do?" said Arabella politely. "I beg your pardon, but the thing is that there has been an accident

to my carriage, and—it is raining, and horribly cold! The
groom has rid in to Grantham, and I daresay will bring
another carriage out directly, but—but Miss Blackburn
here has taken a chill, and we should be very much
obliged if we might wait here in the warm!"

She was stammering and blushing by the time she
came to the end of this speech. Outside, it had seemed
the simplest thing in the world to solicit shelter; under
Mr. Beaumaris's eye, it all at once seemed as though the
request were outrageous. To be sure, he was smiling,
but it was a very different smile from the one his face had
worn when she had entered the room. It was such a very
slight curl of the lips, yet there was some quality in it
which made her feel ruffled and uncomfortable.

But he said with perfect civility: "An unfortunate mishap. You must permit me to send you to Grantham in
one of my carriages, ma'am."

Lord Fleetwood, who had been standing staring in the
frankest admiration at Arabella, was jerked into action
by this speech. Pulling a chair invitingly close to the fire,
he exclaimed, "No, no, come and sit down, ma'am! I can
see you are chilled to the bone! Shocking weather for
traveling! You will have got your feet wet, I daresay, and
that will never do, you know! Robert, where have your
wits gone a-begging? Why don't you desire Brough to
fetch some refreshments for Miss—er—Miss—for the
ladies!"

With a look which Arabella was strongly inclined to
construe as one of resignation, Mr. Beaumaris replied:
"I trust he may be doing so. I beg you will be seated,
ma'am!"

But it was Lord Fleetwood who handed Arabella to
the chair he had placed, saying solicitously: "I am sure
you are hungry and will be glad of something to eat!"

"Well, yes, sir," confessed Arabella, who was very
hungry indeed. "I own I have been thinking of my din-

ner for several miles! And no wonder, for I see it is already past five o'clock!"

This naïve speech made his lordship, who never sat down to his dinner before half past seven at the very earliest, swallow convulsively, but he recovered himself in an instant and replied without a blink: "So it is, by Jupiter! You are famished, then! But never mind! Mr. Beaumaris here was just saying that dinner would be served in a trice. Weren't you, Robert?"

"Was I?" said Mr. Beaumaris. "I have the wretchedest of memories, but I am sure you are right. I beg you will do me the honor of dining with me, ma'am."

Arabella hesitated. She could see from her anguished expression that Miss Blackburn thought she should rather accept Mr. Beaumaris's first offer; and not the most inveterate of optimists could have read into that languid gentleman's voice anything more than a reluctant civility. But this warm, comfortably furnished room was a most welcome change from the traveling carriage, and the aroma of cooking which had assailed her nostrils as she had crossed the hall had considerably whetted her appetite. She looked a little doubtfully at her host. Again it was Lord Fleetwood who, with his friendly smile and easy manners, clinched the matter. "Of course they will dine with us! Now, won't you, ma'am?"

"It would be giving too much trouble, sir!" said Miss Blackburn, in a sort of gasp.

"No trouble in the world, ma'am, I assure you! In fact, we are very much obliged to you, for we had been wishing that we were to have company, eh, Robert?"

"Certainly," agreed Mr. Beaumaris. "Was I not just saying so?"

Miss Blackburn, having undergone a lifetime of slights and snubs, was quick to catch the satirical inflection. She cast him a scared, deprecating look, and colored. His eyes met hers; he stood looking down at her for a moment, and then said in a much kinder tone: "I am afraid

you are not quite comfortable there, ma'am. Will you
not draw nearer to the fire?"

She was thrown into a flutter, and assured him rather
disjointedly that she was perfectly comfortable and himself too good, too obliging! Brough had come into the
room with a tray of glasses and decanters, which he set
down on a table, and Mr. Beaumaris moved toward it,
saying: "You will like to go upstairs with my housekeeper, I daresay, to take off your wet coat, but first you
must let me give you a glass of wine." He began to pour
out some Madeira. "Two extra covers for dinner,
Brough—which you will serve immediately."

Brough thought of the Devonport fowls roasting on
the spits in the kitchen, and of the artist in charge of
them, and was visibly shaken. "Immediately, sir?" he
said, in a failing voice.

"Let us say, within half an hour," amended Mr.
Beaumaris, carrying a glass of wine over to Miss Blackburn.

"Yes, sir," said Brough, and tottered from the room,
a broken man.

Miss Blackburn accepted the wine gratefully, but
when it was offered to Arabella she declined it. Papa did
not like his daughters to taste anything stronger than
porter, or the very mild claret cup served at the Harrowgate Assembly Rooms, and she was a little doubtful of
its possible effect on her. Mr. Beaumaris did not press
her in any way, but set the glass down again, poured out
some sherry for himself and his friend, and returned to
sit beside Miss Blackburn on the sofa.

Lord Fleetwood, meanwhile, had ensconced himself
beside Arabella and was chatting to her in his inconse-
quent, cheerful way, which set her quite at her ease. He
was delighted to hear that she was on her way to London, hoped to have the pleasure of meeting her there—
in the Park, possibly, or at Almack's. He had plenty of
anecdotes of *ton* with which to entertain her, and rattled

on in an agreeable fashion until the housekeeper came to escort the ladies upstairs.

They were taken to a guest chamber on the first floor and handed over there to a housemaid, who brought up hot water for them and bore their damp coats away to be dried in the kitchen.

"Everything in the first style of elegance!" breathed Miss Blackburn. "But we should not be dining here! I feel sure we ought not, my dear Miss Tallant!"

Arabella was a little doubtful on this score herself, but as it was now too late to draw back, she stifled her misgivings and said stoutly that she was persuaded there could be no objection. Finding a brush and comb laid out on the dressing table, she began to tidy her rather tumbled locks.

"They are *most* gentlemanlike," said Miss Blackburn, deriving comfort from this circumstance. "Of the first rank of fashion, I daresay. They will be here for the hunting, depend upon it: I collect this is a hunting box."

"A hunting box!" exclaimed Arabella, awed. "Is it not very large and grand, ma'am, to be that?"

"Oh, no, my dear! Quite a small house! The Tewkesburys, whose sweet children I was engaged to instruct before I removed to Mrs. Caterham's establishment, had one much larger, I assure you. This is the Melton country, you must know."

"Good heavens, are they Melton men, then? Oh, how much I wish Bertram could be here! What I shall have to tell him! I think it is Mr. Beaumaris who owns the house: I wonder who the other is? I thought when I first saw him he could not be quite the thing, for that striped waistcoat, you know, and that spotted handkerchief he wears instead of a cravat makes him look like a groom, or some such thing. But when he spoke, of course I knew he was not a vulgar person at all."

Miss Blackburn, feeling for once in her life pleasantly superior, gave a titter of laughter, and said pityingly:

"Oh, dear me no, Miss Tallant! You will find a great many young gentlemen of fashion wearing much odder clothes than *that!* It is what Mr. Geoffrey Tewkesbury—a very modish young man!—used to call *all the crack!*" She added pensively: "But I must confess that I do not care for it myself, and nor did dear Mrs. Tewkesbury. My notion of a true gentleman is someone like Mr. Beaumaris!"

Arabella dragged the comb ruthlessly through a tangle. "*I* thought him a very proud, reserved man!" she declared. "And not at all hospitable!" she added.

"Oh, no, how can you say so? How very kind and obliging it was of him to place me in the best place, so near the fire! Delightful manners! Nothing high in them at all! I was quite overcome by his condescension!"

It was evident to Arabella that she and Miss Blackburn regarded their host through two very different pairs of spectacles. She preserved an unconvinced silence, and as soon as Miss Blackburn had finished prinking her crimped gray locks at the mirror, suggested that they should go downstairs again. Accordingly they left the room and crossed the upper hall to the head of the stairway. Mr. Beaumaris's fancy had led him to carpet his stairs, a luxury which Miss Blackburn indicated to her charge with one pointing finger and a most expressive glance.

Across the lower hall, the door into the library stood ajar. Lord Fleetwood's voice, speaking in rallying tones, assailed the ladies' ears. "I swear you are incorrigible!" said his lordship. "The loveliest of creatures drops into your lap, like a veritable hone-fall, and you behave as though a gull-groper had forced his way into your house!"

Mr. Beaumaris replied with disastrous clarity: "My dear Charles, when you have been hunted by every trick known to the ingenuity of the female mind, you may more readily partake of my sentiments upon this occasion! I have had beauties hopeful of wedding my fortune swoon in my arms, break their bootlaces outside my London house, sprain their ankles when my arm is there to support them, and now it appears that I am to be pursued even into Leicestershire! An accident to her coach! Famous! What a greenhorn she must believe me to be!"

A small hand closed like a vice about Miss Blackburn's wrist. Herself bridling indignantly, she saw Arabella's eyes sparkling, and her cheeks most becomingly flushed. Had she been better acquainted with Miss Tallant, she might have taken fright at these signs. Arabella breathed into her ear: "Miss Blackburn, can I *trust* you?"

Miss Blackburn would have vigorously assured her that she could, but the hand released her wrist and flew up to cover her mouth. Slightly startled, she nodded. To her amazement, Arabella then picked up her skirts and fled lightly back to the top of the stairs. Turning there, she began to come slowly down again, saying in a clear, carrying voice: "Yes, indeed! I am sure I have said the same, dear ma'am, times out of mind! But do, pray, go before me!"

Miss Blackburn, turning to stare at her, with her mouth at half cock, found a firm young hand in the small of her back and was thrust irresistibly onward.

"But in spite of all," said Arabella, "I prefer to travel with my own horses!"

The awful scowl that accompanied these light words quite bewildered the poor little governess, but she understood that she was expected to reply in kind, and said in a quavering voice: "Very true, my dear!"

The scowl gave place to an encouraging smile. Any one of Arabella's brothers or sisters would have begged her at this point to consider all the consequences of impetuosity; Miss Blackburn, unaware of the eldest Miss Tallant's besetting fault, was merely glad that she had not disappointed her. Arabella tripped across the hall to that half-open door and entered the library again.

It was Lord Fleetwood who came forward to receive her. He eyed her with undisguised appreciation and said: "Now you will be more comfortable! Devilish dangerous to sit about in a wet coat, y'know! But we are yet unacquainted, ma'am! The stupidest thing!—Never can catch a name when it is spoken! That man of Beaumaris's mumbles so that no one can hear him! You must let me make myself known to you, too—Lord Fleetwood, very much at your service!"

"I," said Arabella, a most dangerous glitter in her eye, "am Miss Tallant!"

His lordship, murmuring polite gratification at being made the recipient of this information, was surprised to find his inanities quite misunderstood. Arabella fetched a world-weary sigh and enunciated with a scornful curl of her lip: "Oh, yes! *The* Miss Tallant!"

"Th-*the* Miss Tallant?" stammered his lordship, all at sea.

"The rich Miss Tallant!" said Arabella.

His lordship rolled an anguished and an inquiring eye at his host, but Mr. Beaumaris was not looking at him. Mr. Beaumaris, his attention arrested, was regarding the rich Miss Tallant with a distinct gleam of curiosity, not unmixed with amusement, in his face.

"I had hoped that here at least I might be unknown!" said Arabella, seating herself in a chair a little withdrawn from the fire. "Ah, you must let me make you known to Miss Blackburn, my—my *dame de compagnie!*"

Lord Fleetwood sketched a bow; Miss Blackburn, her countenance wooden, dropped him a slight curtsy, and sat down on the nearest chair.

"Miss Tallant!" repeated Lord Fleetwood, searching his memory in vain for enlightenment. "Ah, yes! Of course! Er—I don't think I have ever had the honor of meeting you in town, have I, ma'am?"

Arabella directed an innocent look from him to Mr. Beaumaris and back again, and clapped her hands together with an assumption of mingled delight and dismay. "Oh, you *did* not know!" she exclaimed. "I need never have told you! But when you looked *so,* I made sure you were as bad as all the rest! Was anything ever so vexatious? I most particularly desire to be quite unknown in London!"

"My dear ma'am, you may rely on me!" promptly replied his lordship, who, like most rattles, thought himself the model of discretion. "And Mr. Beaumaris, you know, is in the same case as yourself, and able to sympathize with you!"

Arabella glanced at her host and found that he had raised his quizzing glass, which hung round his neck on a long black riband, and was surveying her through it. She put up her chin a little, for she was by no means sure that she cared for this scrutiny. "Indeed?" she said.

It was not the practice of young ladies to put up their chins in just that style if Mr. Beaumaris leveled his glass at them: they were more in the habit of simpering, or of trying to appear unconscious of his regard. But Mr. Beaumaris saw that there was a decidedly militant sparkle in this lady's eye, and his interest, at first tickled, was now fairly caught. He let his glass fall, and said gravely: "Indeed! And you?"

"Alas!" said Arabella, "I am fabulously wealthy! It is the greatest mortification to me! You can have no notion!"

His lips twitched. "I have always found, however, that a large fortune carries with it certain advantages."

"Oh, you are a man! I shall not allow you to know anything of the matter!" she cried. "You cannot know what it means to be the object of every fortune hunter, courted and odiously flattered only for your wealth, until you are ready to wish that you had not a penny in the world!"

Miss Blackburn, who had hitherto supposed her charge to be a modest, well-behaved girl, barely repressed a shudder. Mr. Beaumaris, however, said: "I feel sure that you underrate yourself, ma'am."

"Oh, dear me, no!" said Arabella. "I have too often heard myself pointed out as the rich Miss Tallant to be under any illusion, sir! And it is for this reason that I wish to be quite unknown in London."

Mr. Beaumaris smiled, but as the butler came in just then to announce dinner, he said nothing but merely offered his arm to Arabella.

The dinner, which consisted of two courses, seemed to Arabella sumptuous beyond her wildest imaginings. No suspicion crossed her mind that her host, after one swift glance at his board, had resigned himself to the knowledge that the reputations of himself and his cook had been placed in jeopardy; or that that artist in the kitchen, having, with strange Gallic imprecations which made his various assistants quake, rent limb from limb two half-roasted Devonport fowls, and flung them into a pan with a béchamel sauce and some tarragons, was even now, as he arranged a basket of pastry on a dish, undecided whether to leave this dishonored house on the instant or to cut his throat with the larger carving knife. Soup à la Reine was removed with fillets of turbot with an Italian sauce; and the chickens à la Tarragon were flanked by a dish of spinach and croûtons, a glazed ham, two cold partridges, some broiled mushrooms, and a raised mutton pie. The second course presented Arabella with an even more bewildering choice, for there was, besides the baskets of pastry, a Rhenish cream, a jelly, a Savoy cake, a dish of salsify fried in butter, an omelette, and some anchovy toast. Mrs. Tallant had always prided herself on her housekeeping, but such a repast as this, embellished as it was by elegant garnitures and subtle sauces, was quite beyond the range of the Vicarage cook. Arabella could not help opening her eyes a little at the array of viands spread before her, but she managed to conceal her awe and to partake of what was offered to her with a very creditable assumption of unconsciousness. Mr. Beaumaris, perhaps loath to degrade his burgundy, or perhaps with a faint, despairing hope of adding piquancy to this commonplace meal, had instructed Brough to serve champagne. Arabella, having already cast discretion to the winds, allowed her glass to be filled, and sipped her way distastefully through it. It had a pleasantly exhilarating effect upon her. She informed Mr. Beaumaris that she was bound for the town residence of Lady Bridlington; created several uncles for the simple purpose of endowing herself with their fortunes; and at one blow disposed of four brothers and three sisters who might have been supposed to have laid a claim to a share of all this wealth. She contrived, without precisely making so vulgar a boast, to convey the impression that she was escaping from courtships so persistent as to amount to persecution; and Mr. Beaumaris, listening with intense pleasure, said that London was the very place for anyone desirous of escaping attention.

Arabella, embarking recklessly on her second glass of champagne, said that in a crowd one could more easily pass unnoticed than in the restricted society of the country.

"Very true," agreed Mr. Beaumaris.

"*You* never did so!" remarked Lord Fleetwood, helping himself from the dish of mushrooms which Brough presented at his elbow. "You must know, ma'am, that you are in the presence of the Nonpareil—none other! Quite the most noted figure in society since poor Brummell was done up!"

"Indeed!" Arabella looked from him to Mr. Beaumaris with a pretty air of innocent inquiry. "I did not know—I might not have heard the name quite correctly, perhaps?"

"My dear Miss Tallant!" exclaimed his lordship, in mock horror. "Not known the great Beaumaris! The Arbiter of Fashion! Robert, you are quite set down!"

Mr. Beaumaris, whose almost imperceptibly lifted finger had brought the watchful Brough to his side, was murmuring some command into that attentive but astonished ear and paid no heed. His command was passed on to the footman hovering by the side table, who, being quite a young man, and as yet imperfectly in control of his emotions, betrayed in his starting look some measure of the incredulity which shook his trained soul. The coldly quelling eye of his superior recalled him speedily to a sense of his position, however, and he left the room to carry the stupefying command still further.

Miss Tallant, meanwhile, had perceived an opportunity to gratify her most pressing desire, which was to snub her host beyond possibility of his recovery. "Arbiter of Fashion?" she said, in a blank voice. "You cannot, surely, mean one of the *dandy set?* I had thought—Oh, I beg your pardon! I expect that in London that is quite as important as being a great soldier, or a stateman, or—or some such thing!"

Even Lord Fleetwood could scarcely mistake the tenor of this artless speech. He gave an audible gasp. Miss Blackburn, whose enjoyment of dinner had already been seriously impaired, refused the partridge and tried unavailingly to catch her charge's eye. Only Mr. Beaumaris, hugely enjoying himself, appeared unmoved. He replied coolly: "Oh, decidedly! One's influence is so far-reaching!"

"Oh?" said Arabella politely.

"Why, certainly, ma'am! One may blight a whole career by the mere raising of an eyebrow, or elevate a social aspirant to the ranks of the highest *ton* only by leaning on his arm for the length of a street."

Miss Tallant suspected that she was being quizzed, but the strange exhilaration had her in its grip and she did not hesitate to cross swords with this expert fencer. "No doubt, sir, if *I* had ambitions to cut a figure in society *your* approval would be a necessity?"

Mr. Beaumaris, famed for his sword play, slipped under her guard with an unexpected thrust. "My dear Miss Tallant, *you* need no passport to admit you to the ranks of the most sought-after! Even *I* could not depress the claims of one endowed with—may I say it?—your face, your figure, and your fortune!"

The color flamed up into Arabella's cheeks; she choked over the last of her wine, tried to look arch, and only succeeded in looking adorably confused. Lord Fleetwood, realizing that his friend had embarked on yet another of his practiced flirtations, directed an indignant glance at him and did his best to engage the heiress's attention himself. He was succeeding quite well when he was thrown off his balance by the unprecedented behavior of Brough, who, as the second course made its appearance, removed his champagne glass, replacing it with a goblet, which he proceeded to fill with something out of a tall flagon which his lordship strongly suspected was iced lemonade. One sip was enough alike to confirm this hideous fear and to deprive his lordship momentarily of the power of speech. Mr. Beaumaris, blandly swallowing some of the innocuous mixture, seized the opportunity to reengage Miss Tallant in conversation.

Arabella had been rather relieved to see her wineglass removed, for although she would have died rather than have owned to it, she thought the champagne decidedly nasty, besides making her want to sneeze. She took a revivifying draft of lemonade, glad to discover that in really fashionable circles this mild beverage was apparently served with the second course. Miss Blackburn, better versed in the ways of the *haut ton*, now found herself unable to form a correct judgment of her host. To be plunged from a conviction that he was truly gentlemanlike to a shocked realization that he was nothing but a coxcomb, and then back again, quite overset the poor little lady. She knew not what to think, but could not forbear casting him a glance eloquent of the warmest gratitude. His eyes encountered hers, but for such a fleeting instant that she could never afterward be sure whether she had caught the glimmer of an amused smile in them, or whether she had imagined it.

Brough, receiving a message at the door, announced that Madam's groom had brought a hired coach to the house, and desired to know when she would wish to resume her journey to Grantham.

"It can wait," said Mr. Beaumaris, replenishing Arabella's glass. "A little of the Rhenish cream, Miss Tallant?"

"How long," demanded Arabella, recalling Mr. Beaumaris's odious words to his friend, "will it take them to mend my own carriage?"

"I understand, miss, that a new pole will be needed. I could not say how long it will be."

A faint clucking from Miss Blackburn indicated dismay at this intelligence. Mr. Beaumaris said: "A tiresome accident, but I beg you will not distress yourselves! I will send my chaise to pick you up in Grantham at whatever hour tomorrow should be agreeable to you."

Arabella thanked him but was resolute in refusing his offer, for which, she assured him, there was not the slightest occasion. If the wheelwright proved too dilatory for her patience, she would finish her journey post. "It will be quite an experience!" she declared truthfully. "My friends assure me that I am a great deal too old-fashioned in my notions—that quite a respectable degree of comfort is to be found in hired chaises!"

"I perceive," said Mr. Beaumaris, "that we have much in common, ma'am. But I shall not allow a distaste for hired vehicles to be old-fashioned. Let us rather say that we have a little more nicety than the general run of our fellow creatures!" He turned his head toward the butler. "Let a message be conveyed to the wheelwright, Brough, that he will oblige me by repairing Miss Tallant's carriage with all possible expedition."

Miss Tallant had nothing to do but thank him for his kind offices and finish her Rhenish cream. That done, she rose from the table, saying that she had trespassed too long on her host's hospitality, and must now take her leave of him, with renewed thanks for his kindness.

"The obligation, Miss Tallant, is all on my side," he replied. "I am grateful for the chance which has made us acquainted, and shall hope to have the pleasure of calling upon you in town before many days."

This promise threw Miss Blackburn into agitation. As she accompanied Arabella upstairs, she whispered: "My dear Miss Tallant, how *could* you? And now he means to call on you, and you have told him—oh dear, oh dear, what would your Mama say?"

"Pooh!" returned Arabella, brazening it out. "If he is indeed a rich man, he will not care a fig, or think of it again!"

"*If* he is—Good gracious, Miss Tallant, he must be one of the wealthiest men in the country! When I collected that he was in very truth Mr. Beaumaris, I nearly swooned where I stood!"

"Well," said the pot-valiant Arabella, "if he is so very grand and important, you may depend upon it he has not the least intention of calling on me in town. And I am sure I hope he will not, for he is an odious person!"

She refused to be moved from this standpoint, or even to acknowledge that in Mr. Beaumaris's person at least no fault could be found. She said that she did not think him handsome, and that she held dandies in abhorrence. Miss Blackburn, terrified that she might, in this alarming mood, betray her dislike of Mr. Beaumaris at parting, begged her not to forget what the barest civility rendered obligatory. She added that one slighting word uttered by him would be sufficient to wither any young lady's career at the outset, and then wished that she had held her tongue, since this warning had the effect of bringing the militant sparkle back into Arabella's eyes. But when Mr. Beaumaris handed her into the coach, and, with quite his most attractive smile, lightly kissed the tips of her fingers before letting her hand go, she bade him farewell in a shy little voice that gave no hint of her loathing of him.

The coach set off down the drive; Mr. Beaumaris turned, and in a leisurely way walked back into his house. He was pounced on in the hall by his injured friend, who demanded to know what the devil he meant by inflicting lemonade upon his guests.

"I don't think Miss Tallant cared for my champagne," he replied imperturbably.

"Well, if she didn't, she could have refused it, couldn't she?" protested Lord Fleetwood. "Besides, it was no such thing! She drank two glasses of it!"

"Never mind, Charles, there is still the port," said Mr. Beaumaris.

"Yes, by God!" said his lordship, brightening. "And, mind, now! I expect the very best in your cellar! A couple of bottles of that '75 of yours, or—"

"Bring it to the library, Brough—something off the wood!" said Mr. Beaumaris.

Lord Fleetwood, always the easiest preys, rose to the bait without a moment's hesitation. "Here, no, I say!" he cried, turning quite pale with horror. "Robert! No, really, Robert!"

Mr. Beaumaris lifted his brows in the blandest astonishment, but Brough, taking pity on his lordship, said in a soothing tone: "We have nothing like that in our cellars, I assure your lordship!"

Lord Fleetwood, perceiving that he had once more been gulled, said with strong feeling: "You deserve I should plant you a facer for that, Robert!"

"Well, if you think you can—!" said Mr. Beaumaris.

"I don't," replied his lordship frankly, accompanying him into the library. "But that lemonade was a dog's trick to serve me, you know!" His brow puckered in an effort of thought. "Tallant! . . . Did you ever hear the name before, for I'll swear I never did?"

Mr. Beaumaris looked at him for a moment. Then his eyes fell to the snuffbox he had drawn from his pocket. He flicked open the box and took a delicate pinch between finger and thumb. "You have never heard of the Tallant fortune?" he said. "My *dear* Charles—!"

❧ *Chapter 5* ❧

THANKS TO MR. BEAUMARIS'S MESSAGE, which worked so powerfully on the wheelwright as to cause him to ignore the prior claims of three other owners of damaged vehicles, Arabella was only kept waiting for one day in Grantham. Since the Quorn met there on the morning following her encounter with Mr. Beaumaris, she was able, from the window of a private parlor at the Angel and Royal Inn, to see just how he looked on horseback. She could have seen how Lord Fleetwood looked too, had she cared, but curiously enough she never thought of his lordship. Mr. Beaumaris looked remarkably well, astride a beautiful thoroughbred with long, sloping pasterns and shoulders well laid back. She decided that Mr. Beaumaris's seat was as good as any she had ever seen. The tops to his hunting boots were certainly whiter than a mere provincial would have deemed possible.

The hunt having moved off, there was nothing for two delayed travelers to do for the rest of the day but stroll about the town, eat their meals, yawn over the only books to be found in the inn. But by the following morning the Squire's carriage was brought round to the

Angel, with a new pole affixed and the horses well rested, and the ladies were able to set forward betimes on the last half of their long journey.

Even Miss Blackburn was heartily sick of the road by the time the muddied carriage at last drew up outside Lady Bridlington's house in Park Street. She was sufficiently well acquainted with the metropolis to feel no interest in the various sounds and sights which had made Arabella forget her boredom and her fidgets from the moment that the carriage reached Islington. These, to a young lady who had never seen a larger town than York in her life, were at once enthralling and bewildering. The traffic made her feel giddy, and the noise of post bells, of wheels on the cobbled streets, and the shrill cries of itinerant venders of coals, brick dust, door mats, and rattraps quite deafened her. All passed before her wide gaze in a whirl; she wondered how anyone could live in such a place and still retain her sanity. But as the carriage, stopping once or twice for the coachman to inquire the way of nasal and not always polite Cockneys, wound its ponderous way into the more modish part of the town, the din abated till Arabella began even to entertain hopes of being able to sleep in London.

The house in Park Street seemed overpoweringly tall to one accustomed to a rambling two-storied country house; and the butler who admitted the ladies into a lofty hall, whence rose an imposing flight of stairs, was so majestic that Arabella felt almost inclined to apologize for putting him to the trouble of announcing her to her godmother. But she was relieved to find that he was supported by only one footman, and so was able to follow him up with tolerable composure to the drawing room on the first floor.

Here her qualms were put to flight by the welcome she received. Lady Bridlington, whose plump pink cheeks were wreathed in smiles, clasped her to an ample bosom, kissed her repeatedly, exclaimed, just as Aunt Emma had, on her likeness to her Mama, and seemed so unaffectedly glad to see her that all constraint was at an end. Lady Bridlington's good nature extended even to the governess, to whom she spoke with kindness and perfect civility.

When Mama had known Lady Bridlington, she had been a pretty girl, without more than common sense, but with such a respectable portion, and with so much vivacity and good humor that it was no surprise to her friends when she contracted a very eligible match. Time had done more to enlarge her figure than her mind, and it was not many days before her young charge had discovered that under a superficial worldly wisdom there was little but a vast amount of silliness. Her ladyship read whatever new work of prose or verse was in fashion, understood one word in ten of it, and prattled of the whole; doted on the most admired singers at the Opera, but secretly preferred the ballet; vowed there had never been anything to equal Kean's *Hamlet* on the English stage, but derived considerably more enjoyment from the farce which followed this soul-stirring performance. She was incapable of humming a tune correctly, but never failed to patronize the Concerts of Ancient Music during the season, just as she never failed to visit the Royal Academy every year, at Somerset House, where, although her notion of a good picture was a painting that reminded her forcibly of some person or place with which she was familiar, she unerringly detected the hand of a master in all the most distinguished artists' canvasses. Her life seemed to a slightly shocked Arabella to consist wholly of pleasure; and the greatest exertion she ever put her mind to was the securing of her own comfort. But it would have been unjust to have called her a selfish woman. Her disposition was kindly; she liked the people round her to be as happy as she was herself, for that made them cheerful, and she disliked long faces; she paid her servants well, and always remembered to thank them for any extraordinary service they performed for her, such as walking her horses up and down Bond Street in the rain for an hour while she shopped, or sitting up till four or five in the morning to put her to bed after an evening party; and provided she was not expected to put herself out for them, or to do anything disagreeable, she was both kind and generous to her friends.

She expected nothing but pleasure from Arabella's visit, and although she knew that in launching the girl into society she was behaving in a very handsome way, she never dwelled on the reflection, except once or twice a day in the privacy of her dressing room, and then not in any grudging spirit but merely for the gratifying sensation it gave her of being a benevolent person. She was very fond of visiting, shopping, and spectacles; liked entertaining large gatherings in her own house; and was seldom bored by even the dullest Assembly. Naturally, since every woman of fashion did so, she complained of dreadful squeezes or sadly insipid evenings, but no one who had seen her at these functions, greeting a multitude of acquaintances, exchanging the latest *on dits,* closely scanning the newest fashions, or taking eager part in a rubber of whist, could have doubted her real and simple enjoyment of them.

To be obliged, then, to chaperon a young lady making her début to a succession of balls, routs, Assemblies, Military Reviews, balloon ascensions, and every other diversion likely to be offered to society during the season, exactly suited her disposition. She spent the better part of Arabella's first evening in Park Street in describing to her all the delightful plans she had been making for her amusement, and could scarcely wait for Miss Blackburn's departure next day before ordering her carriage to be sent round and taking Arabella on a tour of all the smartest shops in London.

These cast the shops of High Harrowgate into the

shade. Arabella was obliged to exercise great self-restraint when she saw the alluring wares displayed in the windows. She was helped a little by her north-country shrewdness, which recoiled from trifles priced at five times their worth, and not at all by her cicerone, who, having been blessed all her life with sufficient means to enable her to purchase whatever took her fancy, could not understand why Arabella would not buy a bronzegreen velvet hat trimmed with feathers and a broad fall of lace, and priced at a figure which would have covered the cost of all the hats so cleverly contrived by Mama's and Sophia's neat fingers. Lady Bridlington owned that it was an expensive hat, but she held that to buy what became one so admirably could not be termed an extravagance. But Arabella put it resolutely aside, saying that she had as many hats as she required, and explaining frankly that she must not spend her money too freely, since Papa and Mama could not afford to send her any more. Lady Bridlington was quite distressed to think that such a pretty girl should not be able to set her beauty off to the best advantage. It seemed so sad that she was moved to purchase a net stocking-purse and a branch of artificial flowers, and to bestow them on Arabella. She hesitated for a few minutes over a handsome shawl of Norwich silk, but it was priced at twenty guineas, and although this could not be said to be a high price, she remembered that she had one herself, a much better one, for which she paid fifty guineas, which she could very well lend to Arabella whenever she did not wish to wear it herself. Besides, there would be all the expense of Arabella's Court dress to be borne later in the season, and even though a great deal might be found in her own wardrobe which could be converted to Arabella's needs, the cost was still certain to be heavy. A further inspection of the shawl convinced her that it was of poor quality, not at all the sort of thing she would like to give her young charge, so they left the shop without buying it. Arabella was profoundly relieved, for although she would naturally have liked to have possessed the shawl, it made her very uncomfortable to be in danger of costing her hostess so much money.

Her frankness in speaking of her circumstances made Lady Bridlington a little thoughtful. She did not immediately mention the matter, but when the two ladies sat before the fire in the small saloon that evening drinking tea, she ventured to put into words some at least of the thoughts which were revolving in her head.

"You know, my dear," she said, "I have been considering the best way to set to work, and I have made up my mind to it that as soon as you have grown more used to London—and I am sure it will not be long, for you are such a bright, clever little puss!—I should introduce you, quietly, you know! The season has not yet begun, and London is still very thin of company. And I think that will suit us very well, for you are not used to the way we go on here, and a small Assembly—no dancing, just an evening party, with music, perhaps, and cards—is the very thing for your first appearance! I mean to invite only a few of my friends, the very people who may be useful to you. You will become acquainted with some other young ladies, and of course with some gentlemen, and that will make it more comfortable, I assure you, when I take you to Almack's or to some large ball. Nothing can be more disagreeable than to find oneself in a gathering where one does not recognize a single face!"

Arabella could readily believe it, and had nothing but approbation for this excellent scheme. "Oh, yes, if you please, ma'am! It is of all things what I should like, for I know I shall not know how to go on at first, though I mean to learn as fast as I can!"

"Exactly so!" beamed her ladyship. "You are a sensible girl, Arabella, and I am very hopeful of settling you respectably, just as I promised your Mama I would!" She saw that Arabella was blushing, and added: "You won't object to my speaking plain, my love, for I daresay you know how important it is that you should be creditably established. Eight children! I do not know how your poor Mama will ever contrive to get good husbands for your sisters! And boys are such a charge on one's purse! I am sure I do not care to think of what my dear Frederick cost his father and me from first to last! First it was one thing, and then another!"

A serious look came into Arabella's face, as she thought of the many and varied needs of her brothers and sisters. She said earnestly: "Indeed, ma'am, what you say is very just, and I mean to do my best not to disappoint Mama!"

Lady Bridlington leaned forward to lay her pudgy little hand over Arabella's and to squeeze it fondly. "I knew you would feel just as you ought!" she said. "Which brings me to what I had in mind to say to you!" She sat back again in her chair, fidgeted for a moment with the fringe of her shawl, and then said without looking at Arabella: "You know, my love, everything depends on first impressions—at least, a great deal does! In society, with everyone trying to find eligible husbands for their daughters, and so many beautiful girls for the gentlemen to choose from, it is in the highest degree important that you should do and say exactly what is right. That is why I mean to bring you out quietly, and not at all until you feel yourself at home in London. For you must know, my dear, that only rustics appear amazed. I am sure I do not know why it should be so, but you may believe that innocent girls from the country are not at all what the gentlemen like!"

Arabella was surprised, for her reading had taught her otherwise. She ventured to say as much, but Lady Bridlington shook her head. "No, my love, it is not so at all! That sort of thing may do very well in a novel, and I am very fond of novels myself, but they have nothing to do with life, depend upon it! But that was not what I wished to say!" Again she played with the shawl fringe, saying in a little burst of eloquence: "I would not, if I were you, my dear, be forever talking about Heythram and the Vicarage! You must remember that nothing is more wearisome than to be obliged to listen to stories about a set of persons one has never seen. And though of course you would not prevaricate in any way, it is quite unnecessary to tell everyone—or, indeed, anyone!—of your dear Papa's situation! *I* have said nothing to lead anyone to suppose that he is not in affluent circumstances, for nothing, I do assure you, Arabella, could be more fatal to your chances than to have it known that your expectations are very small!"

Arabella was about to reply rather more hotly than was civil when the recollection of her own conduct in Mr. Beaumaris's house came into her mind. She hung her head and sat silent, wondering whether she ought to make a clean breast of the regrettable affair to Lady Bridlington, and deciding that it was too bad to be spoken of.

Lady Bridlington, misunderstanding the reason for her evident confusion, said hastily: "If you should be fortunate enough to engage some gentleman's affection, dear Arabella, of course you will tell him just how you are placed, or I shall, and—and, depend upon it, he will not care a button! You must not be thinking that I wish you to practice the least deception, for it is no such thing! Merely, it would be foolish, and quite unnecessary, for you to be talking of your circumstances to every chance-met acquaintance!"

"Very well, ma'am," said Arabella, in a subdued tone.

"I knew you would be sensible! Well, now, I am sure there is no need for me to say anything more to you on this head, and we must decide whom I shall invite to my evening party. I wonder, my love, if you would see if my tablets are on that little table. And a pencil, if you will be so good!"

These commodities having been found, the good lady settled down happily to plan for the coming party. Since the names she recited were all of them unknown to Arabella, the discussion resolved itself into a gentle monologue. Lady Bridlington ran through the greater part of her acquaintance, murmuring that it would be useless to invite the Farnworths, since they had no children; that Lady Kirkmichael gave the shabbiest entertainments, and could not be depended on to invite Arabella even if she did decide to give a ball for that lanky daughter of hers; that the Accringtons must of course be sent a card, and also the Buxtons—delightful families, both, and bound to entertain largely this season! "And I mean to invite Lord Dewsbury, and Sir Geoffrey Morecambe, my dear, for there is no saying but what one of them might—And I am sure Mr. Pocklington has been hanging out for a wife these two years, not but what he is perhaps a little old—However, we will ask him to come, for there can be no harm in that! Then, I must certainly prevail upon dear Lady Sefton to come, for she is one of the patronesses of Almack's, you know; and perhaps Emily Cowper might—And the Charnwoods, and Mr. Catwick; and, if they are in town, the Garthorpes . . ."

She rambled on in this style, while Arabella tried to appear interested. But as she could do no more than agree with her hostess when she was appealed to, her attention soon wandered, to be recalled with a jerk when Lady Bridlington mentioned a name she did know.

"And I shall send Mr. Beaumaris a card, because it would be such a splendid thing for you, my love, if it were known that he came to your début—for such we may call it! Why, if he were to come, and perhaps talk to you for a few minutes, and seem pleased with you, you would be *made*, my dear! Everyone follows his lead! And perhaps, as there are so few parties yet, he *might* come! I am sure I have been acquainted with him for years, and I knew his mother quite well! She was Lady Mary Caldicot, you know: a daughter of the late Duke of Wigan, and such a beautiful creature! And it is not as though Mr. Beaumaris has never been to my house, for he once came to an Assembly here and stayed for quite half an hour! Mind, we must not build upon his accepting, but we need not despair!"

She paused for breath, and Arabella, coloring in spite of herself, was able at last to say: "I—I am myself a little acquainted with Mr. Beaumaris, ma'am."

Lady Bridlington was so much astonished that she dropped her pencil. "Acquainted with Mr. Beaumaris?" she repeated. "My love, what *can* you be thinking about? When can you possibly have met him?"

"I—I quite forgot to tell you, ma'am," faltered Arabella unhappily, "that when the pole broke—I told you *that!*—Miss Blackburn and I sought shelter in his hunting box, and—and he had Lord Fleetwood with him, and we stayed to dine!"

Lady Bridlington gasped. "Good God, Arabella, and you never told me! Mr. Beaumaris's house! He actually asked you to dine, and you never breathed a word of it to me!"

Arabella found herself quite incapable of explaining why she had been shy of mentioning this episode. She stammered that it had slipped out of her mind in all the excitement of coming to London.

"Slipped out of your mind?" exclaimed Lady Bridlington. "You dine with Mr. Beaumaris, and at his hunting box, too, and then talk to me about the excitement of coming to London? Good gracious, child—But, there, you are such a country mouse, my love, I daresay you did not know all it might mean to you! Did he seem pleased? Did he like you?"

This was a little too much, even for a young lady determined to be on her best behavior. "I daresay he disliked me excessively, ma'am, for *I* thought *him* very proud and disagreeable, and I hope you won't ask him to your party on *my* account!"

"Not ask him to my party, when, if he came to it, everyone would say it was a success! You must be mad, Arabella, to talk so! And do let me beg of you, my dear, never to say such a thing of Mr. Beaumaris in public! I daresay he may be a little stiff, but what is that to the purpose, pray? There is no one who counts for more in society, for, setting aside his fortune, which is immense, my love, he is related to half the houses in England! The Beaumarises are one of the oldest of our families, while on his mother's side he is a grandson of the Duchess of Wigan—the Dowager Duchess, I mean, which of course makes him cousin to the present Duke, besides the Wainfleets, and—But you would not know!" she ended despairingly.

"I thought Lord Fleetwood most amiable and gentlemanlike," offered Arabella, by way of palliative.

"Fleetwood! I can tell you this, Arabella: there is no use in your setting your cap at *him,* for all the world knows that he *must* marry money!"

"I hope, ma'am," cried Arabella, flaring up, "that you do not mean to suggest that I should *set my cap* at Mr. Beaumaris, for nothing would prevail upon me to do so!"

"My love," responded Lady Bridlington frankly, "it would be quite useless for you to do so! Robert Beaumaris may have his pick of all the beauties in England, I daresay! And what is more, he is the most accomplished flirt in London! But I do most earnestly implore you not to set him against you by treating him with the least incivility! You may think him what you please, but, believe me, Arabella, he could ruin your whole career—and mine, too, if it came to that!" she added feelingly.

Arabella propped her chin in her hand, pondering an agreeable thought. "Or he could make everything easy for me, ma'am?" she inquired.

"Of course he could—if he chose to do it! He is the most unpredictable creature! It might amuse him to make you the rage of town—or he might take it into his head to say you were not quite in his style; and if once he says *that,* my dear, what man will look twice at you, unless he has already fallen in love with you, which, after all, we *cannot* expect?"

"My dear ma'am," said Arabella, in dulcet accents, "I hope I should not be so ill-bred as to be uncivil to *any-one*—even Mr. Beaumaris!"

"Well, my dear, I hope not, indeed!" said her ladyship doubtfully.

"I promise I will not be in the least degree uncivil to Mr. Beaumaris, if he should come to your party," said Arabella.

"I am happy to hear you say so, my love, but ten to one he won't come," responded her ladyship pessimistically.

"He said to me at parting that he hoped to have the pleasure of calling on me in town before many days," said Arabella disinterestedly.

Lady Bridlington considered this, but in the end shook her head. "I do not think we should set any store by that," she said. "Very likely he said it for politeness' sake."

"Very likely," agreed Arabella. "But if you are acquainted with him, I wish you will send Lord Fleetwood a card for your party, ma'am, for he was excessively kind, and I liked him!"

"Of course I am acquainted with him!" declared Lady Bridlington, quite affronted. "But do not be setting your heart on him, Arabella, I beg of you! A delightful rattle, but the Fleetwoods are all to pieces, by what I hear, and however much he may flirt with you, I am persuaded he will never make you an offer!"

"Must every man I meet make me an offer?" asked Arabella, controlling her voice with an effort.

"No, my love, and you may depend upon it that they won't!" replied her ladyship candidly. "In fact, I have had it in mind to warn you against setting your ambitions *too* high! I mean to do all I can for you, but there is no denying that suitable husbands do not grow upon every bush! Particularly, my dear—and I know you will not fly into a miff with me for saying it!—when you have no portion to recommend you!"

In face of her ladyship's conviction Arabella hardly liked to betray her feelings, so she bit her lip and was silent. Fortunately, Lady Bridlington's mind was not of a tenacious nature, and as she just then recollected a very important lady whose name must be included among the list of invited persons, she forgot about Arabella's matrimonial chances in explaining why it would be folly to omit Lady Terrington from that list. Nothing more was said about Mr. Beaumaris, her ladyship having been diverted by some chance reference of her own into describing to Arabella the various social treats she had in store for her. In spite of the fact that the season had not yet begun, these were so numerous that Arabella felt almost giddy, and wondered whether, in this round of gaiety, her hostess would find the time to accompany her to church on Sunday. But in doubting whether Lady Bridlington would go to church, she wronged her: Lady Bridlington would have thought it a very odd thing not to be seen in her pew every Sunday morning, unless, as was very often the case, she chose to attend the service at the Chapel Royal, where, in addition to listening to an excellent sermon, she could be sure of seeing all her more distinguished friends, and even, very often, some member of the Royal Family. This good fortune was hers on Arabella's first Sunday in London, and the circumstance made fine reading for the interested brothers and sisters in Yorkshire, following, as it did (most artistically), descriptions of Hyde Park, and St. Paul's Cathedral, and a lively account of the racket and bustle of the London streets.

"We attended Morning Service at the Chapel Royal, St. James's, on Sunday," wrote Arabella in a fine, small hand, and on very thin paper, crossing her lines. "We heard a very good sermon on a text from the Second Epistle to the Corinthians, pray tell dear Papa: 'He that had gathered much had nothing over; and he that had gathered little had no lack.' London is still very thin of company"—not for nothing had Arabella dutifully attended to her godmother's conversation!— "but there were a great many fashionables present, and also the Duke of Clarence, who came up to us afterward, and was very affable, with nothing high in his manner at all." Arabella paused, nibbling the end of her pen and considering the Duke of Clarence. Papa might not care to have his Royal Highness described, but Mama and Sophy and Margaret would most certainly wish to know just what he was like and what he had said. She bent again over her page. "I do not think one would say that he is precisely handsome," she wrote temperately, "but his countenance is benevolent. His head is a queer shape, and he is inclined to corpulence. He made me think of my uncle, for he talks in just that way, and very loud, and he laughs a great deal. He did me the honor to say that I wore a vastly *fetching* hat: I hope Mama will be pleased, for it was the one with her pink feathers which she made for me." There did not seem to be anything more to be said about the Duke of Clarence, except that he talked quite audibly in church, and that was information scarcely likely to please the inhabitants of the Vicarage. She read over what she had written, and felt that it might disappoint Mama and the girls. She added a line. "Lady Bridlington says that he is not near as fat as the Prince Regent, or the Duke of York." On this heartening note she ended her paragraph and embarked on a fresh one.

"I am growing quite accustomed to London, and begin to know my way about the streets, though of course I do not walk out by myself yet. Lady Bridlington sends a footman with me, just as Bertram said she would, but I see that young females do go alone nowadays, only perhaps they are not of the *haut ton.* This is *very important,* and I am in constant dread that I shall do something improper, such as walking down St. James's Street, where all the gentlemen's clubs are, and very *fast,* which of course I do not wish to be thought. Lady Bridlington gives an evening party, to introduce me to her friends. I shall be all of a quake, for everyone is so grand and fashionable, though perfectly civil, and much kinder than I had looked for. Sophy will like to know that Lord Fleetwood, whom I met on the road, as I wrote to you from Grantham, paid us a morning visit, to see how I did, which was very amiable and obliging of him. Also Mr. Beaumaris, but we were out driving in the Park. He left his card. Lady Bridlington was in transports and has placed it above all the rest, which I think nonsensical, but I find that that is the way of the World, and makes me reflect on all Papa has said on the subject of Folly, and the Hollowness of Fashionable Life." That seemed to dispose satisfactorily of Mr. Beaumaris. Arabella dipped her pen in the standish again. "Lady Bridlington is everything that is kind, and I am persuaded that Lord Bridlington is a very respectable young man and not at all abandoned to the Pursuit of Pleasure, as Papa feared. His name is Frederick. He is traveling in Germany, and has visited a great many of the battlefields. He writes very interesting letters to his Mama, with which I am sure Papa would be pleased, for he seems to feel just as he ought, and moralizes on all he sees in a truly elevating way, though rather long." Arabella perceived that there was little room left on her sheet, and added in a cramped fist: "I would write more, only that I cannot get a frank for this and do not wish to put Papa to the expense of paying some sixpences for the second sheet. With my love to my brothers and sisters, and my affectionate duty to dear Papa, I remain your loving daughter Arabella."

Plenty of promising matter there for Mama and the girls to pore over, and to discuss, even though so much remained unwritten! One could not resist boasting a very little about the compliments paid to one by a Royal Duke, or just mentioning that a fashionable peer of the realm had called to see how one did—not to mention the great Mr. Beaumaris, if one had happened to care a fig for that—but one felt quite shy of disclosing even to Mama how very gracious—how amazingly kind—everyone was being to an insignificant girl from Yorkshire.

For so it was. Shopping in Bond Street, driving on clement afternoons in Hyde Park, attending the service at the Chapel Royal, Lady Bridlington naturally encountered friends, and never failed to present Arabella to their notice. Some really forbidding dowagers who might have been expected to have paid scant heed to Arabella unbent in the most gratifying way, quite overpowering her by the kindness of their inquiries, and their insistence that Lady Bridlington should bring her to see them one day. Several introduced their daughters to Arabella, suggesting that she and they might walk in the Green Park some fine morning, so that in less than no time it seemed as though she had a host of acquaintances in London. The gentlemen were not more backward: it was quite a commonplace thing for some stroller in the Park to come up to Lady Bridlington's barouche and stand chatting to her and to her pretty protégée; while more than one sprig of fashion with whom her ladyship was barely acquainted paid her a morning visit on what seemed, even to one so little given to speculation as Lady Bridlington, the slenderest of excuses.

She was a little surprised, but after thinking about it for a few minutes she was as easily able to account for the ladies' civility as the gentlemen's. They were anxious to oblige her. This led her by natural stages to the reflection that she deserved a great deal of credit for having so well advertised Arabella's visit to town. As for the gentlemen, she had never doubted, from the moment of setting eyes on her goddaughter, that that fairy figure and charming countenance must attract instant admiration. Arabella had, moreover, the most enchanting smile, which brought dimples leaping to her cheeks and was at once mischievous and appealing. Any but the most casehardened of men, thought Lady Bridlington enviously, would be more than likely, under its intoxicating influence, to behave in a rash manner, however much he might afterward regret it.

But none of these conclusions quite explained the morning visits of several high-nosed ladies of fashion whose civilities toward Lady Bridlington had hitherto consisted of invitations to their larger Assemblies, and bows exchanged from their respective carriages. Lady Somercote was particularly puzzling. She called in Park Street when Arabella was out walking with the three charming daughters of Sir James and Lady Hornsea, and she sat for over an hour with her gratified hostess. She expressed the greatest admiration of Arabella, whom she had met at the theater with her godmother. "A delightful girl!" she said graciously. "Very pretty behaved, and without the least hint of pretension in her dress or bearing!"

Lady Bridlington agreed to it; and since her mind did not move rapidly, it was not until her guest was well into her next observation that she wondered why Arabella should be supposed to show pretension.

"Of good family, I apprehend?" said Lady Somercote, carelessly, but looking rather searchingly at her hostess.

"Of course!" replied Lady Bridlington, with dignity. "A most respected Yorkshire family!"

Lady Somercote nodded. "I thought as much. Excellent manners, and conducts herself with perfect propriety! I was particularly pleased with the modesty of her bearing: not the least sign of wishing to put herself forward! And her dress too! Just what I like to see in a young female! Nothing vulgar, such as one too often sees nowadays! When every miss out of the schoolroom is decked out with jewelry, it is refreshing to see one with a simple wreath of flowers in her hair. Somercote was much struck. Indeed, he quite took one of his fancies to her! You must bring her to Grosvenor Square next week, dear Lady Bridlington! Nothing formal, you know: a few friends only, and perhaps the young people may find themselves with enough couples to get up a little dance.''

She waited only for Lady Bridlington's acceptance of this flattering invitation before taking her leave. Lady Bridlington was left with her mind in a whirl. She was shrewd enough to know that more than a compliment to herself must lie behind this unexpected honor, and was at a loss to discover the lady's motive. She was the mother of five hopeful and expensive sons, and it was well known that the Somercote estates were heavily mortgaged. Advantageous marriages were a necessity to the Somercotes' progeny, and no one was more purposeful in her pursuit of a likely heiress than their Mama. For a dismayed instant Lady Bridlington wondered whether, in her anxiety to assist Arabella, she had concealed her circumstances too well. But she could not recall that she had ever so much as mentioned them: indeed, her recollection was that she had taken care never to do so.

The Honorable Mrs. Penkridge, calling on her dear friend for the express purpose of bidding her and her protégée to a select Musical Soirée, and explaining, with apologies, how it was due to the stupidity of a secretary that her card of invitation had not reached her long since, spoke in even warmer terms of Arabella. "Charming! Quite charming!" she declared, bestowing her frosted smile upon Lady Bridlington. "She will throw all our beauties into the shade! That simplicity is so particularly pleasing! You are to be congratulated!"

However perplexed Lady Bridlington might be by this speech, issuing, as it did, from the lips of one famed as much for her haughtiness as for her acid tongue, it seemed at least to dispose of the suspicion roused in her mind by Lady Somercote's visit. The Penkridges were a childless couple. Lady Bridlington, on whom Mrs. Penkridge had more than once passed some contemptuous criticism, was not well enough acquainted with her to know that almost the only sign of human emotion she had ever been seen to betray was her doting fondness for her nephew, Mr. Horace Epworth.

This elegant gentleman, complete to a point as regards side whiskers, fobs, seals, quizzing glass, and scented handkerchief, had lately honored his aunt with one of his infrequent visits. Surprised and delighted, she had begged to know in what way she could be of service to him. Mr. Epworth had no hesitation in telling her. "You might put me in the way of meeting the new heiress, ma'am," he said frankly. "Dev'lish fine gal—regular Croesus, too!"

She had pricked up her ears at that, and exclaimed: "Whom can you be thinking of, my dear Horace? If you mean the Flint chit, I have it for a fact that—"

"Pooh! Nothing of the sort!" interrupted Mr. Epworth, waving the Flint chit away with one white and languid hand. "I daresay *she* has no more than thirty thousand pounds! This gal is so rich she puts 'em all in the shade. They call her the Lady Dives."

"Who calls her so?" demanded his incredulous relative.

Mr. Epworth again waved his hand, this time in the direction which he vaguely judged to be northward. "Oh, up there somewhere, ma'am! Yorkshire, or some other of those dev'lish remote counties! Daresay she's a merchant's daughter: wool, or cotton, or some such thing. Pity, but I shan't regard it: they tell me she's charming!"

"I have heard nothing of this! Who is she? Who told you she was charming?"

"Had it from Fleetwood last night, at the Great-Go," explained Mr. Epworth negligently.

"That rattle! I wish you will not go so often to Watier's, Horace! I warn you, it is useless to apply to me! I have not a guinea left in the world, and I dare not ask Mr. Penkridge to assist you again, until he has forgotten the last time!"

"Put me in the way of meeting this gal, and I'll kiss my fingers to Penkridge, ma'am," responded Mr. Epworth, gracefully suiting the action to the word. "Acquainted with Lady Bridlington, ain't you? The gal's staying with her."

She stared at him. "If Arabella Bridlington had an heiress staying with her, she would have boasted of it all over town!"

"No, she wouldn't. Fleetwood particularly told me the gal don't want it known. Don't like being courted for her fortune. Pretty gal, too, by what Fleetwood says. Name of Tallant."

"I never heard of a Tallant in my life!"

"Lord, ma'am, why should you? Keep telling you she comes from some dev'lish outlandish place in the north!"

"I would not set the least store by anything Fleetwood told me!"

"Oh, it ain't him!" said Mr. Epworth cheerfully. "He don't know the gal's name either. It's the Nonpareil. Knows all about the family. Vouches for the gal."

Her expression changed; a still sharper look entered her eyes. She said quickly: "Beaumaris?" He nodded. "If *he* vouches for her—Is she presentable?"

He looked shocked, and answered in protesting accents: " 'Pon my soul, ma'am, you can't be in your senses to ask me such a demned silly question! Now, I put it to you, *would* Beaumaris vouch for a gal that wasn't slap up to the echo?"

"No. No, he would not," she said decidedly. "If it's true, and she has no vulgar connections, it would be the very thing for you, my dear Horace!"

"Just what I was thinking myself, ma'am," said her nephew.

"I will pay Lady Bridlington a morning visit," said Mrs. Penkridge.

"That's it: do the pretty!" Mr. Epworth encouraged her.

"It is tiresome, for I have never been upon intimate terms with her! However, this alters the circumstances! Leave it to me!"

Thus it was that Lady Bridlington found herself the object of Mrs. Penkridge's attentions. Since she had never before been honored with an invitation to one of that lady's more exclusive parties, she was considerably elated and at once seized the opportunity to invite Mrs. Penkridge to her own evening party. Mrs. Penkridge accepted with another of her thin smiles, saying that she knew she could answer for her husband's pleasure in attending the party, and departed, thinking out rapidly some form of engagement for him which would at once spare him an insipid evening and render it necessary for her to claim her nephew's escort.

❧ Chapter 6 ❧

LADY BRIDLINGTON DID NOT EXPECT ARA-
bella's first party to be a failure, since she was a good
hostess and never offered her guests any but the best
wines and refreshments; but that it should prove to be
a wild success had not even entered her head. She had
planned it more with the idea of bringing Arabella to the
notice of other hostesses than as a brilliant social event;
and although she had certainly invited a good many
unattached gentlemen, she had not held out the lure of
dancing, or of cards, and so had little hope of seeing
more than half of them in her spacious rooms. Her main
preoccupation was lest Arabella should not be looking
her best, or should jeopardize her future by some un-
conventional action, or some unlucky reference to that
regrettable Yorkshire vicarage. In general, the child
behaved very prettily, but once or twice she had seriously alarmed her patroness, either by a remark which
betrayed all too clearly the modesty of her circumstances—as when she had asked, in front of the butler,
whether she should help to prepare the rooms for the
party, for all the world as though she expected to be
given an apron and a duster!—or by some impulsive

97

action so odd as to be positively outrageous. Not readily
would Lady Bridlington forget the scene outside the
Soho Bazaar, when she and Arabella, emerging from
this mart, found a heavy wagon stationary in the road,
with the one scraggy horse between its shafts straining
under an unsparing lash to set it in motion. At one
instant a demure young lady had been at Lady Bridlington's side; at the next a flaming fury was confronting the
astonished wagoner, commanding him, with a stamp of
one little foot to get down from the wagon at once—*at
once!*—and not to *dare* to raise his whip again! He got
down, quite bemused, and stood in front of the small
fury, an ox of a man, towering above her while she
berated him. When he had recovered his wits, he attempted to justify himself, but failed signally to pacify
the lady. He was a cruel wretch, unfit to be in charge of
a horse, and a dolt, besides, not to perceive that one of
the wheels was jammed, and through his own bad driving, no doubt! He began to be angry, and to shout
Arabella down, but by this time a couple of chairmen,
abandoning their empty vehicle, came across the square,
expressing, in strong Hibernian accents, their willingness to champion the lady, and their desire to know
whether the wagoner wanted to have his cork drawn.
Lady Bridlington, all this time, had stood frozen with
horror in the doorway of the Bazaar, unable to think of
anything else to do than to be thankful that none of her
acquaintances was present to witness this shocking affair. Arabella told the chairmen briskly that she would
have no fighting, bade the wagoner observe the obstruction against which one of his rear wheels was jammed,
herself went to the horse's head, and began to back him.
The chairmen promptly lent their aid; Arabella addressed a short, pithy lecture to the wagoner on the folly
and injustice of losing one's temper with animals, and
rejoined her godmother saying calmly: "It is mostly ig-
norance, you know!"

And although she did, when shown the impropriety of her behavior, say she was sorry to have made a scene in public, it was evident that she was not in the least penitent. She said that Papa would have told her it was her duty to interfere in such a cause.

But no representations could induce her to say she was sorry for her quite unbecoming conduct two days later, when she entered her bedchamber to find, lighting the fire, a very junior housemaid—with a swollen face. It appeared that the girl had the toothache. Now, Lady Bridlington had no desire that any of her servants should suffer the agonies of toothache, and had she been asked, she would unquestionably have said that at the first convenient moment the girl should be sent off to have the tooth drawn. The mistress of a large household naturally had a duty to oversee the general well-being of her staff. Indeed, some years previously, when inoculation against cowpox had been all the rage, she had with her own hands inoculated all the servants at Bridlington, and most of the tenants on the estate. Nearly every great lady had done so: it had been the accepted order of the day. But to bid the sufferer seat herself in the armchair in the best guest chamber; to give her an Indian silk shawl to wrap round her head; and to disturb one's hostess during the sacred hour of her afternoon nap by bursting in upon her with a demand for laudanum, was carrying benevolence to quite undesirable lengths. Lady Bridlington did her best to convey the sense of this to Arabella, but she spoke to deaf ears.

"The poor girl is in the most dreadful pain, ma'am!"

"Nonsense, my love! You must not let yourself be imposed upon. Persons of her class always make a to-do about nothing. She had better have the tooth drawn tomorrow, if she can be spared from her work, and—"

"Dear ma'am, I assure you she is in no case to be toiling up and down all these stairs with coal scuttles!"

said Arabella earnestly. "She should take some drops of laudanum and lie down on her bed."

"Oh, very well!" said her ladyship, yielding to the stronger will. "But there is no occasion for you to be putting yourself into this state, my dear! And to be asking one of the underhousemaids to sit down in your bedroom, and giving her one of your best shawls—"

"No, no, I have only lent it to her!" Arabella said. "She is from the country, you know, ma'am, and I think the other servants have not used her as they ought. She was homesick, and so unhappy! And the toothache made it worse, of course. I do believe she wanted someone to be kind to her more than anything else! She has been telling me about her home, and her little sisters and brothers, and—"

"Arabella!" uttered Lady Bridlington. "Surely you have not been *gossiping with the servants?*" She saw her young guest stiffen and added hastily: "You should never encourage persons of her sort to pour out the history of their lives into your ears. I expect you meant it for the best, my dear, but you have no notion how encroaching—"

"I hope, ma'am—indeed, I *know!*" said Arabella, her eyes very bright, and her small figure alarmingly rigid, "that not one of Papa's children would pass by a fellow creature in distress!"

It was fast being borne in upon Lady Bridlington that the Reverend Henry Tallant was not only a grave handicap to her daughter's social advancement, but a growing menace to her own comfort. She was naturally unable to express this conviction to Arabella, so she sank back on her pillows, saying feebly: "Oh, very well, but if people were to hear of it they would think it excessively odd in you, my dear!"

Whatever anyone else might think, it soon became plain that the episode had given her ladyship's upper servants the poorest idea of Arabella's social standing.

Her ladyship's personal maid, a sharp-faced spinster who had grown to middle age in her service, and bullied her without compunction, ventured to hint, while she was dressing her mistress's hair that evening, that it was easy to see Miss was not accustomed to living in large and genteel households.

Lady Bridlington allowed Miss Clara Crowle a good deal of license, but this was going too far. A pretty thing it would be if the servants, in that odious way they all had of talking about their betters, were to spread such a thing abroad! It would reach the ears of their employers in less than no time, and then the fat would indeed be in the fire! In a few dignified, well-chosen words Lady Bridlington gave her henchwoman to understand that Miss Tallant came from a mansion of awe-inspiring gentility, and was quite above considering appearances. She added, to clinch the matter, that very different customs obtained in the north from those common in London. Miss Crowle, a little cowed, but with a sting yet left in her tongue, sniffed, and said: "So I have always understood, my lady!" She then encountered her mistress's eyes in the mirror, and added obsequiously: "Not but what I am sure no one would ever suspicion Miss came from the north, my lady, so prettily as she speaks!"

"Certainly not," said Lady Bridlington coldly, and quite forgetful of the fact that she had experienced considerable relief, when Arabella had greeted her on her arrival, at finding that no ugly accent marred her soft voice. The dreadful possibility that she might speak with a Yorkshire burr had more than once occurred to her. Had she but known it, she had the Reverend Henry Tallant to thank for his daughter's pure accent. Papa was far too fastidious and cultured a man to permit his children to be slipshod in their speech, even frowning upon the excellent imitations of the farmhand's conversation achieved by Bertram and Harry in funning humor.

Miss Clara Crowle might be silenced, but Arabella's

reprehensible conduct gave her hostess some serious
qualms, and caused her to anticipate her evening party
with less than her usual placidity.

But nothing could have gone off better. To ensure
that in appearance at least Arabella should do her credit,
Lady Bridlington sent no less a personage than Miss
Crowle herself to put the finishing touches to her toilet,
rounding off the efforts of the housemaid detailed to
wait on her. Miss Crowle was not best pleased when sent
off to offer her services to Arabella, but it was many years
since she had dressed a young and beautiful lady, and in
spite of herself her enthusiasm awoke when she saw how
delightfully Arabella's gown of jonquil crêpe became
her, and how tasteful was the spangled scarf hanging
over her arms. She saw at a glance that she could
scarcely better the simple arrangement of those dark
curls, twisted into a high knot on the top of her head and
with the short ringlets allowed to fall over her ears; but
she begged Miss to permit her to place her flowers more
becomingly. Her cunning hands deftly placed the faggot
of artificial roses at just the right angle, and she was so
well satisfied with the result that she said Miss would be
quite the belle of the evening, being as she was dark, and
the fashion for fair beauties quite outdated.

Arabella, unaware of how greatly Miss Crowle was
condescending to her, only laughed, a piece of uncon-
cern that did her no harm in that critical maiden's eyes.
Arabella was embarking on her first London party enormously heartened by the arrival, not an hour earlier, of
her first London posy of flowers. The exciting box had
been carried up to her room immediately, and when
opened had been found to contain a charming bouquet,
tied up—so fortunately!—with long yellow ribbons.
Lord Fleetwood's card accompanied the tribute, and
was even now propped up against the mirror. Miss
Crowle saw it and was impressed.

Lady Bridlington presently setting eyes on Arabella

just before dinner was announced, was delighted, and reflected that Sophia Theale had always had exquisite taste. Nothing could have set Arabella off to greater advantage than that delicate yellow robe, open down the front over a slip of white satin, and ornamented with clasps of tiny roses to match those in her hair. The only jewelry she wore was the ring Papa had had made for her, and Grandmama's necklet of pearls. Lady Bridlington was half inclined to ring for Clara to fetch down from her own jewel case two bracelets of gold and pearls, and then decided that Arabella's pretty arms needed no embellishment. Besides, she would be wearing long gloves, so that the bracelets would be wasted.

"Very nice, my love!" she said approvingly. "I am glad I sent Clara to you. Dear me, where had you those flowers?"

"Lord Fleetwood sent them, ma'am," replied Arabella proudly.

Lady Bridlington received this information with disappointing composure. "Did he so? Then at all events we may be sure of seeing *him* here tonight. You know, my love, you must not be expecting a squeeze! I am sure I hope to see my drawing rooms respectably filled but it is early in the year still, so you must not be cast down if you do not see as many people as you might have supposed you would."

She might have spared her breath. By half past ten her drawing rooms were crowded to overflowing, and she was still standing at the head of the stairs receiving latecomers. Nothing, she thought dizzily, had ever been like it! Even the Wainfleets, whom really she had not expected to see, were there; while the haughty Mrs. Penkridge, escorted by her dandified nephew, had been among the earliest arrivals, unbending amazingly to Arabella, and begging leave to introduce Mr. Epworth. Lord Fleetwood and his crony Mr. Oswald Warkworth were there, both hovering assiduously near Arabella,

very full of gallantry and good spirits; Lady Somercote
had brought two of her sons, and the Kirkmichaels their
lanky daughter; Lord Dewsbury had failed, but Sir
Geoffrey Morecambe was much in evidence, as were also
the Accringtons, the Charnwoods, and the Seftons. Lady
Sefton, dear creature that she was! had spoken with the
greatest kindness to Arabella, and had promised later on
to send her a voucher admitting her to Almack's Assembly Rooms. Lady Bridlington felt that her cup was full.
It was to overflow. Last of all the guests, arriving after
eleven o'clock, when her ladyship, having long since
released Arabella from her place at her side, was on the
point of abandoning her post and joining her guests in
the drawing rooms, Mr. Beaumaris arrived and came
unhurriedly up the stairs. Her ladyship awaited him with
a bosom swelling beneath its rich covering of purple
satin and her hand, clasping her fan, trembling slightly
under the influence of the accumulated triumphs of this
night. He greeted her with his cool civility, and she replied with tolerable composure, thanking him for his
kind offices, in Leicestershire, toward her goddaughter.

"A pleasure, ma'am," said Mr. Beaumaris. "I trust
Miss Tallant reached town without further mishap?"

"Oh, yes, indeed! So obliging of you to have called to
inquire after her! We were sorry to have been out. You
will find Miss Tallant in one of the rooms. Your cousin,
Lady Wainfleet, too, is here."

He bowed, and followed her into the front drawing
room. A minute later Arabella, enjoying the attentions
of Lord Fleetwood, Mr. Warkworth, and Mr. Epworth,
saw him coming toward her across the room, pausing
once or twice on his way to exchange salutations with his
friends. Until that moment she had thought Mr. Epworth quite the best-dressed man present: indeed, she
had been quite dazzled by the exquisite nature of his
raiment and the profusion of rings, pins, fobs, chains,
and seals which he wore; but no sooner had she clapped

eyes on Mr. Beaumaris's tall, manly figure than she realized that Mr. Epworth's wadded shoulders, wasp waist, and startling waistcoat were perfectly ridiculous. Nothing could have been in greater contrast to the extravagance of his attire than Mr. Beaumaris's black coat and pantaloons, his plain white waistcoat, the single fob that hung to one side of it, the single pearl set chastely in the intricate folds of his necktie. Nothing he wore was designed to attract attention, but he made every other man in the room look either a trifle overdressed or a trifle shabby.

He reached her side, and smiled, and when she put out her hand raised it fleetingly to his lips. "How do you do, Miss Tallant?" he said. "I am happy indeed to have been granted this opportunity of renewing my acquaintance with you."

"Oh, it is too bad—a great deal too bad!" fluted Mr. Epworth, rolling an arch eye at Arabella. "You and Fleetwood have stolen a march on the rest of us, you know—a shameful thing, 'pon my soul!"

Mr. Beaumaris glanced down at him from his superior height, seemed to debate within himself whether this sally was worth the trouble of a reply, to decide that it was not, and turned back to Arabella. "You must tell me how you like London," he said. "It is abundantly plain that London likes you! May I procure you a glass of lemonade?"

This offer brought Arabella's chin up, and made her look at him with a distinct challenge in her eyes. She had had plenty of time to discover that it was not the common practice of hosts to sweep the wine from their table at the end of the first course, and she strongly suspected Mr. Beaumaris of quizzing her. He was looking perfectly grave, however, and met her eyes without a shadow of mockery in his own. Before she could answer him, Lord Fleetwood committed a strategical error and exclaimed:

"Of course! I'll swear you are parched with thirst, ma'am! I will get you a glass immediately!"

"Splendid, Charles!" said Mr. Beaumaris cordially. "Do let me take you a little out of this crush, Miss Tallant!"

He seemed to take her acquiescence for granted, for he did not await a reply but led her to where a sofa standing against one wall was momentarily unoccupied. How he contrived to find a way through the crowd of chattering guests was a mystery to Arabella, for he certainly did not force a passage. A touch on a man's shoulder, a bow and a smile to a lady, and the thing was done. He sat down beside her on the sofa, seated a little sideways, so that he could watch her face, one hand on the back of the sofa, the other playing idly with his quizzing glass. "Does it come up to your expectations, ma'am?" he asked smilingly.

"London? Yes, indeed!" she responded. "I am sure I was never so happy in my life!"

"I am glad," he said.

Arabella remembered that Lady Bridlington had warned her against betraying too much enthusiasm: it was unfashionable to appear pleased. She remembered also that she had promised not to make a bad impression on Mr. Beaumaris, so she added in a languid tone: "It is a shocking squeeze, of course, but it is always diverting to meet new people."

He looked amused, and said with a laugh in his voice: "No, don't spoil it! Your first answer was charming."

She eyed him doubtfully for a moment; then her irrepressible dimples peeped out. "But it is only rustics who own to enjoyment, sir!"

"Is it?" he returned.

"*You,* I am persuaded, do not enjoy such an Assembly as this!"

"You are mistaken: my enjoyment depends on the company in which I find myself."

"That," said Arabella naïvely, having thought it over, "is quite the prettiest thing that has been said to me tonight!"

"Then I can only suppose, Miss Tallant, that Fleet-wood and Warkworth were unable to find words to express their appreciation of the exquisite picture you present. Strange! I formed the opinion that they were paying you all manner of compliments."

She laughed out at that. "Yes, but it was nonsense! I did not believe a word they said!"

"I hope you believe what *I* say, however, for I am very much in earnest."

The light tone he used seemed to belie his words. Arabella found him baffling, and directed another of her speculative glances at him. She decided that he must be answered in kind, and said daringly: "Are you being so obliging as to bring me into fashion, Mr. Beaumaris?"

He let his eyes travel round the crowded room, his brows a little raised. "You do not appear to me to stand in any need of my assistance, ma'am." He perceived that Lord Fleetwood was edging his way past a knot of people, a glass in his hand, and waited for him to reach the sofa. "Thank you, Charles," he said coolly, taking the glass from his lordship, and presenting it to Arabella.

"You," said Lord Fleetwood, with deep feeling, "will receive a message from me in the morning, Robert! This is the most barefaced piracy I ever beheld in my life! Miss Tallant, I wish you will send this fellow about his business: his effrontery goes beyond what is allowable!"

"You must learn not to act on impulse," said Mr. Beaumaris kindly. "A moment's reflection, the least touch of adroitness, and it would have been I who fetched the lemonade and you who had the privilege of sitting beside Miss Tallant on this sofa!"

"But it is Lord Fleetwood who earns my gratitude, for he was the more chivalrous!" said Arabella.

"Miss Tallant, I thank you!"

"You have certainly been amply rewarded, and have now nothing to do but to take yourself off," said Mr. Beaumaris.

"Not for the world!" declared his lordship.

Mr. Beaumaris sighed. "How often I have had to deplore your lack of tact!" he said.

Arabella, sparkling under the influence of all this exciting banter, raised her posy to her nose, and said, with a grateful look cast up at Fleetwood: "I stand *doubly* in Lord Fleetwood's debt!"

"No, no, it is I who stand in yours, ma'am, since you designed to accept my poor tribute!"

Mr. Beaumaris glanced at the posy and smiled slightly, but said nothing. Arabella, catching sight of Mr. Epworth, who was hovering hopefully in the vicinity, suddenly said: "Mr. Beaumaris, who *is* that oddly dressed man?"

He looked round, but said: "There are so many oddly dressed men present, Miss Tallant, that I fear I am at a loss. You do not mean poor Fleetwood here?"

"Of course I do not!" exclaimed Arabella indignantly.

"Well, I am sure it would be difficult to find anything odder than that waistcoat he wears. It is very disheartening, for I have really expended a great deal of time in trying to reform his taste. Ah, I think I see whom you must mean! That, Miss Tallant, is Horace Epworth. In his own estimation, he undoubtedly personifies a set of creatures whom I have reason to believe you despise."

Blushing hotly, Arabella asked: "Is he a—a dandy?"

"He would certainly like you to think so."

"Well, if he is," said Arabella frankly, "I am sure you are no such thing, and I beg your pardon for saying it that evening!"

"Don't apologize to him, ma'am!" said Lord Fleetwood gaily. "It is time someone gave him a set-down, and *that*, I assure you, smote him with stunning effect!

You must know that he thinks himself a notable Corinthian!"

"What is that, pray?" enquired Arabella.

"A Corinthian, ma'am, besides being a very Tulip of Fashion, is an amateur of sport, a master of swordplay, a deadly fellow with a pistol, a Nonpareil among whips, a—"

Mr. Beaumaris interrupted this mock-solemn catalogue. "If you will be such a dead bore, Charles, you will provoke me to explain to Miss Tallant what the world means when it calls you a sad rattle."

"Well?" demanded Arabella mischievously.

"A fribble, ma'am, not worth your attention!" he replied, rising to his feet. "I see my cousin over there, and must pay my respects to her." He smiled, bowed, and moved away, stayed for a minute or two talking to Lady Wainfleet, drank a glass of wine with Mr. Warkworth, complimented his hostess on the success of her party, and departed, having done precisely what he had set out to do, which was to place Miss Tallant's feet securely on the ladder of fashion. The news would be all over town within twenty-four hours that the rich Miss Tallant was the Nonpareil's latest flirt.

"Did you see Beaumaris paying court to that dashed pretty girl?" asked Lord Wainfleet of his wife as they drove away from Lady Bridlington's house.

"Of course I did!" replied his wife.

"Seemed very taken with her, didn't he? Not in his usual style, was she? I wonder if he means anything!"

"Robert?" said his wife, with something very like a snort. "If you knew him as well as I do, Wainfleet, you would have seen at one glance that he was amusing himself. *I* know how he looks in just that humor! Someone ought to warn the child to have nothing to do with him! It is too bad of him, for she is nothing but a baby, I'll swear!"

"They're saying in the clubs that she's as rich as a Nabob."

"So I have heard, but what that has to say to anything I don't know! Robert is quite odiously wealthy, and if ever he marries, which I begin to doubt, it will not be for a fortune, I can assure you!"

"No, I don't suppose it will," agreed his lordship. "Why did we go there tonight, Louisa? Devilish flat, that kind of an affair!"

"Oh, shockingly flat! Robert asked me to go. I own I was curious to see his heiress. He said he was going to make her the most sought-after female in London."

"Sounds like a hum to me," said his lordship. "Why should he do so?"

"Exactly what I asked him! He said it might be amusing. There are times, Wainfleet, when I would like to box Robert's ears!"

❧ Chapter 7 ❧

NOT ONLY IN HIS COUSIN'S BOSOM WERE vengeful thoughts nourished against Mr. Beaumaris. Lady Somercote, not so doting a mother that she supposed any of her sons would be likely to prove more attractive to the heiress than the Nonpareil, could with pleasure have driven the long diamond pin she wore in her hair between his ribs; Mrs. Kirkmichael thought bitterly that he might, considering the number of times she had gone out of her way to be agreeable to him, have bestowed a little of his attention upon her lanky daughter, a gesture which would have cost him nothing, and might have given poor Maria a start in the world; Mr. Epworth, uneasily aware that for some inscrutable reason he was consistently cast in the shade by the Nonpareil, went the round of the clubs saying that he had a very good mind to give Beaumaris a set-down at no very distant date; his aunt recalled that she had once quarreled violently with Lady Mary Beaumaris, and said that it was from his mother Beaumaris had inherited his flirtatious disposition, adding that she was sorry for the woman he eventually married. Even Mr. Warkworth and Lord Fleetwood said that it was rather too bad of the

Nonpareil to trifle with the season's biggest catch; while
several gentlemen who slavishly copied every detail of
Mr. Beaumaris's attire wished him safely underground.

There was one voice which was not raised to swell this
chorus of disapprobation: Lady Bridlington was in raptures over Mr. Beaumaris. She could talk of nothing else
throughout the following day. While he sat beside Arabella, not a smile, not a gesture had escaped the good
lady's anxious eye. He had paid no heed to any other girl
in the room; he had plainly advertised to his world that
he found Miss Tallant charming: there was no one in
London more amiable, more truly polite, more condescending, or more in her ladyship's good graces! Over
and over again she told Arabella that her success was
now assured; it was not until her first transports had
somewhat abated that she could be rational enough to
drop a word of warning in Arabella's ear. But the more
she thought of Mr. Beaumaris's pronounced attentions
to the girl, the more she remembered how many innocent maidens had fallen victims to his spear, the more
she became convinced that it was necessary to put Arabella on her guard. So she said in an earnest voice, and
with a slightly anxious look in her eye: "I am persuaded,
my love, that you are too sensible a girl to be taken in!
But, you know, I stand to you in place of your Mama, and
I think I should tell you that Mr. Beaumaris is a most
accomplished flirt! No one could be more delighted
than I am that he should have singled you out, but it will
never do, my dear, if you were to develop a *tendre* in *that*
direction! I know I have only to drop a word in your ear,
and you will not be offended by it! He is a confirmed
bachelor. I could not tell you the number of hearts he
has broken! Poor Theresa Howden—she married Lord
Congleton some years later—went into a decline, and
was the despair of her afflicted parents! They *did* think—
and I am sure that nothing could have been more pro-

nounced for all one season than—But no! Nothing came of it!"

Arabella had not been the reigning belle for twenty miles round Heythram without learning to distinguish between the flirt and the man who was in earnest, and she replied instantly: "I know very well that Mr. Beaumaris means nothing by his compliments. Indeed, I am in no danger of being taken in like a goose!"

"Well, my love, I *hope* you are not!"

"You may be sure I am not. If you do not see any objection, ma'am, I mean to encourage Mr. Beaumaris's attentions, and make the best use I may of them! *He* believes himself to be amusing himself at my expense; *I* mean to turn him to very good account! But as for losing my heart—no, indeed!"

"Mind, we cannot depend upon his continuing to single you out!" said Lady Bridlington, with unwonted caution. "If he did, it would be beyond anything great, but there is no saying, after all! However, last night's work was enough to launch you, my dear, and I am *deeply* thankful!" She heaved an ecstatic sigh. "You will be invited everywhere, I daresay!"

She was quite right. Within one fortnight, she was in the happy position of finding herself with five engagements for the same evening, and Arabella had had to break into Sir John's fifty-pound bill to replenish her wardrobe. She had been seen at the fashionable hour of the Promenade in the Park, sitting beside the Nonpareil, in his high-perch phaeton; she had been almost mobbed at the theater; she was on nodding terms with all manner of exalted persons; she had received two proposals of marriage; Lord Fleetwood, Mr. Warkworth, Mr. Epworth, Sir Geoffrey Morecambe, and Mr. Alfred Somercote (to mention only the most notable of her suitors) had all entered the lists against Mr. Beaumaris; and Lord Bridlington, traveling by fast post all the way, had returned from the Continent to discover what his mother meant by filling his house with unknown females in his absence.

He expressed himself, in measured terms, as being most dissatisfied with Lady Bridlington's explanation. He was a stocky, somewhat ponderous young man, with more sobriety than properly belonged to his twenty-six years. His understanding was not powerful, but he was bookish and had early formed the habit of acquiring information by the perusal of authoritative tomes, so that by the time he had attained his present age his retentive memory was stocked with a quantity of facts which he was perhaps a little too ready to impart to his less well-read contemporaries. His father's death, while he was still at Eton, coupled with a conviction that his mother stood in constant need of superior male guidance, had added disastrously to his self-consequence. He prided on himself on his judgment; was a careful steward of his fortune; had the greatest dislike of anything bordering on the unusual; and deplored the frivolity of those who might have been expected to have been his cronies. His mother's elation at not having spent one evening at home in ten days found no echo in his heart. He could neither understand why she should want to waste her time at social functions, nor why she should have been foolish enough to have invited a giddy girl to stay with her. He was afraid that the cost of all this mummery would be shocking; had Lady Bridlington asked for his counsel, which she might easily have done, he would have advised most strongly against Arabella's visit.

Lady Bridlington was a trifle cast down by this severity, but since her late husband had left her to the enjoyment of a handsome jointure, out of which she always shared the expenses of the house in Park Street with Frederick, she was able to point out to him that the charge of entertaining Arabella fell upon her and not upon him. He said that the wish to dictate to his Mama

was far from him, but that he must persist in thinking the
affair most ill-advised. Lady Bridlington was fond of her
only son, but Arabella's success had quite gone to her
head, and she was in no mood to listen to sober coun-
sels. She retorted that he was talking a great deal of
nonsense; upon which he bowed, compressed his lips,
and bade her afterward remember his words. He added
that he washed his hands of the whole business. Lady
Bridlington, who had no desire to see him fall a victim
to Arabella's charms, was torn between exasperation
and relief that he showed no sign of succumbing to
them.

"I will allow her to be a pretty enough young female,"
said Frederick fair-mindedly, "but there is a levity in her
bearing which I cannot like, and all this gadding about
which she has led you into is not at all to my taste."

"Well, I can't conceive why you should have come
running home in this foolish way!" retorted his mother.

"I thought it my duty, ma'am," said Frederick.

"It is a great piece of folly, and people will think it
excessively odd in you! No one looked to see you in
England again until July at the earliest!"

She was mistaken. No one thought it in the least odd
of Lord Bridlington to have curtailed his tour. The opinion of society was pithily summed up by Mrs. Penkridge,
who said that she had guessed all along that that schem-
ing Bridlington woman meant to marry the heiress to
her own son. "Anyone could have seen how it would
be!" she declared, with her mirthless jangle of laughter.
"Such odious hypocrisy, too, to hold to it that she did
not expect to see Bridlington in England until the summer! Mark my words, Horace, they will be married
before the season is over!"

"Good gad, ma'am, I don't fear Bridlington's rivalry!"
said her nephew, affronted.

"Then you are a goose!" said Mrs. Penkridge. "Everything is in his favor! He is the possessor of an honored

name, and a title, which you may depend upon it the girl
wants, and—what is a great deal to the point, let me tell
you!—he has all the advantage of living in the same
house, of being always at hand to minister to her wishes,
squire her to parties, and—Oh, it puts me out of all
patience!"

But Miss Tallant and Lord Bridlington, from the very
moment of exchanging their first polite greetings, had
conceived a mutual antipathy which was in no way miti-
gated by the necessity each was under to behave toward
the other with complaisance and civility. Arabella would
not for the fortune she was believed to possess have
grieved her kind hostess by betraying dislike of her son;
Frederick's sense of propriety, which was extremely
nice, forbade him to neglect the performance of any
attention due to his mother's guest. He could appreciate, and, indeed, since he had a provident mind, applaud
Mrs. Tallant's ambition to dispose of her daughters
creditably; and since his own mother had undertaken the
task of finding a husband for Arabella, he was prepared
to lend his countenance to her scheme. What shocked
and disturbed him profoundly was the discovery, within
a week of his homecoming, that every gazetted fortune-
hunter in London was dangling after Arabella.

"I am at a loss, ma'am, to guess what you can possibly
have said to lead anyone to suppose that Miss Tallant is
an heiress!" he announced.

Lady Bridlington, who had several times wondered
much the same thing, replied uneasily: "I never said a
word, Frederick! There is not the least reason why anyone should suppose such an absurdity! I own, I was a
trifle surprised when—But she is a very pretty girl, you
know, and Mr. Beaumaris took one of his fancies to
her!"

"I have never been intimate with Beaumaris," said
Frederick. "I do not care for the set he leads, and must
deplore his making any modest female the object of his

gallantry. The influence he exerts, moreover, over persons whom I should have supposed to have had more—"

"Never mind that!" begged his mother hastily. "You told me yesterday, Frederick! You may think Beaumaris what you please, but even you will not deny that it lies in his power to bring whom he will into fashion!"

"Very likely, ma'am, but I have yet to learn that it lies in his power to prevail upon such men as Epworth, Morecambe, Carnaby, and—I must add!—Fleetwood, to offer marriage to a female with nothing but her face to recommend her!"

"Not Fleetwood!" protested Lady Bridlington feebly.

"Fleetwood!" repeated Frederick in an inexorable tone. "I do not mean to say that he is precisely hanging out for a rich wife, but that he cannot afford to marry a penniless girl is common knowledge. Yet his attentions toward Miss Tallant are more marked even than those of Horace Epworth. And this is not all! From hints dropped in my presence, from remarks actually made to me, I am persuaded that the greater part of our acquaintance believes her to be in the possession of a handsome fortune! I repeat, ma'am: what can you have said to have given rise to this folly?"

"But I didn't!" cried poor Lady Bridlington almost tearfully. "Indeed, I took the greatest pains not to touch on the question of her expectations! It is false to call her penniless, because she is no such thing! With all those children, of course the Tallants can do very little for her upon her marriage, but when her father dies—and Sophia, too, for she has some money as well—"

"A thousand or so!" interrupted Frederick contemptuously. "I beg your pardon, ma'am, but nothing could be more plain to me than that something you have said—inadvertently, I daresay!—has done all this mischief. For mischief I must deem it! A pretty state of affairs it will be if we are to have the world saying—as it will say, once the truth is known!—that you have foisted an impostress upon society!"

This terrible forecast temporarily outweighed in Lady Bridlington's mind the sense of strong injustice the rest of her son's remarks had aroused. She turned quite pale, and exclaimed: "What is to be done?"

"You may rely upon me, ma'am, to do what is necessary," replied Frederick. "Whenever the opportunity offers, I shall say that I have no notion how such a rumor came to be spread about."

"I suppose you must do so," agreed his mother dubiously. "But I do beg of you, Frederick, not to take the whole world into your confidence on the subject! There is not the least need for you to enter into all the details of the poor child's circumstances."

"It would be quite improper for me to do so, ma'am," replied Frederick crushingly. "*I* am not responsible for her visit to London! I must point out to you, Mama, that it is *you* who have engaged yourself—unwisely, I consider—to establish her suitably. I am sure I have no desire to prejudice her chances of matrimony. Indeed, since I understand that you mean to keep her with you until some man offers for her, I shall be happy to see her married as soon as possible!"

"I think you are very disagreeable!" said Lady Bridlington, dissolving into tears.

Her peace of mind was quite cut up. When Arabella came into the room presently, she found her still dabbing at her eyes and giving little sniffs. Quite dismayed, Arabella begged to be told the cause of this unhappiness. Lady Bridlington, glad of a sympathetic audience, squeezed her hand gratefully, and without reflection poured forth the sum of her grievances.

Kneeling beside her chair, Arabella listened in stricken silence, her hand lying slackly within Lady Bridlington's. "It is so unkind of Frederick!" Lady Bridlington complained. "And so unjust, for I assure you, my dear, I never said such a thing to a soul! How could he think I would do so? It would have been quite wicked to have told such lies, besides being so foolish, and vulgar, and everything that is dreadful! And why Frederick should think I could be so lost to all sense of propriety, I am sure I don't know!"

Arabella's head sank; guilt and shame almost overpowered her; she could not speak. Lady Bridlington, misreading her confusion, felt a qualm of conscience at having so unguardedly taken her into her confidence, and said: "I should not have told you! It is all Frederick's fault, and I daresay he has exaggerated everything, just as he so often does! You must not let it distress you, my love, for even if it were true it would be absurd to suppose such a man as Mr. Beaumaris, or young Charnwood, or a great many others I could name, care a button whether you are a rich woman or a pauper! And Frederick will make everything right!"

"How can he do so, ma'am?" Arabella managed to ask.

"Oh, when he sees the opportunity, he will say something to damp such ridiculous notions! Nothing very much, you know, but making light of the story! We need not concern ourselves, and I am sorry I spoke of it to you."

With all her heart Arabella longed for the courage to confess the whole. She could not. Already Lady Bridlington was rambling on, complaining fretfully of Frederick's unkindness, wondering what cause he had to suppose his mother ill-bred enough to have spread a false tale abroad, and wishing that his father were alive to give him one of his famous scolds. She said instead, in a subdued tone: "Is that why—why everyone has been so very polite to me, ma'am?"

"Certainly not!" said Lady Bridlington emphatically. "you must have perceived, my love, how many, many friends I have in London, and you may believe they

accepted you out of compliment to me! Not that I mean
to say—But before you were at all known, naturally it
was my sponsorship that started you in the right way."
She patted Arabella's hand consolingly. "Then, you
know, you are so bright, and pretty, that I am sure it is
no wonder that you are so much sought after. And above
all, Arabella, we must remember that the world always
follows what is seen to be the mode, and Mr. Beaumaris
has made you the fashion by singling you out, even
driving you in his phaeton, which is an honor indeed, I
can tell you!"

Arabella's head was still bowed. "Does—does Lord
Bridlington mean to tell everyone that I—that I have no
fortune at all, ma'am?"

"Good gracious, no, child! That would be a fatal thing
to do, and I hope he would have more sense! He will
merely say it has been greatly exaggerated—enough to
frighten away the fortune-hunters, but what will not
weigh with an honest man! Do not give it another
thought!"

Arabella was unable to obey this injunction. It was
long before she could think of anything else. Her impulse was to fly from London, back to Heythram; but
hardly had she reached the stage of calculating whether
she still possessed enough money to pay her fare on the
first coach than all the difficulties attached to such a
precipitate retreat presented themselves to her. They
were insuperable. She could not bring herself to confess
to Lady Bridlington that her own was the wicked, ill-
bred tongue accountable for the rumor, nor could she
think of any excuse for returning to Yorkshire. Still less
could she face the necessity of telling Papa and Mama of
her shocking behavior. She must remain in Park Street
until the season came to an end, and if Mama was sadly
disappointed at the failure of her scheme, at least Papa
would never blame his daughter for returning to her
home unbetrothed. She perceived clearly that unless

something very wonderful were to happen this must be so, and felt herself guilty indeed.

Not for several hours did her mind recover its tone, but she was both young and optimistic, and after a hearty burst of tears, followed by a period of quiet reflection, she began insensibly to be more hopeful. Something would happen to unravel her difficulties; the odious Frederick would scotch the rumor; people would gradually grow to realize that they had been mistaken. Mr. Beaumaris and Lord Fleetwood would no doubt write her down as a vulgar, boasting miss, but she must hope that they had not actually told everyone that it was she who had been responsible for the rumor. Meanwhile there was nothing to be done but to behave as though nothing were the matter. This, to a naturally buoyant spirit, was not so hard a task as might have been supposed: London was offering too much to Arabella for her to be long cast down. She might fancy all her pleasure destroyed, but she would have been a very extraordinary young woman who could have remembered her difficulties while cards and floral offerings were left every day at the house; while invitations poured in to every form of entertainment known to ingenious hostesses; while every gentleman was eager to claim her hand for the dance; while Mr. Beaumaris took her driving in the Park behind his match-grays, and every other young lady gazed enviously after her. Whatever the cause, social success was sweet; and since Arabella was a very human girl, she could not help enjoying every moment of it.

She expected to see some considerable diminution in her court once Lord Bridlington had let it be known that her fortune had been grossly exaggerated, and braced herself to bear this humiliation. But although she knew from Lady Bridlington that Frederick had faithfully performed his part, still the invitations came in, and still the unattached gentlemen clustered round her. She took

fresh heart, glad to find that fashionable people were
not, after all, so mercenary as she had been led to think.
Neither she nor Frederick had the smallest inkling of the
true state of affairs: she because she was too unsophisticated; Frederick because it had never yet occurred to
him that anyone could doubt what he said. But he might
as well have spared his breath on this occasion. Even Mr.
Warkworth, a charitably minded gentleman, shook his
head over it and remarked to Sir Geoffrey Morecambe
that Bridlington was doing it rather too brown.

"Just what I was thinking myself," agreed Sir Geoffrey, scrutinizing his necktie in the mirror with a dissatisfied eye. "Shabby, I call it. Do you think this way I have
tied my cravat has something of the look of the Nonpareil's new style?"

Mr. Warkworth directed a long, dispassionate stare at
it. "No," he said simply.

"No, no more do I," said Sir Geoffrey, sad but unsurprised. "I wonder what he calls it? It ain't precisely a
Mail-Coach, and it certainly ain't an Osbaldeston, and
though I did think it had something of the look of a *Trône
d'amour,* it ain't that either. I can tie every one of *them.*"

Mr. Warkworth, whose mind had wandered from this
vital subject, said, with a frown: "Damn it, it *is* shabby!
You're right!"

Sir Geoffrey was a little hurt. "Would you say it was
as bad as that, Oswald?"

"I would," stated Mr. Warkworth. "In fact, the more
I think of it the worse it appears to me!"

Sir Geoffrey looked intently at his own image and
sighed. "Yes, it does. I shall have to go home and
change it."

"Eh?" said Mr. Warkworth, puzzled. "Change what?
Good God, dear boy, I wasn't talking about your necktie! Wouldn't dream of saying such a thing to my worst
enemy! Bridlington!"

"Oh, him!" said Sir Geoffrey, relieved. "He's a gudgeon."

"Oughtn't to be gudgeon enough to think everyone else is one. Tell you what: wouldn't do him any good if he did hoax everybody with that bag of moonshine! She's a devilish fine girl, the little Tallant, and if you ask me, she wouldn't have him if he were the only man to offer for her."

"You can't expect him to know that," said Sir Geoffrey. "I shouldn't wonder if he hasn't a suspicion he's a dead bore: in fact, he can't have! Stands to reason: wouldn't prose on as he does, if he knew it!"

Mr. Warkworth thought this over. "No," he pronounced at last. "You're wrong. If he don't know he's a dead bore, why does he want to frighten off everyone else? Haveycavey sort of a business: don't like it! A man ought to fight fair."

"It ain't that," replied Sir Geoffrey. "Just remembered something: the little Tallant don't want it to be known she's as rich as a Nabob. Fleetwood told me: tired of being courted for her money. They were all after her in the north."

"Oh!" said Mr. Warkworth. He asked with vague interest: "Where does she come from?"

"Somewhere up north: Yorkshire, I believe," said Sir Geoffrey, inserting a cautious finger into one of the folds of his necktie and easing it a trifle. "I wonder if that's better?"

"Well, that's a queer thing. Saw Clayton the other day. *He* comes from Yorkshire! Might have been one of those other devilish rural places—Northumberland, or something. Know what I think?"

"No," said Mr. Warkworth.

"Shouldn't be surprised if she's the daughter of some merchant or other, which would account for it."

Mr. Warkworth looked shocked. "No, really, dear old

boy! Nothing of that sort about the girl! Never heard her utter a word that smelled of that shop!"

"Granddaughter, then," said Sir Geoffrey, stretching a point. "Pity if I'm right, but I'll tell you one thing, Oswald! I wouldn't let it weigh with me."

Upon consideration, Mr. Warkworth decided that he would not either.

Since these views were fairly representative, Arabella was not destined to suffer the mortification of seeing her usual gallants hang back when next she attended the Assembly at Almack's. Lord Bridlington was escorting his mother and her guest, for besides being very correct in such matters, he liked Almack's and approved of the severity of the rules imposed on the club by its imperious hostesses. A number of his contemporaries said openly that an evening spent at Almack's was the flattest thing in town, but these were frippery fellows with whom Lord Bridlington had little to do.

His politeness led him to engage Miss Tallant for the first country dance, a circumstance which made the unsuccessful applicants for her hand exchange significant glances. They saw to it that he should have no further opportunity of standing up with her. Not one of them would have believed that he had no desire to do so, much preferring to stroll about the rooms telling as many people as could be got to listen to him all about the travels abroad.

The waltz, which was still looked at askance by old-fashioned persons, had long since forced its way into Almack's, but it was still the unwritten law that no lady might venture to take part in it unless one of the patronesses had clearly indicated her approval. Lady Bridlington had taken care to impress this important convention upon Arabella's mind, so she refused all solicitations to take the floor when the fiddles struck up for the waltz. Papa would certainly not approve of the dance, she knew: she had never dared to tell him that she

and Sophia had learned the steps from their friends the
Misses Caterham, a very dashing pair. So she retired to
a chair against the wall, beside Lady Bridlington's, and
sat fanning herself and trying not to look as though she
longed to be whirling round the floor. One or two more
fortunate damsels, who had watched with disfavor her
swift rise to popularity, cast her glances of such pitying
superiority that she had to recollect a great many of
Papa's maxims before she could subdue the very improper sentiments which entered her breast.

Mr. Beaumaris, who had looked in midway through
the evening—in fact, a bare ten minutes before the
doors were relentlessly shut against latecomers—apparently for no other purpose than to entertain the wife of
the Austrian Ambassador, saw Arabella and was
amused, guessing her emotions correctly. Suddenly he
cast one of his quizzical looks at Princess Esterhazy, and
said: "Shall I ask that chit to dance?"

She raised her delicate black brows, a faint smile
flickering on her lips. "*Here*, my friend, you are not
supreme! I think you dare not."

"I know I dare not," said Mr. Beaumaris, disarming
her promptly. "That is why I ask you, Princess, to present me to the lady as a desirable partner."

She hesitated, glancing from him to Arabella, and
then laughed and shrugged. "Well! She does not put
herself forward, after all, and I find her style excellent.
Come, then!"

Arabella, startled to find herself suddenly confronted
by one of the most formidable patronesses, rose quickly.

"You do not dance, Miss Tallant. May I present Mr.
Beaumaris to you as a very desirable partner?" said the
Princess, with a slightly malicious smile cast at Mr.
Beaumaris.

Arabella could only curtsy, and blush, and be sorry to
find that she was so ill-natured as to be conscious of

feelings of ignoble triumph over the ladies who had been kind enough to look pityingly at her.

Mr. Beaumaris led her on to the floor and encircled her waist with one arm, taking her right hand in a light clasp. Arabella was naturally a good dancer, but she felt extremely nervous, partly because she had never attempted the waltz except in the Misses Caterham's old schoolroom, and partly because it was so strange to be held in such close proximity to a man. For several turns she answered Mr. Beaumaris very much at random, being preoccupied with her feet. She was so much shorter than he that her head only just reached his shoulder, and since she felt shy she did not look up, but steadfastly regarded the top of his waistcoat. Mr. Beaumaris, who was not in the habit of devoting himself to such very young ladies, found this bashfulness amusing, and not unattractive. After he thought she had had time to recover from it a little, he said: "It *is* a nice waistcoat, isn't it, Miss Tallant?"

That did make her look up, and quickly too, her face breaking into laughter. She looked so lovely, and her big eyes met his with such a frank, ingenuous expression in them, that he was aware of a stir of something in his heart that was not mere amusement. But he had no intention of going to dangerous lengths with this or any other pretty chit, and he said, in a bantering tone: "It is customary, you know, to exchange polite conversation during the dance. I have now addressed no fewer than three unexceptionable remarks to you without winning one answer!"

"You see, I am minding my steps," she confided seriously.

Decidedly this absurd child was a refreshing change from the generality of damsels! Had he been a younger man, he reflected, he might easily have succumbed to her charm. It was fortunate that he was thirty, and no longer to be caught by a pretty face and naïve ways, for he knew well that these would pall on him, and that he wanted something more in the lady whom he would one day marry. He had never yet found just what he was looking for, did not even know what it might prove to be, and was perfectly resigned to his bachelordom.

"It is not at all necessary," he said. "You dance delightfully. You do not mean to tell me that this is the first time you have waltzed?"

Miss Tallant certainly did not mean to tell him anything of the sort and was already regretting her impulsive confidence. "Good gracious, no!" she said. "The first time at Almack's, however."

"I am happy to think, then, that mine was the honor of first leading you on to the floor. You will certainly be besieged by every man present, now it is seen that you have no objection to the waltz."

She said nothing, but fell to studying his waistcoat again. He glanced down at her, a hint of mockery in the smile that hovered about his mouth. "How does it feel, Miss Tallant, to be the rage of town? Do you enjoy it, or have your northern triumphs given you a distaste for this sort of thing?"

She raised her eyes, and her chin too. "I am afraid, Mr. Beaumaris, that you betrayed what I—what I begged you not to speak of!"

There was a distinctly sardonic look in his eye, but he replied coolly: "I assure you, ma'am, I have mentioned your circumstances to one person only: Lord Fleetwood."

"Then it is he who—" She broke off, flushing.

"Very probably," he agreed. "You must not blame him, however. Such things are bound to leak out."

Her lips parted, and then closed again. He wondered what she had so nearly said: whether he was to have been treated to her society manners, or whether she had been about to tell him the truth. On the whole, he was glad that she had thought better of it. If she took him into her confidence, he supposed he would be obliged, in mercy, to bring this game to a close, which would be a pity, since it was providing him with a great deal of entertainment. To have elevated an unknown provincial to the heights of society was an achievement which only one who had no illusions about the world he led could properly appreciate. He was deriving much enjoyment too from observing the efforts of his devoted copyists to win the provincial's hand. As for Arabella herself, Mr. Beaumaris shrugged off a momentary compunction, she would no doubt retire in due course to her northern wilds, marry some red-faced squire, and talk for the rest of her life of her brilliant London season. He glanced down at her again, and thought that it would be a pity if she were to retire too soon. Probably by the end of the London season he would be only too thankful to see her go, but for the present he was very well satisfied to gratify her by a little flirtation.

The music ceased, and he led her off the floor to one of the adjoining rooms, where refreshments were served. These were of a very simple nature, the strongest drink offered being a mild claret cup. Mr. Beaumaris procured a glass of lemonade for Arabella, and said: "You must let me thank you for a delightful few minutes, Miss Tallant: I have seldom enjoyed a dance more." He received only a slight smile, and an inclination of the head in answer to this, which were both so eloquent of incredulity that he was delighted. No fool, then, the little Tallant! He would have pursued this new form of sport, in the hope of teasing her into retort, but at that moment two purposeful gentlemen bore down upon them. Arabella yielded to the solicitations of Mr. Warkworth and went off on his arm. Sir Geoffrey Morecambe sighed in a languishing way, but turned his rebuff to good account by seizing the opportunity to ask Mr. Beaumaris what he called the arrangement of his neckcloth. He had to repeat the question, for Mr. Beaumaris, watching Arabella walk away with Mr. Warkworth, was not attending. He brought his gaze to bear on Sir Geoffrey's face, however, at the second time of asking, and raised his brows enquiringly.

"That style you have of tying your cravat!" said Sir Geoffrey. "I don't perfectly recognize it. Is it something new? Should you object to telling me what you call it?"

"Not in the least," replied Mr. Beaumaris blandly. "I call it Variations on an Original Theme."

❧ Chapter 8 ❧

MR. BEAUMARIS'S SUDDEN REALIZATION that the little Tallant was no fool underwent no modification during the following days. It began to be borne in upon him that, charm he ever so wisely, she was never within danger of losing her head over him. She treated him in the friendliest fashion, accepted his homage, and—he suspected—was bent upon making the fullest use of him. If he paid her compliments, she listened to them with the most innocent air in the world, but with a look in her candid gaze which gave him pause. The little Tallant valued his compliments not at all. Instead of being thrown into a flutter by the attentions of the biggest matrimonial prize in London, she plainly considered herself to be taking part in an agreeable game. If he flirted with her, she would generally respond in kind, but with so much the manner of one willing to indulge him that the hunter woke in him, and he was quite as much piqued as amused. He began to toy with the notion of making her fall in love with him in good earnest, just to teach her that the Nonpareil was not to be so treated with impunity. Once, when she was apparently not in the humor for gallantry, she actually had the effrontery to cut him short, saying: "Oh, never mind that! Who was that odd-looking man who waved to you just now? Why does he walk in that ridiculous way, and screw up his mouth so? Is he in pain?"

He was taken aback, for really he had paid her a compliment calculated to cast her into exquisite confusion. His lips twitched, for he had as few illusions about himself as had, to all appearances, the lady beside him. "That," he replied, "is Golden Ball, Miss Tallant, one of our dandies, as no doubt you have been told. He is not in pain. That walk denotes his consequence."

"Good gracious! He looks as though he went upon stilts! Why does he think himself of such consequence?"

"He has never accustomed himself to the thought that he is worth not a penny less than forty thousand pounds a year," replied Mr. Beaumaris gravely.

"What an odious person he must be!" she said scornfully. "To be consequential for such a reason as that is what I have no patience with!"

"Naturally you have not," he agreed smoothly.

Her color rushed up. She said quickly: "Fortune cannot make the man: I am persuaded you agree with me, for they tell me you are even more wealthy, Mr. Beaumaris, and I *will* say this!—you do not give yourself such airs as that!"

"Thank you," said Mr. Beaumaris meekly. "I scarcely dared to hope to earn so great an encomium from you, ma'am."

"Was it rude of me to say it? I beg your pardon!"

"Not at all." He glanced down at her. "Tell me, Miss Tallant!—just why do you grant me the pleasure of driving you out in my curricle?"

She responded with perfect composure, but with that sparkle in her eye which he had encountered several times before: "You must know that it does me a great deal of good socially to be seen in your company, sir!"

He was so much surprised that momentarily he let his

hands drop. The grays broke into a canter, and Miss Tallant kindly advised him to mind his horses. The most notable whip in the country thanked her for her reminder and steadied his pair. Miss Tallant consoled him for the chagrin he might have been supposed to feel by saying that she thought he drove very well. After a stunned moment, laughter welled up within him. His voice shook perceptibly as he answered: "You are too good, Miss Tallant!"

"Oh, no!" she said politely. "Shall you be at the masquerade at the Argyll Rooms tonight?"

"I never attend such affairs, ma'am!" he retorted, putting her in her place.

"Oh, then I shall not see you there!" remarked Miss Tallant with unimpaired cheerfulness.

She did not see him there; but, little though she might have known it, he was obliged to exercise considerable restraint not to cast to the four winds his famed fastidiousness and minister to her vanity by appearing at the ball. He did not do it, and hoped that she had missed him. She had, but this was something she would not acknowledge even to herself. Arabella, who had liked the Nonpareil on sight, was setting a strong guard over her sensibilities. He had seemed to her, when first her eyes had alighted on his handsome person, to be almost the embodiment of a dream. Then he had uttered such words to his friend as must shatter forever her esteem, and had wickedly led her into vulgar prevarication. Now it pleased his fancy to single her out from all the beauties in town, for reasons better known to himself than to her, but which she darkly suspected to be mischievous. No fool, the little Tallant! Not for one moment would she permit herself to indulge the absurd fancy that his court was serious. He might intrude into her meditations, but whenever she was aware of his having done so she was resolute in banishing his image. Sometimes she was strongly of the opinion that he had not believed a word of her boasts on that never-to-be-sufficiently-regretted evening in Leicestershire; at others, it seemed as though she had deceived him as completely as she had deceived Lord Fleetwood. It was impossible to fathom the intricacies of his mind, but one thing was certain: the great Mr. Beaumaris and the Vicar of Heythram's daughter could have nothing to do with one another, so that the less the Vicar's daughter thought about him the better it would be for her. One could not deny his address, or his handsome face, but one could—and one did—dwell on the many imperfections of his character. He was demonstrably indolent, a spoilt darling of society, with no thought for anything but his fleeting pleasure: a heartless, heedless leader of fashion, given over to selfishness and every other vice which Papa's daughter had been taught to think reprehensible.

If she missed him at the masquerade, no one would have guessed it. She danced indefatigably the whole night through, refused an offer of marriage from a slightly intoxicated Mr. Epworth, tumbled into bed at an advanced hour in the morning, and dropped instantly into untroubled sleep.

She was awakened at a most unseasonable hour by the sudden clatter of fire irons in the cold hearth. Since the menial who crept into her chamber each morning to sweep the grate and kindle a new fire there performed her task with trained stealth, this noise was unusual enough to rouse Arabella with a start. A gasp and a whimper, proceeding from the direction of the fireplace, made her sit up with a jerk, blinking at the unexpected vision of a small, dirty, and tearstained little boy, almost cowering on the hearth rug, and regarding her out of scared, dilating eyes.

"Good gracious!" gasped Arabella, staring at him. "Who are you?"

The child cringed at the sound of her voice and returned no answer. The mists of sleep curled away from

Arabella's brain; her eyes took in the soot lying on the floor, the grimed appearance of her strange visitant, and enlightenment dawned on her. "You must be a climbing-boy!" she exclaimed. "But what are you doing in my room?" Then she perceived the terror in the pinched, grimed small face, and she said quickly: "Don't be afraid! Did you lose your way in those horrid chimneys?"

The urchin nodded, knuckling his eyes. He further volunteered the information that old Grimsby would bash him for it. Arabella, who had had leisure to observe that one side of his face was swollen and discolored, demanded: "Is that your master? Does he beat you?"

The urchin nodded again, and shivered.

"Well, he shan't beat you for this!" said Arabella stretching out her hand for the dressing gown that was chastely disposed across the chair beside her bed. "Wait! I am going to get up!"

The urchin looked very much alarmed by this intelligence and shrank back against the wall, watching her defensively. She slid out of bed, thrust her feet into her slippers, fastened her dressing gown, and advanced kindly upon her visitor. He flung up an instinctive arm, cringing before her. He was clad in disgraceful rags, and Arabella now saw that the ends of his frieze nethergarments were much charred, and that his skinny legs and his bare feet were badly burnt. She dropped to her knees, crying out pitifully: "Oh, poor little fellow! You have burnt yourself so dreadfully!"

He slightly lowered his protective arm, looking suspiciously at her over it. "Ole Grimsby done it," he said.

She caught her breath. "What!"

"I'm afraid of going up the chimbley," explained the urchin. "Sometimes there's rats—big, fierce 'uns!"

She shuddered. "And he forces you to do so—like that?"

"They most of 'em does," said the urchin, accepting life as he found it.

She held out her hand. "Let me see! I will not hurt you."

He looked wary, but after a moment appeared to consider that she might be speaking the truth, for he allowed her to take one of his feet in her hand. He was surprised when he saw that tears stood in her eyes, for in his experience the gentler sex was more apt to beat one with a broom handle than to weep over one.

"Poor child, poor child!" Arabella said, a break in her voice. "You are so thin, too! I am sure you are half-starved! Are you hungry?"

"I'm allus hungry," he replied simply.

"And cold too!" she said. "No wonder, in those rags! It is wicked, *wicked!*" She jumped up, and grasping the bell pull that hung beside the fireplace, tugged it violently.

The urchin uttered another of his frightened whimpers and said: "Ole Grimsby'll beat the daylights out of me! Lemme go!"

"He shan't lay a finger on you!" promised Arabella, her cheeks flushed and her eyes sparkling through the tears they held.

The urchin came to the conclusion that she was soft, in her head. "Ho!" he remarked bitterly, "*you* don't know ole Grimsby! Nor you don't know his ole woman! Broke one of me ribs he did, once't!"

"He shall never do so again, my dear," Arabella said, turning aside to pull open a drawer in one of the chests. She dragged out the soft shawl, which had not so long since been swathed round the head of the sufferer from toothache, and put it round the boy, saying coaxingly: "There, let me wrap you up till we have had a fire lit! Is that more comfortable, my little man? Now sit down in this chair, and you shall have something to eat directly!"

He allowed himself to be lifted into the armchair, but his expression was so eloquent of suspicion and terror that it wrung Arabella's tender heart. She smoothed his cropped, sandy hair with one gentle hand and said soothingly: "You must not be afraid of me: I promise you I will not hurt you, nor let your master either. What is your name, my dear?"

"Jemmy," he replied, clutching the shawl about him and fixing her with a frightened stare.

"And how old are you?"

This he was unable to answer, being uninstructed in the matter. She judged him to be perhaps seven or eight years old, but he was so undernourished that he might have been older. While she waited for the summons of the bell to bring her maid to the room, she put more questions to the child. He seemed to have no knowledge of the existence of any parents, volunteering that he was an orphing, on the Parish. When he saw that this seemed to distress her, he tried to comfort her by stating that one Mrs. Balham said he was love-begotten. It appeared that this lady had brought him up until the moment when he had passed into the hands of his present owner. An inquiry into Mrs. Balham's disposition elicited the information that she was a rare one for jackey, and could half murder anyone when under the influence of this stimulant. Arabella had no idea what jackey might be, but she gathered that Jemmy's foster mother was much addicted to strong drink. She questioned Jemmy more closely, and he, gaining confidence, imparted to her, in the most matter-of-fact way, some details of a climbing-boy's life which drove the blood from her cheeks. He told her, with a certain distorted pride, of the violence of one of ole Grimsby's associates, Mr. Molys, a master sweep who only a year before had been sentenced to two years' imprisonment for causing the death of his six-year-old slave.

"Two years!" cried Arabella, sickened by the tale of cruelty so casually unfolded. "If he had stolen a yard of silk from a mercer's factory they would have deported him!"

Jemmy was not in a position to deny or to corroborate this statement, and preserved a wary silence. He saw that the young lady was very angry, and although her wrath did not seem to be directed against himself, his experience had taught him to run no unnecessary risks of being suddenly knocked flying against the wall. He shrank into the corner of the chair therefore, and clutched the shawl more tightly round his person.

A discreet knock fell on the door, and a slightly flustered and considerably startled housemaid entered the room. "Was it you rang, miss?" she asked, in astonished accents. Then her eye alighted on Arabella's visitor, and she uttered a genteel shriek. "Oh, miss! What a turn it gave me! The young varmint to give you such a fright! It's the chimney sweep's boy, miss, and him looking for him all over! You come with me this instant, you wicked boy, you!"

Jemmy, recognizing a language he understood, whined that he had not meant to do it.

"Hush!" Arabella said, dropping her hand on one bony little shoulder. "I know very well it is the sweep's boy, Maria, and if you look at him you will see how he has been used! Go downstairs, if you please, and fetch me some food for him directly—and send someone up to kindle the fire here!"

Maria stared at her as though she thought she had taken leave of her senses. "Miss!" she managed to ejaculate. "A dirty little *climbing-boy?*"

"When he has been bathed," said Arabella quietly, "he will not be dirty. I shall need plenty of warm water, and the bath, if you please. But first a fire, and some milk and food for the poor child!"

The affronted handmaid bridled. "I hope, miss, you do not expect *me* to wash that nasty little creature! I'm sure I don't know what her ladyship would say to such goings-on!"

"No," said Arabella, "I expect nothing from you that

I might expect from a girl with a more feeling heart than yours! Go and do what I have asked you to do, and desire Becky to come upstairs to me!"

"Becky?" gasped Maria.

"Yes, the girl who had the toothache. And when you have brought up food—some bread and butter and some meat will do very well, but do not forget the milk!—you may send someone to tell Lord Bridlington that I wish to see him at once."

Maria gulped, and stammered: "But, miss, his lordship is abed and asleep!"

"Well, let him be wakened!" said Arabella impatiently.

"Miss, I dare not for my life! His orders were no one wasn't to disturb him till nine o'clock, and he won't come, not till he has shaved himself, and dressed, not his lordship!"

Arabella considered the question, and finally came to the conclusion that it might be wiser to dispense with his lordship's assistance for the time being. "Very well," she said. "I will dress immediately, then, and see the sweep myself. Tell him to wait!"

"See the sweep—dress—Miss, you won't never! With that boy watching you!" exclaimed the scandalized Maria.

"Don't be such a fool, girl!" snapped Arabella, stamping her foot. "He's scarcely older than my little brother at home! Go away before you put me out of all patience with you!"

This, however, Maria could not be persuaded to do until she had arranged a prim screen between the wondering Jemmy and his hostess. She then tottered away to spread the news through the house that Miss was raving mad and likely to be taken off to Bedlam that very day. But since she did not dare to thwart a guest so much petted by her mistress, she delivered Arabella's message to Becky, and condescended to carry up a tray of food to her room.

Jemmy, still huddled in the big chair, was bewildered by the unprecedented turn of events and understood nothing of what was intended toward him. But he perfectly understood the significance of a plate of cold beef and half a loaf of bread, and his sharp eyes glistened. Arabella, who had flung on her clothes at random and done up her hair in a careless knot, settled him down to the enjoyment of his meal and sallied forth to do battle with the redoubtable Mr. Grimsby, uneasily awaiting her in the front hall.

The scene, conducted under the open-mouthed stare of a footman in his shirt sleeves, two astonished and giggling maids, and the kitchen boy, was worthy of a better audience. Mr. Beaumaris, for instance, would have enjoyed it immensely. Mr. Grimsby, knowing that the sympathies of those members of the household he had so far encountered were with him, and seeing that his assailant was only a chit of a girl, tried at the outset to take a high line, rapidly cataloguing Jemmy's many vices, and adjuring Arabella not to believe a word the varmint uttered. He soon discovered that what Arabella lacked in inches she more than made up for in spirit. She tore his character to shreds, and warned him of his ultimate fate. She flung Jemmy's burns and bruises in his face, and bade him answer her if he dared. He did not dare. She assured him that never would she permit Jemmy to go back to him, and when he tried to point out his undoubted rights over the boy, she looked so fierce that he backed before her. She said that if he wished to talk of his rights he might do so before a magistrate, and at these ominous words all vestige of fight went out of him. The misfortune which had overtaken his friend Mr. Molys was still fresh in his mind, and he desired to have no dealings with an unjust Law. There was no doubt that a young lady living in a house of this style would have those at her back who could, if she urged them to it, make things very unpleasant for a poor chimney sweep. The course for a prudent man to follow was retreat: climbing-boys were easily come by, and Jemmy had never been a success. Mr. Grimsby, his back bent nearly double, edged himself out of the house, trying to assure Arabella in one breath that she might keep Jemmy, and welcome, and that, whatever the ungrateful brat might say, he had been like a father to him.

Flushed with her triumph, Arabella returned to her room, where she found Jemmy, the plate of meat long since disposed of, eying with a good deal of apprehension the preparations for his ablutions. A capacious hip-bath stood before the fire, into which Becky was emptying the last of three large brass cans of hot water. Whatever Becky might think of climbing-boys, she had conceived a slavish adoration of Arabella, and she declared her willingness to do anything Miss might require of her.

"First," said Arabella briskly, "I must wash him, and put basilicum ointment on his poor little feet and legs. Then I must get him some clothes to wear. Becky, do you know where to procure suitable clothes for a child in London?"

Becky nodded vigorously, twisting her apron between her fingers. She ventured to say that she had sent home a suit for her brother Ben which Mother had been ever so pleased with.

"Have you little brothers? Then you will know just what to buy for this child!" Arabella said. "A warm jacket, and some smalls, and a shirt—oh, and some shoes and stockings! Wait! I will give you the money, and you shall go and procure the things immediately!"

"If you please, miss," said Becky firmly, "I think I ought to help you wash him first." She added sapiently: "Likely he'll struggle, miss—not being used to it."

She was quite right. Jemmy fought like a tiger to defend his person from the intended rape, and was deaf alike to coaxings and to reassurances. But the two damsels before him had not helped to bring up their respective young brothers for nothing. They stripped Jemmy of his rags, heedless of his sobs and his protests, and they dumped him, wildly kicking, in the bath, and ruthlessly washed every inch of his emaciated small person.

It was not to be expected that Jemmy's howls would not be heard beyond the confines of the room. They were lusty, and they penetrated to Lady Bridlington's ears. It was inconceivable to the good lady that they could really be emanating from within her house, as they seemed to be, and she was just about to ring her bell and desire Clara Crowle to send away whatever child it was who was screaming in the street, when the howls ceased (Jemmy had been lifted out of the bath, and wrapped in a warm towel), and she sank back again in her bed. Not long after this, Miss Crowle came softly in with her breakfast tray and with the pleasing intelligence that Miss Arabella was out of her mind and had got a dirty little boy in her room and wouldn't let him go, not whatever anyone said. Hardly had her ladyship grasped the essential points of the story poured into her bemused ears than Arabella herself came in. Her visit made it necessary for Miss Crowle to revive her mistress with hartshorn-and-water, and to burn pastilles, for it brought on a nervous spasm of alarming intensity. Lady Bridlington now understood that she was expected not only to house a boy picked out of the gutter, but to pursue his late master by every means in her power. Arabella talked of the Law, and of magistrates; of cruelties which made it almost impossible for Lady Bridlington even to swallow her coffee; and of what Papa would say must be done in so shocking a case. Lady Bridlington moaned, and said faintly: "But you cannot! The boy must be given back to his master! You don't understand these things!"

"Cannot?" cried Arabella, her eyes flashing. "Cannot, ma'am? I beg your pardon, but it is you who have not understood! When you have seen the dreadful marks on the poor little soul's back—and his ribs almost breaking through his skin!—you will not talk so!"

"No, no, Arabella, for heaven's sake!" begged her godmother. "I won't have you bring him in here! Where is Frederick? My dear, of course it is all very dreadful, and we will see what can be done, but do, pray, wait until I am dressed! Clara, where is his lordship?"

"His lordship, my lady," responded Clara with relish, "having partaken of his breakfast, has gone riding in the Park, as is his custom. His lordship's gentleman happening to mention that Miss had a climbing-boy in her room, his lordship said as how he must be sent off at once."

"Well, he will not be!" said Arabella, not mincing matters.

Lady Bridlington, reflecting that it was just like Frederick to issue orders in this foolish style and leave others to see them carried out, decided to postpone any further discussion until he should be present to lend her his support. She persuaded Arabella to go away, looked with distaste at her breakfast tray, and begged Clara, in a failing voice, to give her her smelling salts.

When Lord Bridlington returned from his morning exercise, he was displeased to learn that nothing had so far been done about the climbing-boy except that Miss had sent one of the under servants out to buy him a suit of clothes. He was still frowning over this when his Mama came downstairs and almost fell upon his neck. "Thank heaven you are come at last!" she uttered. "What can have induced you to go out with the house in this uproar? I am driven nearly distracted! She wants me to employ the boy as a page!"

Frederick led her firmly into the saloon on the ground floor and shut the door upon the interested butler. He then demanded an explanation of an affair which he said he was at a loss to understand. His mother was in the middle of giving him one when Arabella came into the room, leading the washed and clothed Jemmy by the hand.

"Good morning, Lord Bridlington!" she said calmly. "I am glad you are come home, for you will best be able to help me to decide what I ought to do with Jemmy here."

"I can certainly do so, Miss Tallant," he answered. "The boy must of course go back where he belongs. It was most improper of you, if you will permit me to say so, to interfere between him and his master."

He encountered a look which surprised him. "I do not permit anyone, Lord Bridlington, to tell me that in rescuing a helpless child from the brutality of a monster I am doing what is improper!" said Arabella.

"No, no, my dear, of course not!" hastily interposed Lady Bridlington. "Frederick did not mean—But, you see, there is nothing one can do in these sad cases! That is—I am sure Frederick will speak to the man—give him a good fright, you know!"

"Really, Mama—"

"And Jemmy?" demanded Arabella. "What will you do with him?"

His lordship looked distastefully at the candidate for his protection. Jemmy had been well scrubbed, but not the most thorough application of soap and water could turn him into a well-favored child. He had a sharp little face, a wide mouth, from which a front tooth was missing, and a very snub nose. His short, ragged hair was perfectly straight, and his ears showed a tendency to stick out from his head.

"I do not know what you expect me to do!" said his lordship fretfully. "If you had any knowledge of the laws governing apprentices, my dear Miss Tallant, you would

know that it is quite impossible to steal this boy away
from his master!"

"When the master of an apprentice misuses a boy as
this child has been misused," retorted Papa's daughter,
"he renders himself liable to prosecution! What is more,
this man knows it, and I assure you he does not expect
to have Jemmy returned to him!"

"I suppose you think I should adopt the boy!" said
Frederick, goaded.

"No, I do not think that," replied Arabella, her voice
a little unsteady. "I only think that you might—show
some compassion for one so wretchedly circum-
stanced!"

Frederick colored hotly. "Well, of course I am excessively sorry, but—"

"Do you know that his master lights a fire in the grate
beneath him, to force him up the chimney?" interrupted
Arabella.

"Well, I don't suppose he would go up if—Yes, yes,
shocking, I know, but chimneys must be swept, after all,
or what would become of us all?"

"Oh, that Papa were here!" Arabella cried. "I see that
it is useless to talk to you, for you are selfish and heartless, and you care for nothing but your own comfort!"

It was at this inopportune moment that the door was
opened and the butler announced two morning callers.
He afterwards explained this lapse, which he felt quite
as acutely as his mistress, by saying that he had supposed
Miss to be still upstairs with That Boy. Frederick made
a hasty gesture indicative of his desire that the visitors
should be excluded, but it was too late. Lord Fleetwood
and Mr. Beaumaris walked into the room.

Their reception was unusual. Lady Bridlington gave
vent to an audible moan; her son stood rooted to the
floor in the middle of the room, his face flushed, and his
whole appearance that of a man who had been stuffed;
and Miss Tallant, also very much flushed, bit her lip and

turned on her heel, leading a small urchin over to a chair
by the wall and bidding him gently to sit down on it, and
to be a good boy.

Lord Fleetwood blinked upon this scene; Mr.
Beaumaris's brows went up, but he gave no other sign
of surprise, merely bowing over Lady Bridlington's
nerveless hand, and saying: "How do you do? I trust we
don't intrude? I called in the hope of persuading Miss
Tallant to drive to the Botanical Gardens with me. They
tell me the spring flowers are quite a sight there."

"You are very obliging, sir," said Arabella curtly, "but
I have more important affairs to attend to this morning."

Lady Bridlington pulled herself together. "My love,
we can discuss all that later. I am sure it would do you
good to take the air! Do but send that—that child down
to the kitchen, and—"

"Thank you, ma'am, but I do not stir from the house
until I have settled what is to be done with Jemmy."

Lord Fleetwood, who had been regarding Jemmy with
frank curiosity, said: "Jemmy, eh? Er—friend of yours,
Miss Tallant?"

"No. He is a climbing-boy who came by mistake down
the chimney of my bedchamber," Arabella replied. "He
has been most shamefully used, and he is only a child,
as you may see—I daresay not more than seven or eight
years old!"

The warmth of her feelings brought a distinct tremor
into her voice. Mr. Beaumaris looked curiously at her.

"No, really?" said Lord Fleetwood, with easy sympathy. "Well, that's a great deal too bad! Shocking brutes,
some of these chimney-sweeps! Ought to be sent to
jail!"

She said impulsively: "Yes, that is what I have been
telling Lord Bridlington, only he seems not to have the
least understanding!"

"Arabella!" implored Lady Bridlington. "Lord Fleetwood can have no interest in such matters!"

"Oh, I assure you, ma'am!" said his lordship. "I am interested in anything that interests Miss Tallant! Rescued the child, did you? Well, upon my soul, I call it a devilish fine thing to do! Not as though he was a taking brat, either!"

"What does that signify?" said Arabella contemptuously. "I wonder how taking, my lord, you or I should be had we been brought up from infancy by a drunken foster mother, sold while still only babies to a brutal master, and forced into a hateful trade!"

Mr. Beaumaris moved quietly to a chair a little removed from the group in the center of the room and stood leaning his hands on the back of it, his eyes still fixed on Arabella's face.

"No, no! Exactly so!" hastily said Lord Fleetwood.

Lord Bridlington chose, unwisely, to intervene at this point. "No doubt it is just as you say, ma'am, but this is hardly a topic for my mother's sitting room! Let me beg of you—"

Arabella turned on him like a flash, her eyes bright with tears, her voice unsteady with indignation. "I will not be silenced! It is a topic that should be discussed in every Christian lady's sitting room! Oh, I mean no disrespect, ma'am! You have not thought—you cannot have thought! Had you seen the wounds on this child's body you could not refuse to help him! I wish I had made you come into my room when I had him naked in the bath! Your heart must have been touched!"

"Yes, but, Arabella, my heart *is* touched!" protested her afflicted godmother. "Only I don't want a page, and he is much too young, and such an ugly little thing! Besides, the sweep will very likely claim him, because whatever you may think, if the boy is apprenticed to him, which he must be—"

"You may make your mind easy on that score, ma'am! His master will never dare to lay claim to him. He knows very well that he is in danger of being taken before a magistrate, for I told him so, and he did not doubt me! Why, he cringed at the very word, and backed himself out of the house as fast as he could!"

Mr. Beaumaris spoke at last. "Did you confront the sweep, Miss Tallant?" he asked, an odd little smile flickering on his lips.

"Certainly I did!" she replied, her glance resting on him for an indifferent moment.

Lady Bridlington was suddenly inspired. "He must go to the Parish, of course! Frederick, *you* will know how to set about it!"

"No, no, he must not!" Arabella declared. "That would be worse than anything, for what will they do with him, do you suppose, but set him to the only trade he knows? And he is afraid of those dreadful chimneys! If it were not so far away, I would send him to Papa, but how could such a little boy go all that way alone?"

"No, certainly not!" said Lord Fleetwood. "Not to be thought of!"

"Lord Bridlington, surely, surely you would not condemn a child to such a life as he has endured?" Arabella begged, her hands going out in a pleading gesture. "You have so *much!*"

"Of course he wouldn't!" declared Fleetwood rashly. "Now, come, Bridlington!"

"But why should I?" demanded Frederick. "Besides, what could I do with the brat? It is the greatest piece of nonsense I ever had to listen to!"

"Lord Fleetwood, will you take Jemmy?" asked Arabella, turning to him beseechingly.

His lordship was thrown into disorder. "Well, I don't think—You see, ma'am—Fact of the matter is—Dash it, Lady Bridlington's right! The Parish! That's the thing!"

"Unworthy, Charles!" said Mr. Beaumaris.

The much goaded Lord Bridlington rounded on him. "Then, if that is what you think, Beaumaris, perhaps *you* will take the wretched brat!"

Then it was that Mr. Beaumaris, looking across the room at Arabella, all flushed cheeks and heaving bosom, astonished the company and himself as well. "Yes," he said. "I will."

❦ *Chapter 9* ❦

THESE SIMPLE WORDS STRUCK THE EARS OF his audience with stunning effect. Lord Fleetwood's jaw dropped; Lady Bridlington's and her son's rather protuberant eyes started at Mr. Beaumaris; and Arabella stared at him in amazement. It was she who broke the silence. "*You?*" she said, the incredulity in her tone leaving him in no doubt of her opinion of his character.

A rather rueful smile twisted his lips. "Why not?" he said.

Her eyes searched his face. "What would you do with him?" she demanded.

"I haven't the smallest notion," he confessed. "I hope you may be going to tell me what I am to do with him, Miss Tallant."

"If I let you take him, you would throw him on the Parish, like Lord Fleetwood!" she said bitterly.

His lordship uttered an inarticulate protest.

"I have a great many faults," replied Mr. Beaumaris, "but, believe me, you may trust my pledged word! I will neither throw him on the Parish nor restore him to his master."

"You must be mad!" exclaimed Frederick.

149

"You would naturally think so," said Mr. Beaumaris, flicking him with one of his disdainful glances.

"Have you considered what people would be bound to say?" Frederick said.

"No, nor do I propose to burden my head with anything that interests me so little!" retorted Mr. Beaumaris.

Arabella said in a softened voice: "If you mean it indeed, sir, you will be doing the very kindest thing—perhaps the best thing you have ever done, and, oh, I *thank* you!"

"Certainly the best thing I have ever done, Miss Tallant," he said, with that wry smile.

"What will you do with him?" she asked again. "You must not be thinking that I mean you to adopt him as your own, or anything of that nature! He must be brought up to a respectable trade, only I do not know what would be the best for him!"

"Perhaps," suggested Mr. Beaumaris, "he has views of his own on the subject. What, Jemmy, would you choose to do?"

"Yes, what would you like to do when you are a man?" said Arabella, turning to kneel beside Jemmy's chair, and speaking in a coaxing tone. "Tell me!"

Jemmy, who had been following all this with an intent look in his face, had no very clear idea of what it was all about, but his quick cockney mind had grasped that none of these swells, not even the stout, cross one, intended any harm to him. The scared expression in his eyes had given place to one of considerable acuteness. He answered his protectress without hesitation. "Give ole Grimsby a leveler!" he said.

"Yes, my dear, and so you shall, and I hope you will do the same by everyone like him!" said Arabella warmly. "But how would you choose to earn your living?"

Mr. Beaumaris's lips twitched appreciatively. So the little Tallant had brothers, had she?

Lady Bridlington was looking bewildered, and her son disgusted. Lord Fleetwood, accepting Arabella's unconsciously betrayed knowledge of boxing cant without question, looked Jemmy over critically and gave it as his opinion that the boy was not the right build for a bruiser.

"Of course not!" said Arabella. "Think, Jemmy! What could you do, do you suppose?"

The urchin reflected, while the company awaited his pleasure. "Sweep a crossing," he pronounced at last. "I could 'old the gen'lemen's 'orses, then."

"Hold the gentlemen's horses?" repeated Arabella. Her eye brightened. "Are you fond of horses, Jemmy?"

Jemmy nodded vigorously. Arabella looked round in triumph. "Then I know the very thing!" she said. "Particularly since it is you who are to take charge of him, Mr. Beaumaris!"

Mr. Beaumaris waited in deep foreboding for the blow to fall.

"He must learn to look after horses, and then, as soon as he is a little older, you may employ him as your Tiger!" said Arabella radiantly.

Mr. Beaumaris, whose views on the folly of entrusting blood cattle to the guardianship of small boys were as unequivocal as they were well known, replied without a tremor: "To be sure I may. The future now being provided for—"

"But you never drive with a Tiger up behind you!" exclaimed Lord Bridlington. "You have said I know not how many times—"

"I do wish, Bridlington, that you would refrain from interrupting with these senseless comments," said Mr. Beaumaris.

"But that child is far too young to be a Tiger!" pointed out Lady Bridlington.

Arabella's face fell. "Yes, he is," she said regretfully.

"Yet it would be the very thing for him, if only we knew what to do with him in the meantime!"

"I think," said Mr. Beaumaris, "that in the meantime I had better convey him to my own house, and place him in the charge of my housekeeper, pending further discussion between us, Miss Tallant."

He was rewarded with a glowing look. "I did not know you would be so kind!" said Arabella. "It is a splendid notion, for the poor little fellow needs plenty of good food, and I am sure he must get it in your house! Listen, Jemmy, you are to go with this gentleman, who is to be your new master, and be a good boy, and do as he bids you!"

Jemmy, clutching a fold of her dress, was understood to say that he preferred to remain with her. She bent over him, patting his shoulder. "No, you cannot stay with me, my dear, and I am sure you would not like it half so well if you could, for you must know that he has a great many horses, and will very likely let you see them. Did you come here in your curricle, sir?" Mr. Beaumaris bowed. "Well, there, do you hear that, Jemmy?" said Arabella in a heartening tone. "You are to drive away in a carriage, behind a pair of beautiful gray horses!"

"I am driving my chestnuts today," said Mr. Beaumaris apologetically. "I am so sorry, but I feel I should perhaps mention it!"

"You did very right," said Arabella approvingly. "One should never tell untruths to children! Chestnuts, Jemmy, glossy brown horses! How grand you will feel sitting up behind them!"

Apparently the urchin felt that there was much in what she said. He released her gown and directed his sharp gaze upon his new owner. "Proper good 'uns?" he asked suspiciously.

"Proper good 'uns," corroborated Mr. Beaumaris gravely.

Jemmy slid from the chair. "You ain't slumming me? You won't go a-givin' of me back to ole Grimsby?"

"No, I won't do that. Come and take a look at my horses!"

Jemmy hesitated, glancing up at Arabella, who at once took his hand, and said: "Yes, let us go and see them!"

When Jemmy beheld the equipage being led up and down the street, his eyes widened, and he drew a shuddering breath of ecstasy. "That's a bang-up set-out, that is!" he said. "Will I drive them 'orses, guv'nor?"

"You will not," said Mr. Beaumaris. "You may sit up beside me, however."

"Yessir!" said Jemmy, recognizing the voice of authority.

"Up with you, then!" Mr. Beaumaris said, lifting him into the curricle. He turned, and found that Arabella was holding her hand out to him. He took it in his, and held it for a moment.

"I wish I might find the words to thank you!" she said. "You will let me know how he goes on."

"You may rest easy on that head, Miss Tallant," he said, bowing. He took the reins in his hand, and mounted into the carriage and looked down maliciously at Lord Fleetwood, who had accompanied them out of the house and was just taking his leave of Arabella. "Come, Charles!"

Lord Fleetwood started, and said hurriedly: "No, no, I'll walk! No need to worry about me, my dear fellow!"

"Come, Charles!" repeated Mr. Beaumaris gently.

Lord Fleetwood, aware of Arabella's eyes upon him, sighed and said: "Oh, very well!" and climbed into the curricle, wedging Jemmy between himself and Mr. Beaumaris.

Mr. Beaumaris nodded to his gaping groom and steadied the chestnuts as they sprang forward. "Coward," he remarked.

"It ain't that I'm a coward!" protested his lordship.

"But we shall have all the fools in London staring after us! I can't think what's come over you, Robert! You're never going to keep this brat in Mount Street! If it leaks out, and it's bound to, I suppose you know everyone will think it's a by-blow of yours?"

"The possibility had crossed my mind," agreed Mr. Beaumaris. "I am sure I ought not to let it weigh with me: Miss Tallant certainly would not."

"Well, damn it, I think that prosy fool, Bridlington, was right for once in his life! You've gone stark, staring mad!"

"Very true: I have known it this half hour and more."

Lord Fleetwood looked at him in some concern. "You know, Robert, if you're not careful you'll find yourself walking to the altar before you're much older!" he said.

"No, she has the poorest opinion of me," replied Mr. Beaumaris. "I perceive that my next step must be to pursue the individual known to us as 'ole Grimsby.'"

"What?" gasped Fleetwood. "She never asked that of you!"

"No, but I feel she expects it of me." He saw that the mention of the sweep's name had made Jemmy look up at him in quick alarm, and said reassuringly: "No, I am not going to give you to him."

"Robert, never in all the years I've known you have I seen you make such a cake of yourself!" said his friend, with brutal frankness. "First you let the little Tallant bamboozle you into saddling yourself with this horrid brat, and now you talk of meddling with a chimney sweep! *You!* Why, it's unheard of!"

"Yes, and, what is more, I have a shrewd suspicion that a benevolent career is going to prove extremely wearing," said Mr. Beaumaris thoughtfully.

"I see what it is," said Fleetwood, after regarding his profile for a few moments. "You're so piqued she don't favor you, you'll go to any lengths to fix your interest with the girl!"

"I will," said Mr. Beaumaris cordially.

"Well, you'd better take care what you are about!" said his worldly-wise friend.

"I will," said Mr. Beaumaris again.

Lord Fleetwood occupied himself during the rest of the short drive in delivering a severe lecture on the perfidy of those who, without having any serious intentions, attempted to cut out their friends with the season's most notable catch, adding, for good measure, a lofty condemnation of hardened rakes who tried to deceive innocent country maidens.

Mr. Beaumaris listened to him with the utmost amiability, only interrupting to applaud this last flight of eloquence. "That's very good, Charles," he said approvingly. "Where did you pick it up?"

"Devil!" said his lordship, with feeling. "Well, I wash my hands of you—and I hope she will lead you a pretty dance!"

"I have a strong premonition," replied Mr. Beaumaris, "that your hope is likely to be realized."

Lord Fleetwood gave it up, and as Mr. Beaumaris saw no reason to take him into his confidence, what little time was left before Mount Street was reached was occupied in discussing the chances of the newest bruiser in his forthcoming fight with an acknowledged champion.

Mr. Beaumaris, at this stage, would have been chary of confiding in anyone the precise nature of his intentions. He was by no means sure that he knew what they were himself; but that he had called in Park Street for precisely the reasons described by his friend, and, when confronted by the vision of Arabella fighting for the future of her unattractive protégé, had undergone an enlightenment so blinding as almost to deprive him of his senses, was certain. No consideration of the conduct to be expected of a delicately nurtured female had stopped her. She knew no discomfiture when two gentlemen of fashion had arrived to find her embroiled in the concerns of an urchin far beneath the notice of any aspirant to social heights. No, by God! Thought Mr. Beaumaris exultantly, she showed us what she thought of such frippery fellows as we are! We might have gone to the devil for all she cared. *I* might have made her a laughingstock only by recounting the story—as I could! Lord, yes, as I *could!* Did she know it? Would she have cared? Not a farthing, the little Tallant! But I must stop Charles spreading this all over town.

Mr. Beaumaris, hunting now in earnest, was by far too experienced a sportsman to pursue his quarry too closely. He let several days pass before making any attempt to approach Arabella. When next he encountered her it was at a ball given by the Charnwoods. He asked her to stand up with him for one of the country dances, but when the moment for taking their places in the set came, led her to a sofa, saying: "Shall you object to sitting down with me instead? One can never converse in comfort while dancing, and I must consult you about our urchin."

"No, indeed!" she said warmly. "I have been so anxious to know how he goes on!" She seated herself, holding her fan in her clasped hands, and raised her eyes to his face in an inquiring look. "Is he well? Is he happy?"

"As far as I have been able to ascertain," replied Mr. Beaumaris carefully, "he is not only fast recovering the enjoyment of excellent health, but is achieving no common degree of felicity by conduct likely to deprive me of the services of most of my existent staff."

Arabella considered this. Mr. Beaumaris watched appreciatively the wrinkling of her thoughtful brow. "Is he very naughty?" she asked presently.

"According to the report of my housekeeper, Miss Tallant—but I daresay she is not to be at all believed!— he is the embodiment of too many vices for me to enumerate."

JOIN THE
TIMELESS ROMANCE READER SERVICE
AND GET FOUR OF TODAY'S
MOST EXCITING HISTORICAL
ROMANCES FREE,
WITHOUT OBLIGATION!

Imagine getting today's very best historical romances sent directly to your home – at a total savings of at least $2.00 a month. Now you can be among the first to be swept away by the latest from Candace Camp, Constance O'Banyon, Patricia Hagan, Parris Afton Bonds or Susan Wiggs. You get all that – and that's just the beginning.

PREVIEW AT HOME WITHOUT
OBLIGATION AND SAVE.

Each month, you'll receive four new romances to preview without obligation for 10 days. You'll pay the low subscriber price of just $4.00 per title – a total savings of at least $2.00 a month!

Postage and handling is absolutely free and there is no minimum number of books you must buy. You may cancel your subscription at any time with no obligation.

GET YOUR FOUR FREE BOOKS TODAY ($20.49 VALUE)

FILL IN THE ORDER FORM BELOW NOW!

YES! *I want to join the Timeless Romance Reader Service. Please send me my 4 FREE HarperMonogram historical romances. Then each month send me 4 new historical romances to preview without obligation for 10 days. I'll pay the low subscription price of $4.00 for every book I choose to keep — a total savings of at least $2.00 each month — and home delivery is free! I understand that I may return any title within 10 days without obligation and I may cancel this subscription at any time without obligation. There is no minimum number of books to purchase.*

NAME_____

ADDRESS _____

CITY_____STATE_____ZIP_____

TELEPHONE_____

SIGNATURE _____

(If under 18 parent or guardian must sign. Program, price, terms, and conditions subject to cancellation and change. Orders subject to acceptance by HarperMonogram.)

GET
4
FREE
BOOKS
(A $20.49 VALUE)

TIMELESS ROMANCE
READER SERVICE

120 Brighton Road
P.O. Box 5069
Clifton, NJ 07015-5069

She seemed to accept this with unimpaired calm, for she nodded understandingly.

"Pray do not think that I should dream of burdening you with anything so unimportant as the complaints of a mere housekeeper!" begged Mr. Beaumaris. "Nothing but the most urgent of exigencies could have prevailed upon me to open my lips to you upon this subject!" She looked startled, and inquiring. "You see," he said apologetically, "it is Alphonse!"

"Alphonse?"

"My chef," explained Mr. Beaumaris. "Of course, if you say so, ma'am, he shall go! But I must own that his departure would cause me grave concern. I do not mean to say that my life would be shattered, precisely, for no doubt there *are* other chefs who have his way with a soufflé, and who do not take such violent exception to the raids of small boys upon the larder!"

"But this is quite absurd, Mr. Beaumaris!" said Arabella severely. "You must have been indulging Jemmy beyond what is right! I daresay he is excessively ill-behaved: it is always so, unless their spirits are utterly broken, and we must be thankful that his are not!"

"Very true!" agreed Mr. Beaumaris, entranced by this wisdom. "I will at once present this view of the matter to Alphonse."

Arabella shook her head. "Oh, no! It would not be of the least avail, I daresay! Foreigners," she said largely, "have no notion how to manage children! What is to be done?"

"I cannot help feeling," said Mr. Beaumaris, "that Jemmy would benefit by country air."

This suggestion found favor. "Nothing could be better for him!" agreed Arabella. "Besides, there is no reason why he should tease you, I am sure. Only how may it be contrived?"

Much relieved at having so easily cleared this fence, Mr. Beaumaris said: "The notion did just cross my mind, ma'am, that if I were to take him into Hampshire, where I have estates, no doubt some respectable household might be found for him."

"One of your tenants! The very thing!" exclaimed Arabella. "Quite a simple cottage, mind, and a sensible woman to take care of him! Only I am afraid she would have to be paid a small sum to do it."

Mr. Beaumaris, who felt that no sum could be too large for the ridding of his house of one small imp who threatened to disrupt it, bore up nobly under the warning, and said that he had envisaged this possibility and was prepared to meet it. It then occured to Arabella that he might reasonably expect so great an heiress as herself to bear the charge of her protégé; and she embarked on a tangled explanation of why she could not at present do so. Mr. Beaumaris interrupted her speech when it showed signs of becoming raveled beyond hope. "No, no, Miss Tallant!" he cried. "Do not deny me this opportunity to perform a charitable action, I beg of you!"

So Arabella very kindly refrained from doing so, and bestowed so grateful a smile upon him that he felt himself to have been amply rewarded.

"Are you quite in disgrace with Lady Bridlington?" he asked quizzically.

She laughed, but looked a little guilty. "I *was*," she owned. "But since she has seen that the story has not got about, she has forgiven me. She was persuaded that everyone would be laughing at me. As though I would care for such a thing as that, when I had but done my duty!"

"Certainly not!"

"Do you know, I had begun to believe that everyone in town—all the grand people, I mean—were quite heartless and selfish?" she confided. "I am afraid I was not quite civil to you—indeed, Lady Bridlington assures me that I was shockingly rude!—but then, you see, I had no notion that you were not like all the rest. I beg your pardon!"

Mr. Beaumaris had the grace to acknowledge a twinge of conscience. It led him to say: "Miss Tallant, I did it in the hope of pleasing you."

Then he wished that he had curbed his tongue, for her confiding air left her, and although she talked easily for a few more minutes, he was fully aware that she had withdrawn from him again.

He was able to retrieve his position a few days later, and took care not to jeopardize it again. When he returned from a visit to his estates he called in Park Street to give Arabella comfortable tidings of Jemmy, whom he had foisted onto a retired servant of his own. She was a little concerned lest the townbred waif should feel lost and unhappy in the country, but when he informed her that the last news he had of Jemmy, before leaving Hampshire, was that he had let a herd of bullocks out of the field where they were confined, pulled the feathers from the cock's tail, tried to ride an indignant pig round the yard, and eaten a whole batch of cakes newly baked by his kind hostess, she perceived that Jemmy was made of resilient stuff, and laughed, and said that he would soon settle down and learn to be a good boy.

Mr. Beaumaris agreed to it, and then played his trump card. He thought Miss Tallant would like to know that he had taken steps to ensure the well-being of Mr. Grimsby's future apprentices.

Arabella was delighted. "You have brought him to justice!"

"Well, not quite that," confessed Mr. Beaumaris. He saw the disappointed look in her eye and added hastily: "You know, I could not feel that to be appearing in a court of law was just what you would like. Then, too, when it is a question of apprentices one is apt to find oneself confronted with all manner of difficulties in the way of removing boys from their masters. It seemed best, therefore, to drop a word in Sir Nathaniel Conant's ear. He is the Chief Magistrate, and as I have some acquaintance with him the thing was easy. Mr. Grimsby will take care how he disregards a warning from Bow Street, I assure you."

Arabella was a little sorry to think that Mr. Grimsby was not to be cast into jail, but being a sensible girl she readily appreciated the force of Mr. Beaumaris's arguments, and told him that she was very much obliged to him. She sat pondering deeply for some moments, while he watched her, wondering what now was in her head. "It should be the business of people with interest and fortune to inquire into such things!" she said suddenly. "No one seems to care a button in a great city like this! I have seen such dreadful sights since I came to London—such beggary, and misery, and such countless ragged children who seem to have no parents and no homes! Lady Bridlington does not care to have anything of that nature spoken about, but, oh, I would like so much to be able to help such children as poor Jemmy!"

"Why don't you?" he asked coolly.

Her eyes flew to his; he knew that he had been too blunt: she would not tell him the truth about herself. Nor did she. After a tiny pause, she said: "Perhaps, one day, I shall."

He wondered whether her godmother had warned her against him, and when she excused herself from dancing with him at the next Assembly, was sure of it.

But the warning came from Lord Bridlington. Mr. Beaumaris's marked attentions to Arabella, including, as they had, so extraordinary a gesture as the adoption of Jemmy, had aroused the wildest hopes in Lady Bridlington's shallow brain. If any of his previous amatory adventures had led him to perform a comparable deed, she at least had never heard of it. She began to indulge the fancy that his intentions were serious, and had almost written to give Mrs. Tallant a hint of it when Lord Bridlington dashed her hopes.

"You would do well, ma'am, to put your young friend a little on her guard with Beaumaris," he said weightily.

"My dear Frederick, and so I did, at the outset! But he has become so particular in his attentions, showing such a decided preference for her, and trying to fix his interest with her by every means in his power, that I really begin to think he has formed a lasting attachment! Only fancy if she were to form such a connection, Frederick! I declare, I should feel it as much as if she were my own child! For it will be all due to me, you know!"

"You would be very unwise to put such a notion into the girl's head, Mama," he said, cutting short these rhapsodies. "I can tell you this: Beaumaris's intimates don't by any means regard his pursuit of Miss Tallant in that light!"

"No?" she said, in a faltering tone.

"Far otherwise, ma'am! They are saying that it is all pique, because she does not appear to favor him above any other. I must say, I should not have expected her to have shown such good sense! You must know that men of his type, accustomed as he is to being courted and flattered, are put very much on their mettle by a rebuff from any female who has not been so foolish as to pick up the handkerchief he has carelessly tossed toward them. It puts me out of all patience to see anyone so spoiled and caressed! But be that as it may, you should know, Mama, that bets are being laid and taken at White's against Miss Tallant's holding out against this siege!"

"How odious men are!" exclaimed Lady Bridlington indignantly.

Odious they might be, but if they were laying bets of that nature at the clubs, there was nothing for a conscientious chaperon to do but warn her charge once more against lending too credulous an ear to an accomplished flirt. Arabella assured her that she had no intention of doing so.

"No, my dear, very likely not," replied her ladyship. "But there is no denying that he is a very attractive man: I am conscious of it myself! Such an air! Such easy address! But it is of no use to think of that! I am sadly afraid that it is a kind of sport with him to make females fall in love with him."

"*I* shall not do so!" declared Arabella. "I like him very well, but, as I told you before, I am not such a goose as to be taken in by him!"

Lady Bridlington looked at her rather doubtfully. "No, my love, I hope not indeed. To be sure, you have so many admirers that we need not consider Mr. Beaumaris. I suppose—you will not be offended at my asking, I know!— I suppose no eligible gentleman has proposed to you?"

Quite a number of gentlemen, eligible and ineligible, had proposed to Arabella, but she shook her head. She might acquit some of her suitors of having designs on her supposed wealth, but two among them at least would never have offered for her hand, she was very sure, had they known her to be penniless; and the courtships of several notorious fortune-hunters made it impossible for her to believe that Lord Bridlington's well-meaning efforts had in any way scotched that dreadful rumor. She felt her situation to be unhappy indeed. Easter was almost upon them, and there had been plenty of time for her, with the opportunies which had been granted to her, to have fulfilled her Mama's ambitions. She felt guilty, for it had cost Mama so much money, which she could ill afford, to send her to London, so that the least a grateful daughter could have done would have been to have repaid her by accepting some respectable offer of marriage. She could not do it. She cared for none of those who had proposed to her; and although that, she supposed, ought not to weigh too heavily in the scales when balanced against the benefits that would accrue to the dear brothers and sisters, she was resolved to accept no offer from anyone ignorant of her true circumstances. Perhaps there was still to come into her life some suitor to whom it would be possible to confess the whole, but he had not yet appeared, and, pending his arrival, it was with relief that Arabella turned to Mr. Beaumaris, who, whatever his intentions might be, certainly coveted no fortune.

Mr. Beaumaris offered her every facility to turn to him, but he could scarcely congratulate himself on the outcome. The smallest attempt at gallantry had the effect of transforming her from the confiding child he found so engaging into the society damsel who was ready enough to fence lightly with him, but who showed him quite clearly that she wanted none of his practiced love-making. And when Lady Bridlington had repeated much of her son's warning, not omitting to mention the fact that Mr. Beaumaris's friends knew him to be merely trifling, Mr. Beaumaris found Miss Tallant even more elusive. He was reduced to employing an ignoble stratagem, and, having been obliged to visit his estates on a matter of business, sought Arabella out upon his return and told her that he wished to consult her again about Jemmy's future. In this manner he lured her to drive out with him in his curricle. He drove her to Richmond Park, and she raised no objection to this, though he had not previously taken her farther afield than Chelsea. It was a fine, warm afternoon, with the sun so brightly shining that Arabella ventured to wear a very becoming straw hat and to carry a small sunshade with a very long handle, which she had seen in the Pantheon Bazaar and had not been able to resist purchasing. She said, as Mr. Beaumaris handed her up into the curricle, that it was very kind of him to drive her into the country, since she liked it of all things, and was able to think herself, while in that great park, many miles from town.

"Do you know Richmond Park, then?" he asked.

"Oh, yes!" replied Arabella cheerfully. "Lord Fleet-wood drove me there last week; and then, you know, the Charnwoods got up a party and we all went in three barouches. And tomorrow, if it is fine, Sir Geoffrey Morecambe is to take me to see the Florida Gardens."

"I must count myself fortunate, then, to have found you on a day when you had no other engagement," remarked Mr. Beaumaris.

"Yes, I am out a great deal," agreed Arabella. She unfurled the sunshade, and said: "What was it that you wished to tell me about Jemmy, sir?"

"Ah, yes, Jemmy!" he said. "Subject to your consent, Miss Tallant, I am making—in fact, I have made—a tri-fling change in his upbringing. I hear he will never come to any good under Mrs. Buxton's roof, and still more do I fear that if he remained there he would shortly be the death of her. At least, so she informed me when I went down to Hampshire the day before yesterday."

She gave him one of her warm looks. "How very kind that was of you! Did you go all that way on that naughty boy's account?"

Mr. Beaumaris was sorely tempted. He glanced down at his companion, met her innocently inquiring gaze, hesitated, and then said: "Well, no, Miss Tallant! I had business there."

She laughed. "I thought it had been that."

"In that case," said Mr. Beaumaris, "I am glad I did not lie to you."

"How can you be so absurd? As though I should wish you to put yourself to so much trouble! What has Jemmy been doing?"

"It would sadden you to know: Mrs. Buxton is persuaded that he is possessed of a fiend. The language he employs, too, is not such as she is accustomed to. I regret to say that he has also alienated my keepers, who have quite failed to impress upon him the impropriety of disturbing my birds, or, I may add, of stealing pheasants' eggs. I cannot imagine what he can want with them."

"Of course he should be punished for doing so! I daresay he has not enough employment. One must remember that he has been used to work, and should be made to do so now. It is not at all good for anyone to be perfectly idle."

"Very true, ma'am," agreed Mr. Beaumaris meekly.

Miss Tallant was not deceived. She looked sharply up at him, and bit her lip, saying after a moment: "We are speaking of *Jemmy!*"

"I hoped we were," confessed Mr. Beaumaris.

"You are being nonsensical," said Arabella, with some severity. "What is to be done with him?"

"I found, upon inquiry, that the only person who is inclined to regard him favorably is my head groom, who says that his way with the horses is quite remarkable. It appears that he has been forever slipping off to the stables, where, for a wonder, he comports himself unexceptionally. Wrexham was so much impressed by finding him—er—hobnobbing with a bay stallion generally thought to be extremely dangerous, that he came up to represent to me the propriety of handing the boy over to him to train. He is a childless man, and since he expressed his willingness to house Jemmy, I thought it better to fall in with his schemes. I hardly think Jemmy's language will shock him, and I am encouraged to hope, from what I know of Wrexham, that he will know how to keep the boy in order."

Arabella approved so heartily of this arrangement that he took the risk of saying in a melancholy tone: "Yes, but if it succeeds, I shall be at a loss to think of a pretext for getting you to drive out with me."

"Dear me, have I shown myself so reluctant?" said Arabella, raising her eyebrows. "I wonder why you will talk so absurdly, Mr. Beaumaris? You may depend upon

it that I shall take care to be seen every now and then in
your company, for I cannot be so sure of my credit as to
run the risk of having it said that the Nonpareil has
begun to find me a dead bore!"

"You stand in no such danger, Miss Tallant, believe
me." He drew in his horses for a sharp bend in the road,
and did not speak again until the corner was negotiated.
Then he said: "I am afraid that you deem me a very
worthless creature, ma'am. What am I to do to convince
you that I can be perfectly sensible?"

"There is not the least need: I am sure that you can,"
she replied amicably.

After that she became interested in the countryside,
and from that passed to her forthcoming presentation.
This event was to take place in the following week, and
already her dress had been sent home from the skillful
costumier who had altered an old gown of Lady Bridlington's to the present mode. Miss Tallant did not tell
Mr. Beaumaris that, naturally, but she did describe its
magnificence to him, and found him both sympathetic
and knowledgeable. He asked her what jewels she would
wear with it, and she replied, in a very grand way: "Oh,
nothing but diamonds!" and was promptly ashamed of
herself for having said it, although it was perfectly true.

"Your taste is always excellent, Miss Tallant. Nothing
could be more displeasing to a fastidious eye than a
profusion of jewelry. I must congratulate you on having
exerted so beneficial an influence over your contemporaries."

"I?" she gasped, quite startled, and half suspecting
him of quizzing her.

"Certainly. The total lack of ostentation which charac-
terizes your appearance is much admired, I assure you,
and is beginning to be copied."

"You cannot be serious?"

"But of course I am serious! Had you not noticed that
Miss Accrington has left off that shocking collar of sap-

phires, and that Miss Kirkmichael no longer draws attention to the limitations of her figure by a profusion of chains, brooches, and necklaces which I should have supposed her to have chosen at random from an overstocked jewel box?"

There was something so irresistibly humorous to Arabella in the thought that her straitened circumstances had been at the root of a new mode that she began to giggle. But she would not tell Mr. Beaumaris why she sat chuckling beside him. He did not press her for an explanation, but as they had by this time reached the Park, suggested that she might like to walk on the grass for a little way while the groom took charge of the curricle. She assented readily, and while they strolled about, Mr. Beaumaris told her something of that home of his in Hampshire. The bait failed. Miss Tallant confined her remarks on her own home to descriptions of the Yorkshire scene, and would not be lured into exchanging family reminiscences.

"I collect that your father is still alive, ma'am? You mentioned him, as I remember, on the day that you adopted Jemmy."

"Did I? Yes, indeed he is alive, and I wished for him very much that day, for he is the best man in the world, and he would have known just what was right to be done!"

"I shall hope to have the pleasure of making his acquaintance one day. Does he come to London at all?"

"No, never," replied Arabella firmly. She could not imagine that Mr. Beaumaris and Papa would have the least pleasure in one another's acquaintance, thought that the conversation was getting on to dangerous ground, and reverted to her society manner.

This was maintained during most of the drive back to London, but when the open country was left behind and the curricle was passing once more between rows of houses, it deserted her abruptly. In the middle of a narrow street, the grays took highbred exception to a wagon with a tattered and flapping canvas roof, which was drawn up to one side of the road. There was barely room for the curricle to slip past this obstruction, and Mr. Beaumaris, his attention all on his horses, failed to take notice of a group of youths bending over some object on the flagway, or to heed the anguished yelp which made Arabella, casting aside the light rug which covered her legs, cry out: "Oh, stop!" and shut her sunshade with a snap.

The grays were mincing past the wagon, Mr. Beaumaris did indeed pull them up, but Arabella did not wait for the curricle to come to a standstill, but sprang hazardously down from it. Mr. Beaumaris, holding his sidling, snorting pair in an iron hand, took one quick glance over his shoulder, saw that Arabella was dispersing the group on the pavement by the vigorous use of her sunshade, and snapped: "Go to their heads, fool!"

His groom, still perched up behind, and apparently dumbfounded by Miss Tallant's strange conduct, came to himself with a start, jumped down, and ran round to hold the grays. Mr. Beaumaris sprang down and descended swiftly upon the battleground. Having scientifically knocked two louts' heads together, picked up the third lout by his collar and the seat of his frieze breeches and thrown him into the road, he was able to see what had aroused Miss Tallant's wrath. Crouched, shivering and whimpering, on the flag-way was a small, sandy coated mongrel with a curly tail and one ear disreputably flying.

"Those wicked, brutal, *fiends!*" panted Miss Tallant, cheeks and eyes in a glow. "They were *torturing* the poor little thing!"

"Take care! He may snap at you!" Mr. Beaumaris said quickly, seeing her about to kneel down beside the dog. "Shall I thrash them all soundly?"

At these words, the two smaller boys departed precipi-

tately, the two whose heads were still ringing drew cir-
cumspectly out of range of Mr. Beaumaris's long-lashed
whip, and the bruised youth in the road whined that they
weren't doing any harm and that all his ribs were busted.

"How badly have they hurt him?" Miss Tallant asked
anxiously. "He cries when I touch him!"

Mr. Beaumaris pulled off his gloves, and handed them
to her, together with his whip, saying: "Hold those for
me, and I'll see."

She obediently took them, and watched anxiously
while he went over the mongrel. She saw with approval
that he handled the little creature firmly and gently, in
a way that showed he knew what he was about. The dog
whined, and uttered little cries, and cowered, but he did
not offer to snap. Indeed, he feebly wagged his disgraceful tail, and once licked Mr. Beaumaris's hand.

"He is badly bruised, and has one or two nasty sores,
but there are no bones broken," Mr. Beaumaris said,
straightening himself. He turned to where the two remaining youths were standing, poised on the edge of
flight, and said sternly: "Whose dog is this?"

"It don't belong to no one," he was sullenly informed.
"It goes all over, stealing things off of the rubbish heaps:
yus, *and* out of the butcher's shop!"

"I seen 'im in Chelsea once't with 'alf a loaf of bread,"
corroborated the other youth.

The accused crawled to Mr. Beaumaris's elegantly
shod feet and pawed one gleaming Hessian appealingly.

"Oh, see how intelligent he is!" cried Arabella, stoop-
ing to fondle the animal. "He knows he has you to thank
for his rescue!"

"If he knows that, I think little of his intelligence, Miss
Tallant," said Mr. Beaumaris, glancing down at the dog.
"He certainly owes his life to you!"

"Oh, no! I could never have managed without your
help! Will you be so obliging as to hand him up to me,

if you please?" said Arabella, prepared to climb into the curricle again.

Mr. Beaumaris looked from her to the unkempt and filthy mongrel at his feet, and said: "Are you quite sure that you want to take him with you, ma'am?"

"Why, of course! You do not suppose that I would leave him here, for those wretches to torment as soon as we were out of sight! Besides, you heard what they said! He has no master—no one to feed him, or to take care of him! Please give him to me!"

Mr. Beaumaris's lips twitched, but he said with perfect gravity: "Just as you wish, Miss Tallant!" and picked up the dog by the scruff of his neck. He saw Miss Tallant's arms held out to receive her new protégé, and hesitated. "He is very dirty, you know!"

"Oh, what does that signify? I have soiled my dress already, with kneeling on the flag-way!" said Arabella impatiently.

So Mr. Beaumaris deposited the dog on her lap, received his whip and gloves from her again, and stood watching with a faint smile while she made the dog comfortable and stroked its ears and murmured soothingly to it. She looked up. "What do we wait for, sir?" she asked, surprised.

"Nothing at all, Miss Tallant!" he said, and got into the curricle.

Miss Tallant, continuing to fondle the dog, spoke her mind with some force on the subject of persons who were cruel to animals, and thanked Mr. Beaumaris earnestly for his kindness in knocking the horrid boys' heads together, a violent proceeding which seemed to have met with her unqualified approval. She then occupied herself with talking to the dog, and informing him of the splendid dinner he should presently be given, and the warm bath which he would (she said) so much enjoy. But after a time she became a little pensive and relapsed into meditative silence.

"What is it, Miss Tallant?" asked Mr. Beaumaris, when she showed no sign of breaking the silence.

"Do you know," she said slowly, "I have just thought—Mr. Beaumaris, something tells me that Lady Bridlington may not like this dear little dog!"

Mr. Beaumaris waited in patient resignation for his certain fate to descend upon him.

Arabella turned impulsively toward him. "Mr. Beaumaris, do you think—*would* you—?"

He looked down into her anxious, pleading eyes, a most rueful twinkle in his own. "Yes, Miss Tallant," he said. "I would."

Her face broke into smiles. "*Thank* you!" she said. "I knew I might depend upon you!" She turned the mongrel's head gently toward Mr. Beaumaris. "There, sir! That is your new master, who will be very kind to you! Only see how intelligently he looks, Mr. Beaumaris! I am sure he understands. I daresay he will grow to be quite devoted to you!"

Mr. Beaumaris looked at the animal and repressed a shudder. "Do you think so indeed?" he said.

"Oh, yes! He is not, perhaps, a very *beautiful* little dog, but mongrels are often the cleverest of all dogs." She smoothed the creature's rough head, and added innocently: "He will be company for you, you know. I wonder you do not have a dog already."

"I do—in the country," he replied.

"Oh, sporting dogs! They are not at all the same."

Mr. Beaumaris, after another look at his prospective companion, found himself able to agree with this remark with heartfelt sincerity.

"When he has been groomed, and has put some flesh on his bones," pursued Arabella, serene in the conviction that her sentiments were being shared, "he will look very different. I am quite anxious to see him in a week or two!"

Mr. Beaumaris drew up his horses outside Lady Bridlington's house. Arabella gave the dog a last pat and set him on the seat beside his new owner, bidding him stay there. He seemed a little undecided at first, but being too bruised and battered to leap down into the road, he did stay, whining loudly. However, when Mr. Beaumaris, having handed Arabella up to the door and seen her admitted into the house, returned to his curricle, the dog stopped whining and welcomed him with every sign of relief and affection.

"Your instinct is at fault," said Mr. Beaumaris. "Left to myself, I should abandon you to your fate. That, or tie a brick round your neck and drown you."

His canine admirer wagged a doubtful tail and cocked an ear. "You are a disgraceful object!" Mr. Beaumaris told him. "And what does she expect me to do with you?" A tentative paw was laid on his knee. "Possibly, but let me tell you that I know your sort! You are a toadeater, and I abominate toadeaters. I suppose if I sent you into the country my own dogs would kill you on sight."

The severity in his tone made the dog cower a little, still looking up at him with the expression of a dog anxious to understand.

"Have no fear!" Mr. Beaumaris assured him, laying a fleeting hand on his head. "She clearly wishes me to keep you in town. Did it occur to her, I wonder, that your manners, I have no doubt at all, leave much to be desired? Do your wanderings include the slightest experience of the conduct expected of those admitted into a gentleman's house? Of course they do not!" A choking sound from his groom made him say over his shoulder: "I hope you like dogs, Clayton, for you are going to wash this specimen."

"Yes, sir," said his grinning attendant.

"Be very kind to him!" commanded Mr. Beaumaris. "Who knows? He may take a liking to you."

But at ten o'clock that evening, Mr. Beaumaris's butler, bearing a tray of suitable refreshments to the library, admitted into the room a washed, brushed, and fed mongrel, who came in with something as near a prance as could be expected of one in his emaciated condition. At sight of Mr. Beaumaris, seeking solace from his favorite poet in a deep-winged chair by the fire, he uttered a shrill bark of delight and reared himself up on his hind legs, his paws on Mr. Beaumaris's knees, his tail furiously wagging, and a look of beaming adoration in his eyes.

Mr. Beaumaris lowered his Horace. "Now, what the devil—?" he demanded.

"Clayton brought the little dog up, sir," said Brough. "He said as you would wish to see how he looked. It seems, sir, that the dog didn't take to Clayton, as you might say. Very restless, Clayton informs me, and whining all the evening." He watched the dog thrust his muzzle under Mr. Beaumaris's hand, and said: "It's strange the way animals always go to you, sir. Quite happy now, isn't he?"

"Deplorable," said Mr. Beaumaris. "Down, Ulysses! Learn that my pantaloons were not made to be pawed by such as you!"

"He'll learn quick enough, sir," remarked Brough, setting a glass and a decanter down on the table at his master's elbow. "You can see he's as sharp as he can stare. Would there be anything more, sir?"

"No, only give this animal back to Clayton and tell him I am perfectly satisfied with his appearance."

"Clayton's gone off, sir. I don't think he can have understood that you wished him to take charge of the little dog," said Brough.

"I don't think he can have wanted to understand it," said Mr. Beaumaris grimly.

"As to that, sir, I'm sure I couldn't say. I doubt whether the dog will settle down with Clayton, him not having a way with dogs like he has with horses. I'm afraid he'll fret, sir."

"Oh, my God!" groaned Mr. Beaumaris. "Then take him down to the kitchen!"

"Well, sir, of course—if you say so!" replied Brough doubtfully. "Only there's Alphonse." He met his master's eye, apparently had no difficulty in reading the question in it, and said: "Yes, sir. Very French he has been on the subject. Quite shocking, I'm sure, but one has to remember that foreigners are queer and don't like animals."

"Very well," said Mr. Beaumaris, with a resigned sigh, "leave him, then!"

"Yes, sir," said Brough, and departed.

Ulysses, who had been thoroughly, if a little timidly, inspecting the room during this exchange, now advanced to the hearth rug again and paused there, suspiciously regarding the fire. He seemed to come to the conclusion that it was not actively hostile, for after a moment he curled himself up before it, heaved a sigh, laid his chin on Mr. Beaumaris's crossed ankles, and disposed himself for sleep.

"I suppose you imagine you are being a companion to me," said Mr. Beaumaris.

Ulysses flattened his ears and gently stirred his tail.

"You know," said Mr. Beaumaris, "a prudent man would draw back at this stage."

Ulysses raised his head to yawn, and then snuggled it back on Mr. Beaumaris's ankles and closed his eyes.

"You may be right," admitted Mr. Beaumaris. "But I wonder what next she will saddle me with?"

❧ *Chapter 10* ❧

WHEN ARABELLA HAD PARTED FROM MR.
Beaumaris at the door of Lady Bridlington's house, the
butler who had admitted her informed her that two gentlemen had called to see her and were even now awaiting
her in the smaller saloon. This seemed to her a trifle
unusual, and she looked surprised. The butler explained
the matter by saying that one of the young gentlemen
was particularly anxious to see her, since he came from
Yorkshire and would not be unknown to her. A horrid
fear gripped Arabella that she was now to be exposed to
the whole of London, and it was with an almost shaking
hand that she picked up the visiting card from the salver
the butler was holding out to her. But the name elegantly inscribed upon it was unknown to her: she could
not recall ever having heard of, much less met, a Mr.
Felix Scunthrope.

"*Two* gentlemen?" she said.

"The other young gentleman, miss, did not disclose
his name," replied the butler.

"Well, I suppose I must see them," Arabella decided.
"Pray tell them that I shall be downstairs directly! Or is
her ladyship in?"

"Her ladyship has not yet returned, miss."

Arabella hardly knew whether to be glad or sorry. She went up to her room to change her soiled gown, and came down again some few minutes later hoping that she had schooled her face not to betray her inward trepidation. She entered the saloon in a very stately way, and looked rather challengingly across it. There were, as the butler had warned her, two young gentlemen standing by the window. One was a slightly vacuous looking youth, dressed with extreme nicety, and holding, besides his tall hat, an ebony cane and an elegant pair of gloves; the other was a tall, loose-limbed boy, with curly dark hair and an aquiline cast of countenance. At sight of him, Arabella uttered a shriek and ran across the room to cast herself upon his chest. *"Bertram!"*

"Here, I say, Bella!" expostulated Bertram, recoiling. "Mind what you are about, for the lord's sake! My neck-cloth!"

"Oh, I beg your pardon, but I am so *glad* to see you! But how is this? Bertram, Papa is not in town?"

"Good God, no!"

"Thank heaven!" Arabella breathed, pressing her hands to her cheeks.

Her brother found nothing to wonder at in this exclamation. He looked her over critically, and said: "Just as well he ain't, for he'd be bound to give you one of his scolds for dressing up as fine as fivepence! I must say, Bella, you're turned out in prime style! Slap up to the mark, ain't she, Felix?"

Mr. Scunthorpe, much discomposed at being called upon to give an opinion, opened and shut his mouth once or twice, bowed, and looked despairing.

"He thinks you're complete to a shade," explained Bertram, interpreting these signs. "He ain't much of a dab with the petticoats, but he's a great gun, I can tell you! Up to every rig and row in town!"

Arabella looked at Mr. Scunthorpe with interest. He

presented the appearance of a very mild young man; and although his fancy waistcoat bespoke the man of fashion, he seemed to her to lack address. She bowed politely, which made him blush very much and fall into a fit of stuttering. Bertram, feeling that some further introduction might be considered desirable by his sister, said: "You don't know him: he was at Harrow with me. He's older than I am, but he's got no brains, y'know: never could learn anything! I ran into him in the High."

"The High?" repeated Arabella.

"Oxford, you know!" said Bertram loftily. "Dash it, Bella, you can't have forgot I've been up to take Smalls!"

"No, indeed!" she said. "Sophy wrote that you were gone there, and that poor James was unable to accompany you, because of the jaundice. I was so sorry! But how did you go on, Bertram? Do you think you have passed?"

"Lord, I don't know! There was one devilish paper— but never mind that now! The thing is that I met old Felix here, the very man I wanted!"

"Oh, yes?" Arabella said, adding with a civil smile: "Were you up for Smalls too, sir?"

Mr. Scunthorpe appeared to shrink from such a suggestion, shaking his head, and making a sound in his throat which Arabella took to be a negative.

"Of course he wasn't!" said Bertram. "Don't I keep telling you he can't learn anything? He was visiting some friends in Oxford! He found it pretty dull work, too, didn't you, Felix? They would take him to blue-parties, all professors, and Bagwigs, and the poor fellow couldn't follow the stuff they talked. Shabby thing to do to him, for he was bound to make a cake of himself in that sort of company! However, that's not what I want to talk about. The thing is, Bella, that Felix is going to show me all the sights, because he's at home to a peg in London—been on the town ever since they threw him out of Harrow."

"And Papa gave his consent?" exclaimed Arabella.

"As a matter of fact," said Bertram airily, "he don't know I'm here."

"Doesn't know you're here?" cried Arabella.

Mr. Scunthorpe cleared his throat. "Given him the bag," he explained. He added: "Only thing to do."

Arabella turned her eyes wonderingly toward her brother. He looked a little guilty, but said: "No, you can't say I've given him the bag!"

Mr. Scunthorpe corrected himself. "Hoaxed him."

Bertram seemed to be about to take exception to this too, but after beginning to refute it he broke off and said: "Well, in a way I suppose I did."

"Bertram, you must be mad!" cried Arabella, pale with dismay. "When Papa knows you are in town, and without leave—"

"The thing is he won't know it," interrupted Bertram. "I wrote a letter to Mama, telling her I had met my friend Felix, and he had invited me to stay with him. So they won't be in a fret when I don't go back immediately, and they won't know where I am, because I didn't give my direction. And that brings me to what I particularly want to warn you about, Bella! I'm going by the name of Anstey while I'm in town, and while I don't mind if you tell this godmother of yours that I'm a friend of yours, you are not to say I'm your brother! She'd be bound to write and tell my mother, and then the fat would be in the fire!"

"But, Bertram, how can you *dare?*" asked Arabella, in an awed voice. "Papa will be so angry!"

"Yes, I know. I shall get a rare trimming, but I shall have had a bang-up time first, and I can stand a lick or two after," said Bertram cheerfully. "I made up my mind I'd do it, before you came to town. Do you remember my telling you that you might get a surprise? I'll swear you never thought *this* would be it!"

"No, indeed I did not!" Arabella said, sinking into a

chair. "Oh, Bertram, I am quite in a quake! I cannot understand any of it! How can you afford to be staying in London? Are you Mr. Scunthorpe's guest?"

"No, no, poor old Felix ain't standing the huff! I won a ticket in a lottery! Only think of it, Bella! A hundred pounds!"

"A lottery! Good God, what would Papa say if he knew *that?*"

"Oh, he would kick up no end of a bobbery, of course, but I shan't tell him. And, you know, once I had won it, the only thing to be done was to spend it, because you must see I had to get rid of it before Papa found I had it!" He saw that his sister was looking horrified, and said indignantly: "I must say, I don't see why you should grudge it to me! I daresay you are having a capital time yourself!"

"No, no, how could you think I would grudge you *anything*, Bertram? But to have you in town, and to be obliged to pretend I am not your sister, and to deceive Papa and Mama—" She stopped, remembering her own situation. "Oh, Bertram, how *wicked* we are!"

Mr. Scunthorpe looked very much alarmed at this, but Bertram said: "Fudge! It's not telling lies, precisely, just not to mention that you have seen me when you write to Mama!"

"You do not know! It is worse than that!" whispered Arabella. "Bertram, I am in such a scrape!"

He stared at her. "You are? How is this?" He saw her glance toward his friend and said: "You needn't mind Felix: he's no gabster!"

Arabella was easily able to believe this, but she not unnaturally felt reluctant to disclose her story to one who was a stranger to her, even though she had already realized that if he was not to betray her unwittingly, he must be taken some way at least into her confidence. Mr. Scunthorpe tweaked his friend's sleeve. "Must help your

sister out of the scrape, dear boy. Happy to be of service!"

"I am very much obliged to you, sir, but no one can
help me out of it!" said Arabella tragically. "If only you
will be so kind as not to betray me!"

"Of course he won't betray you!" declared Bertram.
"What in thunder have you been about, Bella?"

"Bertram, everyone believes me to be a great heiress!" disclosed Arabella in a stricken tone.

He stared at her for a moment, and then burst out
laughing. "You goosecap! I'll wager they don't! Why,
Lady Bridlington knows you are not! You don't mean
that she put such a tale about?"

She shook her head. "*I* said it!" she confessed.

"*You* said it? What the devil made you do such a thing?
However, I don't suppose anyone believed you!"

"They do believe it. Lord Bridlington says that every
gazetted fortune-hunter in town is dangling after me—
and, oh, Bertram, it is true! I have refused *five* offers
already!"

The idea that there could be found five gentlemen
ready to marry his sister struck Bertram as being exquisitely humorous, and he went off into another burst of
laughter. Arabella was obliged to confess the whole,
since he seemed so incredulous. Her narrative was
rather disjoined, since he interpolated so many questions, and at one point a considerable digression was
caused by Mr. Scunthorpe, who, having regarded her
fixedly for some moments, suddenly became loquacious
and said: "Beg pardon, ma'am, but did you say Mr.
Beaumaris?"

"Yes. He and Lord Fleetwood."

"The Nonpareil?"

"Yes."

Mr. Scunthorpe drew a breath and turned to address
his friend. "You hear that, Bertram?"

"Well, of course I heard it!"

"Didn't think you could have. You see this coat of mine?"

Both Tallants stared at his coat in some bewilderment.

"Got my man to copy the lapels of one Weston made for the Nonpareil," said Mr. Scunthorpe, with simple pride.

"Good God, what has that to say to anything?" demanded Bertram.

"Thought you might be interested," explained Mr. Scunthorpe apologetically.

"Never mind him!" Bertram told his sister. "If it wasn't just like you, Bella, to fly into a miff, and go off into one of your crazy starts! Mind, I don't say I blame you! Did he spread the story over London?"

"I think it was Lord Fleetwood who did that. Mr. Beaumaris told me once that he had not discussed the matter with anyone but Lord Fleetwood. Sometimes I have wondered whether—whether he had guessed the truth, but I cannot believe that he has, for he would despise me dreadfully, I am sure, if he knew how odiously I behaved, and certainly not stand up with me at all the balls—for he very seldom dances!—or take me out driving in his curricle."

Mr. Scunthorpe looked very much impressed. "He does that?"

"Oh, yes!"

Mr. Scunthorpe nodded portentously at Bertram. "You know what, dear boy? All the crack, your sister! Not a doubt of it. Knows all the best people. Drives out with the Nonpareil. Good thing she said she was an heiress."

"Oh, no, no, I wish I had never done so, for it had made everything so uncomfortable!"

"Now, Bella, that's gammon! I know you! Don't you try to tell me you don't like being all the go, because I wouldn't believe you if you did!" said Bertram, with brotherly candor.

Arabella thought it over. Then she gave a reluctant smile. "Well, yes, perhaps I do like it, but when I remember the cause of it, I do indeed wish I had never said such a thing! Only consider what a fix I am in! If the truth were known now I should be utterly discredited! No one would ever *bow* to me, I daresay, and I have the greatest dread that Lady Bridlington would send me home in disgrace! And that Papa would know, and—Bertram, I had almost rather throw myself into the river than have him know such a thing of me!"

"Lord, yes!" he agreed, with a shudder. "But it won't come to that! If anyone asks *me* any prying questions, I shall say you are well known to me, and so will Felix!"

"Yes, but that is not all!" Arabella pointed out. "I never, never accept any offer made to me, and what Mama will think of such selfishness I dare not consider! For she so much hoped that I should form an eligible connection, and Lady Bridlington is bound to tell her that—that quite a number of *very* eligible gentlemen have paid me the most marked attentions!"

Bertram knit his brows over this. "Unless— No, you're right, Bella: devilish awkward fix! You would have to tell the truth, if you accepted an offer, and ten to one he'd cry off. What a tiresome girl you are, to be sure! Dashed if I see what's to be done! Do you, Felix?"

"Very difficult situation," responded Mr. Scunthorpe, shaking his head. "Only one thing to be done."

"What's that?"

Mr. Scunthorpe gave a diffident cough. "Just a little thing that occurred to me. Daresay you won't care about it: can't say I care about it myself, but can't hang back when a lady's in a fix."

"But what *is* it?"

"Mind, only a notion I had!" Mr. Scunthorpe warned him. "You don't like it: you say so! *I* don't like it, but ought to offer." He perceived that the Tallants were quite mystified, blushed darkly, and uttered in a strangled voice: "Marriage!"

Arabella stared at him for a moment, and then went into a peal of mirth. Bertram said scornfully: "Of all the cork-brained notions—! *You* don't want to marry Bella!"

"No," conceded Mr. Scunthorpe. "Promised I would help her out of the scrape, though!"

"What's more," Bertram said severely, "those trustees of yours would never let you! You're not of age."

"Talk them over," said Mr. Scunthorpe hopefully.

However, Arabella, thanking him for his kind offer, said that she did not think they would suit. He seemed grateful, and relapsed into the silence which appeared to be natural to him.

"I daresay I shall hit upon something," said Bertram. "I'll think about it, at all events. Should I stay to do the pretty to this godmother of yours, do you think?"

Arabella urged him strongly to do so. She was inclined to grieve over his necessary incognito, but he told her frankly that it would not at all suit him to be forever gallanting her to the *ton* parties. "Very dull work!" he said. "I know you are gone civility-mad since you came to town, but it's not in my line." He then enumerated the sights he meant to see in London, and since these seemed to consist mostly of such innocuous entertainments as Astley's Amphitheatre, the Royal Menagerie at the Tower, Madame Tussaud's Waxworks, Napoleon's carriage, on view at Bullock's Museum, a look-in at Tattersall's, the departure of the Brighton coaches from the White Horse Cellar, and the forthcoming Military Review in Hyde Park, his anxious sister's worst qualms were allayed. At first sight he had seemed to her to have grown a great deal older, for he was wearing a sophisticated waistcoat and had brushed his hair in a new style; but then he told her about the peer show which had diverted him so much in Coventry Street, and expressed a purely youthful desire to witness that grand spectacle,

The Burning of Moscow (supported by tightrope walking, and an equestrian display) she could feel that he was still boy enough not to hanker after the more sophisticated and by far more dangerous amusements to be found in London. But, then, as he confidentially informed Mr. Scunthorpe when they presently left Park Street together, females took such foolish notions into their heads that it would have been ridiculous to have disclosed to her that he had an equally ardent desire to see a bout of fisticuffs at the Fives Court, to blow a cloud with all the Corinthians at the Daffy Club, to penetrate the mysteries of the Royal Saloon and the Peerless Pool, and certainly to put in an appearance at the Opera—not, he hastened to assure his friend, because he wanted to listen to music, but because he was credibly informed that to stroll in the Fops' Alley was famous sport, and all the go. Since he had decided, very prudently, to put up at one of the City inns, where, if he chose, he could be sure of a tolerable dinner at the Ordinary, which was very moderately priced, he entertained reasonable hopes of being able to afford all these diversions. But first, he perceived, it was necessary to buy a much higher-crowned and more curly-brimmed beaver to set on his head; a pair of Hessians with tassels; a fob, and perhaps a seal; and certainly a pair of natty yellow gloves. Without these adjuncts to a gentleman's costume he would look like a Johnny Raw. Mr. Scunthorpe agreed, and ventured to point out that a driving coat with only two shoulder capes was thought, in well-dressed circles, to be a paltry affair. He said he would take Bertram along to his own man, a devilish clever tailor, even though he had not acquired the fame of a Weston or a Stultz. However, as the great advantage of patronizing this rising man lay in the assurance that he would be willing to rig out any friend of Mr. Scunthorpe's on tick, Bertram raised no objection to jumping into a hackney at once and telling the jarvey to drive with

all speed to Clifford Street. Mr. Scunthorpe vouched for
it that Swindon's art would give his friend quite a new
touch, and as this seemed extremely desirable to Bertram, he thought he could hardly lay out a substantial
sum of money to better advantage. Mr. Scunthorpe then
imparted to him a few useful hints, particularly warning
him against such extravagances of style as must give rise
to the suspicion that he belonged to the extreme dandy
set frowned upon by the real Pinks of the *Ton.* Beyond
question, the finest model for any aspiring gentleman to
copy was the Nonpareil, that Go amongst the Goers.
This put Bertram in mind of something which had been
slightly troubling his mind, and he said: "I say, Felix, do
you think my sister should be driving about the town
with him? I don't mind telling you I don't like it above
half!"

Here Mr. Scunthorpe was able at once to allay his
qualms: for a lady to drive in a curricle or a phaeton, with
a groom riding behind, was unexceptionable. "Mind, it
would not do for a female to go in a tilbury!" he said.

His brotherly concern relieved, Bertram abandoned
the question, merely remarking that he would give a
monkey to see his father's face if he knew how rackety
Bella had become.

Arrived in Clifford Street, they obtained instant audience of Mr. Swindon, who was so obliging as to bring
out his pattern card immediately, and to advise his new
client on the respective merits of Superfine and Bath
Suiting. He thought six capes would be sufficient for a
light drab driving coat, an opinion in which Mr. Scunthorpe gravely concurred, explaining to Bertram that it
would never do for him to ape the Goldfinches, with
their row upon row of capes. Unless one was an acknowledged Nonesuch, capable of driving to an inch, or one
of the Melton men, it was wiser, he said to aim at neat-
ness and propriety rather than at the very height of
fashion. He then bent his mind to the selection of a cloth

for a coat, and although Bertram had not intended to order a new coat, he was persuaded to do so, as much by the assertion of Mr. Swindon that a single-breasted garment of colored cloth, with wide lapels and silver buttons, would set his person off to advantage, as by the whispered assurance of his friend that the snyder always gave his clients long credit. Indeed, Mr. Scunthorpe was rarely troubled with his tailor's account, since that astute man of business was well aware that being a fatherless minor, Mr. Scunthorpe's considerable fortune was held in trust by tight-fisted guardians, who doled him out a beggarly allowance. Nothing so ungenteel as cost or payment was mentioned during the session in Clifford Street, so that Bertram left the premises torn between relief and a fear that he might have pledged his credit for a larger sum than he could afford to pay. But the novelty and excitement of a first visit to the metropolis soon put such untimely thoughts to rout, while a lucky bet at the Fives Court clearly showed the novice the easiest way of raising the wind.

A close inspection of such sprigs of fashion as were to be seen at the Fives Court made Bertram very glad to think he had bespoken a new coat, and he confided to Mr. Scunthorpe that he would not visit the haunts of fashion until his clothes had been sent home. Mr. Scunthorpe thought this a wise decision, and as it was of course absurd to suppose that Bertram should kick his heels at the City inn which enjoyed his patronage, he volunteered to show him how an evening full of fun and gig could be spent in less exalted circles. This entertainment, beginning as it did in the Westminister Pit, where it seemed to the staring Bertram that representatives of every class of society, from the Corinthian to the dustman, had assembled to watch a contest between two dogs; and proceeding by way of the shops of Tothill Fields, where adventurous bucks tossed off noggins of Blue Ruin or bumpers of heavy wet, in company with bruisers, prigs, coal-heavers, Nuns, Abbesses, and apple women, to a coffee shop, ended in the watchhouse, Mr. Scunthorpe having become bellicose under the influence of his potations, Bertram, quite unused to such quantities of liquor as he had imbibed, was too much fuddled to have any very clear notion of what circumstance it was that had excited his friend's wrath, though he had a vague idea that it was in some way connected with the advances being made by a gentleman in Petersham trousers toward a lady who had terrified him earlier in the proceedings by laying a palpable lure for him. But when a mill was in progress, it was not his part to inquire into the cause of it, but to enter into the fray in support of his cicerone. Since he was by no means unlearned in the noble art of self-defense, he was able to render yeoman service to Mr. Scunthorpe, no proficient, and was in a fair way to milling his way out of the shop when the watch, in the shape of several Charleys, all springing their rattles, burst in upon them, and after a spirited set-to overpowered the two peacebreakers, and haled them off to the watchhouse. Here, after considerable parley, conducted for the defense by the experienced Mr. Scunthorpe, they were admitted to bail and warned to present themselves next day in Bow Street, not a moment later than twelve o'clock. The night constable then packed them both into a hackney, and they drove to Mr. Scunthorpe's lodging in Clarges Street, where Bertram passed what little was left of the night on the sofa in his friend's sitting room. He awoke later with a splitting headache, no very clear recollection of the late happenings, but a lively dread of the possible consequences of what he feared had been a very bosky evening. However, when Mr. Scunthorpe's man had revived his master, and he emerged from his bedchamber, he was soon able to allay any such misgivings. "Nothing to be in a fret for, dear boy!" he said. "Been piloted to the lighthouse scores of times. Watchman will produce bro-

ken lantern in evidence—they always do it!—you give
false name, pay fine, and all's right!"

So, indeed, it proved, but the experience a little
shocked the Vicar's son. This, coupled with the extremely unpleasant aftereffects of drinking innumerable
flashes of lightning, made him determine to be more
circumspect in future. He spent several days in pursuing
such harmless amusements as witnessing a badger
drawn in a menagerie in Holborn, losing his heart to
Miss O'Neill from a safe position in the pit, and being
introduced by Mr. Scunthorpe into Gentleman Jackson's
exclusive Boxing School in Bond Street. Here he was
much impressed by the manners and dignity of the proprietor (whose decision in all matters of sport, Mr. Scunthorpe informed him, was accepted as final by patrician
and plebian alike), and was gratified by a glimpse of such
notable amateurs as Mr. Beaumaris, Lord Fleetwood,
young Mr. Terrington, and Lord Withernsea. He had a
little practice with the single-stick with one of Jackson's
assistants, felt himself honored by receiving a smiling
word of encouragement from the great Jackson himself,
and envied the assurance of the Goes who strolled in,
exchanged jests with Jackson (who treated them with
the same degree of civility as he showed to his less exalted pupils), and actually enjoyed bouts with the ex-
champion himself. He was quick to see that no consideration of rank or consequence was enough to induce
Jackson to allow a client to plant a hit upon his person,
unless his prowess deserved such a reward, and from
having entered the saloon with a feeling of superior
superiority he swiftly reached the realization that in the
Corinthian world excellence counted for more than lin-
eage. He heard Jackson say chidingly to the great Nonpareil himself (who stripped to remarkable advantage,
he noticed) that he was out of training; and from that
moment his highest ambition was to put on the gloves
with this peerless master of the art.

At the end of a week, Mr. Swindon, urged thereto by Mr. Scunthorpe, delivered the new clothes, and after purchasing such embellishments to his costume as a tall cane, a fob, and a Marseilles waistcoat, Bertram ventured to show himself in the Park, at the fashionable hour of five o'clock. Here he had the felicity of seeing Lord Coleraine, Georgy à Cock-horse, prancing down Rotten Row on his mettlesome steed; Lord Morton, on his long-tailed gray; and, among the carriages, Tommy Onslow's curricle; a number of dashing gigs and tilburies, the elegant barouches of the ladies; and Mr. Beaumaris's yellow-winged phaeton-and-four, which he appeared to be able to turn within a space so small as to seem impossible to any mere whipster. Nothing would do for Bertram after that but to repair to the nearest jobmaster's stables and to arrange for the hire of a showy chestnut hack. Whatever inperfections might attach to the bearing and style of a young gentleman from the country, Bertram knew himself to be a bruising rider, and in this guise determined to show himself to the society which his sister already adorned.

As luck would have it, he encountered her on the day when he first sallied forth, mounted upon his hired hack. She was sitting up beside Mr. Beaumaris in his famous phaeton, animately describing to him the scene of the Drawing Room in which she had taken humble part. This event had necessarily occupied her thoughts so much during the past week that she had been able to spare very few for the activities of her adventurous brother. But when she caught sight of him, trotting along on his chestnut hack, she exclaimed, and said impulsively: "Oh, it is—Mr. Anstey! Do pray stop, Mr. Beaumaris!"

He drew up his team obediently, while she waved to Bertram. He brought his hack up to the phaeton and bowed politely, only slightly quizzing her with his eyes. Mr. Beaumaris, glancing indifferently at him, caught this arch look, became aware of a slight tension in the trim figure beside him, and looked under his lazy eyelids from one to the other.

"How do you do? How do you go on?" said Arabella, stretching out her hand in its glove of white kid.

Bertram bowed over it very creditably and replied: "Famously! I mean to come—I mean to visit you some morning, Miss Tallant!"

"Oh, yes, please do!" Arabella looked up at her escort, blushed, and stammered: "May I p-present Mr. Anstey to you, Mr. Beaumaris? He—he is a friend of mine!"

"How do you do?" responded Mr. Beaumaris politely. "From Yorkshire, Mr. Anstey?"

"Oh, yes! I have known Miss Tallant since I was in short coats!" grinned Bertram.

"You will certainly be much envied by Miss Tallant's numerous admirers," responded Mr. Beaumaris. "Are you staying in town?"

"Just a short visit, you know!" Bertram's gaze reverted to the team harnessed to the phaeton, all four of them on the fret. "I say, sir, that's a bang-up team you have in hand!" he said, with all his sister's impulsiveness. "Oh, don't look at this hack of mine!—showy, but I never crossed a greater slug in my life!"

"You hunt, Mr. Anstey?"

"Yes, with my uncle's pack, in Yorkshire. Of course, it is not like the Quorn country, or the Pytchley, but we get some pretty good runs, I can tell you!" Bertram confided.

"Mr. Anstey," interrupted Arabella, fixing him with a very compelling look, "I think Lady Bridlington has sent you a card for her ball: I hope you mean to come!"

"Well, you know, Bel—Miss Tallant!" said Bertram, with disastrous lack of gallantry, "that sort of mummery is not much in my line!" He perceived an anguished expression in her eyes and added hastily: "That is, delighted, I am sure! Yes, yes, I shall be there! And I shall hope to have the honor of standing up with you," he ended punctiliously.

Mr. Beaumaris was obliged to pay attention to his team, but he did not miss the minatory note in Arabella's voice as she said: "I collect we are to have the pleasure of receiving a visit from you *tomorrow,* sir!"

"Oh, " said Bertram. "Yes, of course! As a matter of fact, I shall be taking a look-in at Tattersall's, but— Yes, to be sure! I'll come to visit you all right and tight!"

He then doffed his new hat, and bowed, and rode off at an easy canter. Arabella appeared to be conscious that some explanation was called for. She said airily: "You just know, sir, that we have been brought up almost as—as brother and sister!"

"I thought perhaps you had," responded Mr. Beaumaris gravely.

She glanced sharply up at his profile. He seemed to be wholly absorbed in the task of maneuvering the phaeton through a gap between a dowager's landaulet and a smart barouche with a crest on the panel. She reassured herself with the reflection that whereas she favored her Mama, Bertram was said to be the image of what the Vicar had been at the same age, and said: "But I was telling you about the Drawing Room, and how graciously the Princess Mary smiled at me! She was wearing the most magnificent toilet I ever saw in my life! Lady Bridlington tells me that when she was young she was thought to be the most handsome of all the princesses. I thought she looked to be very good-natured."

Mr. Beaumaris agreed to it, reserving to himself his enjoyment in hearing this innocent description of the Regent's most admired sister. Miss Tallant, entrancing him with one of her unguarded moments of naïvety, then told him of the elegant, gilt-edged card of invitation which had arrived that very day in Park Street from no less a personage than the Lord Chamberlain, who

informed Lady Bridlington that he was commanded by
his Royal Highness the Prince Regent to invite her, and
Miss Tallant, to a dress party at Carlton House on
Thursday next, to have the honor of meeting (in large
capitals) Her Majesty The Queen. He said that he should
be on the lookout for her at Carlton House, and refrained from observing that the Regent's parties,
planned as they were on a magnificent scale which offended the taste of such arbiters of true elegance as
himself, were among the worst squeezes in town, and
had ever been known to include such vulgarities as a
fountain playing in the middle of the dinner table, to
which he had himself been bidden.

   He entered into her feelings upon this event with far
more sympathy than did Bertram when he presented
himself in Park Street on the following afternoon. Lady
Bridlington having retired, as she always did, to her
couch, to recruit her energies for an evening to be spent
at no fewer than four different parties, Arabella was able
to enjoy the luxury of a tête-à-tête with her favorite
brother. While acknowledging handsomely that he was
glad to think of her being invited to Carlton House, he
said that he supposed there would be a vast rout of
fashionables present, and that for himself he preferred
to spend his evenings in a simpler style. He further
begged her not to favor him with a description of the
gown she meant to wear. She perceived that he was not
much interested in her social triumphs, and turned willingly enough to his own chosen amusements. He was
slightly evasive on this subject, replying to her questions
in general terms. His experience of the female sex had
not led him to indulge his imagination with the belief
that even an adoring sister would regard with favor such
delights as a visit to Cribb's Parlor, where he had actually handled the Champion's famous silver cup, presented to him after his last fight, some years previously,
against Molyneux, the Black; the blowing of a cloud at

the Daffy Club, surrounded by young Bloods of the
Fancy, veterans of the ring, promising novices, and an
array of portraits hanging round the walls of past cham-
pions whose very names filled him with awe; or a lounge
through the famous Saloon at Covent Garden, where
the bold, ogling glances of the Cyprians who made this
haunt their hunting ground both shocked and terrified
him. Nor did he tell her of an assignation he had made
with a new acquaintance, encountered at Tattersall's
that very morning. He had seen at a glance that Mr. Jack
Carnaby was quite the thing—almost a Tulip of Fashion,
in fact, if dress and air were anything to judge by—but
something warned him that Arabella would regard with
horror his approaching introduction into a smug little
gaming house under the auspices of this gentleman. It
would be of very little use to assure her that he was going
merely for the experience and had not the least intention of gaming away his precious blunt; even his knowledgeable cicerone had shaken his head over his new
scheme, and had uttered cryptic warnings against ivory-
turners and Greek banditti, adding that his uncle and
principal trustee held that it was a good flat that was
never down. He said that he had himself proved the
truth of this excellent maxim, but since he owned, upon
inquiry, that nothing was known to Mr. Carnaby's dis-
credit, Bertram paid scant heed to his advice. Mr. Carnaby led him to a discreet house in Pall Mall, where,
upon knocking in a certain fashion on the door, they
were inspected through a grille and finally admitted.
Nothing could have been further removed from Bertram's expectations of what a gaming hell would be like
than the decorous house in which he found himself. The
various servants were all very respectable men with quiet
manners, and it would have been hard to have found a
more civil or obliging host than the proprietor. Never
having indulged in any game more dashing than whist,
Bertram spent some time in looking on, but when he

thought he had mastered the rules governing hazard, he ventured to join that table, armed with a modest rouleau. He soon perceived that Mr. Scunthorpe had been quite at fault in his talk of Fulhams and uphills, for he enjoyed a run of astonishing luck and came away at last with his pocket so full of guineas that he had no longer any need to worry over his growing expenses. A lucky bet at Tattersall's on the following day put him in a fair way to thinking himself at home on the Turf and at the Table, and it was not to be expected that he would lend any but an impatient ear to Mr. Scunthorpe's dark prophecy that having got into Tow Street he would end up in the clutch of a bum-trap.

"Know what my uncle says?" Mr. Scunthorpe demanded. "They always let a flat win the first time he goes to a hell. Hedge off, dear boy! They'll queer you on that suit!"

"Oh, fudge!" retorted Bertram. "I hope I'm not such a gudgeon as to dip too deeply! I'll tell you what, Felix, I *would* like to play just once at Watier's, if you could contrive it for me!"

"What?" gasped Mr. Scunthorpe. "Dear old boy, they would never let you set foot inside the Great-Go, upon my honor they would not! Why, I've never played there myself! Much better go to Vauxhall! Might meet your sister there! See the Grand Cascade! Listen to the Pandean band! All the crack, you know!"

"Oh, dull work, when I might be trying my luck at faro!" said Bertram.

❧ *Chapter 11* ❧

FROM THE DAFFY CLUB TO LIMMER'S HOTEL
in Conduit Street was an inevitable step for any young
gentleman interested in the fancy to take. Here were to
be found all the Pets of the Ring, and the Corinthians
who patronized them. Bertram went there under the
auspices of Mr. Scunthorpe, who was anxious to turn his
friend's thoughts away from more dangerous haunts. He
had begun to acquire acquaintances in London, and was
thus in the proud position of exchanging greetings with
several of the men present. He and Mr. Scunthorpe sat
down in one of the boxes, and Mr. Scunthorpe painstakingly pointed out to him all the notabilities he could see,
including a very down-the-road-looking man who, he
whispered, could be trusted to tip a man the office what
to back in any race. He then excused himself and bore
down upon this knowledgeable person, and became absorbed in conversation with him. While he was thus
engaged, Bertram saw Mr. Beaumaris stroll in with a
party of friends, but as he had by this time fully grasped
the exalted position occupied by the Nonpareil, he was
flattered beyond measure when, after raising his glass
and regarding him through it for a moment, Mr.

Beaumaris walked across the sanded floor and sat down at his table, saying with a slight smile: "Did I not meet you in the Park the other day? Mr.—er—Anstey, I believe?"

Bertram acknowledged it, flushing shyly, but when Mr. Beaumaris added casually: "You are related to Miss Tallant, I collect?" he made haste to deny any relationship, adding that Miss Tallant was quite above his touch. Mr. Beaumaris accepted this without comment and asked him where he was putting up in town. Bertram saw no harm in disclosing his direction, or even in telling Mr. Beaumaris that this was his first visit to the metropolis.

It was the expressed opinion of Mr. Jack Carnaby that the Nonpareil was a haughty, disagreeable kind of a man, but Bertram was unable to trace the least sign of haughtiness or of reserve in his manners. Mr. Beaumaris's intimates could have informed Mr. Tallant that while no one could be more snubbing, no one, on the other hand, could be—when he chose—more sympathetic. In less than no time, Bertram, forgetting his bashfulness, was confiding far more to his grand new acquaintance than he had the least idea of. Mr. Beaumaris, himself a Melton man, complimented him on his seat on a horse, and any barrier Bertram might have raised between himself and the author of his sister's predicament crumbled at this touch. He was led on to describe the country over which he hunted, the exact locality of Heythram, and his own impossible ambitions, without having the smallest suspicion that all this information was being skillfully extracted from him. He told Mr. Beaumaris about Smalls and his hopes of adorning the Home Office, and when Mr. Beaumaris said, with a humorous lift to one eyebrow that he should not have supposed him to have had parliamentary ambitions, he blurted out his real ambition ending by saying wistfully: "But it can't be, of course. Only I would have liked of all things to have been able to have joined a cavalry regiment!"

"I think you would do very well in a cavalry regiment," agreed Mr. Beaumaris, rising, as Mr. Scunthorpe came back to the table. "Meanwhile, do not draw the bustle with too much of a vengeance during this visit of yours to London!" He nodded to Mr. Scunthorpe and walked away, leaving that gentleman to explain to Bertram with the utmost earnestness just how greatly he had been honored.

But Mr. Beaumaris, quelling the ecstatic advances of his canine admirer an hour or two later, said: "If you had any real regard for me, Ulysses, you would be greeting me with condolences rather than with these uncalled-for raptures."

Ulysses, considerably plumper, and with his flying ear more rebellious than ever and his tail even more tightly curled over his back, stretched worshipfully before the god of his idolatry, and uttered an encouraging bark. After that he bustled to the door of the library and plainly invited Mr. Beaumaris to enter and partake of refreshment there. Brough, tenderly relieving his master of his long cloak and his hat and gloves, remarked that it was wonderful how knowing the little dog was.

"It is wonderful what encouragement he has received from my staff to continue to burden me with his unwanted presence in my house!" retorted Mr. Beaumaris acidly.

Brough, who had dealt with Mr. Beaumaris for many years, permitted himself to give what in a lesser personage would have been a grin, and to say: "Well, sir, if I had *known* you wanted him chased off, I'm sure I'd have done my best! Not but what he's so devoted to you that I doubt if he'd have gone, setting aside that it would go to my heart to chase off a dog that handles Alphonse like this one does."

"If that misbegotten animal has been upsetting Alphonse, I'll wring his neck!" promised Mr. Beaumaris.

"Oh, no, sir, nothing of that sort! When you're out, and Ulysses comes downstairs (as come he does), he behaves to Alphonse as though he hadn't had a bite to eat in a month, nor wouldn't think of touching so much as a scrap of meat he found on the kitchen floor. Well, as I said to Mrs. Preston, if ever a dog could speak, that one does, telling Alphonse as plain as a Christian that he's the only friend he's got in the world. Quite won Alphonse over, he has. In fact, when two nice loin chops was found missing, Alphonse would have it the under-cook was accusing the dog of having stolen them only to cover up his own carelessness, and Ulysses sitting there looking as if he didn't know what a chop tasted like. He buried the bones under the rug in your study, sir, but I have removed them."

"You are not only an ill-favored specimen," Mr. Beaumaris informed Ulysses severely, "but you have all the faults of the underbred: toadeating, duplicity, and impudence!"

Ulysses sat down to relieve the irritation of a healing wound by a hearty scratch. He was rebuked, and since he had heard that note in Mr. Beaumaris's voice before—as when he had expressed a vociferous desire to share his bedchamber with him—he stopped scratching and flattened his ears placatingly.

Mr. Beaumaris poured himself out a glass of wine and sat down with it in his favorite chair. Ulysses sat before him and sighed deeply. "Yes, I daresay," said Mr. Beaumaris, "but I have something better to do than to spend my time spreading ointment on your sores. You should remember, moreover, that you cannot be permitted to meet your benefactress again until you are entirely healed." Ulysses yawned at him and lay down with his head on his paws, as one who found the conversation tedious. Mr. Beaumaris stirred him with one foot. "I wonder if you are right?" he mused. "A month ago I should have been sure of it. Yet I let her saddle me with a foundling brat, and a mongrel cur—you will forgive my plain speaking, Ulysses!—and I am now reasonably certain that neither of you is destined to be the most tiresome of my responsibilities. Do you suppose that that wretched youth is masquerading under a false name for reasons of his own, or in support of her pretensions? Do not look at me like that! You may consider that experience should have taught me wisdom, but I do not believe that it was all a clever plot to inveigle me into declaring myself. I am not even sure that she regards me with more than tolerance. In fact, Ulysses, I am not very sure of anything—and I think I will pay my grandmother a long overdue visit."

In pursuance of this resolve, Mr. Beaumaris sent for his curricle next morning. Ulysses, who had shared his breakfast, bundled ahead of him down the steps of his house, leaped into the curricle, and disposed himself on the passenger's seat with all the air of a dog born into the purple.

"*No!*" said Mr. Beaumaris forcibly. Ulysses descended miserably from the curricle and prostrated himself on the flag-way. "Let me tell you, my friend," said Mr. Beaumaris, "that I have a certain reputation to maintain, which your disreputable appearance would seriously jeopardize! Do not be alarmed!—I am not, alas, going out of your life forever!" He climbed into the curricle, and said: "You may stop grinning, Clayton, and let 'em go!"

"Yes, sir!" said his groom, obeying both these behests, and swinging himself expertly up on to the curricle as it passed him. After a minute or two, having twice glanced over his shoulder, he ventured to inform Mr. Beaumaris that the little dog was following him.

Mr. Beaumaris uttered an oath and reined in his reluctant pair. The faithful hound, plodding valiantly along with heaving ribs and several inches of tongue hanging

from his parted jaws, came up with the curricle and once
more abased himself on the road. "Damn you!" said Mr.
Beaumaris. "I suppose you are capable of following me
all the way to Wimbledon! It now remains to be seen
whether my credit is good enough to enable me to carry
you off. Get up!"

Ulysses was very much out of breath, but at these
words he mustered up enough strength to scramble into
the curricle once more. He wagged a grateful tail,
climbed on to the seat beside Mr. Beaumaris, and sat
there panting blissfully. Mr. Beaumaris read him a short
lecture on the evils of blackmail, which sorely tried the
self-control of his groom, discouraged him peremptorily
from hurling a challenge at a mere pedestrian dog in the
gutter, and proceeded on his way to Wimbledon.

The Dowager Duchess of Wigan, who was the terror
of four sons, three surviving daughters, numerous
grandchildren, her man of business, her lawyer, her phy-
sician, and a host of dependents, greeted her favorite
grandson characteristically. He found her imbibing
nourishment in the form of slices of toast dipped in tea,
and bullying the unmarried daughter who lived with her.
She had been a great belle in her day, and the vestiges
of her former beauty were still discernible in the delicate
bones of her face. She had a way of looking at her visitors
with an eaglelike stare, had never been known to waste
politeness on anyone, and was scathingly contemptuous
of everything modern. Her children were inordinately
proud of her, and lived in dread of her periodical commands to them to present themselves at her house.
Upon her butler's ushering Mr. Beaumaris into her
morning room, she directed one of her piercing looks at
him and said: "Oh! So it's you, is it? Why haven't you
been to see me since I don't know when?"

Mr. Beaumaris, bowing deeply over her hand, replied
imperturbably: "On the occasion of my last visit, ma'am,

you told me you did not wish to see me again until I had mended my ways."

"Well, have you?" said the Duchess, conveying another slip of soaked toast to her mouth.

"Certainly, ma'am: I am in a fair way to becoming a philanthropist," he replied, turning to greet his aunt.

"I don't want any more of *them* about me," said her grace. "It turns my stomach enough already to have to sit here watching Caroline at her everlasting knitting for the poor. In *my* day, we gave 'em vails, and there was an end to it. Not that I believe you. Here, take this pap away, Caroline, and ring the bell! Maudling one's inside with tea never did any good to anyone yet, and never will. I'll tell Hadleigh to fetch up a bottle of Madeira— the lot your grandfather laid down, not that rubbish Wigan sent me t'other day!"

Lady Caroline removed the tray, but asked her parent in a shrinking tone if she thought that Dr. Sudbury would approve.

"Sudbury's an old woman, and you're a fool, Caroline!" replied the Duchess. "You go away, and leave me to talk to Robert! I never could abide a pack of females hangin' round me!" She added, as Lady Caroline gathered up her knitting: "Tell Hadleigh the *good* Madeira! He knows. Well, sir, what have you to say for yourself now you *have* had the impudence to show your face here again?"

Mr. Beaumaris, closing the door behind his aunt, came back into the room and said with deceptive meekness that he was happy to find his grandmother in such excellent health and spirits.

"Graceless jackanapes!" retorted the Duchess with relish. She ran her eye over his handsome person. "You look very well—at least, you would if you didn't make such a figure of yourself in that rig! When I was a girl, no gentleman would have dreamed of paying a social call without powder, let me tell you! Enough to make your grandfather turn in his grave to see what you've all come to, with your skimpy coats, and your starched collars, and not a bit of lace to your neckcloth or your wristbands! If you can sit down in those skin-tight breeches, or pantaloons, or whatever you call 'em, do so!"

"Oh, yes, I can sit down!" said Mr. Beaumaris, disposing himself in a chair opposite to hers. "My pantaloons, like Aunt Caroline's gifts to the poor, are knitted, and so adapt themselves reasonably well to my wishes."

"Ha! Then I'll tell Caroline to knit you a pair for Christmas. That'll send her into hysterics, for a bigger prude I never met!"

"Very likely, ma'am, but as I am sure that my aunt would obey you, however much her modesty was offended, I must ask you to refrain. The embroidered slippers which reached me last Christmas tried me high enough. I wonder what she thought I should do with them?"

The Duchess gave a cackle of laughter. "Lord bless you, she don't *think!* You shouldn't send her handsome gifts."

"I send you very handsome gifts," murmured Mr. Beaumaris, "but you never reciprocate!"

"No, and I never shall. You've got more than's good for you already. What have you brought me this time?"

"Nothing at all—unless you have a fancy for a mongrel dog?"

"I can't bide dogs, or cats either. Fifty thousand a year if you've a penny, and you don't bring me as much as a posy! Out with it, Robert! What did you come for?"

"To ask you whether you think I should make a tolerable husband, ma'am."

"What?" exclaimed her grace, sitting bolt upright in her chair, and grasping the arms with her frail, jeweled hands. "You're never going to offer for the Dewsbury girl?"

"Good God, no!"

"Oh, so that's yet another idiot who's wearing the willow for you, is it?" said her grace, who had her own ways of discovering what was going on in the world from which she had retired. "Who is it now? One of these days you'll go a step too far, mark my words!"

"I think I have," said Mr. Beaumaris.

She stared at him, but before she could speak her butler had entered the room, staggering under a specimen of the ducal plate which her grace had categorically refused to relinquish to the present Duke, on the two-fold score that it was her personal property and that he shouldn't have married anyone who gave his mother such a bellyache as that die-away ninny he had set in her place. This impressive tray Hadleigh set down on the table, casting, as he did so, a very expressive look at Mr. Beaumaris. Mr. Beaumaris nodded his understanding, and rose, and went to pour out the wine. He handed his grandmother a modest half glass, to which she instantly took exception, demanding to know whether he had the impertinence to suppose that she could not carry her wine.

"I daresay you can drink me under the table," replied Mr. Beaumaris. "But you know very well it's extremely bad for your health, and also that you cannot bully me into pandering to your outrageous commands." He then lifted her disengaged hand to his lips and said gently: "You are a rude and an overbearing old woman, ma'am, but I hope you may live to be a hundred, for I like you so much better than any other of my relatives!"

"I daresay that's not saying much," she remarked, rather pleased by this audacious speech. "Sit down again, and don't try to hoax me with any of your faradiddles! I can see you're going to make a fool of yourself, so you needn't wrap it up in clean linen! You haven't come here to tell me you're going to marry that brass-faced lightskirt you had in keeping when I last saw you?"

"I have not!" said Mr. Beaumaris.

"Just as well, for laced mutton being brought into the family is what I won't put up with! Not that I think you're fool enough for that."

"Where *do* you learn your abominable expressions, ma'am?" demanded Mr. Beaumaris.

"*I* don't belong to your mealy-mouthed generation, thank God! Who is she?"

"If I did not know from bitter experience, ma'am, that nothing occurs in London but what you are instantly aware of it, I should say that you had never heard of her. She is—or at any rate, she says she is—the latest heiress."

"Oh! Do you mean the chit that that silly Bridlington woman had staying with her? I'm told she's a beauty."

"She *is* beautiful," acknowledged Mr. Beaumaris. "But that's not it."

"Well, what is it?"

He reflected. "She is the most enchanting little wretch I ever encountered," he said. "When she is trying to convince me that she is up to every move in the social game, she contrives to appear much like any other female, but when, as happens all too often for my comfort, her compassion is stirred, she is ready to go to any lengths to succor the object of her pity. If I marry her, she will undoubtedly expect me to launch a campaign for the alleviation of the lot of climbing-boys, and will very likely turn my house into an asylum for stray curs."

"Oh, she will, will she?" said her grace, staring at him with knit brows. "Why?"

"Well, she has already foisted a specimen of each on to me," he explained. "No, perhaps I wrong her. Ulysses she certainly foisted on to me, but the unspeakable Jemmy I actually offered to take under my protection."

The Duchess brought her hand down on the arm of her chair. "Stop trying to gammon me!" she commanded. "Who is Ulysses, and who is Jemmy?"

"I have already offered to make you a present of Ulysses," Mr. Beaumaris reminded her. "Jemmy is a small climbing-boy whose manifest wrongs Miss Tallant is determined to set right. I wish you might have heard her telling Bridlington that he cared for nothing but his own comfort, like all the rest of us; and asking poor Charles Fleetwood to imagine what his state might now be had he been reared by a drunken foster mother, and sold into slavery to a sweep. Alas that I was not privileged to witness her encounter with the sweep! I understand that she drove him from the house with threats of prosecution. I am not at all surprised that he cowered before her: I have seen her disperse a group of louts."

"She sounds to me an odd sort of a gal," remarked her grace. "Is she a lady?"

"Unquestionably."

"Who's her father?"

"That, ma'am, is a mystery I have hopes that you may be able to unravel."

"I?" she exclaimed. "I don't know what you think I can tell you!"

"I have reason to believe that her home is within easy reach of Harrowgate, ma'am, and I recall that you visited that watering place not so very long ago. You may have seen her at an Assembly—I suppose they do have Assemblies at Harrowgate?—or have heard her family spoken of."

"Well, I didn't!" replied her grace bitterly. "What's more I don't want to hear anything more about Harrowgate! A nasty, cold, shabby-genteel place, with the filthiest waters I ever tasted in my life! They did me no good at all, as anyone but a fool like that sniveling leech of mine would have known from the outset! Assemblies, indeed! It's no pleasure to me to watch a parcel of country dowds dancing this shameless waltz of yours! Dancing! *I* could give you another name for it!"

"I have no doubt that you could, ma'am, but I must

beg you to spare my blushes! Moreover, for one who is forever railing against the squeamishness of the modern miss, your attitude toward the waltz seems a trifle inconsistent."

"I don't know anything about consistency," retorted her grace, with perfect truth, "but I do know indecency when I see it!"

"We are wandering from the point," said Mr. Beaumaris firmly.

"Well, I never met any Tallants in Harrowgate, or anywhere else. When I wasn't trying to swallow something that no one is ever going to make me believe wasn't drained off from the kennels, I was sitting watching your aunt knot a fringe in the most uncomfortable hole of a lodging I've been in yet! Why, I had to take all my own bed linen with me!"

"You always do, ma'am," said Mr. Beaumaris, who had several times been privileged to see the start of one of the Duchess's impressive journeys. "Also your own plate, your favorite chair, your steward, your—"

"I don't want any of your impudence, Robert!" interrupted her grace. "I don't always *have* to take 'em!" She gave her shawl a twitch. "It's nothing to me whom you marry," she said. "But why you must needs dangle after a wealthy woman beats me!"

"Oh, I don't think she has any fortune at all!" replied Mr. Beaumaris coolly. "She only said she had to put me in my place."

He came under her eagle stare again. "Put you in your place? Are you going to tell me, sir, that she ain't tumbling over herself to catch you?"

"Far from it. She holds me at arm's length. I cannot even be sure that she has even the smallest *tendre* for me."

"Been seen in your company often enough, hasn't she?" said her grace sharply.

"Yes, she says it does her a great deal of good socially to be seen with me," said Mr. Beaumaris pensively.

"Either she's a devilish deep 'un," said her grace, a gleam in her eye, "or she's a good gal! Lord, I didn't think there was one of these niminy-piminy modern gals alive that had enough spirit not to toadeat you! Should I like her?"

"Yes, I think you would, but to tell you the truth, ma'am, I don't care a button whether you like her or not."

Surprisingly, she took no exception to this, but nodded and said: "You'd better marry her. Not if she ain't of gentle blood, though. You ain't a Caldicot of Wigan, but you come of good stock. I wouldn't have let your mother marry into your family if it hadn't been one of the best—not for five times the settlements your father made on her!" She added reminiscently: "A fine gal, Maria: I liked her better than any other of my brats."

"So did I," agreed Mr. Beaumaris, rising from his chair. "Shall I propose to Arabella, risking a rebuff, or shall I address myself to the task of convincing her that I am not the incorrigible flirt she has plainly been taught to think me?"

"It's no use asking me," said her grace unhelpfully. "It wouldn't do you any harm to get a good set-down, but I don't mind your bringing the gal to see me one day." She held out her hand to him, but when he had punctiliously kissed it and would have released it, her talonlike fingers closed on his and she said: "Out with it, sir! What's vexing you, eh?"

He smiled at her. "Not precisely that, ma'am—but I have the stupidest wish that she would tell me the truth!"

"Poor, why should she?"

"I can think of only one reason, ma'am. That is what vexes me!" said Mr. Beaumaris.

❧ *Chapter 12* ❧

ON HIS WAY HOME FROM WIMBLETON, MR.
Beaumaris drove up Bond Street and was so fortunate
as to see Arabella, accompanied by a prim-looking maid-
servant, come out of Hookham's Library. He pulled up
immediately, and she smiled and walked up to the curricle exclaiming: "Oh, how much better he looks! I told
you he would! Well, you dear little dog, do you remember me, I wonder?"

Ulysses wagged his tail in a perfunctory manner, suffered her to stretch up a hand to caress him, but yawned.

"For heaven's sake, Ulysses, try to acquire a little polish!" Mr. Beaumaris admonished him.

Arabella laughed. "Is that what you call him? Why?"

"Well, he seemed, on the evidence, to have led a rov-
ing life, and judging by the example we saw, it must have
been adventurous," explained Mr. Beaumaris.

"Very true!" She watched Ulysses look up adoringly
into his face, and said: "I knew he would grow to be
attached to you: only see how he looks at you!"

"His affection, Miss Tallant, threatens to become a
serious embarrassment."

"Nonsense! I am sure you must be fond of him, or you
would not take him out with you!"

"If that is what you think, ma'am, you can have no idea of the depths to which he can sink to achieve his own ends. Blackmail is an open book to him. He is well aware that I dare not deny him, lest I should lose what little reputation I may have in your eyes."

"How absurd you are! I knew, as soon as I saw how well you handled him, that you know just how to use a dog. I am so glad you have kept him with you."

She gave Ulysses a last pat and stepped back on to the flag-way. Mr. Beaumaris said: "Will you not give me the pleasure of driving you to your door?"

"No, indeed, it is only a step!"

"No matter: send your maid home! Ulysses adds his entreaties to mine."

As Ulysses chose this moment to scratch one ear, this made her laugh.

"Mere bashfulness," explained Mr. Beaumaris, stretching down his hand. "Come!"

"Very well—since Ulysses wishes it so much!" she said, taking his hand and climbing into the curricle. "Mr. Beaumaris will see me home, Maria."

He spread a light rug across her knees and said over his shoulder: "I have recalled, Clayton, that I need something from the chemist's. Go and buy me a—a gum plaster! You may walk home."

"Very good, sir," said the groom, at his most wooden, and sprang down into the road.

"A *gum plaster?*" echoed Arabella, turning wide eyes of astonishment upon Mr. Beaumaris. "What in the world can you want with such a thing, sir?"

"Rheumatism," said Mr. Beaumaris defiantly, setting his horses in motion.

"*You?* Oh, no, you must be quizzing me!"

"Not at all. I was merely seeking an excuse to be rid of Clayton. I hope Ulysses will prove himself an adequate chaperon. I have something to say to you, Miss Tallant, for which I do not desire an audience."

She had been stroking the dog, but her hands were stilled at this, and the color receded from her cheeks. Rather breathlessly, she asked: "What is it?"

"Will you do me the honor of becoming my wife?"

She was stunned, and for a moment she could not utter a word. When she was able to control her voice a little, she said: "I think you *must* be quizzing me."

"You must know that I am not."

She trembled. "Yes, yes, let us say that that was all it was, if you please! I am very much obliged to you, but I cannot marry you!"

"May I know why you cannot, Miss Tallant?"

She was afraid that she was about to burst into tears, and answered in a shaken tone: "There are many reasons. Pray believe it is impossible!"

"Are you quite sure that these reasons are insuperable?" he asked.

"Quite, quite sure! Oh, please do not urge me further! I had never dreamed—it never entered my head—I would not for the world have given you cause to suppose— Oh, *please* say no more, sir!"

He bowed, and was silent. She sat staring down at her clasped hands in great agitation of spirit, her mind in a turmoil, tossed between surprise at such a declaration, coming from one whom she had believed to have been merely amusing himself, and the shock of realizing, for the first time, that there was no one she would rather marry than Mr. Beaumaris.

After a slight pause, he said in his usual calm way: "I believe there is always a little awkwardness attached to such situations as this in which we now find ourselves. We must strive not to allow it to overcome us. Is Lady Bridlington's ball to rank among the season's greatest squeezes?"

She was grateful to him for easing the tension, and all the discomfort of the moment, and tried to reply naturally. "Yes, indeed, it is! I am sure quite three hundred cards of invitation have been sent out. Shall—shall you find time to look in, I wonder?"

"Yes, and shall hope that even though you will not *marry* me, you may be persuaded to *dance* with me."

She replied she scarcely knew what: it was largely inaudible. He shot a quick look at her averted profile, hesitated, and then said nothing. They had reached Park Street by this time, and in another moment he had handed her down from the curricle.

"Do not come with me to the door! I know you do not like to leave your horses!" she said, in a hurried tone. "Good-bye! I shall see you at the ball."

He waited until he had seen her admitted into the house, and then got into the curricle again and drove off. Ulysses nudged his nose under his arm. "Thank you," he said dryly. "Do you think I am unreasonable to wish that she would trust me enough to tell me the truth?"

Ulysses sighed heavily; he was rather sleepy after his day in the country.

"I suppose I shall end by telling her that I have known it all along. And yet— Yes, Ulysses, I am quite unreasonable. Did it seem to you that she was not as indifferent to me as she would have had me believe?"

Understanding that something was expected of him, his admirer uttered a sound between a yelp and a bark, and furiously wagged his tail.

"You feel that I should persevere?" said Mr. Beaumaris. "I was, in fact, too precipitate. You may be right. But if she had cared at all, would she not have told me the truth?"

Ulysses sneezed.

"At all events," remarked Mr. Beaumaris, "she was undoubtedly pleased with me for bringing you out with me."

Whether it was due to the circumstance, or to Ulysses' unshakable conviction that he was born to be a carriage dog, Mr. Beaumaris continued to take him about. Those of his intimates who saw Ulysses, once they had recovered from the initial shock, were of the opinion that the Nonpareil was practicing some mysterious jest on society, and only one earnest imitator went so far as to adopt an animal of mixed parentage to ride in his own carriage. He thought that if the Nonpareil was setting a new fashion, it would become so much the rage that it might be difficult hereafter to acquire a suitable mongrel. But Mr. Warkworth, a more profound thinker, censured this act as being rash and unconsidered. "Remember when the Nonpareil wore a dandelion in his buttonhole three days running?" he said darkly. "Remember the kick-up there was, with every saphead in town running round to all the flower women for dandelions?—which they hadn't got, of course. Stands to reason you couldn't buy dandelions! Why, poor Geoffrey drove all the way to Esher looking for one, and Altringham went to the trouble of rooting up half a dozen out of Richmond Park, and having a set-to with the keeper over it, and then planting 'em in his window boxes. Good idea, if they *had* become the mode: clever fellow, Altringham!—but of course the Nonpareil was only hoaxing us! Once he had the whole lot of us decked out with them, he never wore one again, and a precious set of gudgeons we looked! Playing the same trick again, if you ask me!"

Only in one quarter did unhappy results arise from the elevation of Ulysses. The Honorable Frederick Byng, who had for years been known by the sobriquet of Poodle Byng from his habit of driving everywhere with a very highly bred and exquisitely shaved poodle sitting up beside him, encountered Mr. Beaumaris in Piccadilly one afternoon, and no sooner clapped eyes on his disreputable companion than he pulled up his horses all standing, and spluttered out: "What the devil—?"

Mr. Beaumaris reined in his own pair and looked inquiringly over his shoulder. Mr. Byng, his florid countenance suffused by an angry flush, was engaged in

backing his curricle, jibbing at his horses' mouths in a
way that showed how greatly moved he was. Once alongside the other curricle, he glared at Mr. Beaumaris, and
demanded an explanation.

"Explanation of what?" said Mr. Beaumaris. "If you
don't take care, you'll go off in an apoplexy one of these
days, Poodle! What's the matter?"

Mr. Byng pointed a trembling finger at Ulysses.
"What's the meaning of *that*?" he asked belligerently.
"If you think I'll swallow any such damned insult—!"

He was interrupted. The two dogs, who had been
eying one another measuringly from their respective
vehicles, suddenly succumbed to a mutual hatred, uttered two simultaneous snarls, and leaped for one another's throats. Since the curricles were too far apart to
allow them to come to grips, they were obliged to vent
their feelings in a series of hysterical objurgations,
threats, and abuse, which drowned the rest of Mr.
Byng's furious speech.

Mr. Beaumaris, holding Ulysses by the scruff of his
neck, laughed so much that he could hardly speak: a
circumstance which did nothing to mollify the outraged
Mr. Byng. He began to say that he should know how to
answer an attempt to make him ridiculous, but was
obliged to break off in order to command his dog to be
quiet.

"No, no, Poodle, don't call me out!" said Mr. Beaumaris, his shoulders still shaking. "Really, I had no such
intention! Besides, we should only make fools of ourselves, going out to Paddington in the cold dawn to
exchange shots over a pair of dogs!"

Mr. Byng hesitated. There was much in what Mr.
Beaumaris said; moreover Mr. Beaumaris was acknowledged to be one of the finest shots in England, and to
call him out for a mere trifle would be an act of sheer
foolhardiness. He said suspiciously: "If you're not doing
it to make a laughingstock of me, why *are* you doing it?"

"Hush, Poodle, hush! You are treading on delicate ground!" said Mr. Beaumaris. "I cannot bandy a lady's name about in the open street!"

"What lady? I don't believe a word of it! Why can't you make that damned mongrel be quiet?"

In lamentable contrast to his well-trained adversary, who was now seated virtuously beside his master again and affecting a maddening deafness, Ulysses, convinced that he had cowed the contemptible dandy, was hurling extremely ignoble taunts at him. Mr. Beaumaris cuffed him, but although he cowered under the avenging hand he was quite unrepentant and resumed his threats with unabated fervor.

"It is all jealousy, Poodle!" Mr. Beaumaris said soothingly. "The hatred of the vulgar for the aristocrat! I think we had better part, don't you?"

Mr. Byng gave an angry snort and drove off. Mr. Beaumaris unleased Ulysses, who shook himself, sighed his satisfaction, and looked up for approbation. "Yes, you will, I perceive, ruin me yet," said Mr. Beaumaris severely. "If I am any judge of the matter, you picked your language up in the back slums, and have probably been the associate of dustmen, coalheavers, bruisers, and other such low persons! You are quite unfit for polite circles."

Ulysses lolled his tongue out and grinned cheerfully.

"At the same time," said Mr. Beaumaris, relenting, "I daresay you would have made mincemeat of the creature, and I must own that I am not entirely out of sympathy with you. But poor Poodle will certainly cut me for a week at least."

However, at the end of five days Mr. Byng unbent, adopting a tolerant attitude toward Ulysses. It had been borne in upon him that to drive past the Nonpareil's curricle staring rigidly ahead was provocative of just the amusement among his acquaintances which he particularly wished to discourage.

Mr. Beaumaris and Miss Tallant met again in the dazzling splendor of the Circular Room at Carlton House, on the night of the Regent's dress party. Arabella was so much impressed by the elegance of the sky-blue draperies, and the almost intolerable glare of a huge cut-glass chandelier, reflected, with its myriads of candles, in four large pier glasses, that she momentarily forgot her last meeting with Mr. Beaumaris and greeted him by saying impulsively: "How do you do? I have never seen anything like it in my life! Each room is more magnificent than the last!"

He smiled. "Ah, but have you yet penetrated to the Conservatory, Miss Tallant? Our Royal host's *chef d'ouevre*, believe me! Let me take you there!"

By this time she had recollected under what circumstances they had parted, so short a time previously, and her color had risen. Many tears had been shed over the unhappy circumstance which had made it impossible for her to accept Mr. Beaumaris's suit, and it had required all the excitement of a party at Carlton House to make her forget for one evening that she was the most miserable girl alive. She hesitated now, but Lady Bridlington was nodding and beaming, so she placed her hand on Mr. Beaumaris's arm and went with him through a bewildering number of apartments, all full of people, up the grand stairway, and through several saloons and antechambers. In the intervals of bowing to acquaintances and occasionally exchanging a word of greeting, Mr. Beaumaris entertained her with an account of Ulysses' quarrel with Mr. Byng's poodle, and this made her laugh so much that a good deal of her constraint vanished. The Conservatory made her open her eyes very wide indeed, as well it might. Mr. Beaumaris watched her, a look of amusement in his face, while she gazed silently round the extraordinary structure. Finally she drew a breath and uttered one of her unexpectedly candid remarks. "Well, I don't know why he should call it a Conservatory, for it is a great deal more like a cathedral, and a very bad one too!" she said.

He was delighted. "I thought you would be pleased with it," he said, with deceptive gravity.

"I am not at all pleased with it," replied Arabella severely. "Why is there a veil over that statue?"

Mr. Beaumaris leveled his glass at Venus Asleep under a shroud of light gauze. "I can't imagine," he confessed. "No doubt one of Prinny's flashes of taste. Would you like to ask him? Shall I take you to find him?"

Arabella declined the offer hastily. The Regent, an excellent host, had already managed to spend a minute or two in chat with nearly every one of his guests, and although Arabella was storing up the gracious words he had uttered to her and meant to send home to the Vicarage an exact account of his amiability, she found conversation with such an exalted personage rather overpowering. So Mr. Beaumaris took her back to Lady Bridlington, and after staying beside her for a few minutes was buttonholed by a gentleman in very tight satin knee breeches who lisped that the Duchess of Edgeware commanded his instant attendance. He bowed, therefore, to Arabella, and moved away, and although she several times afterward caught a glimpse of him, he was always engaged with friends and did not again approach her. The rooms began to seem hot and overcrowded: the company the most boring set of people imaginable; and the vicacious, restless, and scintillating Lady Jersey, who flirted with Mr. Beaumaris for quite twenty minutes, an odious creature.

Lady Bridlington's ball was the next social event of importance. This promised to be an event of more than ordinary brilliance, and although the late Lord Bridlington, to gratify an ambitious bride, had added a ballroom and a conservatory to the back of the house, it seemed unlikely that all the guests who had accepted her ladyship's invitation could be accommodated without a degree of overcrowding so uncomfortable as to mark the evening as an outstanding success. An excellent band had been engaged for the dancing, Pandean pipes were to play during supper, extra servants were hired, police officers and link boys warned to make Park Street their special objective, and refreshments to supplement the efforts of Lady Bridlington's distracted cook ordered from Cunter's. For days before the event, housemaids were busy moving furniture, polishing the crystal chandeliers, washing the hundreds of spare glasses unearthed from a storeroom in the basement, counting and recounting plates and cutlery, and generally creating an atmosphere of bustle and unrest in the house. Lord Bridlington, who combined an inclination for ceremonious hospitality with a naturally frugal mind, was torn between complacency at having drawn to his house all the most fashionable persons who adorned the *ton*, and a growing conviction that the cost of the party would be enormous. The bill for wax candles alone threatened to rise to astronomical heights, and not his most optimistic calculations of the number of glasses of champagne likely to be drunk reduced the magnums that must be ordered to a total he could contemplate with anything but gloom. But his self-esteem was too great to allow of his contemplating for more than a very few minutes the expedient of eking out the precious liquor by making it into an iced cup. Cups there must certainly be, as well as lemonade, orgeat, and such milder beverages as would please the ladies; but unless the party were to fall under the stigma of having been but a shabby affair after all, the best champagne must flow throughout the evening in unlimited quantities. His mind not being of an order to question his own consequence, his gratification on the whole outweighed his misgivings, and if a suspicion did enter his head that he had Arabella to thank for the flattering number of acceptances which poured into the house, he was easily

able to banish it. His mother, rather shrewder than he,
gave honor where it was due, and in a fit of reckless
extravagance was moved to order a new gown for Arabella from her own expensive dressmaker. But she was
not, after all, so sadly out of pocket over the transaction,
since a very few words whispered into the ear of Mme.
Dumaine were enough to convince that astute woman of
business that the *réclame* of designing a toilette for the
great Miss Tallant would fully justify her in making a
substantial reduction in the price of a gown of figured
lace over a white satin robe with short, full, plaited
sleeves, fastened down the front with pearl buttons to
match the edging of pearls to the overdress. Arabella,
ruefully surveying the depredations caused by a succession of parties to her glove drawer, was obliged to purchase a new pair of long white gloves, as well as new
satin sandals and a length of silver net to drape round
her shoulders in the style known as *à l'Ariane*. There was
not very much left, by this time, of the Squire's handsome present to her; and when she considered how impossible her own folly had made it for her to requite her
family's generosity in the only way open to a personable
young female, she was overcome by feelings of guilt and
remorse, and could not refrain from shedding tears. Nor
could she refrain from indulging her fancy with the con-
templation of the happiness which might even now have
been hers, had she not allowed her temper to lead her
so grossly to deceive Mr. Beaumaris. This was a thought
more bitter than all the rest, and it was only by the
resolute exercise of her common sense that she was able
to regain some degree of calm. It was not to be supposed
that the haughty Mr. Beaumaris, related as he was to so
many noble houses, so distinguished in his bearing, so
much courted, and so much pursued, would ever have
looked twice at a girl from a country vicarage, with neither fortune nor connection to recommend her to his
notice.

It was therefore with mixed feelings that Arabella awaited the arrival of the first guests on the appointed night. Lady Bridlington, thinking that she looked a little hagged (as well she might, after a week of such nerve-racking preparation) had tried to persuade her to allow Miss Crowle to rub a little—a *very* little!—rouge into her cheeks, but after one look at the result of this delicate operation, Arabella had washed it away, declaring that never would she employ such aids to beauty as must, could he but see them, destroy forever Papa's affection for his eldest daughter. Lady Bridlington pointed out, very reasonably, that there could be no fear of Papa's seeing them, but as Arabella remained adamant, and showed alarming signs of being about to burst into tears, she pressed her no more, consoling herself with the reflection that even without her usual blooming color, her goddaughter could not fail to appear lovely in the exquisite gown of Mme. Dumaine's making.

One cause at least for satisfaction was granted to Arabella: although some guests might arrive early and leave betimes to attend another function, and others walk in past two o'clock, having relegated Lady Bridlington's ball to the third place on their list of the evening's engagements, so that the ball was rendered chaotic by the constant comings and goings, and Park Street echoed hideously for hours to the shouts of My lord's carriage! of My lady's chair! and heated police officers quarreled with vociferous link boys, and chairmen exchanged insults with coachmen, Bertram arrived punctually at ten o'clock, and nobly remained throughout the proceedings.

He had recklessly ordered an evening dress from the obliging Mr. Swindon, rightly deeming the simple garments he had brought with him from Heythram quite inadequate to the occasion. Mr. Swindon had done well by him, and when Arabella saw him mount the stairway between the banks of flowers, which she had helped all

day to revive by frequent sprinklings of water, her heart
swelled with pride in his appearance. His dark blue coat
set admirably across his shoulders; his satin knee
breeches showed scarcely a crease; and nothing could
have been more chaste than his stockings or his waistcoat. With his dark, curly locks rigorously brushed into
the fashionable Brutus, his handsome, aquiline countenance interestingly pale from the nervousness natural to
a young gentleman attending his first *ton* party, he
looked almost as distinguished as the Nonpareil himself.
Arabella, fleetingly clasping his hand, bestowed on him
so speaking a look of admiration that he was betrayed
into a grin so boyish and attractive as to cause another
early arrival to demand of her companion, Who was that
handsome boy?

Emboldened by the intensive coaching of a noted
French dancing master, whom he had found the time to
visit, he claimed his sister's hand for the first waltz, and
being a graceful youth, taught by the athletic sports at
Harrow to move with precision and a complete control
over his limbs, acquitted himself so well that Arabella
was moved to exclaim: "Oh, Bertram, how elegantly you
dance! Do, pray, let us make up a set for the quadrille
and dance together in it!"

This, however, he did not feel himself capable of
doing. It was true that he had acquired the rudiments of
the more simple steps, but he doubted his ability to go
through the *grande ronde* or the *pas de zéphyr* without
muffing these figures. Gazing up into his face, it occurred to Arabella that he, too, was looking a trifle hagged.
She anxiously asked him if he were quite well, and he
assured her that he had never been better in his life, very
creditably refraining from confiding to her that his adventurous career had made so deep a hole in his purse
that the question of how he was to meet his liabilities had
been causing him some sleepless nights. Since she had
not seen him since a furtive assignation in the Mall one

morning, under the vague chaperonage of the nurse-
maids who aired their charges there and bought glasses
of milk for them, fresh from the cows that lent so rural
an air to the scene, she could not but feel uneasy about
him. The faint rakishness that now hung about him did
nothing to allay her fears, and she rather unjustly
blamed Mr. Scunthorpe for setting his feet upon a path
Papa would certainly not have wished him to tread. She
had formed no very favorable opinion of Mr. Scunthorpe, and with the praiseworthy notion of introducing
Bertram into better company, now made him known to
one of the most disinterested of her admirers, young
Lord Wivenhoe, heir to an affluent earldom, and known
to the greater part of London as Chuffy Wivenhoe, an
affectionate sobriquet earned for him by his round,
good-humored countenance. This lively young nobleman, although he had not so far offered for her hand,
formed one of Arabella's court and was one of her favor-
ites, being blessed with ingenuous manners and an overflowing friendliness. She introduced Bertram to him
with the best of intentions, but had she known that the
engaging Chuffy had been reared by a misguided parent
according to the principles laid down by the late Mr.
Fox's father, she might have refrained from so doing. In
spite of every evidence to disprove them, the Earl of
Chalgrove held Lord Holland's maxims in high esteem
and blandly encouraged his heir to indulge in every
extravagance that captured his erratic fancy, discharging
his gaming debts as cheerfully as he discharged the bills
that poured in from his tailor, his coachbuilder, his hat-
ter, and a host of other tradesmen who enjoyed his patronage.

  The two young gentlemen took an instant liking to
one another. Lord Wivenhoe was some years Bertram's
senior, but his mind was as youthful as his countenance,
whereas Bertram's aquiline features, and superiority of
intellectual attainment, added several years to his true

age. They found themselves with much in common, and
before they had enjoyed one another's society for more
than a very few minutes had arranged to go together to
a forthcoming race meeting.

Meanwhile, Miss Tallant's pleasure in dancing with
her young friend from Yorkshire had not passed unnoticed. Gloom was struck into several hearts that had
cherished hopes of winning the heiress, for not the most
sanguine among her suitors could persuade himself that
she had ever smiled up into his face with such unshad-
owed affection as she bestowed upon Bertram, or had
talked so much or so confidentially to him. It struck that
acute observer, Mr. Warkworth, that there was an elusive resemblance between the pair. He mentioned the
matter to Lord Fleetwood, who had been so fortunate as
to secure the promise of Arabella's hand for the quadrille and was being incorrigibly blind to the claims of the
less well-favored damsels who had not been solicited to
waltz, and were consequently chatting animatedly together in gilt chairs placed round the walls of the ballroom.

Lord Fleetwood stared hard at the Tallants for a minute or two, but could perceive no likeness, which, indeed, existed more in an occasional expression than in
their lineaments. "No, dash it!" he said. "The little Tallant ain't got a beak of a nose!"

Mr. Warkworth acknowledged it, and excused his
lapse by explaining that it was only a sudden notion he
had taken into his head.

Mr. Beaumaris did not arrive until after midnight, and
consequently failed to secure a waltz with Arabella. He
seemed to be in one of his more inaccessible moods, and
having exerted himself to say a few civil things to his
hostess, to dance once with a lady to whom she presented him, and once with his cousin, Lady Wainfleet,
occupied himself in strolling through the various saloons, talking languidly to acquaintances and surveying

the company through his quizzing glass with a faintly
bored air. After about half an hour, when two sets were
forming for a country dance, he went in search of Arabella, who at the end of the last dance had disappeared
from the ballroom in the direction of the conservatory,
accompanied by Mr. Epworth, who protested that there
had never been such a jam in the history of London balls
and offered to procure her a cooling glass of lemonade.
Whether he redeemed this promise or not, Mr. Beaumaris never knew, but when he walked into the conservatory a few minutes later, it was to find Arabella shrinking
back in a chair in a state of the greatest discomfort, and
trying to disengage her hands from the fervent clasp of
Mr. Epworth, romantically on his knees before her. Everyone else having left the conservatory to take their
places in the new sets, the enterprising Mr. Epworth,
fortified by liberal doses of Lord Bridlington's champagne, had seized the opportunity once more to press
his suit upon the heiress. Mr. Beaumaris entered in time
to hear her utter in a tone of distress: "Oh, pray do not!
Mr. Epworth, I implore you, get up! I am very much
obliged to you, but I shall never, never change my mind!
It is ungentlemanly of you to tease me like this!"

"Do try not to be such a dead bore, Epworth!" said
Mr. Beaumaris, with all his usual *sang-froid.* "I came to
ask you if you would stand up with me for the next
dance, Miss Tallant."

She was blushing furiously, and returned rather an
incoherent answer. Mr. Epworth, considerably mortified
at having been found in such a posture by one whose
contempt he dreaded, got to his feet, muttered something about taking his leave, and left the conservatory.
Mr. Beaumaris, taking her fan from Arabella's hand,
unfurled it, and began gently to wave it beside her
heated countenance. "How many times has he proposed
to you?" he inquired conversably. "How very ridiculous
he looked, to be sure!"

She was obliged to laugh, but said warmly: "He is the most odious little man, and seems to think he has only to persevere to make me receive his advances with complaisance!"

"You must make allowances for him," said Mr. Beaumaris. "If he did not believe you to be a wealthy woman, he would cease to trouble you."

Her bosom swelled; she said in a low, shaking voice: "Had it not been for *you*, sir, he would never have known it!"

He was silent, as much from disappointment as from the rueful knowledge that although Fleetwood's had been the tongue which had spread the rumor, it had been his own idly malicious words which had convinced Fleetwood of the truth of Arabella's claim.

After a moment, she said in a subdued tone: "Shall we take our places in the set?"

"No, the numbers must by now be made up," he replied, continuing to fan her.

"Oh! Well—well, perhaps we should go back into the ballroom, at all events!"

"Don't be alarmed!" said Mr. Beaumaris, with a touch of asperity. "I have not the smallest intention of embarrassing you by kneeling at your feet!"

Her color rushed up again; she turned away her head in confusion, her lip slightly trembling. Mr. Beaumaris shut the fan, and gave it back to her. He said gently: "I am not, I hope, such a coxcomb as to distress you by repeated solicitations, Miss Tallant, but you may believe that I am still of the same mind as I was when I made you an offer. If your sentiments should undergo a change, one word—one look!—would be sufficient to apprise me of it." She lifted her hand in a gesture imploring his silence. "Very well," he said. "I shall say no more on that head. But if you should stand in need of a friend at any time, let me assure you that you may depend upon me."

These words, delivered, as they were, in a more earnest tone than she had yet heard him use, almost made her heart stand still. She was tempted to take the risk of confessing the truth; hesitated, as the dread of seeing his expression change from admiration to disgust took possession of her; turned her eyes toward him; and then hurriedly rose to her feet, as another couple entered the conservatory. The moment was lost; she had time not only to recollect what might be the consequences if Mr. Beaumaris treated her second confidence with no more respect than he had treated her first; but also to recall every warning she had received of the danger of trusting him too far. Her heart told her that she might do so, but her scared brain recoiled from the taking of any step that might lead to exposure and to disgrace.

She went back into the ballroom with him; he relinquished her to Sir Geoffrey Morecambe, who came up to claim her; and within a very few minutes had taken leave of his hostess and left the party.

❧ *Chapter 13* ❧

*BERTRAM'S ACQUAINTANCE WITH LORD WI-*venhoe prospered rapidly. After a day spent together at the races, each was so well pleased with the other that further assignations were made. Lord Wivenhoe did not trouble to inquire into his new friend's age, and Bertram naturally did not confess that he was only just eighteen years old. Wivenhoe drove him to Epsom in his curricle, with a pair of dashing bays harnessed in the bar, and finding that Bertram was knowledgeable on the subject of horseflesh, good-naturedly offered to hand over the ribbons to him. So well did Bertram handle the pair, and at such a spanking pace did he drive them, showing excellent judgment in the feathering of his corners, and catching the thong of his whip just as the Squire had taught him, that he needed no other passport to Wivenhoe's favor. Any man who could control the kind of prime cattle his lordship liked must be a capital fellow. When he could do so without abating his cheerful conversation, he was clearly a right 'un, at home to a peg, and worthy of the highest regard. After some very interesting exchanges of reminiscences about incurable millers, roarers, lungers, half-bred blood cattle, gingers, and slugs, which led inevitably to still more interesting stories of the chase, during the course of which both gentlemen found themselves perfectly in accord in their contempt of such ignoble persons as roadsters and skirters, and their conviction that the soundest of all maxims was, Get over the ground if it breaks your neck, formality was at an end between them, and his lordship was not only begging Bertram to call him Chuffy, as everyone else did, but promising to show him some of the rarer sights in town.

Bertram's fortunes, ever since he had come to London, had fluctuated in a bewildering manner. His first lucky evening with what he had swiftly learned to refer to as St. Hugh's Bones had started him off on a career that seriously alarmed his staider friend, Mr. Scunthorpe. He had been encouraged by his luck to order a great many things from the various shops and warehouses where Mr. Scunthorpe was known, and although a hat from Baxter's, a pair of boots from Hoby's, a seal from Rundell and Bridge, and a number of trifling purchases such as a walking cane, a pair of gloves, some neckcloths, and some pomade for his hair were none of them really expensive, he had discovered, with a slight shock, that when added together they reached rather an alarming total. There was also his bill at the inn to be taken into account; but since this had not so far been presented, he was able to relegate it to the very back of his mind.

The success of that first evening's play had not been repeated: in fact, upon the occasion of his second visit to the discreet house in Pall Mall he had been a substantial loser and had been obliged to acknowledge that there might have been some truth in Mr. Scunthorpe's dark warning. He was quite shrewd enough to realize that he had been a pigeon among hawks, but he was inclined to think that the experience would prove of immense value to him, since he was not one to be twice

caught with the same lure. Playing billiards with Mr.
Scunthorpe at the Royal Saloon, he was approached by
an affable Irishman who applauded his play, offered to
set him a main or two, or to accompany him to a snug
little ken where a penchant for faro or *rouge et noir* could
be enjoyed. It was quite unnecessary for Mr. Scunthorpe
to whisper in his ear that this was a nibble from an
ivory-turner: Bertram had no intention of going with the
plausible Irishman, had scented a decoy the moment he
saw him, and was very well pleased with himself for
being no longer a flat, but, on the contrary, a damned
knowing one. A pleasantly convivial evening at Mr.
Scunthorpe's lodging, with several rubbers of whist to
follow an excellent dinner, convinced him that he had a
natural aptitude for cards, a belief that was by no means
shaken by the vicissitudes of fortune which followed this
initiation. It would be foolish, of course, to frequent
gaming hells; but once a man has made friends in town,
there were plenty of unexceptionable places where he
could enjoy every form of gaming, from whist to rou-
lette. On the whole, he rather thought he was lucky at
the tables. He was quite sure that he was lucky on the
turf, for he had several very good days. It began to be
a regular habit with him to look in at Tattersall's to
watch how the sporting men bet their money there, and
sometimes to copy them, in his modest way, or at others
to back his own choice. When he became intimate with
Chuffy Wivenhoe, he accompanied him often, either to
advise him on the purchase of a prad, to watch some
ruined man's breakdowns being sold, or to lay out his
blunt on a forthcoming race. Once he had fallen into the
way of going with Wivenhoe, it was impossible to resist
spending a guinea for the privilege of being made free
of the subscription room; and once the very safe man
whom his lordship patronized saw the company he kept,
it was no longer necessary for him to do more than
record his bets, just as the Bloods did, and wait for

settling day either to receive his gains or to pay his losses. It was all so pleasant, and every day was so full of excitement, that it went to his head, and if he was sometimes seized by panic and felt himself to be careering along at a pace he could no longer control, such frightening moments could not endure when Chuffy was summoning him to come and try the paces of a capital goer, or Jack Carnaby carrying him off to the theater, or the Fives Court or the Daffy Club. None of his new friends seemed to allow pecuniary considerations to trouble them, and since they all appeared to be constantly on the brink of ruin, and yet contrived, by some fortunate bet or throw of the dice, to come about again, he began to fall insensibly into the same way of life, and to think that it was rustic to treat a temporary insolvency as more than a matter for jest. It did not occur to him that the tradesmen who apparently gave Wivenhoe and Scunthorpe unlimited credit would not extend the same consideration to a young man whose circumstances were unknown to them. The first hint he received of the different light in which he was regarded came in the form of a horrifying bill from Mr. Swindon. He could not believe at first that he could possibly have spent so much money on two suits of clothes and an overcoat, but there did not seem to be any disputing Mr. Swindon's figures. He asked Mr. Scunthorpe, in an airy way, what he did if he could not meet his tailor's account. Mr. Scunthorpe replied simply that he instantly ordered a new rig-out; but however much Bertram had been swept off his feet, he retained enough native shrewdness to know that this expedient would not answer in his case. He tried to get rid of a very unpleasant feeling at the pit of his stomach by telling himself that no tailor expected to be paid immediately, but Mr. Swindon did not seem to be conversant with this rule. After a week he presented his bill a second time, accompanied by a courteous letter indicating that he would be much obliged by an early

settlement of his account. And then, as though they had
been in collusion with Swindon, other tradesmen began
to send in their bills, so that in less than no time one of
the drawers in the dressing table in Bertram's bedroom
was stuffed with them. He managed to pay some of
them, which made him feel much easier, but just as he
was convincing himself that with the aid of a judicious
bet, or a short run of luck, he would be able to clear
himself from debt altogether, a polite but implacable
gentleman called to see him, waited a good hour for him
to come in from a ride in the Park, and then presented
him with a bill which he said he knew had been over-
looked. Bertram managed to get rid of him, but only by
giving him some money on account, which he could ill
spare, and after an argument which he suspected was
being listened to by the waiter hovering round the cof-
fee-room door. This fear was shortly confirmed by the
landlord's sending up his account with the Red Lion
next morning. Matters were becoming desperate, and
only one way of averting disaster suggested itself to
Bertram. It was all very well for Mr. Scunthorpe to advise against racing and gaming: what Mr. Scunthorpe
did not understand was that merely to abstain from
these pastimes would in no way solve the difficulty. If
Mr. Scunthorpe found himself at *Point Non Plus,* he had
trustees who, however much they might rate him, would
certainly come to his rescue. It was quite unthinkable
that Bertram should appeal to his father for assistance:
he would rather, he thought, cut his throat, for not only
did the very thought of laying such a collection of bills
before the Vicar appall him, but he knew very well that
the settlement of them must seriously embarrass his father. Nor would it any longer be of any use to sell his
watch, or that seal he had bought, or the fob that hung
beside it from his waistband: in some inexplicable way
his expenses seemed to have been growing ever larger
since he had begun to frequent the company of men of

fashion. A vague and rather dubious notion of visiting
a moneylender was vetoed by Mr. Scunthorpe, who told
him that since the penalties attached to the lending of
money at interest to minors were severe, not even Jew
King could be induced to advance the smallest sum to
a distressed client under age. He added that he had once
tried that himself, but that the cents-per-cent were all as
sharp as needles and seemed to smell out a fellow's age
the moment they clapped eyes on him. He was concerned, though not surprised, to learn of Bertram's having got into Queer Street, and had the quarter not been
so far advanced that he himself was at a standstill, he
would undoubtedly have offered his friend instant relief,
for he was one, his intimates asserted, who dropped his
blunt like a generous fellow. Unfortunately he had no
blunt to drop, and knew from past experience that an
application to his trustees would result in nothing but
unfeeling advice to him to rusticate at his house in Berkshire, where his Mama would welcome him with open
arms. To do him justice, Bertram would have been ex-
ceedingly reluctant to have accepted pecuniary assistance from any of his friends, since he saw no prospect,
once he had returned to Yorkshire, of being able to
reimburse them. There was only one way of getting
clear, and that was the way of the Turf and the Table.
He knew it to be hazardous; but as he could not see that
it was possible for him to be in a worse case than he was
already, it was worth the risk. Once he had paid his
debts, he rather thought that he should bring his visit to
London to an end, for although he had enjoyed certain
aspects of it enormously, he by no means enjoyed insolvency and was beginning to realize that to stand continu-
ally on the edge of a financial precipice would very soon
reduce him to a nervous wreck. An interview with a
creditor who was not polite at all, but on the contrary,
extremely threatening, had shaken him badly: unless he
made a speedy recovery, it could only be a matter of days

before the tipstaffs would be on his heels, even as Mr.
Scunthorpe had prophesied.

It was at this stage in his career that two circumstances
occurred which seemed to hold out hopes of delivery. A
fortunate evening playing faro for modest stakes encouraged him to think that his luck had turned again;
and Chuffy Wivenhoe, earwigged by a jockey at Tattersall's, passed on to him the name of the *certain bet* thus
disclosed. It really seemed as though Providence was at
last aiding Bertram. It would be madness not to bet a
substantial amount on the horse, for if it won he would
have solved all his difficulties at one blow, and would
have enough money left over to pay for his fare back to
Yorkshire on the stagecoach. When Wivenhoe laid his
own bet, he followed suit, and tried not to think of the
predicament he would be in on settling day if that infalli-
ble jockey had for once in his life been mistaken in his
judgment.

"I'll tell you what, Bertram," said Wivenhoe, as they
strolled out of the subscription room together, "if you
should care for it, I'll take you along with me to the
Nonesuch Club tonight: all the go, y'know, and devilish
exclusive, but they'll let you in if you come with me."

"What is it?" Bertram asked.

"Oh, faro and hazard, for the most part! It was started
by some of the great guns only this year, because Watier's is becoming damned flat: they say it won't last
much longer—never been the same since Brummell had
to run for it! The Nonesuch is devilish good sport, I can
tell you. There ain't many rules, for one thing, and
though most of the men bet pretty heavily, the patrons
fixed the minimum stake at twenty guineas, and there's
only one faro table. What's more, it ain't a shabby business enterprise, like half the gaming clubs, and if you
want to play hazard, you appoint the croupier from
among your set, and someone will always volunteer to
call the odds. None of these paid croupiers and groom

porters, which make the Great-Go more like a hotel than a social club. The whole idea is to make it a friendly affair, keep out the scaff and raff, and do away with all the rules and regulations which get to be such a dead bore! For instance, there's no damned syndicate running the faro bank: they take it in turns, the well-breeched swells, like Beaumaris, and Long Wellesley Pole, and Golden Ball, and Petersham, and the rest of that set. Oh, it's the Pink of the Mode, I can tell you—the top-of-the-trees!''

"I'd like to go with you," Bertram said, "only— Well, the fact is I'm none too plump in the pocket just now! Had a shocking run of luck!''

"Oh, no need to fret over that!" said his insouciant friend. "I keep telling you it ain't like Watier's! No one cares whether you bet twenty guineas or a hundred! You come: a man's luck is bound to change if he sticks to it—one of the things my governor told me, and *he* should know!''

Bertram was undecided, but since he was already engaged to dine at Long's Hotel with Lord Wivenhoe, there was no need for him to return a definite answer to the invitation until he had thought it over rather more carefully. His lordship said that he should depend upon him, and there the matter for the moment rested.

It was not to be supposed that Bertram's protracted sojourn in London was causing his sister no anxiety. Arabella was very anxious indeed, for although she was not taken into his confidence, she could not doubt, from his appearance, that he was spending money far more lavishly than the winning of a hundred pounds in a lottery justified him in doing. She seldom set eyes on him, and when they did meet, she could not think that he was looking well. Late nights, unaccustomed potations, and worry were taking their toll. But when she told him that he was looking fagged to death, and implored him to return to Yorkshire, he was able to retort with a good

deal of truth that she was not particularly blooming herself. It was true. Her bright color had faded a little, and
her eyes had begun to seem a trifle large for her face,
etched in, as they were, with shadows. Lord Bridlington,
observing this, ascribed it to the absurd exigencies of a
London season and moralized on the folly of females
with social ambitions. His mother, who had not failed to
take note of the fact that her charge was no longer driving in the Park so frequently with Mr. Beaumaris and
had developed a habit of evading his visits to the house,
drew more correct conclusions but failed signally to induce Arabella to confide in her. Whatever Frederick
chose to say, Lady Bridlington was by this time convinced that the Nonpareil was very much in earnest, and
she could not imagine what could be holding Arabella
back from encouraging his advances. Divining that her
reasons would be quite inexplicable to the good lady,
Arabella preferred to keep her own counsel.

It had not escaped the notice of the Nonpareil that his
tiresome love was not enjoying her customary good
looks and spirits, nor was it unknown to him that she had
lately refused three advantageous offers of marriage,
since the rejected suitors made no secret of the fact that
their hopes were quite cut up. She had excused herself
from dancing with him at Almack's, but three times during the course of the evening he had been aware that her
eyes were following him.

Mr. Beaumaris, rhythmically drawing Ulysses' flying
ear through his hand—a process which reduced Ulysses
to a state of blissful idiocy—said meditatively: "It is a
melancholy reflection, is it not, that at my age I can be
such a fool?"

Ulysses, his eyes half closed, his senses swooning in
ecstasy, gave a sigh which his god might, if he chose,
interpret as one of sympathy.

"What if she proves to be the daughter of a trades-
man?" said Mr. Beaumaris. "I do owe something to my

name, you know. It might even be worse, and surely I am
too old to be losing my head for a pretty face!"

Since his hand was still, Ulysses nudged him. Mr.
Beaumaris resumed his steady pulling of that shameful
ear, but said: "You are quite right: it is not her pretty
face. Do you believe her to be entirely indifferent to me?
Is she really afraid to confess the truth to me? She must
not be—no, Ulysses, she must not be! Let us look on the
darker side! Is she ambitious to acquire a title? If that is
so, why, then, has she sent poor Charles to the right
about? You believe her to be aiming higher? But she
cannot suppose that Witney will come up to scratch! Nor
do I think that your suspicions are correct, Ulysses."

Ulysses, catching the note of severity in his voice,
cocked an anxious eye at him. Mr. Beaumaris took his
muzzle in his hand and gently shook it. "What do you
advise me to do?" he asked. "It appears to me that I have
reached *Point Non Plus*. Should I—" He broke off and
rose suddenly to his feet, and took a turn about the
room. "What a saphead I am!" he said. "Of course!
Ulysses, your master is a fool!" Ulysses jumped up to
place his forepaws against those elegant pantaloons and
uttered a protesting bark. All this walking about the
room, when Mr. Beaumaris might have been better employed, was not at all to his taste. "Down!" commanded
Mr. Beaumaris. "How many more times am I to request
you not to sully the purity of my garments by scabbling
at them with your ignoble, and probably dirty, paws?
Ulysses, I shall be leaving you for a space!"

Ulysses might find this a little beyond him, but he fully
understood that his hour of bliss was at an end, and so
lay down in an attitude of resignation. Mr. Beaumaris's
subsequent actions filled him with vague disquiet, for
although he was unacquainted with portmanteaus, some
instinct warned him that they boded no good to little
dogs. But these inchoate fears were as nothing when
compared to the astonishment, chagrin, and dismay

suffered by that peerless gentleman's gentleman, Mr. Painswick, when he apprehended that his employer proposed to leave town without the support and expert ministrations of a valet whom every Tulip of Fashion had at one time or another attempted to suborn from his service. He had accepted with equanimity that his master was going out of town for perhaps as long as a week, and was already laying out, in his mind, the raiment suitable for a sojourn at Wigan Park, or Woburn Abbey, or Belvoir, or perhaps Cheveley, when the full horror of the event burst upon him. "Put up enough shirts and neckcloths to last me for seven days," said Mr. Beaumaris. "I'll travel in riding dress, but you may as well pack the clothes I have on, in case I should need them. I shan't take you with me."

It took a full minute for the sense of this pronouncement to penetrate to the mind of his valet. He was shocked, and could only gaze at Mr. Beaumaris in stupefaction.

"Tell 'em to have my traveling chaise, and the bays, at the door by six o'clock," said Mr. Beaumaris. "Clayton can accompany me for the first couple of stages and bring the horses home."

Mr. Painswick found his voice. "Did I understand you to say, sir, that you would not be requiring me?" he asked.

"You did," responded Mr. Beaumaris.

"May I inquire, sir, who then is to wait upon you?" demanded Mr. Painswick, in a voice of ominous quiet.

"I am going to wait upon myself," replied Mr. Beaumaris.

Mr. Painswick accorded his attempt at humor the perfunctory smile it deserved. "Indeed, sir? And who, if you please, will press your coat for you?"

"I suppose they are accustomed to pressing coats at the posting houses," said Mr. Beaumaris indifferently.

"If you can call it pressing," said Mr. Painswick darkly.

"Whether you will be pleased with the result, sir, is, if I may be permitted to say so, another matter."

Mr. Beaumaris then said something so shocking that it gave his henchman, as he afterward reported to Brough, a Very Nasty Spasm. "I daresay I shan't," he said, "but it won't signify."

Mr. Painswick looked searchingly at him. He did not bear the appearance of one bordering on delirium, but there could be little doubt that his case was serious. Mr. Painswick spoke in the tone of one soothing a refractory patient. "I think sir, it will be best for me to accompany you."

"I have already told you that I don't need you. You may have a holiday."

"I should not, sir, have the heart to enjoy it," returned Mr. Painswick, who invariably spent his holidays in indulging nightmarish visions of his understudy's sending Mr. Beaumaris forth with his clothes improperly brushed, his boots dulled by neglect, or worst of all, a speck of mud on the skirts of his driving coat. "If I may say so without offense, sir, you cannot go alone!"

"And if *I* may say so without offense, Painswick," retorted Mr. Beaumaris, "you are being foolish beyond permission! I will readily own that you keep my clothes in excellent order—I should not continue to bear with you, if you did not—and that the secret of imparting a gloss to my Hessians, which you so jealously guard, makes you not wholly undeserving of the extortionate wage I pay you; but if you imagine that I am unable to dress myself creditably without your assistance, your powers of self-deception must be greater than even I was aware of! Upon occasion—and merely to reward you!—I have permitted you to shave me; I allow you to help me into my coats and to hand me my neckcloth. But at no time, Painswick, have I allowed you to dictate to me what I should wear, to brush my hair, or to utter a word—a sound!—while I am engaged in arranging that neck-

cloth! I shall do very well without you. But you must put
up enough neckcloths to allow for some failures."

Mr. Painswick swallowed these insults but tried one
last, desperate throw. "Your boots, sir! You will never
use a *jack!*"

"Certainly not," said Mr. Beaumaris. "Some menial
shall pull them off for me."

Mr. Painswick gave a groan. "With greasy hands, sir!
And only I know what it means to get a thumb mark off
your Hessians!"

"He shall handle them through gloves," promised Mr.
Beaumaris. "You need not lay out my knee breeches: I
am going to the Nonesuch Club tonight." He added,
possibly to atone for his harshness: "Don't wait up for
me, but call me at five o'clock tomorrow morning!"

Mr. Painswick responded in a voice trembling with
suppressed passion: "If, sir, you choose to dispense with
my services upon your journey, I am sure it is not for me
to utter a word of criticism, not would I so far demean
myself as to remonstrate with you, whatever my feelings
may be. But retire from my post before I have put you
to bed, sir, and removed your raiment for proper attention, nothing will prevail upon me to do!"

"As you please," said Mr. Beaumaris, unmoved. "Far
be it from me to interfere in your determination to
become a martyr in my cause!"

Mr. Painswick could only throw him a look of searing
reproach, being, as he afterward confided to Brough,
unable to trust himself to say more. It had been touch
and go with him, he said, whether he remained another
day in the service of one so lost to the sense of what was
due to himself and his valet. Brough, who was perfectly
well aware that wild horses would not have parted his
colleagues from Mr. Beaumaris, sympathized in suitable
terms and produced a bottle of Mr. Beaumaris's second-
best port. The healing properties of port, when mixed
with a judicious quantity of gin, soon exercised a

beneficial effect upon Mr. Painswick's wounded feelings, and remarking that there was nothing like a glass of flesh-and-blood for setting a man up, he settled down to discuss with his crony and rival all the possible reasons that might be supposed to underlie Mr. Beaumaris's rash and unbecoming conduct.

Mr. Beaumaris, meanwhile, after dining at Brooks's, strolled across St. James's Street toward Ryder Street, where the Nonesuch Club was established. Thus it was that when, rather later in the evening, Bertram Tallant entered the faro room under the protective chaperonage of Lord Wivenhoe, Mr. Beaumaris was afforded an excellent opportunity of estimating in just what manner Miss Tallant's enterprising young relative had been spending his time in London.

Two circumstances had decided Bertram in favor of visiting the Nonesuch Club. The first was the news that that sure winner, Fear-not-Victorious, had been unplaced in his race; the second the discovery of a twenty-pound bill among the tangle of accounts in the dressing table. Bertram had sat staring at it quite numbly for some minutes, not even wondering how he had come to mislay it. He had suffered a terrible shock, for he had argued himself into believing that Fear-not-Victorious was bound to win, and had not seriously considered how he was to meet his creditor at Tattersall's on Monday if the animal were unplaced. The utter impossibility of meeting him at all burst upon him with shattering effect, so that he felt sick with apprehension and could see nothing but a hideous vision of the Fleet Prison, where he would no doubt languish for the rest of his days, since it did not appear to him that his father could be expected to do more for so depraved a son than to expunge his name from the family tree and forbid all mention of him at the Vicarage.

Rendered reckless by his last and most crushing blow, he rang the bell for the waiter and demanded a bottle of

brandy. It was then borne upon him that orders had
been issued in the tap not to supply him with any liquor
for which he did not put down his blunt. Flushing darkly,
he drove his hand into his breeches pocket and dragged
out his last remaining handful of coins. Throwing one of
these on the table, he said: "Fetch it, damn you!—and
you may keep the change!"

This gesture a little relieved his feelings, and the first
glass of brandy, tossed at one gulp down his throat, had
a still more heartening effect upon him. He looked again
at the twenty-pound bill, still clasped between his fingers. He remembered that Chuffy had named twenty
pounds at the minimum stake permitted to punters at
the Nonesuch. Such a coincidence was surely too
marked to be ignored. The second glass of brandy convinced him that here in his hand lay his last chance of
saving himself from irretrievable ruin and disgrace.

Not being accustomed to drinking neat brandy, he was
obliged before setting out for Long's Hotel to swallow
a damper in the form of a glass of porter. This had a
sobering effect, and the walk through the streets to
Long's put him in tolerable shape to do justice to *mainte-
non* cutlets and the hotel's famed Queensberry hock. He
had made up his mind to be guided by Fate. He would
lay down his twenty guineas upon a card chosen at random from the livret: if it turned up, he would take it for
a sign that his luck had changed at last, and play on until
he had covered all his debts; if it lost, he would be very
little worse off than he was already, and could, at the
worst, cut his throat, he supposed.

When he and Lord Wivenhoe entered the faro room
at the Nonesuch, Mr. Beaumaris, holding the bank, had
just completed a deal and had tossed the pack onto the
floor. He raised his eyes as a waiter laid a fresh pack
before him and looked straight across to the door. The
lure of hazard had drawn all but one other of the club's

doyens from the room, and that one, Lord Petersham, was lost in one of his fits of deep abstraction.

Damn Petersham! thought Mr. Beaumaris, on the horns of a dilemma. Why must he choose this of all moments to dream of tea?

That amiable but vague peer, perceiving Lord Wivenhoe, smiled upon him with the doubtful air of one who seemed to recollect seeing his face before. If he took notice of a youthful stranger within the sacred precincts of the club, he gave no sign of it. Mr. Warkworth stared very hard at Bertram and then glanced toward the head of the table. Lord Fleetwood, filling his glass, frowned and also looked to the Nonpareil.

Mr. Beaumaris gave an order to the waiter to bring him another bottle of burgundy. One blighting word from him, and the stranger would have nothing to do but bow himself out with what dignity he could muster. There was the rub: the boy would be unbearably humiliated, and one could not trust that young fool, Wivenhoe, to smooth over the rebuff. He would be far more likely to kick up a dust over the exclusion of one of his friends, placing the unhappy Bertram in a still more intolerable position.

Lord Wivenhoe, finding places for himself and Bertram at the table, was casually making Bertram known to his neighbors. One of these was Fleetwood, who favored Bertram with a curt nod and again looked under his brows at the Nonpareil; the other, like most of the men in the room, was content to accept any friend of Chuffy's without question. One of the older men said something under his breath about babes and sucklings, but not loudly enough to be overheard.

Mr. Beaumaris glanced round the table. "Stakes, gentlemen," he said calmly.

Bertram, who had changed his bill for one modest rouleau, thrust it in a quick movement toward the Queen in the livret, which happened to be the card nearest to

his hand. Other men were placing their bets; someone
said something which made his neighbor laugh; Lord
Petersham sighed deeply, and deliberately pushed forward several large rouleaus and ranged them about his
chosen cards; then he drew a delicately enameled
snuffbox from his pocket and helped himself to a pinch
of his latest blend. A pulse was beating so hard in Bertram's throat that it almost hurt him; he swallowed, and
fixed his eyes on Mr. Beaumaris's hand, poised above
the pack before him.

The boy has been having some deep doings, thought
Mr. Beaumaris. Shouldn't wonder if he's rolled up!
What the devil possessed Chuffy Wivenhoe to bring him
here?

The bets were all placed; Mr. Beaumaris turned up the
first card and placed it to the right of the pack.

"Scorched again!" remarked Fleetwood, one of
whose bets stood by the card's counterpart.

Mr. Beaumaris turned up the *Carta Anglaise*, and laid
it down to the left of the pack. The Queen of Diamonds
danced before Bertram's eyes. For a dizzy moment he
could only stare at the card; then he looked up, and met
Mr. Beaumaris's cool gaze, and smiled waveringly. That
smile told Mr. Beaumaris quite as much as he had need
to know, and did nothing to increase his enjoyment of
the evening ahead of him. He picked up the rake beside
him, and pushed two twenty-guinea rouleaus across the
table. Lord Wivenhoe called for wine for himself and his
friend, and settled down to plunge with his usual reck-
lessness.

For half an hour the luck ran decidedly in Bertram's
favor, and Mr. Beaumaris was encouraged to hope that
he would rise from the table a winner. He was drinking
fairly steadily, a flush of excitement in his cheeks, his
eyes, glittering a little in the candlelight, fixed on the
cards. Lord Wivenhoe sat cheerfully losing beside him.
He was soon punting on tick, scrawling his vowels, and

tossing them over to the bank. Other men, Bertram noticed, did the same. There was quite a pile of paper before Mr. Beaumaris.

The luck veered. Three times did Bertram bet heavily on the bank's card. He was left with only two rouleaus, and staked them both, sure that the bank could not win his money four times in succession. It could. To his own annoyance, Mr. Beaumaris turned up the identical card.

From then on, he accepted, with an unmoved countenance, vowel upon vowel from Bertram. It was quite impossible to tell the boy either that he would not take his vouchers, or that he would be well advised to go home. It was even doubtful whether Bertram would have listened to him. He was in the grip of a gamester's madness, betting recklessly, persuaded by one lucky chance that the luck smiled upon him again, convinced, when he lost, that ill fortune could not last. That he had the least idea of the sum he already owed the bank, Mr. Beaumaris cynically doubted.

The evening broke up rather earlier than usual, Mr. Beaumaris having warned the company that he did not sit after two o'clock, and Lord Petersham sighing that he did not think he should take the bank over tonight. Wivenhoe, undaunted by his losses, said cheerfully: "In the basket again! What do I owe, Beaumaris?"

Mr. Beaumaris silently handed his vowels to him. While his lordship did rapid sums in mental addition, Bertram, the flush dying out of his cheeks, sat staring at the paper still lying in front of Mr. Beaumaris. He said jerkily: "And I?" and stretched out his hand.

"Dipped, badly dipped!" said Wivenhoe, shaking his head. "I'll send you a draft on my bank, Beaumaris. The devil was in it tonight!"

Other men were totting up their losses; there was a noise of lighthearted conversation dinning in Bertram's ears; he found that his vowels totaled six hundred pounds, a sum that seemed vast to him, almost incredible. He pulled himself together, pride coming to his rescue, and rose. He looked very white now, and ridiculously boyish, but he held his head well up and spoke to Mr. Beaumaris perfectly calmly. "I may have to keep you waiting for a few days, sir," he said. "I—I have no banking accommodation in London and must send to Yorkshire for funds!"

What do I do now? wondered Mr. Beaumaris. Tell the boy the only use I have for his vowels is as shaving papers? No; he would enact me a Cheltenham tragedy. Besides, the fright may do him a world of good. He said: "There is no hurry, Mr. Anstey. I am going out of town tomorrow for a week, or five days. Come and see me at my house—let us say, next Thursday. Anyone will tell you my direction. Where are you putting up?"

Bertram replied mechanically: "At the Red Lion, in the City, sir."

"Robert!" called Fleetwood, from the other side of the room, where he was engaged in a lively argument with Mr. Warkworth. "Robert, come and bear me out! *Robert!*"

"Yes, in a moment!" Mr. Beaumaris returned. He detained Bertram a moment longer. "Don't fail!" he said. "I shall expect to see you on Thursday."

He judged it to be impossible to say more, for there were people all round them, and it was plain that the boy's pride would not brook a suggestion that his gaming debts should be consigned to the flames.

But he was still frowning when he reached his house, some time later. Ulysses, gamboling and squirming before him, found that his welcome was not receiving acknowledgment, and barked at him. Mr. Beaumaris bent and patted him absent-mindedly. "Hush! I am not in the mood for these transports!" he said. "I was right when I told you that you were not destined to be the worst of my responsibilities, was I not? I think I ought to have set the boy's mind at ease: one never knows, with boys of that age—and I didn't like the look in his face. All to pieces, I have little doubt. At the same time, I'll be damned if I'll go out again at this hour of night. A night's reflection won't hurt him."

He picked up the branch of candles that stood upon the hall table and carried it into his study, and to his desk by the window. Seeing him sit down and open the ink standish, Ulysses indicated his sentiments by yawning loudly. "Don't let me keep you up!" said Mr. Beaumaris, dipping a pen in the standish and drawing a sheet of paper toward himself.

Ulysses cast himself on the floor with a flop, gave one or two whines, bethought him of a task left undone, and began zealously to clean his forepaws.

Mr. Beaumaris wrote a few rapid lines, dusted his sheet, shook off the sand, and was just about to fold the missive when he paused. Ulysses looked up hopefully. "Yes, in a minute," said Mr. Beaumaris. "If he has quite outrun the constable—" He laid down the paper, drew out a fat pocketbook from his inner pocket, and extracted from it a bill for a hundred pounds. This he folded up in his letter, sealed the whole with a wafer, and directed it. Then he rose, and to Ulysses' relief indicated that he was now ready to go to bed. Ulysses, who slept every night on the mat outside his door, and regularly, as a matter of form, challenged Painswick's right to enter that sacred apartment each morning, scampered ahead of him up the stairs. Mr. Beaumaris found his valet awaiting him, his expression a nice mixture of wounded sensibility, devotion to duty, and long-suffering. He gave the sealed letter into his hand. "See that that is delivered to a Mr. Anstey, at the Red Lion, somewhere in the City, tomorrow morning," he said curtly. "In person!" he added.

❧ *Chapter 14* ❧

NOT FOR THREE DAYS DID ANY NEWS OF THE disaster which had overtaken Bertram reach his sister. She had written to beg him to meet her by the Bath Gate in the Green Park, and had sent the letter by the Penny Post. When he neither appeared at the rendezvous nor replied to her letter, she began to be seriously alarmed, and was trying to think of a way of visiting the Red Lion without her godmother's knowledge when Mr. Scunthorpe sent up his card, at three o'clock one afternoon. She desired the butler to show him into the drawing room and went down immediately from her bedchamber to receive him.

It did not at once strike her that he was looking preternaturally solemn; she was too eager to learn tidings of Bertram, and went impetuously toward him with her hand held out, exclaiming: "I am so very glad you have called to see me, sir! I have been so much worried about my brother! Have you news of him? Oh, do not tell me he is ill?"

Mr. Scunthorpe bowed, cleared his throat, and grasped her hand spasmodically. In a somewhat throaty voice he replied: "No, ma'am. Oh, no! Not *ill*, precisely!"

Her eyes eagerly scanned his face. She now perceived that his countenance wore an expression of deep melancholy, and felt immediately sick with apprehension. She managed to say: "Not—not—*dead?*"

"Well, no, he ain't dead," replied Mr. Scunthorpe, but hardly in reassuring tones. "I suppose you might say it ain't as bad as that. Though, mind you, I wouldn't say he won't be dead, if we don't take care, because when a fellow takes to— But never mind that!"

"Never mind it?" cried Arabella, pale with alarm. "Oh, what can be the matter? Pray, pray tell me instantly!"

Mr. Scunthorpe looked at her uneasily. "Better have some smelling salts," he suggested. "No wish to upset a lady. Nasty shock. Daresay you'd like a glass of hartshorn-and-water. Ring for a servant!"

"No, no, I need nothing! Pray do not! Only put me out of this agony of suspense!" Arabella implored him, clinging with both hands to the back of a chair.

Mr. Scunthorpe cleared his throat again. "Thought it best to come to you," he said. "Sister. Happy to be of service myself, but at a standstill. Temporary, of course, but there it is. Must tow poor Bertram out of the River Tick!"

"River?" gasped Arabella.

Mr. Scunthorpe perceived that he had been misunderstood. He made haste to rectify this. "No, no, not drowned!" he assured her. "Swallowed a spider!"

"Bertram has swallowed a spider?" Arabella repeated, in a dazed voice.

Mr. Scunthorpe nodded. "That's it," he said. "Blown up at *Point Non Plus.* Poor fellow knocked into horsenails!"

Arabella's head was by this time in such a whirl that she was uncertain whether her unfortunate brother had fallen into the river, or had been injured in some explosion, or was, more mildly, suffering from an internal

disorder. Her pulse was tumultuous; the most agitating
reflections made it impossible for her to speak above a
whisper. She managed to utter: "Is he dreadfully hurt?
Have they taken him to a hospital?"

"Not a case for a hospital, ma'am," said Mr. Scunthorpe. "More likely to be screwed up."

This pronouncement, conjuring up the most horrid
vision of a coffin, almost deprived Arabella of her
senses. Her eyes started at Mr. Scunthorpe in a look of
painful inquiry. "Screwed up?" she repeated faintly.

"The Fleet," corroborated Mr. Scunthorpe, sadly
shaking his head. "Told him how it would be. Wouldn't
listen. Mind, if the thing had come off right, he could
have paid down his dust and no harm done. Trouble
was, it didn't. Very rarely does, if you ask me."

The gist of this speech, gradually penetrating to Arabella's understanding, brought some of the color back to
her face. She sank into a chair, her legs trembling violently, and said: "Do you mean he is in *debt?*"

Mr. Scunthorpe looked at her in mild surprise. "Told
you so, ma'am!" he pointed out.

"Good God, how could I possibly guess—? Oh, I have
been so afraid that something of the sort must happen!
Thank you for coming to me, sir! You did very right!"

Mr. Scunthorpe blushed. "Always happy to be of service!"

"I must go to him!" Arabella said. "Will you be so
kind as to escort me? I do not care to take my maid on
such an errand, and I think perhaps I should not go
alone."

"No, wouldn't do at all." Mr. Scunthorpe agreed.
"But better not go, ma'am! Not the thing for you. Delicate female—shabby neighborhood! Take a message."

"Nonsense! Do you think I have never been to the
City? Only wait until I have fetched a bonnet and a
shawl! We may take a hackney and be there before Lady
Bridlington comes downstairs."

"Yes, but— Fact is, ma'am, he ain't at the Red Lion!" said Mr. Scunthorpe, much disturbed.

She had sprung up from her chair, but at this she paused. "Not? But how is this? Why has he left the inn?"

"Couldn't pay his shot," explained Mr. Scunthorpe apologetically. "Left his watch. Silly thing to do. Might have come in useful."

"Oh!" she cried out, horror in her voice. "Is it as bad as *that*?"

"Worse!" said Mr. Scunthorpe gloomily. "Got queered sporting his blunt on the table. Only hadn't enough blunt. Took to signing vowels, and ran aground."

"*Gaming!*" Arabella breathed, in a shocked voice.

"Faro," said Mr. Scunthorpe. "Mind, no question of any Greeking transactions! No fuzzing, or handling the concave suit! Not but what it makes it worse, because a fellow has to be dashed particular in all matters of play and pay, if he goes to the Nonesuch. All the go, I assure you: Corinthian club—best of good *ton!* They play devil-ish high there—above my touch!"

"Then it was not you who took him to such a place!"

"Couldn't have been," said Mr. Scunthorpe simply. "Not a member. Chuffy Wivenhoe."

"Lord Wivenhoe! Oh, what a fool I have been!" cried Arabella. "It was I who made him known to Lord Wivenhoe!"

"Pity," said Mr. Scunthorpe, shaking his head.

"But how wicked of him to have led Bertram to such a place! Oh, how could he have done so? I had no suspicion—I thought him so agreeable, and gentlemanlike—!"

"Polite to a point," agreed Mr. Scunthorpe. "Very good sort of a man: very well liked. Daresay he did it for the best."

"How could he think so?" Arabella said hotly.

"Very exclusive club," he pointed out.

She said impatiently: "It is of no use for us to argue on that head. Where is Bertram?"

"Don't think you'd know the place, ma'am. It's—it's near Westminister!"

"Very well, let us go there at once!"

In considerable agitation, Mr. Scunthorpe said: "No, dash it! Can't take a lady to Willow Walk! You don't quite understand, ma'am! Poor Bertram—couldn't pay his shot—not a meg on him—duns in his pocket—tip-staffs after him—had to give 'em all the bag! Can't quite make out exactly how it was, but think he must have gone back to the Red Lion when he left the Nonesuch, because he has his portmanteau with him. Seems to have bolted for it to Tothill Fields. Very low back slum, ma'am. Silly fellow ought to have come and knocked me up—happy to have given him my sofa!"

"Good God, why did he not?"

He coughed in an embarrassed way. "Might have been a little bit on the go," he said diffidently. "Scared of being pounded by the tipstaffs, too. Come to think of it, might easily be if he stayed with me. Dashed tradesmen know he's a friend of mine! At all events, he ain't with me—didn't send me word where he was till this morning—feeling too blue-deviled, I daresay. Don't blame him: would myself!"

"Oh, poor Bertram, poor Bertram!" she cried, wringing her hands. "I do not care where he is, see him I must, if I have to go to this Willow Walk alone!"

"Good God, ma'am, mustn't do that!" he exclaimed, appalled. "Very rough set of coves in Willow Walk! Besides—" He paused, looking acutely uncomfortable. "Not quite himself!"

"Oh, he must be ill with worry and despair! Nothing would keep me from him at such a time! I will fetch my bonnet, and we may be off directly!"

"Ma'am, he won't like it!" Mr. Scunthorpe said desperately. "Very likely be ready to murder me only for telling you! You *can't* see him!"

"Why can I not?"

"He's been in the sun a trifle! You see—very understandable thing to do!—shot the cat!"

"Shot the cat?"

"Can't blame him!" Mr. Scunthorpe pleaded. "Wouldn't have told you, if you hadn't been so set on seeing him! Felt desperate—shot the cat—felt better—kept on swallowing balls of fire—result, looking as queer as Dick's hatband, when I saw him!"

"Do you mean that he has been drinking?" demanded Arabella. "What, in heaven's name, is a ball of fire?"

"Brandy," said Mr. Scunthorpe. "Devilish bad brandy too. Told him to make Blue Ruin the preferred suit. Safer."

"Every word you say makes me the more determined to go to him!" declared Arabella.

"Assure you much better to send him some blunt, ma'am!"

"I will take him all I have, but oh, it is so little! I cannot think yet what is to be done!"

Mr. Scunthorpe pointed significantly to the ceiling. "You don't think the old lady—?" he suggested delicately.

She shook her head. "Oh, no, no! Impossible!"

Mr. Scunthorpe looked a little thoughtful. "In that case, ma'am, better take you to him. Talking very wildly this morning. No saying what he might do."

She almost ran to the door. "We have not a moment to waste, then!"

"No, no!" he assured her. "No need to be on the fret! Won't cut his throat today! Told the girl to hide his razor."

"What girl?"

He became very much confused, blushed, and ut-

tered: "Girl he sent to my lodging with a message. Been
looking after him."

"Oh, God bless her!" Arabella cried fervently. "What
is her name? How much I must owe her!"

As the lady in question had introduced herself to Mr.
Scunthorpe as Leaky Peg, he was obliged to take refuge
in prevarication and to hope devoutly that they would
not encounter her in Willow Walk. He said that he had
not caught her name. Arabella seemed a little disappointed, but since this was no time for wasting over
trifles, she said no more but ran out of the room to fetch
her bonnet and shawl.

It was impossible for her to leave the house without
the butler's being aware of it; but although he looked
surprised, he made no comment, and in a few minutes'
time she and Mr. Scunthorpe were seated in a ram-
shackle hackney coach, which seemed as though, many
years before, it had formed part of a nobleman's equipage, but which had fallen into sad decay. The coverings
to the seats and the squabs were tattered and dirty, and
the vehicle smelled strongly of beer and old leather.
These evils Arabella scarcely noticed, in such a turmoil
was her mind. It was a struggle to support her spirits at
all; she felt ready to sink, and was unable, while in such
a state of agitation, to form any plan for Bertram's relief.
The only solution which had so far presented itself to
her mind was an instinctive impulse, no sooner thought
of than recoiled from, to send off an express to Heythram. Mr. Scunthorpe's suggestion of applying to Lady
Bridlington she well knew to be useless, nor would her
pride tolerate the putting of herself under such added
obligation to her grandmother. Wild notions of selling
Mama's diamonds and the pearl necklet that had belonged to Grandmama Tallant could not, she knew, be
entertained, for these trinkets were not hers to dispose
of at will.

Beside her, Mr. Scunthorpe, feeling vaguely that her

spirits required support, tried to entertain her by pointing out, conscientiously, the various places of interest
the hackney drove past. She scarcely heeded him, but
when they reached Westminister began to look about
her a little, insensibly cheered by the respectability of
the neighborhood. But the hackney lumbered on, and in
a surprisingly short space of time, it was hard to realize
that she must be within a stone's throw of the Abbey, so
squalid were her surroundings. An unlucky attempt
made by Mr. Scunthorpe to divert her, by pointing out
an ugly brick structure which he said was the Tothill
Fields Bridewell, made her shudder so alarmingly that
he hastily informed her that it was so crammed to overflowing with felons that there was no room for another
soul behind its walls. A row of squat almshouses was the
next object of interest to be seen. This was followed by
a charity school, but the district seemed to Arabella to
be largely composed of wretched hovels, ancient man-
sions fallen into depressing decay, and a superfluity of
taverns. Frowsy-looking women stood in the doorways
of some of the hovels; half-naked urchins turned cart-
wheels on the dirty cobbles, in the hope of gaining largesse from persons well breeched enough to travel in
hackney coaches; at one corner a fat woman seated behind an iron caldron appeared to be dispensing tea to
a curiously ill-assorted crowd of persons, ranging from
bricklayers to bedizened young women; various street
cries echoed in the narrow streets, from offers of coal to
entreaties for old iron; and the male population seemed
to consist entirely of scavengers, sweeps, and unidenti-
fiable persons with blue jowls and mufflers round their
necks in place of collars.

After passing the entrances to several noisome alleys,
the hackney turned into Willow Walk and proceeded
down it for some way before drawing up outside a dingy
house whose windows showed, besides fluttering odd-
ments of washing hung out to dry, several broken panes

of glass. In the open doorway an old woman sat in a rocking chair puffing at a clay pipe and engaged in conversation with a younger female who held a squalling infant on one arm, which she from time to time shook, or refreshed from a black bottle, from which she herself took frequent pulls. Arabella had no positive knowledge of what was in that black bottle, but that it must contain strong liquor she felt convinced. The thought of Bertram was momentarily banished from her head; as Mr. Scunthorpe handed her down from the hackney and punctiliously brushed off the straws that clung to the flounce of her simple cambric dress, she opened her reticule, hunted in it for a shilling, and astonished the mother of the infant by pressing it into her hand, and saying earnestly: "Pray buy the baby some milk! Oh, pray do not give it that horrid stuff!"

Both women stared at her with fallen jaws. The old Irishwoman, the first to regain command over her faculties, burst into a cackle of mirth and informed her that she was talking to no less a personage than Quartern Sue. This conveyed little to Arabella, but while she was still puzzling over the appellation, Quartern Sue, recovering from her stupefaction, had launched forth into a catalogue of her embarrassments and was holding her hand cupped suggestively. Mr. Scunthorpe, beads of sweat standing upon his brow, took it upon himself to hustle his charge into the house, whispering to her that she must not get into talk with such ill-famed women. Quartern Sue, never one to let slip an opportunity, followed them, her beggar's whine rising to a crescendo, but was repulsed at the foot of a rickety, uncarpeted stairway by a strapping young woman with a tousle of greasy yellow hair, a countenance which not all the ravages of gin had entirely deprived of comeliness, and a tawdry dress, stained in various places, and with the bodice cut so low as to reveal glimpses of a dirty shift. This lady, having driven Quartern Sue forth by a series of remarks not one of which was intelligible to Arabella, turned and confronted the genteel visitors with a belligerent look on her face and her arms set widely akimbo. She demanded of Mr. Scunthorpe, with whom she appeared to be acquainted, what he meant by bringing a flash mort to the ken. Mr. Scunthorpe uttered the one word, Sister! in strangled accents, upon which the blonde beauty turned a pair of fierce, bloodshot eyes upon Arabella and ejaculated: "Ho! Sister, is it?"

"Girl who brought me the message!" exclaimed Mr. Scunthorpe in a blushful aside to Arabella.

The blonde beauty needed no other passport to Arabella's favor. If she was conscious—as she could hardly have failed to have been—of the strong aroma of daffy which hung about the person of Leaky Peg, she gave no sign of it but started forward, with her hands held out and impulsive words on her lips. "Oh, are you the girl who has been kind to my brother? You must let me thank you! I can never, never repay you! Mr. Scunthorpe here has been telling me that it was you who took care of him when he—when he came to this place!"

Leaky Peg stared very hard at her for a moment and then said pugnaciously: "I found the covey on the mop, blue as megrim, see? and him no more than a mouth! Half flash and half foolish, that's him. Strike me, I don't know what I see in the hick!"

"Miss Tallant, better come upstairs!" said the anguished Mr. Scunthorpe, to whom Leaky Peg's vocabulary was rather more intelligible than to Arabella.

"You dub your mummer, you death's head on a mopstick!" Leaky Peg advised him. "Leave me and the swell mort be!" She turned back to Arabella and said roughly: "Lurched, ain't he? He tells me there's a fastener out after him. He hadn't so much as a meg in his truss when I come up with him in the boozing ken. I took him along with me—strike me if I know why!" She jerked her thumb toward the stairs. "You want to take him away:

this ain't his lay, nor it ain't mine neither! Spouting a kid's mish all to buy him mutton and smash, which he don't eat! Me! You take him off; you're welcome!"

Gathering from these words that Leaky Peg had been keeping Bertram supplied with food, Arabella, tears standing in her eyes, seized one of her hands and pressed it fervently between both her own, saying: "How good you are! Indeed, I thank you! He is only a boy, you know, and what must have become of him without you I dare not think!"

"Well, it's little enough I got from it!" remarked Leaky Peg caustically. "You and him with your break-teeth words! You get up them dancers, you and that molder alongside you that looks like a toothdrawer! First door on the right: stale drunk, he is, but he ain't back yet!"

With these heartening words she turned on her heel and strode out of the house, driving before her Quartern Sue, who had the temerity to venture onto the threshold again. Mr. Scunthorpe made haste to usher Arabella up the stairs, saying reproachfully: "Shouldn't talk to her, ma'am! Not at all the thing! Assure you!"

"The thing!" she exclaimed scornfully. "She has a kind heart, sir!"

Abashed, Mr. Scunthorpe begged pardon, and tapped at a door at the head of the stairs.

Bertram's voice sounded from within the room, and without waiting for her escort to usher her in, Arabella lifted the latch and quickly entered.

The apartment, which looked out onto a filthy yard where lean cats prowled among garbage heaps, was small, rather dark, and furnished with a sagging bed pushed up against one wall, a deal table, two wooden chairs, and a strip of threadbare carpet. The remains of a loaf of bread, a heel of cheese, together with a glass, a jug, and an empty bottle stood on the table; and on the mantel shelf, presumably placed there by Leaky Peg, was a cracked mug containing a wilting bunch of flowers. Bertram, who was stretched on the bed, raised himself on his elbow as the door opened, an apprehensive look on his face. He was fully dressed, but was wearing a handkerchief knotted round his neck and looked both ill and unkempt. When he saw Arabella, he uttered something like a sob, and struggled up and to his feet. "Bella!"

She was in his arms on the word, unable to prevent herself from bursting into tears, but passionately clasping him to her. His breath reeked of spirits, but although this shocked her, she did not recoil from him but hugged him more tightly still.

"You should not have come!" he said unsteadily. "Felix, how *could* you have brought her here?"

"Warned her she wouldn't like it," Mr. Scunthorpe excused himself. "Very set on seeing you!"

Bertram gave a groan. "I did not mean you to know!"

She disengaged herself, wiped her tears away, and sat down on one of the chairs. "Bertram, you know that is nonsense!" she said. "Whom should you turn to if not to me? I am so sorry! What you must have suffered in this dreadful house!"

"Pretty, ain't it?" he said jeeringly. "I don't know how I came here: Leaky Peg brought me. You may as well know, Bella, I was so foxed I don't remember anything that happened after I bolted from the Red Lion!"

"No, I quite see," she said. "But, Bertram, pray do not go on drinking! It is all so bad, and that makes it worse! You look sadly out of sorts, and no wonder! Have you a sore throat, dearest?"

He flushed, his hand going instinctively to the hand-kerchief round his neck. "This! Oh, no! Gammoning the draper, my dear!" He saw her look of bewilderment, and added with a short laugh: "You would be surprised at the cant I have learnt from my hosts here! I've become a spouter—at least Peg manages the business for me!

Pawned, Bella, pawned! Shan't have a rag to my back soon—not that that will signify!"

Mr. Scunthorpe, seated on the edge of the bed, exchanged a meaning look with Arabella. She said briskly: "It would signify very much! We must think what is to be done. Only tell me what you owe!"

He was reluctant to divulge the sum, but she insisted, and after a little while he blurted out: "It comes to more than seven hundred pounds! There is no possibility of my being able to get clear!"

She was aghast, for she had not supposed that he could owe nearly so much. The sum seemed vast beyond belief, so that she could not be surprised when Bertram, casting himself into the other chair, began to talk in a wild way of putting a period to his existence. She let him run on, guessing that his despair needed the relief of just such mad outpourings, and having no very real fear that he would put his violent threats into execution. While he talked, she cudgeled her brains for a solution to his difficulties, only lending half an ear to him but patting his hand soothingly from time to time. Mr. Scunthorpe intervened at last, saying with great common sense: "Don't think you ought to jump into the river, dear old boy. Sister wouldn't like it. Bound to leak out. Your governor might not like it either: never can tell!"

"No, indeed!" Arabella said. "You must not talk of it any more. Bertram. You know how wicked it would be!"

"Well, I suppose I shan't kill myself," Bertram said, a shade sulkily. "Only, I can tell you this; I'll never face my father with *this!*"

"No, no!" she agreed. "Seven hundred pounds! Bertram, how has it been possible?"

"I lost six hundred at faro," he said, dropping his head in his hands. "The rest—well, there was the tailor, and the horse I hired, and what I owe at Tatt's, and my shot at the inn—oh, a dozen things! Bella, what am I to do?"

He sounded much more like the younger brother she knew when he spoke like that, a scared look on his face, and in his voice an unreasoning dependence on her ability to help him out of a scrape.

"Bills don't signify," pronounced Mr. Scunthorpe. "Leave town: won't be followed. Not been living under your own name. Gaming debts another matter. Got to raise the wind for that. Debt of honor."

"I know it, curse you!"

"But all debts are debts of honor!" Arabella said. "Indeed, you should pay your bills first of all!"

A glance passed between the two gentlemen, indicative of their mutual agreement not to waste breath in arguing with a female on a subject she would clearly never understand. Bertram passed his hand over his brow, heaving a short sigh and saying: "There's only one thing to be done. I have thought it all over, Bella, and I mean to enlist, under a false name. If they won't have me as a trooper, I'll join a line regiment, I should have done it yesterday when I first thought of it, only that there's some thing I must do first. Affair of honor. I shall write to my father, of course, and I daresay he will utterly cast me off, but that can't be helped!"

"How can you think so?" Arabella cried hotly. "Grieved he must be—oh, I dare not even think of it!— but you must know that never, never would he do such an unchristian thing as to cast you off! Oh, do not write to him yet! Only give me time to think what I can do! If Papa knew that you owed all that money, I am very sure he would pay every penny of it, though it ruined him!"

"How can you suppose I could be such a gudgeon as to tell him *that*? No! I shall tell him that my whole mind is set on the army, and I had as lief start in the ranks as not!"

This speech struck far more dismay into Arabella's heart than his previous talk of committing suicide, for to take the King's shilling seemed to her a likely thing for him to do. She uttered, hardly above a whisper: "No, no!"

"It must be, Bella," he said. "I'm sure the army is all I'm fit for, and I cannot show my face again with a load of debt hanging over me. Particularly a debt of honor! Oh God, I think I must have been mad!" His voice broke, and he could not speak for a moment. In the end he contrived to summon up the travesty of a smile, and say: "Pretty pair, ain't we? Not that *you* did anything as wrong as I have."

"Oh, I have behaved so dreadfully!" she exclaimed. "It is even my fault that you are reduced to these straits! Had I never presented you to Lord Wivenhoe—"

"That's fudge!" he said quickly. "I had been to gaming houses before I met him. He was not to know I wasn't as well blunted as that set of his! I ought not to have gone with him to the Nonesuch. Only I had lost money on a race, and I thought—I hoped— Oh, talking pays no toll! But to say it was your fault is all gammon!"

"Bertram, who won your money at the Nonesuch?" she asked.

"The bank. It was faro."

"Yes, but someone holds the bank!"

"The Nonpareil."

She stared at him. "Mr. Beaumaris?" she gasped. He noded. "Oh, no, do not say so! How could he have let you— No, no, Bertram!"

She sounded so much distressed that he was puzzled. "Why the devil shouldn't he?"

"You are only a boy! He must have known! And to accept notes of hand from you! Surely he might have refused to do so much at least!"

"You don't understand!" he said impatiently. "I went there with Chuffy, so why should he refuse to let me play?"

Mr. Scunthorpe nodded. "Very awkward situation, ma'am. Devilish insulting to refuse a man's vowels."

She could not appreciate the niceties of the code evidently shared by both gentlemen, but she could accept that they must obtain in male circles. "I must think it wrong of him," she said. "But never mind! The thing is that he is—that I am particularly acquainted with him! Don't be in despair, Bertram! I am persuaded that if I were to go to him, explain that you are not of age, and not a rich man's son, he will forgive the debt!"

She broke off, for there was no mistaking the expressions of shocked disapprobation in both Bertram's and Mr. Scunthorpe's faces.

"Good God, Bella, what will you say next!"

"But, Bertram, indeed he is not proud and disagreeable, as so many people think him! I—I have found him particularly kind and obliging!"

"Bella, this is a *debt of honor!* If it takes me my life long to do it, I must pay it, and so I shall tell him!"

Mr. Scunthorpe nodded judicial approval of this decision.

"Spend your life paying six hundred pounds to a man who is so wealthy that I daresay he regards it no more than you would a shilling?" cried Arabella. "Why, it is absurd!"

Bertram looked despairingly at his friend. Mr. Scunthorpe said painstakingly: "Nothing to do with it, ma'am. Debt of honor is a debt of honor. No getting away from that."

"I cannot agree! I own, I do not like to do it, but I *could* do it, and know he would never refuse me!"

Bertram grasped her wrist. "Listen, Bella! I daresay you don't understand—in fact, I can see that you don't!—but if you dared to do such a thing I swear you'd never see my face again! Besides, even if he did tear up my vowels I should still think myself under an obligation to redeem them! Next you will be suggesting that you should ask him to pay those damned tradesmen's bills for me!"

She colored guiltily, for some such idea had just crossed her mind. Suddenly, Mr. Scunthorpe, whose face a moment before had assumed a cataleptic expression, uttered three pregnant words. "Got a notion!"

The Tallants looked anxiously at him, Bertram with hope, his sister more than a little doubtfully.

"Know what they say?" Mr. Scunthorpe demanded. "Bank always wins!"

"I know that," said Bertram bitterly. "If that's all you have to say—"

"Wait!" said Mr. Scunthorpe. "Start one!" He saw blank bewilderment in the two faces confronting him, and added, with a touch of impatience: "Faro!"

"Start a faro bank!" said Bertram incredulously. "You must be mad! Why even if it were not the craziest thing I ever heard of, you can't run a faro bank without capital!"

"Thought of that," said Mr. Scunthorpe, not without pride. "Go to my trustees. Go at once. Not a moment to be lost."

"Good God, you don't suppose they would let you touch your capital for such a cause as that?"

"Don't see why not!" argued Mr. Scunthorpe. "Always trying to add to it. Preaching at me forever about improving the estate! Very good way of doing it: wonder they haven't thought of it for themselves. Better go and see my uncle at once."

"Felix, you're a gudgeon!" said Bertram irritably. "No trustee would let you do such a thing! And even if they would, good God, we neither of us want to spend our lives running a faro bank!"

"Shouldn't have to," said Mr. Scunthorpe, sticking obstinately by his guns. "Only want to clear you of debt! One good night's run would do it. Close the bank then."

He was so much enamored of this scheme that it was some time before he could be dissuaded from trying to promote it. Arabella, paying very little heed to the argument, sat wrapped in her own thoughts. That these were by no means pleasant would have been apparent even to Mr. Scunthorpe, had he been less engrossed in the championing of his own plans, for not only did her hands clench and unclench in her lap, but her face, aways very expressive, betrayed her. But by the time Bertram had convinced Mr. Scunthorpe that a faro bank would not answer, she was sufficiently mistress of herself again to excite no suspicion in either gentleman's breast.

She turned her eyes toward Bertram, who had sunk back, after his animated argument, into a state of hopeless gloom. "I shall think of something," she said. "I *know* I shall contrive to help you! Only please, please do not enlist, Bertram! Not yet! Only if I should fail!"

"What do you mean to do?" he demanded. "I shan't enlist until I have seen Mr. Beaumaris, and—and explained to him how it is! That I *must* do. I—I told him I had no funds in London and should be obliged to send into Yorkshire for them, so he asked me to call at his house on Thursday. It is of no use to look at me like that, Bella! I couldn't tell him I was done up and had no means of paying him, with them all there listening to what we were saying! I would have died rather! Bella, have you any money? Could you spare me enough to get my shirt back'? I can't go to see the Nonpareil like this!"

She thrust her purse into his hand. "Yes, yes, of course! If only I had not bought those gloves, and the shoes, and the new scarf! There are only ten guineas left, but it will be enough to make you more comfortable until I have thought how to help you, won't it? Do, do remove from this dreadful house! I saw quite a number of inns on our way, and one or two of them looked to be respectable!"

It was plain that Bertram would be only too ready to change his quarters, and after a brief dispute, in which he was very glad to be worsted, he took the purse, gave her a hug, and said that she was the best sister in the

world. He asked wistfully whether she thought Lady Bridlington might be induced to advance him seven hundred pounds, on a promise of repayment over a
protracted period; but although she replied cheerfully
that she had no doubt that she could arrange something
of the sort, he could not deceive himself into thinking it
possible, and sighed. Mr. Scunthorpe, prefixing his remark with one of his deprecating coughs, suggested that
as the hackney had been told to wait for them, he and
Miss Tallant ought, perhaps, to be taking their leave.
Arabella was much inclined to go at once in search of a
suitable hostelry for Bertram, but was earnestly dissuaded, Mr. Scunthorpe promising to attend to this matter himself, and also to redeem Bertram's raiment from
the pawnbroker's shop. The brother and sister then
parted, clinging to one another in such a moving way
that Mr. Scunthorpe was much affected by the sight and
had to blow his nose with great violence.

Arabella's first action on reaching Park Street again
was to run up to her bedchamber, and without pausing
to remove her bonnet to sit down at the little table in the
window and prepare to write a letter. But in spite of the
evident urgency of the matter, she had no sooner written
her opening words than all inspiration appeared to des-
ert her, and she sat staring out of the window, while the
ink dried on her pen. At last she drew a breath, dipped
the pen in the standish again, and resolutely wrote two
lines. Then she stopped, read over, tore up the paper,
and drew a fresh sheet toward her.

It was some time before she had achieved a result that
satisfied her, but it was done at last and the letter sealed
up with a wafer. She then rang the bell pull, and upon
a housemaid's coming in answer to the summons, desired the girl to send Becky to her if she could be spared
from her duties. When Becky presently appeared, shyly
smiling and twisting her hands together in her apron,
Arabella held out the letter and said: "If you please,

Becky, do you think you could contrive to slip out, and— and carry that to Mr. Beaumaris's house? You might say that I have asked you to go on an errand for me, but— but I shall be very much obliged to you if you will not disclose to anyone what it is!"

"Oh, miss!" breathed the handmaid, scenting a romance. "As though I would say a word to a living soul!"

"Thank you! If—if Mr. Beaumaris should be at home, I should be glad if you would wait for an answer to the letter!"

Becky nodded her profound understanding of this, assured Arabella that she might trust her through fire and water, and departed.

Nothing could have been more conspiratorial than her manner of entering Arabella's room half an hour later, but she brought bad news: Mr. Beaumaris had gone into the country three days ago, and had said he might be away from London for a week.

❧ *Chapter 15* ❧

MR. BEAUMARIS RETURNED TO HIS LONDON
house in time to partake of a late breakfast on Tuesday
morning, having been absent for six days. It had been
considered probable by his dependents that he would be
away for a full week, but as he rarely gave any positive
information on his movements, counted no cost, and
had accustomed his highly paid servants to live in a
constant state of expectation of being obliged, at a moment's notice, to provide suitable entertainment for
himself, or for a score of guests, his premature arrival
caused no one any dismay. It caused one member of his
household a degree of joy bordering on delirium. A
ragged little mongrel, whose jauntily curled tail had
been clipped unhappily between his legs for six intermi-
nable days, and who had spent the major part of this
time curled into a ball on the rug outside his master's
door, refusing all sustenance, including plates of choice
viands prepared by the hands of the great M. Alphonse
himself, came tumbling down the stairs, uttering canine
shrieks, and summoned up enough strength to career
madly round in circles before collapsing in an ex-
hausted, panting heat at Mr. Beaumaris's feet. It spoke

volumes for the light in which Mr. Beaumaris's whims were regarded by his retainers that the condition to which his disreputable protégé had willfully reduced himself brought every member of the household who might have been considered in some way responsible into the hall to exonerate himself from all blame. Even M. Alphonse mounted the stairs from his basement kingdom to describe to Mr. Beaumaris in detail the chicken broth, the ragout of rabbit, the shin of beef, and the marrowbone with which he had tried to tempt Ulysses' vanished appetite. Brough broke in on his Gallic monologue to assure Mr. Beaumaris that he for one had left nothing undone to restore Ulysses' interest in life, even going to the lengths of importing a stray cat into the house, in the hope that this outrage would galvanize one notoriously unsympathetic toward all felines to activity. Painswick, with a smug air that rendered him instantly odious to his colleagues, drew attention to the fact that it had been his superior understanding of Ulysses' processes of thought which Mr. Beaumaris had to thank for his finding himself still in possession of his lowborn companion: he had conceived the happy notion of giving Ulysses one of Mr. Beaumaris's gloves to guard.

Mr. Beaumaris, who had picked Ulysses up, paid no heed to all these attempts at self-justification but addressed himself to his adorer. "What a fool you are!" he observed. "No, I have the greatest dislike of having my face licked and must request you to refrain. Quiet, Ulysses! Quiet! I am grateful to you for your solicitude, but you must perceive that I am in the enjoyment of my customary good health. I would I could say the same of you. You have once more reduced yourself to skin and bone, my friend, a process which I shall take leave to inform you I consider as unjust as it is ridiculous. Anyone setting eyes on you would suppose that I grudged you even the scraps from my table!" He added, without

the slightest change of voice, and without raising his
eyes from the creature in his arms: "You would also
appear to have bereft my household of its senses, so that
the greater part of it, instead of providing me with the
breakfast I stand in need of, is engaged in excusing itself
from any suspicion of blame, and—I may add—doing
itself no good thereby."

Ulysses, to whom the mere sound of Mr. Beaumaris's
voice was ecstasy, looked adoringly up into his face and
contrived to lick the hand that was caressing him. On his
servants, Mr. Beaumaris's voice operated in quite another fashion: they dispersed rapidly, Painwick to lay out
a complete change of raiment; Brough to set the table
in the breakfast parlor; Alphonse to carve at lightning
speed several slices of a fine York ham and to cast eggs
and herbs into a pan; and various underlings to grind
coffee beans, cut bread, and set kettles on to boil. Mr.
Beaumaris tucked Ulysses under one arm, picked up the
pile of letters from the table in the hall, and strolled with
them into his library. To the zealous young footman who
hastened to fling open the door for him, he said: "Food
for this abominable animal!"—a command which,
relayed swiftly to the kitchen, caused M. Alphonse to
command his chief assistant instantly to abandon his
allotted task and to prepare a dish calculated to revive
the flagging appetite of a Cambacérès.

Mr. Beaumaris, tossing a pile of invitations and bills
aside, came upon a billet which had not been delivered
through the medium of the Penny Post, and which was
superscribed, *Urgent.* The writing, certainly feminine,
was unknown to him. "Now, what have we here,
Ulysses?" he said, breaking the wafer.

They had not very much. "Dear Mr. Beaumaris," ran
the missive, "I should be *very much obliged to you* if you
would do me the honor of calling in Park Street *as soon
as may be convenient to you,* and requesting the butler to

inform *me* of the event. I remain, Ever yours most sincerely, Arabella Tallant."

This model of the epistolary art, which had caused Miss Tallant so much heart-searching and so many ruined sheets of hot-pressed note paper, did not fail of its effect. Mr. Beaumaris cast aside the rest of his correspondence, set Ulysses down on the floor, and bent his powerful mind to the correct interpretation of these few, heavily underlined words. He was still engaged on this task when Brough entered the room to announce that his breakfast awaited him. He carried the letter into the parlor and propped it against the coffee pot, feeling that he had not yet got to the bottom of it. At his feet, Ulysses, repairing with enthusiasm the ravages of his protracted fast, was rapidly consuming a meal which might have been judged excessive for the satisfaction of the appetite of a boa constrictor.

"This," said Mr. Beaumaris, "was delivered here three days ago, Ulysses!"

Ulysses, whose keen olfactory sense had discovered the chicken giblets cunningly hidden in the middle of his plate, could spare no more than a perfunctory wag of the tail for this speech; and to Mr. Beaumaris's subsequent demand to know what could be in the wind, he returned to answer at all. Mr. Beaumaris pushed away the remains of his breakfast, a gesture which was shortly to operate alarmingly on the sensibilities of the artist below stairs, and waved aside his valet, who had just entered the room. "My town dress!" he said.

"I have it ready, sir," responded Painswick with dignity. "There was just one matter which I should perhaps mention."

"Not now," said Mr. Beaumaris, his eyes still bent upon Miss Tallant's tantalizing communication.

Painswick bowed, and withdrew. The matter was not, in his fastidious estimation, of sufficient importance to justify him in intruding upon his employer's evident preoccupation; nor did he broach it when Mr. Beaumaris presently came upstairs to change his riding dress for the blue coat, yellow pantaloons, chaste waistcoat, and gleaming Hessians with which he was wont to gratify the eyes of beholders in the metropolis. This further abstention was due, however, more to the sense of irretrievable loss which had invaded his soul on the discovery that a shirt was missing from Mr. Beaumaris's execrably packed portmanteau than from a respect for his master's abstraction. He confined his conversation to bitter animadversions on the morals of inn servants and the depths of depravity to which some unknown boots had sunk in treating Mr. Beaumaris's second-best pair of Hessians with a blacking fit only to be used on the footwear of country squires. He could hardly flatter himself that Mr. Beaumaris, swiftly and skillfully arranging the folds of his neckcloth in the mirror, or delicately paring his well-cared-for fingernails, paid the least heed to his discourse, but it served in some measure to relieve his lacerated feelings.

Leaving his valet to repair the damage to his wardrobe, and his faithful admirer to sleep off the effects of a Gargantuan meal, Mr. Beaumaris left the house and walked to Park Street. Here he was met by the intelligence that my lord, my lady, and Miss Tallant had gone out in the barouche to the British Museum, where Lord Elgin's much disputed marbles were now exhibited, in a wooden shed built for their accommodation. Mr. Beaumaris thanked the butler for this information, called up a passing hackney, and directed the jarvey to drive him to Great Russell Street.

He found Miss Tallant, her disinterested gaze fixed upon a sculptured slab from the Temple of Nike Apteros, enduring a lecture from Lord Bridlington, quite in his element. It was Lady Bridlington who first perceived his tall, graceful figure advancing across the saloon, for since she had naturally seen the collection of

antiquities when it was on view at Lord Elgin's residence
in Park Lane, and again when it was removed to Burling-
ton House, she felt herself to be under no obligation to
look at it a third time, and was more profitably engaged
in keeping a weather eye cocked for any of her acquaintances who might have elected to visit the British Museum that morning. Upon perceiving Mr. Beaumaris,
she exclaimed in accents of delight: "Mr. Beaumaris!
What a lucky chance, to be sure! How do you do? How
came you not to be at the Kirkmichael's Venetian breakfast yesterday? Such a charming party! I am persuaded
you must have enjoyed it! Six hundred guests—only
fancy!"

"Amongst so many, ma'am, I am flattered to know
that you remarked my absence," responded Mr.
Beaumaris, shaking hands. "I have been out of town for
some days, and only returned this morning. Miss Tallant! 'Servant, Bridlington!"

Arabella, who had started violently upon hearing his
name uttered, and quickly turned her head, took his
hand in a clasp which seemed to him slightly convulsive
and raised a pair of strained, inquiring eyes to his face.
He smiled reassuringly down into them, and bent a
courteous ear to Lady Bridlington, who was making
haste to assure him that she had come to the Museum
merely to show the Grecian treasures to Arabella, who
had not been privileged to see them on their *first* showing. Lord Bridlington, not averse from any aggrandize-
ment to his audience, began in his consequential way to
expound his views on the probably artistic value of the
fragments, a recreation which would no doubt have occupied him for a considerable period of time had Mr.
Beaumaris not cut him short by saying, in his most languid way: "The pronouncements of West, and of Sir
Thomas Lawrence, must, I imagine, have established
the aesthetic worth of these antiquities. As to the *propri-*

ety of their acquisition, we may, each one of us, hold to our own opinion."

"Mr. Beaumaris, do you care to visit Somerset House with us?" interrupted Lady Bridlington. "I do not know how it comes about that we were not there upon Opening Day, but such a rush of engagements have we been swept up in that I am sure it is a wonder we have time to turn round! Arabella, my love, I daresay you are quite tired of staring at all these sadly damaged bits of frieze, or whatever it may be called—not but what I declare I could feast my eyes on it forever!—and will be glad to look at pictures for a change!"

Arabella assented to it, throwing so beseeching a look at Mr. Beaumaris that he was induced to accept a seat in the barouche.

During the drive to the Strand, Lady Bridlington was too much occupied in catching the eyes of chance acquaintances, and drawing their attention to the distinguished occupant of one of the back seats by bowing and waving to them, to have much time for conversation. Arabella sat with her eyes downcast and her hand fidgeting with the ribands tied round the handle of her sunshade; and Mr. Beaumaris was content to watch her, taking due note of her pallor and the dark shadows beneath her eyes. It was left to Lord Bridlington to entertain the company, which he did very willingly, prosing uninterruptedly until the carriage turned into the courtyard of Somerset House.

Once inside the building, Lady Bridlington, whose ambitions had for some time been centered on promoting a match between Arabella and the Nonpareil, seized the first opportunity that offered of drawing Frederick away from the interesting pair. She stated her fervent desire to see the latest example of Sir Thomas Lawrence's art, and dragged him away from a minute inspection of the President's latest enormous canvas to search for this fashionable masterpiece.

"In what way can I serve you, Miss Tallant?" said Mr. Beaumaris quietly.

"You—you had my letter?" faltered Arabella, glancing fleetingly up into his face.

"This morning. I went instantly to Park Street, and, apprehending that the matter was of some urgency, followed you to Bloomsbury."

"How kind—how *very* kind you are!" uttered Arabella, in accents which could scarcely have been more mournful had she discovered him to have been a monster of cruelty.

"What is it, Miss Tallant?"

Bearing all the appearance of one rapt in admiration of the canvas before her, she said: "I daresay you may have forgot all about it, sir, but—but you told me once—That is, you were so obliging as to say—that if my sentiments underwent a change—"

Mr. Beaumaris mercifully intervened to put an end to her embarrassment. "I have certainly not forgotten it," he said. "I perceive Lady Charnwood to be approaching, so let us move on! Am I to understand, ma'am, that your sentiments *have* undergone a change?"

Miss Tallant, obediently walking on to stare at one of the new Associate's *Probationary Picture* (described in her catalogue as "An old Man soliciting a Mother for Her Daughter who was shewn Unwilling to consent to so disproportionate a match"), said baldly: "Yes."

"My surroundings," said Mr. Beaumaris "make it impossible for me to do more than assure you that you have made me the happiest man in England, ma'am."

"Thank you," said Arabella, in a stifled tone. "I shall try to be a—to be a comfortable wife, sir!"

Mr. Beaumaris's lips twitched, but he replied with perfect gravity: "For my part, I shall try to be an unexceptionable husband, ma'am!"

"Oh, yes, I am *sure* you will be!" said Arabella naïvely. "If only—"

"If only—?" prompted Mr. Beaumaris, as she broke off.

"Nothing!" she said hastily. "Oh, dear, there is Mr. Epworth!"

"A common bow in passing will be enough to damp his pretensions," said Mr. Beaumaris. "If that does not suffice, I will look at him through my glass."

This made her give an involuntary gurgle of laughter, but an instant later she was serious again, and evidently struggling to find the words with which to express herself.

"What very awkward places we do choose in which to propose to one another!" remarked Mr. Beaumaris, guiding her gently toward a red plush couch. "Let us hope that if we sit down and appear to be engrossed in conversation, no one will have the bad manners to interrupt us!"

"I do not know what you must think of me!" said Arabella.

"I expect I had better not tell you until we find ourselves in a more retired situation," he replied. "You always blush so delightfully when I pay you compliments that it might attract attention to ourselves."

She hesitated, and then turned resolutely toward him, tightly gripping her sunshade, and saying: "Mr. Beaumaris, you do *indeed* wish to marry me?"

"Miss Tallant, I do *indeed* wish to marry you!" he asserted.

"And—and you are so wealthy that my—my fortune can mean nothing to you?"

"Nothing at all, Miss Tallant."

She drew an audible breath. "Then—will you marry me at once?" she asked.

Now, what the devil's the meaning of this? thought Mr. Beaumaris, startled. Can that damned young cub have been getting up to more mischief since I left town?

"At once?" he repeated, voice and countenance quite impassive.

"Yes!" said Arabella desperately. "You must know that I have the greatest dislike of—of all *formality,* and—and the nonsense that always accompanies the announcement of an engagement! I—I should wish to be married very quietly—in fact, in the strictest secrecy—and before anyone has guessed—that I have accepted your very obliging offer!"

The wretched youth must have been deeper under the hatches than I guessed, thought Mr. Beaumaris, and still she dare not tell me the truth! Does she really mean to carry out it? A virtuous man would undoubtedly, at this juncture, disclose that there is not the smallest need for these measures. What very unamusing lives virtuous men must lead!

"You may think it odd of me, but I have always thought it would be so very romantic to elope!" pronounced Papa's daughter defiantly.

Mr. Beaumaris, whose besetting sin was thought by many to be his exquisite enjoyment of the ridiculous, turned a deaf ear to the promptings of his better self and replied instantly: "How right you are! I wonder I should not have thought of an elopement myself! The announcement of the engagement of two such notable figures as ourselves must provoke a degree of comment and congratulation which would not be at all to our taste!"

"Exactly so!" nodded Arabella, relieved to find that he saw the matter in so reasonable a light.

"Consider, too, the chagrin of such as Horace Epworth!" said Mr. Beaumaris, growing momently more enamored of the scheme. "You would be driven to distraction by their ravings!"

"Well, I do think I might be," said Arabella.

"There is not a doubt of it. Moreover, the formality of making application to your father for permission to address you is quite antiquated, and we shall do well to dispense with it. If some little feeling still exists in the minds of old-fashioned persons against marrying minors out of hand, it need not concern us, after all."

"N-no," agreed Arabella, rather doubtfully. "Do you think people will—will be very much shocked, sir?"

"No," said Mr. Beaumaris, with perfect truth. "No one will be in the least shocked. When would you like to elope?"

"Would tomorrow be too soon?" asked Arabella anxiously.

Mr. Beaumaris might wish that his love would give him her confidence, but it would have been idle to have denied that he was hugely enjoying himself. Life with Arabella would contain few dull moments; and although her estimate of his morals was unflattering enough to have discomposed any man of sensibility, it left his withers unwrung, since he was well aware that her assumption of his readiness to behave in so improper a fashion sprang from an innocence which he found enchanting. He replied with great promptness: "Not a moment too soon! But for the recollection that there are one or two preparations which perhaps I should make, I should have suggested that we should leave this building together at once."

"No, that would be impossible," said Arabella seriously. "In fact—I do not know very much about such things, but I cannot but feel that it will be excessively difficult for me to escape from Park Street without anyone's knowing! For I must carry a valise with me, at least, besides my dressing case, and how may it be contrived? Unless I crept out at dead of night, of course, but it would have to be very late indeed, for the porter always waits up for Lord Bridlington to come in. And I might fall asleep," she added candidly.

"I have a constitutional dislike of eloping at dead of night," said Mr. Beaumaris firmly. "Such exploits entail the use of rope ladders, I am credibly informed, and the thought of being surprised perhaps by the Watch in the very act of throwing this up to your window I find singularly unnerving."

"Nothing," said Arabella, "would prevail upon me to climb down a rope ladder! Besides, my bedroom is at the back of the house."

"Perhaps," said Mr. Beaumaris, "you had better leave me to make the necessary arrangements."

"Oh, yes!" responded Arabella gratefully. "I am sure you will know just how it should be contrived!"

This reflection upon his past career Mr. Beaumaris bore with an unmoved countenance. "Just so, Miss Tallant," he said gravely. "Now, it occurs to me that, tomorrow being Wednesday, there will be a gala night at Vauxhall Gardens."

"Yes, Lady Bridlington thought at one time of taking me to it," agreed Arabella. "But then, you know, she recalled that it is the night of the party at Uxbridge House."

"A very dull affair, I have no doubt. I shall invite Lady Bridlington—and Bridlington, I suppose—to do me the honor of joining *my* party at Vauxhall. You will naturally be included in this invitation, and at a convenient moment during the course of the evening, we shall slip away together to the street entrance, where my chaise will be awaiting us."

Arabella considered this proposition, and discovered two objections to it. "Yes, but how very odd it would seem to Lady Bridlington if you were to go away in the middle of your own party!"

The reflection that Lady Bridlington might well deem this eccentricity the least odd feature of the affair, Mr. Beaumaris kept to himself. He said: "Very true. A note shall be delivered to her after our departure."

"Well, I suppose that would be better than nothing," Arabella conceded. "Oh, will she ever forgive me for treating her so?" This involuntary exclamation seemed to escape her without her knowledge. She raised the second of her objections. "And in any event it will not answer, because I cannot take a valise to Vauxhall!"

"That you will also leave to me," said Mr. Beaumaris.

"But you cannot call in Park Street to fetch it!" she pointed out.

"Certainly not."

"And I will *not* elope without a change of clothes, or my hairbrushes, or my tooth powder!" declared Arabella.

"Most improper," agreed Mr. Beaumaris. "All these things shall be forthcoming."

"You cannot buy such things for me!" gasped Arabella, shocked.

"I assure you I should enjoy doing it."

She stared at him, and then exclaimed wretchedly: "How dreadful it all is! I never, never thought I should come to this! I daresay it seems the merest commonplace to you, but to me—But I see that it is of no use to cavil!"

The telltale muscle at the corner of Mr. Beaumaris's mouth quivered and was sternly repressed. "Well, perhaps not precisely commonplace," he said. "It so happens that I have not previously eloped with anyone. However, to a man of ordinary ingenuity, the affair should not prove impossible to achieve creditably, I trust. I perceive Mrs. Penkridge, who is hoping to catch either your eye or mine. We shall permit her to do so, and while she asks you to say if you do not think Nollekins's bust over there most like, I shall go in search of Lady Bridlington, and engage her to bring you to Vauxhall tomorrow evening."

"Oh, pray do not! I dislike Mrs. Penkridge excessively!" she whispered.

"Yes, an odious woman, but impossible to avoid," he returned.

Seeing him rise to his feet, Mrs. Penkridge bore down upon him, her acidulated smile on her lips. Mr. Beaumaris greeted her with his smooth civility, stayed for perhaps a minute, and then, to Arabella's indignation, made his bow and went off in the direction of the next room.

Either Lady Bridlington proved hard to find, or he must have fallen a victim to her garrulity, Arabella thought, for it seemed a very long time before she set eyes on him again. When he did reappear, Lady Bridlington was walking beside him, wreathed in smiles. Arabella made her excuses to Mrs. Penkridge, and went across to her godmother, who greeted her with the cheerful intelligence that Mr. Beaumaris had formed the most delightful scheme for an evening at Vauxhall. "I did not scruple to accept, my love, for I knew you would like it of all things!" she said.

"Yes," said Arabella, feeling that she was now committed to an irrevocable and reprehensible course which she would no doubt regret her life long. "I mean, oh, yes! How very agreeable!"

❧ Chapter 16 ❧

UPON LEAVING SOMERSET HOUSE, MR.
Beaumaris got into a hackney and drove to the Red Lion
inn. What he learned at that hostelry threw abundant
light onto Arabella's conduct. Since he had his own reasons for believing Arabella's heart to have been won
long since, he was not in the least wounded by the discovery that she proposed to marry him as a means of
rescuing her brother from debt, but on the contrary
considerably amused. Having paid Bertram's bill at the
inn, and received his watch back from the landlord, he
returned to his own house in yet another hackney.

The same delight in the ridiculous which had made
him wear a dandelion in his buttonhole for three consec-
utive days for no better purpose than to enjoy the discomfiture of his misguided friends and copyists made
him deeply appreciative of the situation in which he now
found himself; and he beguiled the tedium of the drive
to Mount Street in wondering when it would cross his
absurd love's mind that the disclosure, following hard
upon the wedding ceremony, that she required a large
sum of money from him without a moment's loss of
time, might be productive of a little awkwardness. He

could not resist picturing the scene, and was still laughing softly when he reached his house, a circumstance which surprised his butler.

"Send round to the stables for my tilbury, will you, Brough?" he said. "And desire Painswick—oh, you're there, are you?" he added as his valet descended the stairs. "I want to hear no more about missing shirts, on which excessively boring subject I can see from your expression you are prepared to discourse at length, but you may tell me this! Where is the letter I gave into your hands to be delivered at the Red Lion, to a Mr. Anstey, and why did you not tell me that it had not been so delivered?"

"You may perhaps recall, sir," said Painswick reproachfully, "that I mentioned to you while you sat at breakfast that there was a matter which I deemed it my duty to bring to your notice. Upon which, sir, you said, Not now."

"Did I? I had no idea you could be so easily silenced. Where is the letter?"

"I placed it, sir, at the bottom of the pile that was awaiting you on the table here," replied Painswick, tacitly disclaiming further responsibility.

"In that case it is in the library. Thank you: that is all."

Ulysses, who had been lying stretched out in the library, enjoying the sleep of the replete, awoke at Mr. Beaumaris's entrance, yawned, got up, shook himself, sneezed several times, stretched, and indicated by his cocked ears and wagging tail that he was now ready for any adventure.

"I am glad to see you restored to your usual self," said Mr. Beaumaris, running through the mass of his neglected correspondence and picking up his own letter to Bertram. "You know, you should not have dissuaded me from going out again that evening! Just look what has come of it! And yet I don't know. I would not have missed this morning's interview for a thousand pounds!

I suppose you think that I am behaving very badly? I am, of course, but do me the justice to own that she deserves it for being such an adorable little fool!''

Ulysses wagged his tail. He was not only willing to do Mr. Beaumaris justice, but presently indicated his readiness to accompany him on whatever expedition he had in mind.

"It would be useless to suggest, I suppose, that you are occupying Clayton's seat?'' said Mr. Beaumaris, mounting into his tilbury.

Clayton, grinning, expressed himself as being agreeable to taking the little dog on his knees, but Mr. Beaumaris shook his head.

"No, no, I fear he would not like it. I shan't need you,'' he said, and drove off, remarking to his alert companion: "We are now faced with the wearing task of tracking down that foolish young man's inarticulate friend, Felix Scunthorpe. I wonder whether, in the general medley, there is any bloodhound strain in you?''

He drew blank at Mr. Scunthorpe's lodging, but on being informed that Mr. Scunthorpe had mentioned that he was going to Boodle's, drove at once to St. James's Street, and was so fortunate as to catch sight of his quarry walking up the flag-way. He reined in and called imperatively: "Scunthorpe!''

Mr. Scunthorpe had naturally perceived who was driving a spanking chestnut between the shafts of the tilbury, but as he had no expectation of being recognized by the Nonpareil, this summons surprised him very much. He was even a little doubtful and said cautiously: "Me, sir?''

"Yes, you. Where is young Tallant?'' He saw an expression of great wariness descend upon Mr. Scunthorpe's face and added impatiently: "Come, don't be more of a fool than you can help! You don't suppose I am going to hand him over to the tipstaffs, do you?''

"Well, he's at the Cock,'' disclosed Mr. Scunthorpe reluctantly. "That is to say,'' he corrected himself, suddenly recalling his friend's incognito, "he is, if you mean Mr. Anstey."

"Have you any brothers?" demanded Mr. Beaumaris.

"No," said Mr. Scunthorpe, blinking at him. "Only child."

"You relieve my mind. Offer my congratulations to your parents!"

Mr. Scunthorpe thought this over, with knit brow, but could make nothing of it. He put Mr. Beaumaris right on one point. "Only one parent," he said. "Father died three months after I was born."

"Very understandable," said Mr. Beaumaris. "I am astonished that he lingered on for so long. Where is this Cock you speak of?"

"Thing is—not sure I ought to tell you!" said Mr. Scunthorpe.

"Take my word for it, you will be doing your misguided friend an extremely ill turn if you don't tell me!"

"Well, it's at the corner of Duck Lane, Tothill Fields," confided Mr. Scunthorpe, capitulating.

"Good God!" said Mr. Beaumaris and drove off.

The Cock inn, however, though a small, squat building, proved to be more respectable than its situation had led Mr. Beaumaris to suppose. Duck Lane might abound in filth of every description, left to rot in the road, but the Cock seemed to be moderately clean and well kept. It even boasted an ostler, who emerged from the stable to gape at the tilbury. When he understood that the swell handling the ribbons had not merely stopped to inquire the way but really did desire him to take charge of his horse and carriage, a vision of enormous largesse danced before his eyes, and he hastened to assure this noble client that he was ready to bestow his undivided attention on the equipage.

Mr. Beaumaris then descended from the tilbury and walked into the tap of the inn, where his appearance caused a waterman, a jarvey off duty, two bricklayer's

laborers, a scavenger, and the landlord to break off their
conversation in mid-sentence to stare at him.

"Good morning!" said Mr. Beaumaris. "You have a
Mr. Anstey putting up here, I think?"

The landlord, recovering from his surprise, came forward, bowing several times. "Yes, your honor! Oh, yes,
indeed, your honor!— Chase that cur out of here, Joe!—
If your honor will—"

"Do nothing of the sort, Joe!" interrupted Mr.
Beaumaris.

"Is he *yours,* sir?" gasped the landlord.

"Certainly he is mine. A rare specimen: his family tree
would surprise you! Is Mr. Anstey in?"

"He'll be up in his room, sir. Keeps hisself *to* hisself,
in a manner of speaking. If your honor would care to
step into the parlor, I'll run up and fetch him down
before the cat can lick her ear."

"No, take me up to him," said Mr. Beaumaris.
"Ulysses, do stop hunting for rats! We have no time to
waste on sport this morning! Come to heel!"

Ulysses, who had found a promising hole in one corner of the tap and was snuffing at it in a manner calculated to keep its occupant cowering inside it for the
next twenty-four hours at least, regretfully obeyed this
command and followed Mr. Beaumaris up a steep, narrow stairway. The landlord scratched on one of the three
doors at the top of this stair, a voice bade him come in,
and Mr. Beaumaris, nodding dismissal to his guide,
walked in, shut the door behind him, and said cheerfully:
"How do you do? I hope you don't object to my dog?"

Bertram, who had been sitting at a small table trying
for the hundredth time to hit upon some method of
solving his difficulties, jerked up his head and sprang to
his feet, as white as his shirt. *"Sir!"* he uttered, grasping
the back of his chair with one shaking hand.

Ulysses, misliking his tone, growled at him, but was
called to order. "How many more times am I to speak

to you about your total lack of polish, Ulysses?" said Mr.
Beaumaris severely. "Never try to pick a quarrel with a
man under his own roof! Lie down at once!" He drew
off his gloves and tossed them onto the bed. "What a
very tiresome young man you are!" he told Bertram
amiably.

Bertram, his face now as red as a beetroot, said in a
choked voice: "I was coming to your house on Thursday, as you bade me!"

"*I'm* sure you were. But if you hadn't been so foolish
as to leave the Red Lion so—er—hurriedly, there would
not have been the slightest need for this rustication of
yours. *You* would not have worried yourself halfway to
Bedlam, and *I* should not have been obliged to bring
Ulysses to a locality you can see he does not care for."

Bertram glanced in a bewildered way toward Ulysses,
who was sitting suggestively by the door, and said: "You
don't understand, sir. I—I was rolled up! It was that,
or—or prison, I suppose!"

"Yes, I rather thought you were," agreed Mr.
Beaumaris. "I sent a hundred-pound bank note to you
the next morning, together with my assurance that I had
no intention of claiming from you the vast sums you lost
to me. Of course, I should have done very much better
to have told you so at the time—and better still to have
ordered you out of the Nonesuch at the outset! But you
will agree that the situation was a trifle awkward."

"Mr. Beaumaris," said Bertram, with considerable
difficulty, "I c-can't redeem my vowels now, but I pledge
you my word that I *will* redeem them! I was coming to
see you on Thursday, to tell you the whole, and—and to
beg your indulgence!"

"Very proper," approved Mr. Beaumaris. "But it is
not my practice to win large sums of money from school-
boys, and you cannot expect me to change my habits
only to accommodate your conscience, you know. Shall
we sit down, or don't you trust the chairs here?"

"Oh, I beg pardon!" Bertram stammered, flushing vividly. "Of course! I don't know what I was thinking about! Pray, will you take this chair, sir? But it will do! I must and I will— Oh, can I offer you any refreshment? They haven't anything much here, except beer, and porter, and gin, but if you would care for some gin—"

"Certainly not, and if that is how you have been spending your time since last I saw you, I am not surprised that you are looking burned to the socket."

"I haven't been—at least, I did at first, only it was brandy—but not—not lately," Bertram muttered, very shamefaced.

"If you drank the brandy sold in this district, you must have a constitution of iron to be still alive," remarked Mr. Beaumaris. "What's the sum total of your debts? Or don't you know?"

"Yes, but— *You* are not going to pay my debts, sir!" A dreadful thought occurred to him; he stared very hard at his visitor, and demanded: "Who told you where I was?"

"Your amiable but cork-brained friend, of course."

"*Scunthorpe?*" Bertram said incredulously. "It was not—it was not someone else?"

"No, it was not someone else. I have not so far discussed the matter with your sister, if that is what you mean."

"How do you know she is my sister?" Bertram said, staring at him harder than ever. "Do you say that Scunthorpe told you that too?"

"No, I guessed it from the start. Have you kept your bills? Let me have them!"

"Nothing would induce me to!" cried Bertram hotly. "I mean, I am very much obliged to you, sir, and it's curst good of you, but you must *see* that I couldn't accept such generosity! Why, we are almost strangers! I cannot conceive why you should think of doing such a thing for me!"

"Ah, but we are not destined to remain strangers!" explained Mr. Beaumaris. "I am going to marry your sister."

"Going to marry *Bella?*" Bertram said.

"Certainly. You perceive that that puts the whole matter on quite a different footing. You can hardly expect me either to win money from my wife's brother at faro, or to bear the odium of having a relative in the Fleet. You really must consider my position a little, my dear boy."

Bertram's lip quivered. "I see what it is! She *did* go to you, and *that* is why— But if you think, sir, that I have sunk so low I would let Bella sacrifice herself only to save me from disgrace—"

Ulysses, taking instant exception to the raised voice, sprang to Mr. Beaumaris's side and barked a challenge at Bertram. Mr. Beaumaris dropped a hand on his head. "Yes, very rude, Ulysses," he agreed. "But never mind! Bear in mind that it is not everyone who holds me in such high esteem as you do!"

Much confused, Bertram stammered: "I didn't mean— I beg your pardon! I only meant— She never said a word of this to me!"

"Didn't she? How secretive females are, to be sure! Perhaps she felt that her parents should be the first persons to learn the news."

"Well, I suppose she *might,*" Bertram said doubtfully. "But considering she said she couldn't marry anyone, because she made 'em all think she was an heiress—"

"She didn't make me think anything of the sort," said Mr. Beaumaris.

"Oh, I *see!*" said Bertram, his brow clearing. "Well, I must say, sir, I'm dashed glad, because I had a notion she liked you more than all the rest! I—I wish you very happy! And, of course, I do see that it makes a difference to my debt to *you,* only I don't think I should let you pay the other debts, because it is not in the least your affair, and—"

"Now, don't let us go into all that again!" begged Mr. Beaumaris. "Just tell me what you propose to do if I don't pay your debts!"

"I thought of enlisting in a cavalry regiment, if they would take me," confessed Bertram. "Under an assumed name, of course!"

"I should think that a cavalry regiment would suit you very well," said Mr. Beaumaris. "But it will be very much more comfortable for you, and for all of us, if you join it under your own name, and as a cornet. What do you want? A Hussar regiment?"

These incredible words made Bertram turn first red and then white, swallow convulsively, and finally blurt out: "You *c-couldn't* mean that! After *this!* I—oh, sir, *do* you mean it?"

"Yes, of course, but give me your bills!"

"I don't deserve anyone should do anything for me!" Bertram said, overcome.

"The bills!"

Bertram, already floating in some beatific dream, started, and said: "The bills? Oh! Oh, yes, I have them all here—only you will be very much shocked to see how much I have spent, and—"

"Nothing ever shocks me," replied Mr. Beaumaris, holding out a hand. He stuffed the sheaf of crumpled papers into the pocket of his driving coat and said: "I will settle all these so that none of your creditors will know that it was not you who paid them. Do you owe anything in this neighborhood beyond your shot here?"

Bertram shook his head. "No, for Bella gave me all the money she had, when she came to see me. I am afraid you would not have liked her doing so, sir, and nor did I, but Felix brought her, like the saphead he is! It—it was a horrid place, and I think I ought to tell you that it was all my fault that she ever went to such a back slum!"

"You fill me with dismay," said Mr. Beaumaris. "I do trust she did not set eyes on any destitute person whom she may feel it to be her duty to befriend?"

"Well, I don't *think* she did," Bertram replied. "Felix did say that she told a woman they all call Quartern Sue not to give her baby gin to drink, and gave her a shilling to buy it some milk. And I am excessively sorry, sir, and I would not have had it happen for the world, but Felix says that they walked smash into Leaky Peg, who—who took me to the place when I was so castaway I didn't know even where I was, or how I came there. She—she *was* very good to me, in her way, you know, and Bella got it into her head she owed her a debt of gratitude for looking after me! But that's all right, because I gave Peg five pounds out of the money Bella left for me!"

"Heaven help me!" said Mr. Beaumaris. "She will undoubtedly expect me to house this doxy! *Leaky Peg,* did you say? Good God!"

"No, no, sir, of course she won't!" exclaimed Bertram. "Why *should* she?"

"Because that is her invariable practice," said Mr. Beaumaris bitterly. "You don't suppose, do you, that I voluntarily adopted that animal over there?"

"You don't mean Bella gave him to you? Well, that's a great deal too bad of her! I must say, I thought it was a queer sort of a dog for *you* to have, sir!"

"The whole of London thinks it is a queer sort of a dog for me to have. Even the landlord of this tavern tried to chase him from the taproom!" He drew out his pocketbook and extracted from it several bank notes and pushed them across the table. "There you are: pay your shot here, redeem whatever lies in pawn, and book yourself the box seat on the first stage to Harrowgate. I believe the northern-bound coaches leave at some godless hour of the morning, so you had better spend tonight at whatever inn they set out from. A few days in the fresh air will, I trust, repair the ravages of all the brandy

you imbibed and make it possible for you to meet your
father without arising suspicion."

Bertram tried to speak, failed, tried once more, and
managed to say in a very gruff voice: "I c-can't thank you
as I should, and of course I know it is for Bella's sake!
But I *can* do one thing, and I will! I shall confess the
whole to my father, sir, and—and if he says I may not
join a Hussar regiment, after behaving so badly, well—
well, it will serve me right!"

"Yes," said Mr. Beaumaris, "that is very noble of you,
of course, but I have always found it to be an excellent
plan, before one indulges in an orgy of expiation, to
consider whether the recipient of the sort of confession
you have in mind may not be made to suffer a great deal
of quite unnecessary pain."

Bertram was silent for a moment as this sank into his
brain. "You don't think I should tell my father, sir?"

"I not only don't think you should: I utterly forbid you
to mention the matter to him."

"I don't quite like to deceive him," Bertram said shyly.
"You see—"

"I am sure you don't, so if your mind is set on doing
penance, that will serve your turn excellently. You have
been staying in Berkshire with Scunthorpe. Just bear
that in mind, and forget that you have ever been within
ten miles of London!" He rose, and held out his hand.
"Now I must go. Don't harrow yourself with thinking
that you have broken all the ten commandments! You
have only done what four out of five young fools do, if
set loose upon the town. Incidentally, you have acquired
a deal of valuable experience, and when next you come
to London you will do much better."

"I shall never be able to show my face in London
again, sir," said Bertram wistfully. "But thank you!"

"Nonsense! A few years' service and you will become
a dashing captain, I daresay, with a fine pair of military
whiskers. No one will recognize you. By the way, don't

call to take leave of your sister: she is very much occupied today. I will tell her that you are safely dispatched to Yorkshire. Ulysses, stop scratching! Do try to be a little more worthy of me! Yes, we are going, but it is quite unnecessary, and, indeed, extremely uncivil, to caper about in that joyful fashion!" He picked up his gloves, shook hands, and walked to the door, but bethought him of something and put a hand into his inner pocket. "Association with that hound—the boon companion of every prig in town, I have not the least doubt—is fast undermining my morals. Your watch, Bertram!"

❧ *Chapter 17* ❧

MR. BEAUMARIS'S SUBSEQUENT PROCEED-ings, during the short space of time that elapsed before his elopement, were many and varied, but although they included precise instructions to his coachman, and his postilion, and a drive out of London, there was one curious omission: he took no steps to procure a special license, so that it was to be inferred that he contemplated a flight to the Border and a ceremony performed across the anvil at Gretna Green: a departure from the canons of good taste which would have staggered any of his associates who had had the least suspicion of his clandestine intentions. But as no one who met him detected anything out of the ordinary in his demeanor, no one except his prospective bride speculated at all on the course of action he meant to pursue.

Arabella, naturally enough, employed every moment that was unoccupied by social engagements in a great deal of speculation, but as she was wholly ignorant of the rules governing hasty marriages, the need of a special license did not occur to her. She certainly supposed that she would be driven to Gretna Green, and having once accepted this hateful necessity, resolutely turned her thoughts away from it. Romantic though such an adventure might be, no young lady, reared, as she had been, in the strictest propriety, could embark on it without feeling herself to have sunk to irreclaimable depths of depravity. How she was ever to explain such conduct to the satisfaction of Papa was an unanswerable question. Only the thought of Bertram's predicament in any way sustained her. She snatched ten minutes between seeing a balloon ascent and dressing for a more than ordinarily splendid ball in scribbling a letter to Bertram, assuring him that he need only wait patiently at the Cock for a few more days before he should infallibly be rescued from all his embarrassments.

Of Mr. Beaumaris she saw nothing until she met him at Vauxhall Gardens. He was not present at the ball on the night previous to their assignation, a circumstance of which she hardly knew whether to be glad or sorry.

Perhaps it was fortunate that Lady Bridlington's plans for their amusement left her with so little time for reflection. The indulgence of a quiet hour or two in her own bedchamber was not granted her. Try as she would, she was unable to stay awake after that splendid ball, and only awoke next morning when Maria drew back her window blinds. The day was full to overflowing with engagements: she was dressing for Mr. Beaumaris's Vauxhall Gardens party before, as it seemed to her, she well realized what she was about.

It so happened that through the press of invitations which had showered down upon the house in Park Street, Arabella had never before visited the famous gardens. They took sculls across the river, to enter by the water gate, and at any other time she must have been transported by the sight which met her eyes. The gardens, which were laid out in groves and colonnades, were lit (as Lord Bridlington instructively informed her) by no fewer than thirty-seven thousand lamps, some of them suspended in graceful festoons between the pillars

of the colonnades. The orchestra, detected across the
principal grove, was established in a giant kiosk, glittering all over with colored lights; there was a spacious
pavilion, lined with mirrors, which formed the principal
supper room for those who did not care to go to the
expense of hiring one of the boxes which opened onto
the various colonnades; a rotunda, where excellent concerts were held throughout the season; several magnificent fountains; and innumerable walks where lovers
could lose themselves at will.

Mr. Beaumaris met his guests at the water entrance
and conducted them to the Rotunda, where, since it was
past eight o'clock, the concert was already in progress.
Arabella could scarcely meet his eyes, but forced herself
to look up once, very fleetingly, into his face. He smiled
at her, but no private speech passed between them.

After the first act of the concert, at about ten o'clock,
a bell rang, and those who had no ear for music poured
into the Rotunda to witness the marvels of the Grand
Cascade. Even though feelings of guilt were in danger
of overcoming her, Arabella could not help uttering an
exclamation of delight when a dark curtain arose to reveal a rural scene, done in miniature, but amazingly
lifelike, of a cascade, a water mill, a bridge, and a succession of coaches, wagons, and other vehicles passing with
every appearance of verisimilitude across the stage.
Even the sound of the wheels and the rush of the waters
were ingeniously counterfeited, so that she thought it no
matter for wonder that people should visit Vauxhall
three and four times only to see the marvel.

When the curtain descended again, Mr. Beaumaris
suggested that his guests might like to partake of supper
instead of waiting to hear the second part of the concert.
This being agreed to, they edged their way out of the
row where they were sitting and strolled down one of the
colonnades to the supper box which had been hired for
their accommodation. This was in an excellent position,

not so close to the orchestra in the kiosk as to make conversation a labor, and commanding a splendid view of the principal grove. No one, of course, could visit Vauxhall without eating the wafer-thin slices of ham for which the suppers were famous, or tasting the rack punch; but in addition to these delicacies Mr. Beaumaris had ordered a meal so excellently chosen as to tempt the most fugitive appetite. Even Arabella, whose appetite had deserted her several days before, could enjoy the chicken, cooked before her eyes in a chafing dish; and was persuaded to toy with a trifle. Mr. Beaumaris prepared a peach for her with his own hands, and since an imminent elopement was no excuse, she believed, for a present lapse of good manners, she ate this too, smiling shyly and gratefully at him. She found little to say beyond the merest commonplace throughout supper, but this silence passed unnoticed in the spate of Lord Bridlington's discourse. He kindly explained to the ladies the mechanism which produced the wonders of the Grand Cascade; sketched the history of the Gardens; extensively examined their claim to be considered a development of the old Spring Gardens; and disposed of the tradition which linked the district with the name of Guy Fawkes. He was only interrupted when it became necessary to exchange greetings with some acquaintance who happened to walk past the box; and since his mother murmured encouraging remarks every now and then, and Mr. Beaumaris, with great self-control, forbore to utter one of his blighting snubs, he enjoyed himself very much and was sorry when his host suggested that Miss Tallant would like to see the fireworks.

He was allowed to take Arabella on his arm on their way to the part of the grounds whence these could best be seen, while Mr. Beaumaris followed beside Lady Bridlington; but just as he had secured two excellent places, he found himself, quite how he did not know, supplanted, and was obliged to attend to his Mama, who did

not like her situation and insisted on his finding her a
place where her view of the set pieces would not be
obscured by the headdress of a lady who favored immensely tall ostrich plumes.

Arabella momentarily forgot her troubles in enchant-
ment, and clapped her hands when the rockets soared
skywards and burst into stars. Mr. Beaumaris, inured to
fireworks, derived even more entertainment through
watching her round-eyed delight; but after the first of
the set pieces had burned itself out, he consulted his
watch and said gently: "Shall we go, Miss Tallant?"

These words brought her to earth with a shock. An
impulse to tell him that she had changed her mind had
to be sternly repressed, and all the miseries poor Bertram must be enduring recalled. She clutched her taffeta
cloak round her and said nervously: "Oh, yes! Is it already time? Yes, let us go at once!"

There was not the least difficulty in detaching themselves unnoticed from a crowd of persons all intent upon
the evolutions of a giant Catherine wheel; Arabella laid
a cold hand on Mr. Beaumaris's arm and went with him
down an alley, past the Fountain of Neptune, most taste-
fully illuminated, along one of the colonnades, and so to
the land entrance. Several carriages were awaiting their
owners here, and among them Mr. Beaumaris's traveling chaise, with a pair of horses harnessed to it and his
head coachman and one postilion in attendance. Neither
of these individuals betrayed the smallest surprise at
seeing a lady on his master's arm, and although Arabella
was too much embarrassed to raise her eyes, she was
aware that they were conducting themselves as though
this elopement were an everyday occurrence in their
lives. They sprang to well-trained activity as soon as they
saw their master; the cloths were swept from the backs
of Mr. Beaumaris's highly bred horses; the steps of the
chaise were let down, the doors opened, and Mr.
Beaumaris handed his bride tenderly up into the luxuri-

ous vehicle. So little time had she been kept waiting in the road that she did not even look to see whether any baggage was strapped to the back of the chaise. Mr. Beaumaris paused only to exchange a word with the coachman, and then sprang up and took his place beside Arabella on the comfortably cushioned seat; the doors were shut on them; the postilion swung himself into the saddle, and the equipage moved forward.

Mr. Beaumaris spread a soft rug over Arabella's legs and said: "I have a warmer cloak here: may I put it round your shoulders?"

"Oh, no, thank you! I am quite warm!" Arabella said nervously.

He took her hand and kissed it. After a moment she drew it away, and sought desperately for something to say to relieve the tension of the moment.

"How very well sprung your chaise is, sir!" she achieved.

"I am glad you are pleased with it," he responded, in the same polite tone which she had used. "I remembered, of course, that we are alike in detesting hired vehicles."

"Are—are we?" she said doubtfully. "I mean, of course—"

"We exchanged opinions, the first time we met, on the only tolerable way of travel," Mr. Beaumaris reminded her.

This recollection not unnaturally deprived her of speech. Mr. Beaumaris, most obligingly, forbore to press her for an answer, but talked agreeably about the concert they had heard that night. Arabella, who had experienced a few moments' panic on finding herself shut up with her bridegroom in a chaise, traveling to an unknown but probably remote destination, was overwhelmingly grateful to him for behaving precisely as though he were escorting her home from some place of entertainment. She had been much afraid that he would

perhaps have tried to make love to her. She had not
much experience in such matters, but it had occurred to
her that a gentleman starting on an elopement might
expect some demonstration of affection from his be-
loved. A week earlier, safe in the darkness of her bedchamber, her cheek on a damp pillow, Arabella had
owned to herself that life could hold no greater happiness for her than for Mr. Beaumaris to take her in his
arms; now, miserably conscious of her duplicity, she
could imagine nothing more unnerving. But Mr.
Beaumaris, surely the calmest of runaway bridegrooms,
showed no desire to succumb to his ardor. Finding that
he was being answered in monosyllables, he presently
gave up trying to engage Arabella in genteel conversation, and leaned back in his corner of the chaise, his head
a little turned against the squabs behind it toward her,
so that he could watch her face in the dim moonlight that
penetrated into the vehicle. Arabella was scarcely aware
that he had stopped talking to her. She was lost in her
own thoughts, seated bolt upright and clinging with one
hand to the strap that hung from the wall of the chaise
beside her. She could see the postilion bobbing up and
down before her, and when the cobbles were left behind,
was vaguely conscious of having left the streets and to
be driving through the countryside. In what direction
they were traveling, or where she would find herself at
the first halt, she had no idea, nor were these the questions that troubled her mind. The impropriety of her
conduct she had from the start known to be unforgiv-
able; what now filled her with repugnance was the sudden realization that in marrying Mr. Beaumaris while he
still labored under a misapprehension, she was treating
him so shabbily that it was doubtful if he would ever
pardon her, much less continue to regard her with even
a shred of affection. At this melancholy reflection a small
sob escaped her, which had the effect of making Mr.
Beaumaris say: "What is it, my love?"

"Nothing! Nothing!" whispered Arabella, much agitated.

To her relief, he appeared to accept this, for he said no more. She decided, in a wave of remorse, that he was the greatest gentleman of her acquaintance, with the best manners, the most delicate forbearance, and quite the kindest disposition. It was at this point that the moment for which Mr. Beaumaris had been waiting arrived. All at once Arabella wondered how soon after the wedding ceremony she could break the news to him that she required him not only to forgive her brother's debt to him but also to bestow a hundred pounds on him for the settlement of all his other liabilities; and what words she could find with which most unexceptionably to express this urgent necessity. There were no such words, as a very little cudgeling of her brain sufficed to convince her. She could not imagine how she could ever have been foolish enough to have supposed that the thing could be done, or that such a confession could be made without afterward rendering it impossible for her to convince him that she did indeed love him.

These, and still more disagreeable thoughts, were jostling one another in Arabella's frightened mind when the pace at which they were traveling seemed sensibly to slacken. The chaise swung round at so sharp an angle that only her clutch on the strap saved Arabella from being thrown onto Mr. Beaumaris's shoulder. It proceeded for a very little way, and then drew up. Arabella turned toward the dupe beside her, and said breathlessly: "I cannot! I cannot! Mr. Beaumaris, I am *very* sorry, but it was all a mistake! Please take me back to London at once! Oh, please take me back!"

Mr. Beaumaris received this daunting request with a remarkable degree of composure, merely replying, as the doors of the chaise were opened: "Shall we discuss this matter in a more private spot? Let me assist you to alight, my love!"

"Please take me back! I—I don't want to elope, after all!" said Arabella, in an urgent whisper.

"Then we won't elope," returned Mr. Beaumaris reassuringly. "I must own that I think it quite unnecessary for us to do so. Come!"

Arabella hesitated, but since he seemed determined that she should descend from the chaise, and perhaps wanted to rest his horses, she allowed him to hand her down. They seemed to be standing before a large building, but it showed none of the welcoming lights to be expected of a posting inn, nor had the chaise driven into a courtyard. At the top of a flight of broad, shallow stone steps a large door opened, and a beam of light from the interior of the building showed Arabella neat flower beds flanking the entrance. Before she had recovered from the surprise of finding herself at what was plainly a private residence, Mr. Beaumaris had led her up the steps and into a lofty hall, furnished in a massive style and lit by candles in wall chandeliers. An elderly butler bowed them in, and said: "Good evening, sir." One powdered and liveried footman divested Mr. Beaumaris of his cloak, another relieved him of his hat and gloves.

Arabella stood turned to stone as all the implications of her surroundings burst upon her. Mr. Beaumaris's soothing assurance to her that they would not elope now became invested with the most sinister significance, and it was a pathetically white and frightened face which she turned toward him. He smiled at her, but before either of them had time to speak, the butler had informed Mr. Beaumaris that he would find the Yellow Saloon in readiness; and a most respectable-looking housekeeper, with neat white hair under a starched cap, had appeared upon the scene and was dropping a curtsy to Arabella.

"Good evening, miss! Good evening, Mr. Robert! Please to take miss into the saloon, while I see that the maids unpack her trunk! You will find a nice fire, for I am sure miss must be chilled after the drive, so late as

it is. Let me take your cloak, miss! I shall bring you up
a glass of hot milk directly: I am sure you will be glad
of it."

The promise of a glass of hot milk, which hardly
seemed to be in keeping with the hideous vision of se-
duction and rape which had leapt to her mind, a little
reassured Arabella. One of the footmen had thrown
open a door at the back of the hall; Mr. Beaumaris possessed himself of a trembling, icy little hand and said: "I
want to make you known to Mr. Watchet, my love, who
is a very old friend of mine. Indeed, one of my earliest
allies!"

"Now, Master Robert! I'm sure I am very happy to see
you here, miss—and mind, now, don't let Master Robert
keep you out of your bed till all hours!"

The fear that Master Robert had quite different intentions receded still further. Arabella summoned up a
smile, said something in a shy little voice, and allowed
herself to be led into a saloon fitted up in the first style
of elegance and offering her all the comfort of a small
fire, burning in a brightly polished grate.

The door was softly closed behind them; Mr. Beaumaris drew a chair invitingly forward, and said: "Come and
sit down, Miss Tallant! You know, I cannot but be glad
that you have decided after all not to elope with me. To
tell you the truth, there is one circumstance at least that
makes me reluctant to proceed with you to Scotland—a
journey that would occupy six or seven days, I daresay,
before we found ourselves back in London."

"Oh!" said Arabella, sitting down primly on the edge
of the chair and regarding him out of scared, doubtful
eyes.

"Yes," said Mr. Beaumaris. "Ulysses!"

Her eyes widened. "Ulysses?" she repeated blankly.

"The animal you were so obliging as to bestow upon
me," he explained. "Most unfortunately, he has developed so marked a predilection for my society that he

frets himself to skin and bone if I am absent from him
for more than a night. I did not quite like to bring him
with me upon our elopement, for I can discover no
precedent for taking a dog with one upon such an occasion, and one scarcely cares to violate the conventions
at such a moment."

The door opened just then to admit Mrs. Watchet,
who came in carrying a glass of steaming milk on a silver
tray. This, with a plate of macaroons, she set down on
a small table at Arabella's elbow, telling her that when
she had drunk it and said good night to Master Robert,
she should be escorted upstairs to her bedchamber.
With a slightly severe injunction to Mr. Beaumaris not
to keep miss talking to him too long, she then curtsied
herself out of the room.

"Sir!" said Arabella desperately, as soon as they were
alone again: "What is this house to which you have
brought me?"

"I have brought you to my grandmother's house, at
Wimbledon," he replied coolly. "She is a very old lady
and keeps early hours, so you must forgive her for not
being downstairs to receive you. You will meet her tomorrow morning. My aunt, who lives with her, would
undoubtedly have sat up to receive you had she not gone
a few days ago to stay with one of her sisters for a short
time."

"Your grandmother's house?" exclaimed Arabella, almost starting from her chair. "Good God, why have you
brought me to such a place, Mr. Beaumaris?"

"Well, you know," he explained, "I could not but feel
that it was possible you might think better of that notion
of eloping. Of course, if, after a night's repose, you still
believe we should go to Gretna Green, I assure you I
shall escort you there, whatever Ulysses' claims upon me
may be. For myself, the more I consider the matter, the
more I am convinced that we should do better to steel
ourselves to meet the felicitations of our friends and

announce our betrothal in the columns of the society journals in the accepted manner."

"Mr. Beaumaris," interrupted Arabella, pale but resolute, "I cannot marry you!" She added, on another of her small sobs: "I don't know why you should ever have wanted to marry me, but—"

"I have lost my entire fortune on 'Change, and must instantly repair it," he interrupted promptly.

Arabella rose jerkily and confronted him. "I have not a penny in the world!" she announced.

"In that case," responded Mr. Beaumaris, maintaining his calm, "you really have no choice in the matter: you must obviously marry me. Since we are being frank with one another, I will confess that my fortune is still intact."

"I deceived you! I am not an heiress!" Arabella said, feeling that he could not have understood her words.

"You never deceived me for a moment," said Mr. Beaumaris, smiling at her in a way which made her tremble still more violently.

"I *lied* to you!" cried Arabella, determined to bring him to a sense of her iniquities.

"Most understandable," agreed Mr. Beaumaris. "But I am really quite uninterested in heiresses."

"Mr. Beaumaris," said Arabella earnestly, "the whole of London believes me to be a wealthy woman!"

"Yes, and since the whole of London must certainly continue in that belief, you have, as I have already pointed out to you, no choice but to marry me," he said. *"My* fortune, happily, is so large that *your* lack of fortune need never be suspected."

"Oh, why didn't you tell me you knew the truth?" she cried, wringing her hands.

He possessed himself of them, and held them lightly. "My dearest goose, why didn't you trust me when I assured you that you might?" he countered. "I have cherished throughout the belief that you would confide

in me, and you see I was quite right. So certain was I that
you would not, when the time actually came, run off with
me in this absurd fashion, that I visited my grandmother
yesterday and told her the whole story. She was very
much diverted, and commanded me to bring you to stay
for a few days with her. I hope you will not object to this:
she frightens half the world, but you will have me to
support you through the ordeal."

Arabella pulled her hands resolutely away, and turned
from him to hide her quivering lips and suffused eyes.
"It is worse than you know!" she said, in a stifled tone.
"When you know all the truth, you will not wish to marry
me! I have been worse than untruthful: I have been
shameless! I can never marry you, Mr. Beaumaris!"

"This is not disturbing," he said. "Not only have I
sent the notice of our betrothal to the *Gazette*, and the
Morning Post, but I have obtained your father's consent
to our marriage."

At this, she spun round to face him again, a look of
utter astonishment in her face. "*My father's consent?*" she
repeated incredulously.

"It is usual, you know," explained Mr. Beaumaris
apologetically.

"But you do not know my father!"

"On the contrary. I made his acquaintance last week,
and spent two most agreeable nights at Heythram," he
said.

"But— Did Lady Bridlington tell you?"

"No, not Lady Bridlington. Your brother let slip the
name of his home once, and I have an excellent memory.
I am sorry, by the way, that Bertram should have been
having such an uncomfortable time during my absence
from town. That was quite my fault: I should have
sought him out and settled his difficulties before I left
for Yorkshire. I did write to him, but he had unfortunately departed from the Red Lion before the delivery
of my letter. However, you won't find that the experi-

ence has harmed him, so I must hope to be forgiven."

Her cheeks were now very much flushed. "You know it all, then! Oh, what must you think of me? I asked you to marry me because—because I wanted you to give me seven hundred pounds to save poor Bertram from a debtor's prison!"

"I know you did," said Mr. Beaumaris cordially. "I don't know how I contrived to keep my countenance. When did it occur to you, my ridiculous little love, that to demand a large sum of money from your bridegroom as soon as the ring was on your finger might be a trifle awkward?"

"Just now—in your chaise!" she confessed, covering her face with her hands. "I couldn't do it! I have behaved very, very badly, but when I realized what I was about— oh, indeed, I knew I could never do it!"

"We have both behaved very badly," he agreed. "I encouraged Fleetwood to spread the news that you were a great heiress: I even allowed him to suppose that I knew all about your family. I thought it would be amusing to see whether I could make you the rage of London—and I blush to confess it, my darling: it *was* amusing! Nor do I really regret it in the least, for if I had not set out on this most reprehensible course we might never have come much in one another's way again, after our first meeting, and I might never have discovered that I had found the very girl I had been looking for for so long."

"No, no, how can you say so?" she exclaimed, large tears standing on the ends of her lashes. "I came to London in the hope of—of contracting an eligible marriage, and I asked you to marry me because you are so very rich! You *could* not wish to marry such an odious creature!"

"No, perhaps I couldn't," he replied. "But although you may have forgotten that when I first addressed myself to you, you declined my offer, I have not. If wealth was all your object, I can't conceive what should have induced you to do so! It seemed to me that you were not entirely indifferent to me. All things considered, I decided that my proper course was to present myself to your parents without further loss of time. And I am very glad I did so, for not only did I spend a very pleasant time at the Vicarage, but I also enjoyed a long talk with your mother. By the way, do you know how much you resemble her? More, I think, than any of your brothers and sisters, though they are all remarkably handsome. But, as I say, I enjoyed a long talk with her, and was encouraged to hope, from what she told me, that I had not been mistaken in thinking you were not indifferent to me."

"I never wrote a word to Mama, or even to Sophy, about—about—not being indifferent to you!" Arabella said involuntarily.

"Well, I do not know how that may be," said Mr. Beaumaris, "but Mama and Sophy were not at all surprised to receive a visit from me. Perhaps you may have mentioned me rather frequently in your letters, or perhaps Lady Bridlington gave Mama a hint that I was the most determined of your suitors."

The mention of her godmother made Arabella start, and exclaim: "Lady Bridlington! Good God, I left a letter for her on the table in the hall, telling her of the dreadful thing I had done, and begging her to forgive me!"

"Don't disturb yourself, my love. Lady Bridlington knows very well where you are. Indeed, I found her most helpful, particularly when it came to packing what you would need for a brief sojourn at my grandmother's house. She promised that her own maid should attend to the matter while we were listening to that tedious concert. I daresay she has long since told that son of hers that he may look for the notice of our engagement in tomorrow's *Gazette*, together with the intelligence that we have both of us gone out of town to stay with the Dowager Duchess of Wigan. By the time we reappear in London, we must hope that our various acquaintances will have grown so accustomed to the news that we shall not be quite overwhelmed by their astonishment, their chagrin, or their felicitations. But I am strongly of the opinion that you should permit me to escort you home to Heythram as soon as possible: *you* will naturally wish your father to marry us, and *I* am extremely impatient to carry off my wife without any loss of time. My darling, what in the world have I said to make you cry?"

"Oh, nothing, nothing!" sobbed Arabella. "Only that I don't deserve to be so happy, and I n-never was indifferent to you, though I t-tried very hard to be, when I thought you were only trifling with m-me!"

Mr. Beaumaris then took her firmly into his arms, and kissed her, after which she derived much comfort from clutching the lapel of his elegant coat and weeping into his shoulder. None of the very gratifying things which Mr. Beaumaris murmured into the curls that were tickling his chin had any other effect on her than to make her sob more bitterly than ever, so he presently told her that even his love for her could not prevail upon him to allow her to ruin his favorite coat. This changed her tears to laughter, and after he had dried her face and kissed her again, she became tolerably composed and was able to sit down on the sofa beside him, and to accept from him the glass of tepid milk which he told her she must drink if she did not wish to incur Mrs. Watchet's displeasure. She smiled mistily and sipped the milk, saying after a moment: "And Papa gave his consent! Oh, what will he say when he knows the whole? What did you tell him?"

"I told him the truth," replied Mr. Beaumaris.

Arabella nearly dropped the glass. "All the truth?" she faltered, dismay in her face.

"All of it—oh, not the truth about Bertram! His name did not enter into our conversation, and I strictly

charged him, when I sent him off to Yorkshire, not to
divulge one word of his adventures. Much as I like and
esteem your father, I cannot feel that any good purpose
would be served by distressing him with *that* story. I told
him the truth about you and me."

"Was he—dreadfully displeased with me?" asked Arabella, in a small, apprehensive voice.

"He was, I fear, a little grieved," owned Beaumaris.
"But when he understood that you would never have
announced yourself to have been an heiress had you not
overheard me talking like a coxcomb to Charles Fleetwood, he was soon brought to perceive that I was even
more to blame for the deception than you."

"*Was* he?" said Arabella doubtfully.

"Drink your milk, my love! Certainly he was. Between
us, your Mama and I were able to show him that without
my prompting, Charles would never have spread the
rumor abroad, and that once the rumor had been so
spread, it was impossible for you to deny it, since naturally no one ever asked you if it were true. I daresay he
may give you a little scold, but I am quite sure you are
already forgiven."

"Did he forgive you too?" asked Arabella, awed.

"*I* had all the merit of making the confession," Mr.
Beaumaris pointed out virtuously. "He forgave me
freely. I cannot imagine why you should look so much
surprised. I found him in every way delightful, and have
seldom enjoyed an evening more than the one I spent
conversing with him in his study, after your Mama and
Sophy had gone to bed. Indeed, we sat talking until the
candles guttered in their sockets."

Arabella's awed expression became even more
marked. "Dear sir, why—what did you talk *about?*" she
inquired, quite unable to visualize Papa and the Nonpareil hobnobbing together.

"We discussed certain aspects of Wolf's *Prolegomena ad
Homerum,* a copy of which work I chanced to see upon

his bookshelf," replied Mr. Beaumaris calmly. "I myself picked up a copy when I was in Vienna last year, and was much interested in Wolf's theory that more than one hand was employed in the writing of the *Iliad* and the *Odyssey*."

"Is—is *that* what the book is about?" asked Arabella.

He smiled, but replied gravely: "Yes, that is what it is about—though your father, a far more profound scholar than I am, found the opening chapter, which treats of the proper methods to be used in the recension of ancient manuscripts, of even more interest. He took me a little out of my depth there, but I hope I may have profited by his very just observations."

"Did you *enjoy* that?" demanded Arabella, much impressed.

"Very much. In spite of my frippery ways, you know, I do occasionally enjoy rational conversation, just as I can spend a very agreeable evening playing at lottery tickets with Mama, and Sophy, and the children."

"You did not do *that!*" she cried. "Oh, you are quizzing me! You must have been shockingly bored!"

"Nothing of the sort! The man who could be bored in the midst of such a lively family as yours must be an insufferable fellow, above being pleased by anything. By the bye, if that uncle of yours does not come up to scratch, we must do something toward helping Harry to achieve this burning ambition to become a second Nelson. Not the eccentric uncle who died and left you his entire fortune, but the one who still lives."

"Oh, pray don't speak of that dreadful fortune ever again!" begged Arabella, hanging down her head.

"But I must speak of it!" objected Mr. Beaumaris. "Since I presume that we shall frequently be inviting the various members of your family to stay with us, and can hardly pass them all off as heirs and heiresses, *some* explanation of your superior circumstances must be forthcoming! Your Mama—an admirable woman!—and I

decided that the eccentric uncle would serve our turn
very well. We were further agreed, quite tacitly, you
know, that it will be unnecessary, and, indeed, quite
undesirable, to mention the matter to Papa."

"Oh no, it would never do to tell him that!" she said
quickly. "He would not like it at all, and when he is
grieved with any of us— Oh, if only he does not discover
the scrape Bertram fell into, and if only Bertram didn't
fail to pass that examination at Oxford, which I am much
afraid he may have, because it did not sound to me as
though—"

"It is not of the slightest consequence," he interrupted. "Bertram—though Papa does not yet know it—
is not going to Oxford: he is going to join a good cavalry
regiment, where he will feel very much more at home,
and, I daresay, become a great credit to us all."

At this, Arabella caught his hand in her free one, and
kissed it, exclaiming, with a sob in her voice: "How good
you are! How much, much *too* good you are, my *dear* Mr.
Beaumaris!"

"Never," said Mr. Beaumaris, snatching his hand away,
and taking Arabella into his arms so urgently that the
rest of the milk in the glass was spilt over her gown,
"Never, Arabella, dare to do such a thing again! And
don't talk such fustian to me, or persist in calling me Mr.
Beaumaris!"

"Oh, I must!" protested Arabella, into his shoulder.
"I can't call you—I can't call you—Robert!"

"You have called me Robert very prettily, and you will
find, if you persevere, that it will rise quite easily to your
lips in a very short space of time."

"Well, if it will please you, I will *try* to say it," said
Arabella. She sat up suddenly, as a thought occurred to
her, and said in her impulsive way: "Oh, Mr. Beau—I
mean, dear Robert!—there was an unfortunate female,
called Leaky Peg, in that horrid house where I went to

see poor Bertram, and she was so very kind to him! Do you think—?"

"No, Arabella," said Mr. Beaumaris firmly. "I do not!"

She was disappointed, but docile. "No?" she said.

"No," said Mr. Beaumaris, drawing her back into his arm.

"I thought we might have taken her away from that dreadful place," suggested Arabella, smoothing his coat lapel with a coaxing hand.

"I am quite sure you did, my love, but while I am prepared to receive into my household climbing-boys and stray curs, I must draw the line at a lady rejoicing in the name of Leaky Peg."

"You don't think she might learn to become a house-maid, or something of that sort? You know—"

"I only know two things," interrupted Mr. Beaumaris. "The first is that she is not going to make the attempt in any house of mine; and the second, and by far the more important, is that I adore you, Arabella!"

Arabella was so much pleased by this disclosure that she lost interest in Leaky Peg, and confined herself to the far more agreeable task of convincing Mr. Beaumaris that his very obliging sentiments were entirely reciprocated.

Georgette Heyer, author of over 50 novels, was seventeen when she started writing her first book. Although she is primarily known for her historical romances set in Regency London, she also wrote eleven detective stories. Ms. Heyer died in July, 1974, at the age of 71.

☙ HarperPaperbacks *By Mail*

YESTERDAY'S SHADOWS
by Marianne Willman

Bettany Howard was a young orphan traveling west searching for the father who left her years ago. Wolf Star was a Cheyenne brave who longed to know who abandoned him—a white child with a jeweled talisman. Fate decreed they'd meet and try to seize the passion promised. 0-06-104044-4

MIDNIGHT ROSE by Patricia Hagan

From the rolling plantations of Richmond to the underground slave movement of Philadelphia, Erin Sterling and Ryan Youngblood would pursue their wild, breathless passion and finally surrender to the promise of a bold and unexpected love. 0-06-104023-1

WINTER TAPESTRY
by Kathy Lynn Emerson

Cordell vows to revenge the murder of her father. Roger Allington is honor bound to protect his friend's daughter but has no liking for her reckless ways. Yet his heart tells him he must pursue this beauty through a maze of plots to win her love and ignite their smoldering passion. 0-06-100220-8